Mrs. Bundle Takes A Hike:

The Case of the Singing Swans

❧ ❧

ALLISON CESARIO PATON

To Phylis an

Allison Cesario Paton

© 2006 by Bundle Publishing. All rights reserved.
Design: Univoice, Portland, Maine
Illustrations: Donna Stackhouse Illustration and Design
ISBN 10: 0-9790270-0-4   ISBN 13: 978-0-9790270-0-0

*for more information about the
Mrs. Bundle series, please contact*

Bundle Publishing
23 Woodside Drive, Scarborough, Maine 04074
1-207-883-4231
acesari1@maine.rr.com

∾⤬∾

*This book is dedicated
to my husband, John,
who found me in Vermont
and whose love forever nurtures me.
Thank you for your support,
which empowers my imagination
to have no boundaries.*

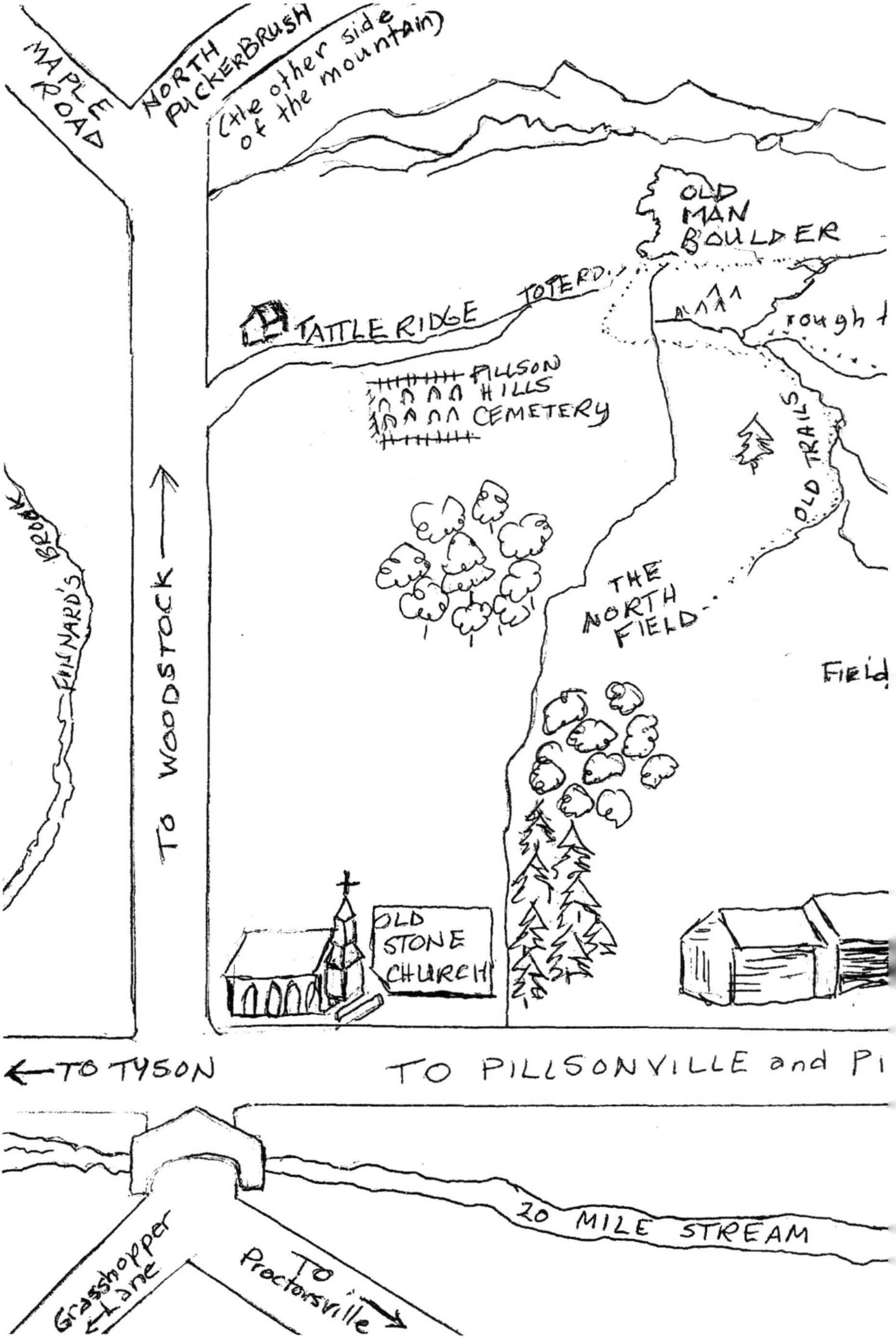
MAPLE ROAD
NORTH PUCKERBRUSH
(the other side of the mountain)
OLD MAN BOULDER
TATTLE RIDGE
TOTERD.
rough t
PILLSON HILLS CEMETERY
OLD TRAILS
KINNARD'S BROOK
TO WOODSTOCK
THE NORTH FIELD
Field
OLD STONE CHURCH
TO TYSON
TO PILLSONVILLE and Pi
20 MILE STREAM
Grasshopper Lane
TO Proctorsville

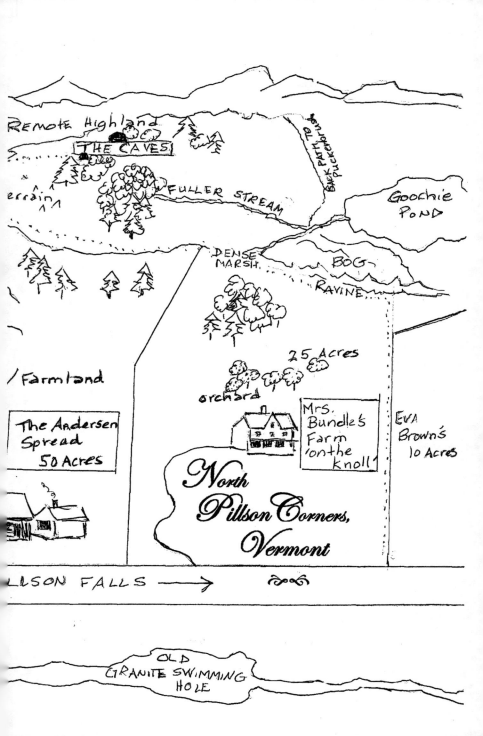

Acknowledgements

THIS IS A WORK OF FICTION; all characters are imagined. No one character is based upon any one person, living or dead. Some locations, local landmarks and stores, municipalities, and other areas are real, and are used solely as an authentic framework for the author's intention of telling this fictional tale.

A special thank you to our dear neighbors and friends in Vermont, and to the people of Vermont, whose kind hearts and interesting, witty stories reinforce that true life is much better than fiction.

To my large extended family, whose interest in my creative endeavors and love for me makes my heart happy.

Thank you to the Honorable Kenneth Cooper, Asst. Judge, Superior Court, Windsor County, Vermont for taking time from his busy day to provide historical information, along with a personal tour of the Woodstock Correctional Center facility.

I am ever indebted to Elsie Whidden, Editor, whose teacher hand has gently touched the pages of Mrs. Bundle's world and whose kind spirit has made the editing process fun.

PROLOGUE

LOOKING OUT OVER THE EXPANSIVE LONDON SKYLINE from the extravagant Canary Wharf penthouse quarters, he feebly reached for the one-hundred-and-twenty-fifth cigarette of the day. The yellowed skeletal fingers grabbed on, as though to a lifeline, and held tightly, and the old man's cracked dry lips caressed the unfiltered end. *Pleasure and pain, pleasure and pain,* he thought, as the first smoke greedily filled his lungs. *Ahhh…* sweet charcoal elixir.

The wracking, choked coughs followed, as usual, one grueling hacking after another, and his frail aged torso convulsed in the wheelchair, once again activating his private nurse, who came running from the anteroom.

"Are you all right, Mr. Wesley, sir?" she asked, her soft voice fearful. Her overriding professionalism and responsible nature dominated her fear, enough so to risk his wrath, and she attempted once more to make him comfortable. An oxygen tank stalwartly stood nearby and, as she reached for the mask, he waved her away.

"Go away!" he shouted amidst his horrible wracking and spitting. "Of course, I'm all right, you silly prat! Leave it! *Arggh…!* Sod off!"

The room was hazy with smoke, a mini-cloud hovering above him, and she gagged behind his back, the fusion of smells engulfing her senses. Usually, she could withstand the most vile of onslaughts to the senses that her job brought with it, but today, the decaying stench combined with the reek of heavy tobacco was so malodorous it was almost more than she could bear.

She looked at the nearby 18th century Norfolk wall clock, noted the time, comparing it to her own watch. She made little clicking noises with her tongue. Good! Only one more hour left in her shift. How the hours dragged! She was glad she would soon be heading home to her nice warm bedsit and a cozy pot of tea. Having now become desensitized to her employer's harsh and cruel demeanor, she didn't bother responding in any way to his abusive comments. Instead, she simply faded back into the darker corners of the room and left him to indulge in the hellhole of his noxious, stale cloud.

As his body became accustomed to the one-hundred-and-twenty-fifth invasion of the day, he sat back, out of breath and relaxing in his addiction, thoroughly enjoying his solitary tapered companion. He reached over and picked up the nearby photograph and studied it again for the umpteenth time, carefully examining it for several minutes.

His feeble, red-rimmed eyes moved slightly upward and, without having to adjust his debilitated body, his range of vision encompassed Londinium in all its glory. Perched in his nest in the highest of three buildings in London and all of Europe, he could see everything within a twenty-mile radius. Canary Wharf, the huge skyscraper where he resided, had been built over the original Docklands of London—the expansive Port of London—which was the original point of departure for merchants from the 1500's to the 1970's. Although the skyscraper primarily housed urban office and retail space for many large corporations, the addition of his small but lavish penthouse living quarters had been constructed so that he could control his business ventures twenty-four hours a day.

He looked out over the skyline at the vast empire he had accumulated, bit by bit, methodically picking out each of the buildings he owned. He never tired of looking at the urban scene, now showcased by the backdrop of twilight's rosy horizon. Remarkably, he had spent his whole life accumulating and collecting this world of cement, steel, brick, and glass, building after building, section by section.

He shifted his miserly gaze down the snaking River Thames, all the way to the Chelsea Bridge section and the area around Battersea Wharf where he had grown up in the early 20th century. His old neighborhood, once squalid and dirty, had been restored and improved over the last few decades, to the extent that it now was considered a trendy and posh area to live.

He closed his tired lizard-like eyes, still holding the magnificent vista in his mind's eye. *Sidney Lambdin Johns Wesley, III, entrepreneur extraordinaire,* he thought triumphantly, but also with an acerbic tinge. Not only was he one of the richest and most powerful men in all of Great Britain, but he was also well known by anyone of distinction for his philanthropic society endowments. He gloated to himself, satisfied with the knowledge that he had beaten them all. That nebulous entity of social elitists he had clawed his way toward and with whom he had strived to be a part of all his life, to "belong". Of course, it was all a sham, this glamorized bogus front, this false identity he had created long ago.

Where he had originally come from had been obliterated from all records. Only he knew his miserable beginnings, his early recollections full of dark secrets and horrible conditions. The true secret of his wretched derivation was that he was born out of wedlock to an alcoholic mother and never recognized by his lowlife father. He had fought like a rabid cat, first through childhood and then later through adolescence, to virtually pull himself out of the infested and toxic environment into which he had been born.

His business beginnings were sketchy for a reason. Methodically, slowly, he had extricated himself from his miserable London ghetto existence to first toil in the London factories at age 15, scrupulously saving every penny he could put by.

There was no time for merriment, no extras, and no room for emotions, closeness, or intimacy. Eating, drinking, and sleeping his dream of wealth and power, he had purchased his first London tenement at a city auction for 100 pounds. He then saved for his second building, adding a third and fourth, and so on. He never improved or repaired the structures, just quietly continued buying up more and more London real estate, all in the most depressed of neighborhoods. By age twenty-five he had reached his goal of acquiring a net worth of a million dollars and, realizing his dream had come to fruition, he started on the next phase of his objective. Systematically, he began the process of removing any links, any traces at all, to his sordid past.

With the profits from his first fortune, he began to quietly amass an array of big waterfront district projects, emerging as a significant player behind the redevelopment plans in the distressed wharf areas. Obtaining contract after contract, his fortune grew by leaps and bounds, and his corporation's anonymity allowed him to gradually modify his identity. One piece at a time, like the massive structures that he constructed brick by brick over those years, he reinvented himself, creating the new identity complete with socially acceptable lineage.

The new persona he masterfully contrived conveniently neutralized his squalid true origin. He flawlessly fabricated a most glowing biography, based purely on hearsay, innuendo, and legend, at the same time carving out an insulated and very arcane life. Finally he had resurfaced, like a propitious butterfly emerging from the chrysalis, as the corporate heavyweight and multimillionaire entrepreneur he was known as today. No one seemed to question this morphing of his identity, his massive wealth having opened and closed the appropriate doors essential to achieve this final result.

From then on, his obsession with respectability and culture had been his primary focus, and he'd amassed more and more money, more and more *things*, and, of course, more and more real estate. Everything he touched had turned to gold and multiplied twofold, and his penchant for making more money, then more, fed his greedy soul.

His only weakness was, *well*….he thought pleasurably, then paused, reflecting on his one affinity.

Opening his weary eyes, he glanced ambivalently around the room. He was like an ancient, crusty Komodo dragon, flicking his yellow tongue, deadly in his silent review. Here, he deteriorated in his 90's now, a recluse closeted alone with his wealth.

The room was heavy, suffocating with dark oak and ornate mahogany, so very elaborate and so magnificently pretentious. Lavish, padlocked heirloom cherry cabinets held precious collectibles, rare glassware, and jewelry. Regency rosewood inlaid cases, engraved chinese lacquer cabinets, brass-escutcheoned chests; all held various hidden treasures of untold value.

He looked at the photograph once more. Finally! *After all this time,* he thought with an air of self-satisfied anticipation.

He picked up the phone and hit speed dial 2. It was immediately picked up at the other end.

He spoke quietly, gasping, yet authoritative, into the receiver.

"Did you receive it? It's clear? Splendid. Proceed as planned."

Listening intently, he replied, "Yes, as usual." There was another pause. "Of course! Whatever you have to do."

He hung up the phone. Professional, brief, impassive. The entire call had taken all of thirty seconds. Economy of speech. The way he liked it. *His* way of doing business.

So, he observed smugly, *if all went well, the final piece would fall into place.* He sat back, thoroughly exhausted now, but protected and surrounded by his Rembrants, his Sargents, and his Renoirs. *We want more, and more,* this fraternity of priceless paintings seemed to entreat him. He blinked once again, reptilian-style. He would have it…at all costs. At any cost.

Pleasure and Pain, he thought, a distant memory causing him to wince slightly as he stubbed out the black cold end of the poisonous cigarette. Immediately reaching for number one-hundred-and-twenty-six, he coughed, clearing his congested throat as best he could.

Yes, another wonderful stick of pain, he mused, lighting it masterfully and sending the inhaled smoke once again directly to his waiting, craving arteries and lungs. *Ahhhh.* He looked at the photograph once more, this time with glazed eyes, and a sinister smile lacerated his parched, hoary lips.

Chapter One

The Beginning of the Journey

Wham! The door to the cookstove closed with a loud bang.

"Dang!" Mrs. Bundle cried, looking at Cracker, hands on her hips, but certainly not soliciting a response. Cracker looked up from his throne on the comfy rocking chair and stretched his sleek body, his long talons widespread. He opened his mouth broadly into a silent big yawn.

"You're just as bored as I am, aren't you?" she asked.

Mrs. Bundle fiddled with the hefty stovetop kettle, agitating the bottled herbs and spices on the shelf above, and then kicked the logs beside the oven, which sent them crashing like fiddlesticks onto the habitually foot-scuffed linoleum floor. Its yellow-and-black diamond pattern had worn through in spots, giving it the multi-hued patina that only years of wear and tear can produce. She sighed, bending over to straighten and laboriously rearrange the logs one at a time until they once again resembled a neat pyramid, and then sat down next to Cracker.

"What do you think, old P-Cat? Here we are together again with not a dang exciting thing going on in our life. Nothing to keep us occupied. Zip, zero, nada!"

Cracker jumped off the chair, gently rubbing against Mrs. Bundle's leg. Then, on soft cat feet he went lazily to his empty milk bowl and methodically licked the last driblet from its depths.

Bored to tears, he meandered back to his special warm spot beside the shiny green enamel cookstove.

Crack! The pine cupboard doors slammed loudly, one at a time, as Mrs. Bundle opened, then closed, them, looking for she-didn't-know-what on each shelf. She finally settled on one of her favorite tea biscuits from the flowered black tin. She munched while she stood glowering at her favorite companion.

Hampered by a mouthful of dry cookie, she mumbled resignedly, "You're goin' (mumble) make me do all the work on this one, Cracker-cat, (mumble) you?" Cracker leapt onto the butcher-block counter. Moving quicker than a cornered mouse, he sniffed at the crumbs left lingering there and then meowed loud and long.

"Dang!" Mrs. Bundle said again, this time accentuating it long and loud, so much so that it resonated throughout the cozy interior of their abode. Absentmindedly, she picked up the top book from the piled assortment of latest library treasures, all of which were of the mystery genre. Scattered throughout her house were books piled upon other books, like a politician's most patient constituents waiting for their turn to be heard. She grasped the bookmark and opened to where last she was reading.

Her latest "read" was Sue Grafton's *P is for Peril,* and she reveled in the slightly askew world of Detective Kinsey Milhone. Mrs. Bundle just loved "that Kinsey", as she affectionately called her. It was a real hoot to see how Kinsey got herself into, and then out of, her alphabetically-sequenced private eye scrapes. She imagined Henry, Kinsey's beloved elderly landlord, as an exciting and fascinating, vital individual. She had to admit she had even daydreamed about Henry and his coveted baking skills, especially since her husband had passed away. She read along, trying to concentrate, but to no avail. She plunked the book down onto the table.

"Oh, *double* dang!" she hollered, hearing her voice reverberate through the lonely house. A chuckle erupted from her throat and she said, "Here's an old lady talking to herself! My Lord! And her cat has to listen to it, too, for heaven's sake."

She paused, then continued her one-sided conversation. "No! I just won't have it! C'mon, C.C.…let's go!"

With that, she yanked off her apron, simultaneously grabbing the old tweed cap from the wrought iron hook. It was the hat that her husband Arthur had worn for many years and she paused, then replaced the hat's former site with the apron, fondly looping the worn gingham companion over the hook.

She sniffed the inside label of the hat, inhaling the wonderfully lingering aromas of pipe tobacco, Old Spice Aftershave, and woodsmoke. *Wish you were here, my darling man*, she thought. She walked out into the breezeway shed and sighed, then plopped the hat lopsided on her head, and looked for the oversized deerskin gloves she used for outside chores. Not finding them in their usual spot, she grabbed two mismatched mittens, one red, one green, drew on her walking boots and headed outside into the crisp clean Vermont air.

"You know, you're a good old companion, and you've got a lot of spunk, too!" Mrs. Bundle admitted, sighing, as she and Cracker hiked out over the lower field, now dull brown with intermittent flecks of multihued greens and ochers. She continued down the hill, away from the familiar 1830's Vermont farmhouse they both called home.

Cracker had always had the uncanny ability, even as a kitty, to be able to read Mrs. Bundle's thoughts, especially during the toughest of times, and he knew what was really on her mind now. *Now, my dear,* he replied in cat-thought (as he always did when Mrs. Bundle talked to him) *we've been through a lot together, and I miss Arthur, too.*

Everything about Cracker was sleek and to the point, from the tips of his delicately accentuated ears to his perfectly shaped, ebony, triangular nose. The clean, dapper line of his prim whiskers neatly framed his pristine wide mouth and luxuriously long pink tongue, a tongue which he obsessively employed, keeping his appearance in remarkably tidy condition.

His tongue also occasionally got him in trouble with Mrs. Bundle. Cracker's basic nature was that of a realist, not unlike most cats. He was born with a no-nonsense, straight-ahead mentality and was not one to mince his thoughts. He felt Mrs. Bundle often relied upon him to give her his honest assessment of any given situation. He knew this was important to Mrs. Bundle, especially after Arthur's death when she had become solely responsible for making her own decisions. But the fact of the matter was, sometimes Cracker gave his opinion too freely, embellishing and extemporizing, sometimes *ad infinitum.*

No doubt, she and Cracker had their little squabbles occasionally, but they always worked things out. When he and Mrs. Bundle disagreed, Cracker always believed, at least intially, that he was right. He would flick his long black tail neatly in the air as he left the room in a huff. Not long for pouting, he would return after a short time. Usually, he would circumnavigate the room, slowly wending his way toward her location, until finally, he would find a comfy spot nearby her. Often as not, his loyalty, along with a very forgiving spirit and their combined affection for each other, enabled them to compromise on any subject. And so it went; they were a pair—through thick and thin.

This time of year Mrs. Bundle's farm on the knoll was as beautiful as ever. These last few days of autumn were now on the cusp of winter, no snow as yet, but coming any day. The air was frosty and as sharp as the teeth of a saw. It was that time of year when it was fun to run or do an outside work project to achieve the exhilarating sensation of maintaining one's body warmth. The dry dull leaves swirled and turned in the wind, transformed from the brilliant colors they had recently been to nature's dusty *crepe de chine.*

As she moved along at a steady pace, Mrs. Bundle remembered all the days of all the years she had lived here in Pillsonville.

Actually, the farm was in North Pillson Corners, the more rural area about three miles north of Pillsonville. North Pillson Corners was not to be confused with Pillsonville, Pillson Junction, or Pillson Falls, all of which were nearby hamlets.

In 1761, Governor Benning Wentworth of New Hampshire had commissioned a certain George Hartland Pillson to go to the newly chartered area in remote southern Vermont, thereby instituting the modest beginnings of Pillsonville. Before too many years passed, Pillsonville expanded to become the smaller communities of North Pillson Corners (the uppermost rural section of Pillson), Pillson Junction (created when the train service came to Vermont in the 1800's), and Pillson Falls, now primarily a community of artists. These smaller villages all fell under the municipal umbrella of Pillsonville and the whole area was commonly known as "Pillson" to the locals. All told, there were 735 residents in its entirety, sparsely spread out over a twenty-mile radius. Originally, Pillsonville had been a tanning factory village on Twenty Mile Stream but, through the course of many generations, the area around Pillson (as in most of Vermont) turned to the land for sustenance and it became predominantly a farming community.

Now the area had metamorphosed into a collection of eclectic inhabitants, most of who commuted to jobs in other neighboring towns. One thing Mrs. Bundle knew for sure; Pillson had been a wonderful place to have spent her life. She mused that even now, in what would be considered the last half of her life span, she never had regrets about not leaving the area. Growing up here, marrying and raising children (both of whom had now gone their individual ways), and now, still here after all these years.

There was only one problem. She had to admit that these days, now that she was alone in the oversized rambling dwelling at North Pillson Corners, life did not seem as laden with adventure. Ostensibly retired, she spent Wednesday and Sunday afternoon volunteering for the Good Neighbor Food Shelf at the Old

Stone Schoolhouse just up the road, helping prepare hot meals for the needy and elderly and assist with the grocery distribution program. Other than that, she had no specific reason to get out of bed in the morning, no profound reason to feel fulfilled at the end of the day.

Oh, the memories! It had been a contented, complete life on the farm with Arthur and the kids. She smiled as she envisioned the family's activities over the years: playing summer badminton in the backyard and swimming in the back pond just over the ravine, gathering pumpkins to carve into grotesque faces in the fall, cross-country skiing winters over the many miles of area foothills. So many, many memories! She thought of Arthur. As usual, her heart began to ache a bit as she visualized her husband strumming his acoustic guitar and singing to her quietly in the evening after the kids had gone to bed. *"You are my sunshine, my only sunshine…"* oh, his sweet masculine voice traced through her mind, the melody softly playing in her head. Oh, so much to look back on, to love remembering the special times they all spent together.

But now, the kids were on their own, grown and far away, both doing their own thing as they should be, she reminded herself. And, she looked around resignedly, here she and Cracker were, alone on the farm, wishing for…what?

As Mrs. Bundle trudged along past the Old Stone Church, Cracker followed at a fair distance. He stopped to snuffle and then stuck his paw into the chipmunk hole in the ground. He gingerly sniffed the air for anything exciting or interesting and then, nonchalantly tripped along to catch up with his friend and her thoughts.

"What does a mature woman," she expounded, eyeballing Cracker,"what does a *mature* woman do for excitement around here? Cracker-cat, I ask you. Where do we go from here? We need a challenge, I know that for sure. Goodness knows I am not ready to sit in a rocking chair and knit little newborn baby caps.

No way. I have the rest of my life in front of me, with things to accomplish. I've been thinking about this a long time, and…I want things to do! But, what, I haven't a clue….and, how do I find something when I don't know what I want? Oh, *dang!*" Her words ended in a puddle of open-ended feelings.

Cracker looked up at her, his whiskers askance as he twitched his cold black nose. Truth be told, he was rather out of sorts, too. *You sure love that word, 'dang',* he fussed peevishly. Frankly, he thought the word gauche and terribly overused in these parts. Of course, he knew Arthur had often used the other *stronger* words. But, he also noted, Mrs. B had always just humored him, saying affectionately, "*Shush,* dear!" *Anyway, dear lady,* Cracker cat-thought, *I'm rarin' to go! I'm ready whenever you are. So what are we waiting for? Let's do it!*

He assessed her appearance as only a cat can, in that clinical matter-of-fact way. He noted her solid well-built frame, still long and trim, outfitted in her comfortable, unpretentious farm attire. Quite an athlete in her day, she continued the daily regimen of walking and lifting hand weights, which allowed her to maintain sturdy, healthy arms and legs. Her notably hearty face was softly outlined with the chapters of her life, the dancing youthful dark brown eyes still sharp and bright. Lovely almond eyes, a square chin, classic Roman nose, she was still a beautiful woman. These days she preferred the natural look of "no makeup", except for a touch of lipstick now and then. Brilliantly long, silver-brown braids were wrapped neatly around her head in an intricate circle, crowning her extraordinary features, completing the picture. Today, with the old tweed cap perched off-kilter atop the twisted plaits, she resembled an interesting eclectic mix of "class", "country", and a touch of eccentricity. She moved along nimbly, the gnarled walking stick grabbing at the ground as she headed up the steep rural hill. Natural lanolin from handling sheep's wool had kept her hands soft and smooth, far younger-looking than their true age. Tall, hardy, and quite extraordinary looking, she defied the average description of someone of her generation. In conclusion, she exuded vitality.

No doubt about it, she's a corker, he cat-thought proudly.

As they crossed the wooden covered bridge toward Grasshopper Lane, Cracker spotted Sweetness and Moo Shue in the distant meadow up the hill. The stallion and mare were slowly moving and munching, stopping to look up expectantly from their routine, ruminating to see who was coming up the road.

*Hello, friends…*Cracker acknowledged the two horses and they nodded in reply. Mrs. Bundle leaned over the fence, digging deep in her pocket for something she knew they'd fancy. She first came up with a scrawny tissue that had seen better days, then a peppermint candy secure in its cellophane, and finally, a juicy carrot, which she broke in half. Mrs. Bundle whistled low, and then issued the familiar gentle, whispered greeting, "Hello, beauties." Moo Shue blew air through her nostrils, threw back her head, and her huge horse teeth smiled salutations.

Mrs. Bundle placed one piece of carrot on the fence, the other she held up in the palm of her hand. This daily game, which had developed and improved over the years between her and the equines, was now a treat, in and of itself, for all of them. First Sweetness stuck his lips out, emitting a loud whinny, then slobbering them in and around the treat. He secured it tightly in his big rubbery lips, yanking it from Mrs. Bundle's outstretched hand.

Moo Shue, not to be outdone, moved toward her human friend, nodding her impressive dark chocolate-brown head emphatically and voraciously took her carrot half, too. Having captured the tasty vegetable firmly, she chewed loudly, big horse chews.

Mrs. Bundle opened the peppermint plastic covering with her teeth. Whistling again, more shrilly this time, she said dramatically to her captive chewing audience, "So, what's the general consensus in the horse world? I'm desperate for some ideas! Cracker and I need a challenge, a goal, something wonderfully mysterious…

Dang!" She popped the candy into her mouth with emphasis, like an exclamation point ending a thought.

She looked at them expectantly but received no answers to her questions from the staring audience. *Oh well,* she thought, chuckling to herself, *horses are never much help when you're trying to brainstorm.* As the large, placid animals cogitated, then turned away apathetically, Cracker hopped onto the nearby fence post. Jumping to the next bare oak bough hanging just above, he sidled along the limb, halting just inches from the lone sparrow on the branch above. He remained in place, frozen in anticipation, not necessarily longing to harm the bird, more just playing the customary waiting game. *Yes, this gets old, too,* he cat-thought.

Ultimately, the general attitude was catching and Cracker hopped down to the frozen gravel. *G'bye, mates,* he signed off, then followed Mrs. Bundle, who had meandered up the dirt lane.

They walked along in silence for awhile, traversing over the backland engrossed in their own endeavors. A half hour later, they passed Finnard's Brook heading home. Mrs. Bundle stopped in her tracks, then whispered to Cracker, "Listen!"

She could hear a very distant voice cutting through the bucolic silence with the sweetness of a nightingale. Yes, it was singing she was hearing, unclear but quite lyrical tender strains. She stopped to listen, her ears straining, and, at last, she distinctly heard the lyrics:

> " *Yes you did, so you did, so did he and so did I.*
> *And the more I think about it sure the nearer I'm to cry.*
> *Oh, wasn't it the happy days when troubles we had not…*
> *And our mothers made Colcannon in the little skillet pot.* "

*Hmmm…*Mrs. Bundle thought, *I've heard that song before… Scottish? Or…maybe Irish-sounding… yes, I think so!* Specific memories escaped her, but she knew it from somewhere, maybe from the trip to Ireland she and Arthur had taken before he had become too ill to travel. How that country's Gaelic music had delighted them both! Afterward, they'd sit together quietly in the parlor and listen to their Celtic music tapes, reminiscing about their travels.

But, she thought, *who could that be singing now?* The voice was young and bright, and the far off tune continued, echoing, the words indistinct. She cocked her head, smiling, as she continued listening a few seconds longer, humming along until the music abruptly stopped.

She looked into the dark woods and, quite some distance away, saw a faint dusky movement. *What was that?* She squinted through the forest, thick with the late fall underbrush along with a backdrop of majestic pine, cedar, hemlock and spruce. She barely glimpsed a figure, elflike and small, hustling quickly into the woods. The movements were likened to the quickness and agility of a pixie or even an elusive leprechaun. She lost sight immediately as the fleeting figure disappeared into the darkened thicket. Curious by nature, Mrs. Bundle was inclined to take pursuit into the forest; she wondered who on earth could be cavorting in this neck of the woods at this time in the late afternoon. And, during hunting season, too! Of course, in these parts everyone knew everyone, so this was truly an uncommon event. A mystery, she mused...here in our little world! *Hmmm, I wonder,* she thought. A germ of an idea was formulating in her mind.

The red-orange sun slipped down behind the distant trees. Absentmindedly humming the catchy jingle she'd overheard, she called out, "C'mon Cracker-cat!" and the two of them hiked back to their warm hearth.

———⬥———

Across the world, two cunning lizard eyes stared out: cold, calculating, and ruthlessly focused.

Chapter Two
Ready or not...

The next morning she lay in bed luxuriously, slowly waking to the autumn morning sun, and then drew back the covers just a bit. Opening one eye nonchalantly, she peered out at her cozy bedroom. Opening the other eye, she lazily surveyed the surroundings, evaluating her private space. Here was where she spent most of her life now, she thought wryly. Most of her activities had become commonplace, revolving around pleasant but mediocre pastimes such as reading, watching PBS or BBC television shows, and sometimes even taking a dinner tray up to "her nest" in the early evening. She loved her room. So comfortable and safe; it was all very tidy and neat with everything in its place.

The wall shelves and bureau tops were neatly laden with all the years of collecting whimsical items. She loved history and antiques, especially if she could learn the story attached to the bygone item. Curious little carved wooden and pressed tin boxes, bunches of unusual costume jewelry, multi-shaped old perfume bottles, sweet colorful lacy hankies, and a multitude of other bits and pieces shared her space in happy harmony. She just loved old paraphernalia, and mostly, she loved sharing it with others who appreciated it, too.

And, there were all her books. Situated in neat piles like mini-mountains, they awaited her fond touch. These books were like her oldest and dearest chums. From authors Agatha Christie and Sara Paretsky to Lauri R. King and Ngaio Marsh, books abounded in her room and fulfilled her need for adventure and intrigue. These mysteries were diversions into another world outside of rural Vermont where, often as not, life was more than a bit mundane. She lived vicariously through the women detectives she loved so dearly. Women of substance like Mary Russell, and Amelia Peabody, not to mention her Kinsey.

Although their respective choice of genres had been different, accumulating books was a passion both she and Arthur had shared. He had reveled in his collection of old and treasured historical novels, many of which still lined the library walls downstairs. But now, he was gone, and she felt like one of those dated artifacts on the shelves. *I hate feeling as though I'm being put away on a shelf,* she thought stubbornly. *If I have anything to say about it—and I do—my own story has a lot more chapters!*

She felt an inert weight at her feet and looked down to see Cracker's glossy black body curled in a circle. His contented purring interrupted her thoughts; she could feel the warmth of his catbody through the covers.

He looked up expectantly, waiting for the usual routine of his mistress gently sending him on his way to the cold floor. Instead, Mrs. Bundle grabbed her rimless glasses from the bedside table, sat up and reached for her satiny pink quilted bed jacket. *Brrrr! It was chilly this morning!* Quickly slipping it on, she gathered her still-lovely silvery brown hair into the routine morning loose bun at the nape of her neck, pushing the hairpins in one at a time until the chignon was secure. Later, she would style her hair into the customary pile of long winding braids "pillbox-style" around the crown of her head. Without hesitating, she picked up the phone and dialed quickly. *Better do it now, before I have time to change my mind,* she thought.

"Hi Allie!" she said excitedly into the phone.

"L! Is that you?" came back the musical voice, the voice she had known for almost five decades. Althea Swain had been her best friend through middle school, high school, through Mrs. Bundle's long married life, and all the years since. "Allie" (for short) was a remarkable woman who had spent most of her life in service, always vital, always searching for interesting projects. A year younger than Althea, Mrs. Bundle had always looked up to her, admiring her keen ability to be proactive in any crisis.

Althea had led a very interesting life. When she was just 17, her sweetheart, Chaunce Cookson, had enlisted in the Army and, after basic training, had been immediately shipped off to the Korean War. PFC Chauncey Cookson, known as "Kickapoo" for his stellar football career at Woodstock High School, had died two months before the war ended when he was all of nineteen years old. Chaunce had just returned to Korea from Pillson Falls, where he had been on leave visiting his father and proposing to Althea. Thrilled to be his fiancée and looking forward to marrying him after she graduated, Althea was the happiest Mrs. Bundle had ever seen her.

Sadly, the marriage was not to be. Chaunce had jumped on top of a fellow soldier to protect him from an incoming grenade, saving the other soldier's life but losing his own. Althea was severely traumatized by his death and spent the first year after high school in a funk, unable to focus or find meaning in her life. Finally, she decided to become a nurse. By the end of her college years, she had made an unbending commitment to make a change in the world. She had gone on to work in the Peace Corps in Africa in the early 60's. During the Vietnam War she was an infantry nurse caring for the incoming wounded. Later in the 70's, she had thrown herself into public service working with the Ak-Chin Indians at their Arizona reservation. Over time, her activist nature dominated her private needs and she became accustomed to being independent and alone. Choosing never to marry, Althea remained focused in her commitment to help the less fortunate. As the next two decades flew by, she seldom rested before her next big undertaking. Now, having taken an early retirement, she spent her time volunteering; her only other love was her newfound hobby of watercolor painting.

Mrs. Bundle was just "L" to Allie (the single letter name being short for Letitia, a name that Mrs. Bundle had endured with painful chagrin throughout her younger years. Letitia Elizabeth Bundle. Nowadays, most of the world called her "Lettie", although she was known to some as "Mrs. B", or to others as "Mrs. Bundle". But never Letitia. In her adult life, no one had ever called her Letitia, except for one very special person, her sweet husband, Arthur. Mrs. Bundle had always secretly adored the sweet way he would call to her, "Letitia, dear…" or, in his deep singsong voice say, "Letitia Elizabeth, my darling girl…")

This morning, Althea didn't have to wait more than a heartbeat before Mrs. Bundle dove right in. "Allie, I need to bounce something off you. I've been tossing and turning all night. And I've got this idea…."

"L, hold on, girl!" Althea's voice was slow and sleepy, "Good grief! Do you know what time it is?"

"Oh, I'm sorry, honey. What time is it?"

"Hmmm," Althea yawned, "Let's see.. in my California world, it's 4:24 AM! What's up?" Her groggy voice became clearer instantly; years of handling emergencies had steeled her to instant action. "Is everything okay?"

"Yes, fine, dear, no emergency, except…" Mrs. Bundle paused, straightening her bed jacket, taking in a breath, then proceeding with deliberate drama, "This is big, Allie." She took another big breath, and then out it came in a loud, deliberate rush. *"I-think-I'm- going-to-start-a-Detective-Agency!"*

Cracker jumped, his body electrified by her proclamation.

There was a slight pause, just a momentary blip in which Althea recovered quickly. She quipped, "You don't say! L, you never cease to amaze me. You always did need a challenge, something to do, something fun. So, you're bored, right?"

"You know me so well...yes, but, it's more than that, Allie."

They had their own way of communicating—the way all best friends have. Their love of nature and their adventuresome spirits had drawn them together from the beginning. They had braided each other's long hair as young girls, had been on many escapades throughout their childhood, had shared all their secrets and, as chums, the best and worst of their life happenings over their many years.

"Okay...detecting. *Hmmm.* Let's see, that would mean problem solving and intrigue, and mystery, yeah. Uh-*huh.* I can see you doing it." Althea let the idea sink into her tired brain. "But, L, have you thought about the possibility of danger, and might I add very delicately," she cleared her throat, "at your age?" (She placed intentional emphasis on the last three words.)

"Well, yes, I have, as a matter of fact. But then I thought, well, maybe I could use a bit of danger in my life...Things have been so...so..." she searched, "ordinary...and normal.. and mundane, yes, mundane the last few years. I need to shake things up here in my little world. I need something to do at this stage of my life. You, of all people, must understand what I mean."

"'Course, I do. You only go around once in life, that's for sure. Heck, things are too tame here in California, too! I may just come back to my old stomping ground and join in. You know I'll always be a Vermonster." They both chuckled at the old expression combining "Vermonter" and "Monster". "Yes, I can picture this...ooh, yes...." she pronounced in her best soothsayer's voice, as though peering into a crystal ball, "I can see it all now. I envision success and intrigue for you in this new enterprise." She stopped abruptly. "Wait. Of course, the kids know what you're up to, right?"

"Nuh-huh. Not yet, Allie. You're the first one I've told, actually the first person I wanted to bounce the idea off of. I think for now I'll keep it 'on the Q-T.' There's no need to alarm the kids. They've become so protective over the last few years to the point of being exasperating at times, especially since their Dad is gone.

Of course, they mean well, and I understand and appreciate it, but sometimes…well, don't you just want to cut loose? I mean, do something out of the realm of everyday life? You know, step outside the box, as they say—get a little wild. I'm tired of being…. just who I am."

"Uh-huh. I think I know what you're talking about." At any rate, Althea sounded like she was trying to understand.

Mrs. Bundle's voice became excited. "Allie, remember the summer we climbed to the top of Okemo and stayed overnight? There we were, two young girls, barely in our teens, alone on the mountain. Lots of 'spunk' is what they used to call it. Remember the big black bear? Cat's granny! Were we scared! There you were, trying to be so brave with that dang skillet in one hand and the lantern in the other, yelling at that bear! I daresay they heard your hollering all the way to Ludlow! And me, jumping up and down like a banshee throwing our whole food basket as far into the woods as I could! Between the two of us, two young girls too foolish to not back down! Thank goodness our machinations spooked that bear enough to turn on his heel and run headlong back to where he came from!"

They laughed spontaneously, both vividly remembering the escapade.

"Gaw, weren't we foolish!"

"We stayed up the rest of the night scared to death! At first we were hysterical, and then we laughed ourselves silly!" Mrs. Bundle chuckled. "And petrified? I tell you what! We were sure that big old bear was going to come back—"

"—and eat us alive! But we made it through the night, what an adventure!"

Mrs. Bundle sighed. "Anyway, that's what I'm feeling now. I need…more adventures to make even more memories. And goodness knows, Cracker and I could use more fun!"

Althea's second yawn was followed by a sleepy chuckle. "Oh, L…adventure! You mean, like how we used to always find ourselves in a pickle? Remember spelunking in the caves up past Tattle Ridge and getting lost? And, hey! How 'bout the time we took that old rowboat out onto Hapgood Pond, and that stinker Dusty Greene stole our oars? How we had to jump in and swim to shore so we wouldn't hit the Big Falls—remember?"

For a split second they were both silent in their thoughts and then both murmured simultaneously, "Where does all the time go?"

It was followed by a unison "*Owe me coke!*" They both laughed, automatically responding with the customary girlish expression for saying the same thing at the same time.

Althea's voice became serious once more. "Well, all I can say to you, L, is…go for it! And, have fun doing it. You know I'm here for you—I've got your back, right?"

"Right! And I've got yours!"

They agreed to email each other daily, as usual, and Mrs. Bundle promised to keep Althea abreast of each newfound adventure.

As Mrs. Bundle hung up the phone, she gave a satisfied "Hmm." *There*, she acknowledged thoughtfully, *that was relatively painless. Ready or not, we're off on our quest for something new and exciting.* She patted the nearby Cracker absentmindedly.

Having taken it all in, he sat up and shook his impeccably polished body. The involuntary shudder began at his head and the rippling effect continued all the way down until it reached his fine long tail. Then, with an air of impetuosity he'd not recently experienced, he meowed loudly. *Ooooh, baby, here we go….*

Chapter Three

... And Here We Come!

B AND C DETECTIVES
At Your Service
555-888-4231
North Pillson Corners
"no job too big or too small"
(fees reasonable)

"There, that says it all!" Mrs. Bundle said to Cracker as she read the little classified ad she had put into the local paper, *The State Standard*, the previous day. "We'll have to have some professional cards made up, and then, who knows? Let's see what comes through the door, as they say! Right, Cracker?" She put the paper down, looking at the cat over her spectacles. As she grinned at her business partner, the phone rang. *Well, that was fast*, she thought. She answered the hallway phone.

"Hey, Mrs. B, how's the world treatin' ya?"

"Well, Walter, I can't complain. It's nice to hear your voice. How have things been?" Walter Andersen owned the next farm over. He had worked it his whole life as his father and grandfather had before in previous generations. Now, he had relinquished most of the hard work to his twin sons, Carl and Clay. (His beloved wife Angelina, the war bride he'd brought back from Italy in 1947, had died after only a bit more than a decade of their wedded bliss.

Walter and Angelina had tried to have children throughout their marriage but had been unsuccessful. When they finally gave up, Angelina, at age 33, became pregnant, and they were ecstatic. Although it was a difficult pregnancy, Angelina couldn't wait for the day—and when she gave birth to identical twin boys, it was the happiest day of her life. Sadly, complications developed, and she went into a coma. Twenty-four hours later, Angelina Andersen was dead. Walter was left alone, bereft, to learn how to parent two babies. The community had pitched in and helped as best they could during the twin's young lives, and the boys had fared quite well. The twins had always loved the farming life and had stayed close to home, helping their father with the livestock and the crops.)

"Oh, fair to middlin'," he said. "The boys and me been keepin' busy." (He still called them "The Boys" even though they were now middle-aged men.) "The danged snow machine ain't workin' up to puff yet. Consequently and so forth, we're fixin' to get it ready before the first Nor'Easter. It'll be comin' in before too long."

Walter bore a remarkable resemblance to Mr. Green Jeans, the benevolent sidekick of Captain Kangaroo. Mrs. Bundle could envision his face now, the craggy laugh lines crinkling like comical rivulets. His sandy-white wisps of hair sprouted like errant hayseed shoots from the top of his balding dome, which Mrs. Bundle bet was covered, per usual, with his favorite chapeau: either a John Deere or International Harvester hat. Overalls or suspender jeans were his everyday attire, although, on a rare occasion Mrs. Bundle had seen him in his steel-gray, worsted wool suit.

Neither of Walter's boys had ever been too far from home, except for Clay's move to New York City, an uncommon episode, when he was 25. Almost a year later to the day, Clay had returned under somewhat mysterious circumstances. He showed up back at the farm with something quite extraordinary. Clay had returned from the big city and he'd brought with him a little bundle called Angela. That was in 1986. His newborn baby girl, the offspring of a mysterious tryst from "away", had brought absolute joy to father, uncle, and grandfather throughout the subsequent years. Clay had been a devoted father and the baby had flourished under his tender care. Angela, called Angie for short, was the spitting image of her beautiful Italian grandmother, and was now all of 16 years old. No one in the village had ever really learned the full story of how she had come to be, of course mainly because Clay was as quiet, introverted, and undemonstrative as his brother. Surely no one ever asked—that was the way it was in Pillson. If you wanted people to know something, you would tell them.

"So, what's new with the boys? How did Carl do at the Quebec Music Festival?" she asked.

Walter's other son, Carl, had also never made a trip to the wedding alter, laboring solidly on the farm all these years. His one passion, other than farming, appeared to be his love of music. He played the bugle in the local village band, The Pillson Rhythmares, playing weekly concerts on the Village Green at Town Square on warm summer nights. Dressed in the traditional blue band uniforms, the small local group would play everything from Sousa marches to the Standards, along with Carl's personal favorites, the *salsa* or *merengue* tunes. Nowadays, any traveling he did revolved around the town band, playing parades and festivals throughout the Tri-State area and Canada when time and work permitted. He also taught trumpet, saxophone, and clarinet on the side.

Although both boys were decidedly on the reserved and quiet side, Carl's behavior changed markedly on the bandstand. It was as though the rhythm took over and possessed his otherwise sedate demeanor. His body swaying with abandon, he would become animated, almost exuberant, as he blew on his beloved horn, his cheeks puffing in and out like a hornpout in heat. Always in musical nirvana when he was playing his horn, he genuinely enjoyed the crowd's reaction of tapping feet, clapping hands, and spontaneous dancing. Mrs. Bundle had often heard the bugle strains waft like ear candy through the country air from the Andersen farm, spanning the airspace distance with clarity and melodious substance. He was known to play a pretty mean guitar, too, strumming sonorous chords to the standards, blues, and bluegrass melodies in informal gatherings.

"Oh, he had a grand time as usual. Saw the sights, ate some of that French chow, you know, tortie pie and *qweesh* and the like. Stayed at one of them fancy board and breakfasts, him and the other fellas. And, by God, he got home next day in time for the afternoon milkin'. Said he'll be goin' back down to Canada again next year."

Mrs. Bundle knew Walter well, having had many conversations with him over the years. Sometimes it was a bit of a teaser for her, like a fun cryptogram, to try to figure out what exactly Walter was talking about. While she still continued to unravel his words, he pressed on.

"By the by," he said, "we was wonderin' if you'd noticed anythin' missin' lately?"

Funny thing, Mrs. Bundle thought as she pondered the question, and then asked, "Why, what's gone missing over *there,* Walter?"

"A ham." He let the word lie there, then continued, "Don't make sense, though. It ain't the whole ham, just one piece hacked off the side. Left it out t' the back shed to cure. Flustrates the hell out of me. The boys cain't figure it for nothin'." He sniffed. "Whoever it were, they wasn't selfish. Took what they needed, looks like to me, left the rest for us. Nice of 'em."

Mrs. Bundle made a light huffing sound. "Uh-huh. *Hmm,* a ham. Sounds rather peculiar…I haven't really noticed anything…..but, I'll have to check around here to see if anything's disappeared. Have you noticed anything else unusual?"

"Well, Angie said lately that her gas money, you know, the change she keeps in the truck from her tip money at the *L 'n B?* It's been disappearin'. I thought she was pullin' my leg at first, but now that I ponder on it, that truck ain't ever locked, so any body could help theirself." His granddaughter worked two Sunday mornings a month bussing tables at Bette's Lunch and Breakfast Diner. The part-time job kept her in pocket money.

"I'm thinkin' that someone with sticky fingers is makin' the rounds. I was goin' to call O'Malley, 'ceptin' he's up north getting his deer. Weezy Bunton said he ain't comin' back' til next week on account of he'll be stopping over to Burlington at Lizzie's for Turkey Day."

Sheriff Will O'Malley (or, as he was known by the locals, "Sheriff Will O") had grown up down the road in Tyson Corners and was one of Mrs. Bundle's dearest friends. He and Arthur had been buddies in high school, football teammates, and fishing companions. They had joined the service together and had served their country in the Korean War. Later, when they were young married men, they had played in the same softball league. Will had returned from the service to his hometown and entered law enforcement; he was considered by all to be "a local boy who had made good". First starting as a Constable, he had worked his way up through the ranks and then had run for the county sheriff position. Sheriff now for over 20 years, Will was well known throughout the surrounding countryside; his presence gave a sense of security to the couple dozen small communities that made up Windsor County. Although past the age of retirement, he still continued to be a driving force in law enforcement. He carried his 6' 3" rotund torso nimbly even though he was pushing 270 pounds; he also knew every part of his large territory like the back of his stocky hand.

Business aside, he was especially proud of his newly born first grandchild Amelia and visited Lizzie, his daughter, in Burlington when time permitted. Grandfather, daughter, and granddaughter all had the O'Malley long jowls, ruddy complexion, bright red hair, and robust figure.

"Yes," Mrs. Bundle countered, "It might be wise to wait until Will is back, especially with Bette being up at Hitchcock Medical.

I think Zack is pretty preoccupied with taking care of her right now." (Zachary Benois was Pillson's public safety alternative and husband to Bette from Bette's Lunch and Breakfast.)

"Hell's bells! I ain't about to call Old Zack! He's about as slow as molasses running up Gobby Hill and jeesum crowbars! Most of the time he ain't got that thingy in his ear so he cain't hear for nothin'! Well, I reckon it can wait, seeing as Will ain't *assessible* right now..." he trailed off. Before Mrs. Bundle had a chance to respond, he concluded, "Not to mention you cain't never get nary a word in sideways with old Zack. Talks your dang ear off!"

Yes, she thought, *I know what you mean.* She winked at Cracker.

Constable Zack spent most of his twenty hour work week behind a radar gun, patiently awaiting offenders who might unwittingly speed by the rickety old cruiser stationed discreetly behind the bridge in Pillsonville. Zack was all of seventy-five years old and had been Pillson's constable for over forty years. Zackary no longer heard as well or moved as reliably as he used to, causing considerable consternation to anyone who might be in a hurry. And, everyone knew how much Zack liked to talk. He had a habit of doing his job exceedingly well—often being described as "overzealous" in his meandering cross-examinations. As beloved by the community as Zack was, no one wanted to be the target of Zack's sense of civic duty. A Bull Terrier alter-personality emerged whenever he suited up for the job, superceding an otherwise calm nature. Nicknamed affectionately "The Mother of all Constables", his small frame was completely lost inside the constable uniform he'd worn for many years, the police badge shining forth like a lighthouse beacon. Pulling his scrawny body to full height with his trademark Constable hat perched just above his shaggy eyebrows and indubitably balanced precariously on large cauliflower ears, he would immediately become The Enforcer.

"I think Zack's skills are much better served trolling for speeders, don't you?"

"The Rec department thinks so — I know that for a fact!" Walter guffawed. "*Ha!* Every little bit helps!"

They both knew Zack's SOP (standard operating procedure) was to endlessly grill unsuspecting people (mostly from downcountry) once they were trapped in his web, ordering the alleged offender to hand over his or her identification. In his methodical, Vermonter intonation, he would inquire where they were from, if they were visiting in the area or just passing through — all the time executing his questions gently, in a quiet non-threatening way. As the time ticked by with excruciating tediousness, Zack acquired all the information in hearing-challenged spurts and starts, frequently saying, "Eh? You say what?" Finally, he would let the culprit go with a warning, asking only that they stop at Town Hall and make a "contribution" in any amount they saw fit to the Pillson Volunteer Fire Department, The Christmas Giving Project, or the Pillson Recreation Fund. Zack typically would go the extra mile and offer an official escort over to Town Hall to the exhausted party, at which point he would then kindly show them where to put their donation. Most offenders gladly paid, considering themselves lucky to be free of Constable Benois' skilled interrogation techniques. Ironically, Zackary was a pushover when he was out of uniform, most pleasant, and as sociable as a mayor at a town picnic. "You can't get much by old Zack!" the locals chuckled, deferentially staying out of his way when he was in his official capacity and respecting his commitment to enforce speed limits and benign law and order in the village.

For heavier offenses, everyone in the area pretty much depended on Sheriff Will O' and his department, calling the county dispatcher twenty miles away in White River Junction whenever there was a big problem.

Walter sighed. "Good 'ol Zack. Anyways — it's not like it's the crime of the century. But, truth be told! Makes you feel kind of *quingy* when things ain't safe in your own home." Walter had a way of making up his own words, which was sometimes confusing but often endearing. Not infrequently, he just combined two words into one meaning, like an efficient wordsmith. Often, the word meanings were close to accurate, but just a tad off their true mark. Over the many years of their friendship, Mrs. Bundle had observed Walter's hiccups of the English vocabulary. She and Cracker had come to privately refer to them (with great affection, mind you) as "*Walterisms*".

"Queer thing is, what we found on the blasted hill up yonder. Don't know if it's got anything to do with t'other. Snatch me baldheaded, ain't it the oddest thing! It's some kind of strange piece of jewelry. Clay's totally disconfused, but Carl thinks it's got some kind of whammy- hex symbol markings with these stone eyeballs peepin' out at you. Looks foreign and it's heavier than a ton of backyard rocks, too!"

"Hold on, Walter. You found something, but you don't know what it is."

"Uh-huh."

"A piece of jewelry with strange *whammy* things on it…" Her voice trailed off with anticipation.

"That's what I said."

"Is it a medallion, or ornamental talisman, or an amulet of some kind?"

"No, it ain't no kind of animal, for sure—and I got no idea about Tasmanian whatzit. It's a…well, for the life of me, I cain't really decipher it. But, Angie'll be glad to bring t'over later today if you want so you can take a look-see. Looks old, real old. *Hey!* I know you always like that antique *parafennaylee*. God knows who it rightly belongs to, it bein' way up there in the williwags. You gonna be around later this afternoon per usual?"

"Yes, I'll be right here, as usual." She rolled her eyes in frustration at Cracker. Didn't she say she was too predictable?

"Good. I reckon she can bring t'over then."

Well, Mrs. Bundle considered as she hung up the phone. *Well, well!*

"Fantastical!" she pronounced loudly.

Smiling at Cracker, she put her glasses on and sat down at the computer.

Here it comes, he cat-thought ruefully.

Little does Walter know, she thought. *This is going to be our... First Case!*

Great, Cracker cat-thought back, *detective work at its finest.* His mouth opened wide as he gave a huge *Mee-ooww! Move over, Miss Marple, V.I. Warshawski, and yes, you too, Mary Russell,* he cat-thought. *Here comes Mrs. Bundle and her cat protégé to the rescue! Read all about it! 'The Case of the Missing Ham.' No, wait! Not even the whole ham—just a piece 'hacked off the side'. Hallelujah, Horatio!*

But, wait a minute. His topaz eyes turned to thin slits as he lay deep in thought. *That mysterious, foreign-looking thingamabob,* Cracker cat-conjectured, *and the mysterious singing, too. Now, there are two conundrums with some promise...*his wide cat mouth formed a huge grin and his whiskers twitched in delicious speculation.

He stretched out on the oh-so-comfy rug. Cracker had always fashioned himself somewhat of a warrior, a stealth combatant and fearless protagonist incorporating physical prowess and mental strength. His cat mind wandered as his fantasy world began to consume him. *Hmmm, jujitsu or karate—which would it be today?* His almond eyes narrowed into barely perceptible slivers and his fantasy mind took him through the slow, intricate movements. *Hi-Ya!* His left hind leg jerked backward involuntarily. In his dreams, his young, svelte body expertly executed the deliberate martial arts moves. Before too long he was deep into his afternoon catnap, dreaming of younger, more adventurous times.

Chapter 4
"Who's Got the Ham?"

L ater that afternoon, Mrs. Bundle was sitting in the den, deeply engrossed in her mystery, exploring (with Kinsey) the latest escapade into the darker side of the human soul. A small comfortable room off the parlor, the den consisted of a soft blue plaid loveseat and matching oversized swivel tub chair, two end tables, a rectangular combination ottoman-coffee table, a small footstool, and, last but not least, the old comfortable wicker rocking chair. This was her favorite place to curl up and read. Sitting patiently on the table beside her was the latest Mary Russell novel, another adventure waiting to be read. She tapped her foot to Sarah McLachlin's "Angel", totally absorbed in her reading. She absentmindedly hummed along to the CD and for a half-hour or so time was lost with her and Kinsey. When she heard the old Ford truck come rumbling up the road, she closed her book.

Slam! The porch screen door resonated, then the familiar light footsteps could be heard in the back shed. "Mrs. B? It's me!"

"I'm in here, luv," she called back, watching for the girl that was like a daughter to her.

Angie's head appeared around the corner, looking as excited and energetic as ever.

"Hi!" she said, giving Mrs. Bundle a hug with one arm, the

other holding a big basket. It seemed wherever Angie was, there was an air of energy and fun.

"Gumpy wanted me to give you this," pushing the basket out to Mrs. Bundle. Her face was filled with spontaneous, infectious enthusiasm.

Mrs. Bundle peeked inside. She could see three sparkling canned jars of glorious homemade mincemeat, a huge Hubbard squash, bumpy and mottled green, and a small jar of freshly grated horseradish.

"Oh, wonderful. Thank your Granddad for me, will you, Angie?"

She nodded and flopped her lean muscular frame down into the generous tub chair next to Mrs. Bundle, taking Cracker in her lap and nuzzling him. Her face was aglow, her golden skin and rose-colored cheeks invigorated by the unseasonably chilly air. By any standard she was a natural beauty; her classic Italian and Scandinavian features combined to create a lovely, already-developed face. It was a strong, interesting face with intelligence and a blossoming comeliness that Mrs. Bundle delighted in seeing, having known Angie since she was a baby.

Cracker loved Angie, especially because of the attention she lavished on him, and he purred peacefully.

"Well, girl-child, catch your breath. I swear, you're always running. Of course, I've never known you to be any different. From the time you were a little girl, you have never stopped! Here, pass me your cup, would you, luv?" A dainty tray, laden with all the sweet treasures for afternoon tea, sat on the ottoman in front of Mrs. Bundle. She removed the satin tea cozy from the porcelain floral teapot and poured the rich liquid into Angie's cup.

This was a ritual Angie and Mrs. Bundle had shared since Angie was a little girl. Many late afternoons after returning from school and her practices, Angie would come to the farm. She and "Mrs. B" would share stories, discuss current events, and have their special "tea time". On those occasions any number and combination of jams or jellies, biscuits or scones, shortbread, cookies, cucumber and various other finger sandwiches, along with copious pots of hot, luscious tea (with delectable clover honey from Weezy Bunton's farm and tiny pitchers of fresh cream) would be lavishly consumed. And always lots of glorious butter... mmmm! (Of course, as Mrs. Bundle had been a vegetarian for years, she always enjoyed dairy-free soymilk with her tea and soy margarine instead of butter with her scones.)

Angie had come often, at first on her own, as though yearning for the female fellowship she had found lacking at the Andersen house. They had grown to depend on their time together, and now it was part of their routine, often two or three times a week during the colder months. Angie knew without asking that Mrs. Bundle would be there at that time for Afternoon Tea, and Mrs. Bundle knew that Angie would arrive around that time for a visit. And, with Karen grown and gone, it was like having another child again. Their talks elicited a close bond between the two; Mrs. Bundle often the life mentor, the listener, and Angie the bundle of energy, the vessel soaking up every bit of knowledge.

Early on, she asked Mrs. Bundle to show her how to serve the tea properly, "like they do in England." They would laugh together as they pretended, sharing in their love for the formality and ceremony of high tea, and always delighting in the use of Mrs. B's best china teacups and assorted teapots. And, of course, the homemade biscuits and scones that Mrs. Bundle made were "dee-lish!" as Angie always exclaimed as she took her first delicious bites.

"So, how are you, girl?" Mrs. Bundle asked eagerly, knowing that Angie always had interesting news to share with her about her most recent endeavors. She put her feet up on the nearby needlepoint footstool, sat back, and waited to hear what Angie's latest news might be.

As a child, Angie had been a true tomboy, doing anything any boy could do and better. Whether it was running, jumping, swimming (or even fighting, for that matter, if she had to) she was the best at whatever she attempted. She moved like a slender gazelle as a child, beautifully fit, and bright as a sunburst. She also had a soft spot in her heart for anyone downtrodden or mistreated. In essence, she had an innocence about her, offset by a solid no-nonsense attitude like her grandfather, father, and uncle.

Mrs. Bundle remembered Angie coming to her one day after school when she was eight years old sporting a bruised and black eye—the result of having jumped Monky Brushwein. Monky was the biggest bully in the school. Evidently, he had been terrorizing little Jimmy Lazareth, and Angie had taken it upon herself (when no one else dared to intercede) to leap onto Monky's back, hanging on gallantly through his direct punch to her eye. She sunk her nails into his gullet and, unable to catch his breath, he gave up, exhausted. She had gained new respect on the playground that day, and Monky had steered clear of her the rest of the school year.

Angie had learned early on from her family of men about standing up for oneself under adversity and, if necessary, suffering the consequences afterward. As Mrs. Bundle quietly nursed her black eye, they had discussed the merits of involving an adult in the fracas, at which point Angie had said, very patiently and with complete earnestness, in her little-girl voice, "Yes, but, Mrs. B., *sometimes* you just have to take matters into your own hands!"

Mrs. Bundle had walked her home, helping ease the shock and anger that ensued when her father, uncle, and grandfather learned their pride and joy had been injured. Of course, fighting was all well and good for the Andersen men as long as their "Angie-girl" didn't get hurt, and they were tempted to go find Monky and string him up by his ankles. That was, until they learned that Angie had come out the unabashed winner in the fracas. At that point, they all had a good laugh about the event.

Angie continued, "Well, everyone's winding down for next week, and we're in the soccer finals. And, I've been gearing up for the winter sports schedule. And, of course, I'm lifting so that I'll be ready for lacrosse in the spring."

Mrs. Bundle and Arthur had always gone to every sports-related event Angie had been in, from T-Ball at age 6, then soccer, softball, basketball, and now lacrosse, Angie's favorite sport and one which she had achieved All-American status. Mrs. Bundle had always enjoyed her spunk and never-give-up attitude, and the rough sport of lacrosse suited her to a "T". Originating with the Indians and the oldest game on the North American continent, lacrosse was a game the Indians played not only for recreation, but also to settle tribal disputes and to toughen warriors for fighting. Modern lacrosse (called the fastest game on two feet) was a combination of football, hockey and basketball, a grueling test of stamina, and Angie played it well.

Truth be told, Angie reminded Mrs. Bundle of herself at that age. Mrs. Bundle's agility, combined with expertise, had translated to her own great athletic ability on the softball field and had helped win her high school's State Softball Championship during her senior year.

As she looked at Angie, she was startled to realize to what end she was coming into her own now. Her comely, large brown eyes held green-yellow flecks (they had always reminded Mrs. Bundle of a dewy fawn's appearance), and her beautifully golden olive complexion (a combination of her grandmother's skin tone and her Norwegian paternal heritage) shone with young vibrancy. Her hair was a rich chestnut brown, with streaks of blonde, pulled back lazily today into the current pony tail style, wisps flying all over and framing her excited face. She wore the everyday uniform of young adults nowadays: hooded sweatshirt, overly long faded jeans, and sneakers.

"Oh, yeah! You wouldn't believe what's been going on, Mrs. B! Coach Conklin has made arrangements for me to meet the

Lacrosse coach at Bates College! I'm so excited—it would be so cool to go there, or Bowdoin. I'm so psyched! Of course, it seems like it's light-years away…but Dad said it's not too early to start looking at colleges—even though it's still my junior year. What do you think?" Angie asked, her eyes big and wide.

Cracker jumped off her lap and stood at attention at her feet. *Good going, girl*, he cat-thought proudly.

"Oh, honey, what a wonderful prospect for you. And, both are wonderful schools, too! You have so much opportunity to do well in life with a college education and, to be able to play lacrosse, too, would be the best of both worlds." Mrs. Bundle smiled back at Angie, excited to see her enthusiasm. "So, what else has been going on?" They caught up quickly on the rest of all the local news and current events, and then Mrs. Bundle said, "By the way, what's this about things going missing over at your house?"

Angie bit into a scone, melted butter frothing on her lips, "Yuh, Gumpy's all in a freak about it—oopsey! Sorry…"(she picked up a crumb from her lap and popped it in her mouth), "…strange things have been happening, quite bizarre, really. Like the 'Ham Thing'," (she put up her long fingers in quotes signals), "and, I know for a fact my gas money in the truck is being pilfered, and…. Uncle Carl says he can just… feel… that someone's been watching him. He says, 'Something pesky is boring a hole in my backside!' It's a hoot, Mrs. B! When he's outside doing chores, he keeps reeling around, quick-like, convinced that someone's behind him." She rolled her spirited eyes. "He hasn't caught anyone watching him yet." She took a couple more bites and said again, "*Mmmm, de-lish!*"

She continued thoughtfully, "It's little things, though, like… I can't find Binkie's horse blanket—I know I left it in the stable on the rack, and," she put her hand to her head in thought, "this is really bizarre. The colander has disappeared off the back porch! Isn't that weird? Now, what on earth does someone need a colander for?"

Mrs. Bundle pondered the last blast of information and sat back, peering at a ladybug crawling on the ceiling. Thinking out loud she cogitated, "A piece of ham, spare change, a warm blanket, and a colander...well, the colander has me stumped, but...wait a minute! Add a pair of deerskin gloves to that list!" she said, surprised to have come up with another missing item. She poured another cup of tea for Angie and herself. Dripping honey from the spoon into her cup, her hand froze in mid-air.

"And," Mrs. Bundle paused as she screwed up her face in that thinking-mode gaze. Then she exclaimed, "add a personage of unknown identity, age, or gender singing in the woods!"

"Huh?"

"Yes, that's right, luv. Yesterday Cracker and I heard the loveliest singing on our hike—no idea who it was, though...they ran off before we could get a look. Actually, it sounded as if it came from out of nowhere."

Cracker yawned from his spot on the floor, cat-thinking, *Finally! How long was it going to take, my dear, to put that together? Sometimes, I wonder that you're ignoring my finely tuned, steel trap of a mind on purpose.*

She continued, "The music was lovely, lilting, and somewhat familiar to me. I know I'd heard it before.....It was Irish, I think!"

Angie looked at Mrs. B. in surprise. "Irish?"

"Yes, and I'm missing Arthur's deerskin gloves, the ones I always wear. Let's see, I haven't seen them since...let me think...Sunday! Yes, now that I think on it, that's the last time I wore them."

She paused, reveling in her realization, which she shared with Angie dramatically. "It appears we have a mystery here, my dear."

Angie pulled a hard rubber ball from her pocket. She absentmindedly started tossing it in the air, a habit she had developed over the years whenever she needed to concentrate. It was a lacrosse ball, made of solid rubber, slightly smaller than a baseball but just as hard. Often, she bounced it on the floor between tosses, distractedly catching it in one hand, then the other. She had become very adept at throwing and catching the little globe. It was almost as though the sturdy white ball was an extension of her hands; tricking the ball through her nimble fingers, skillfully balancing it and then popping it into the air and catching it.

"All I know is, it feels a little creepy having things go missing, especially around here where everyone knows everyone, and I'd feel better knowing it's nothing serious." She gulped. "Oh m' gosh! I almost forgot the most important thing!"

She put the ball back into her pocket.

"Take a look at this, Mrs. B." she said as she reached into her other pocket and pulled out a lovely, old but crumpled, lace hankie delicately wrapped around a hard, bumpy object. Faint clinking noises came from inside as she carefully uncovered the item. Then, she handed over the object to Mrs. Bundle's waiting, eager hands. It appeared to be a pendant of some weight and considerable age.

"Is this what Walter was talking about this morning, Angie? Let me see….why, it *is* a necklace of some sort, isn't it? Oh, well, look here, it's quite old by the looks of it, and the design is really ornate, just as he tried to tell me."

"Dad found it on the top of Old Man Boulder when he was hunting—it was just laying there, on the rocks."

Both were familiar with the spot, far into the high land of North Pillson Corners. Old Man Boulder was a huge granite rock formation northwest of the Andersen property. If one stood at the very top of the stone monument, there was a magnificent view of sweeping patchwork quilt landscapes, miles of farms, multileveled forests, and mountain ranges. As one approached Old Man Boulder from a distance, the slabs of convoluted rock configuration looked like the deeply-lined craggy face of a very old man. It was a wonderfully quiet spot that many of the locals appreciated, not only for the spectacular views of the far mountain ridge but also for the solitude that gently rocked one's senses into a peacefully meditative state.

Mrs. Bundle pulled out her little magnifying glass from the side table drawer next to her. The glass had a variety of uses, from helping to see while darning socks, to viewing splinters needing to be tenderly pulled out.

She looked at the huge pendant carefully. "It's silver, I think, very old and look at that patina! It's larger than normal, about four inches in circumference I'd say. There are some stones in the piece, rather dirty, not sure if they're real or fake. Let's see, red, green, blue, and yellow. They're set in to look like eyes, I think. Can you see it, Angie?"

She held the magnifying glass over the item for Angie to see. They spied delightfully through the magnifying glass together, their heads close, both intently fascinated with this new treasure.

Mrs. Bundle paused, then continued, "It looks like four birds' heads, somewhat intertwined. Geese, or swans is what I think they are, their long necks interlinked. Yes, and then surrounded by braiding of some sort, very ornate, ancient-looking designs to me."

"Don't those things at the bottom look like waves to you?"

"Yes! And, see, Angie, that looks like the shape of a…bell. There! Yes, clear as day. That's a bell of some sort."

"Yes, I noticed that. That's what I thought, too! It's set in—almost like a puzzle piece. Hey, like a secret piece of some sort. Mrs. B, do you think this could be a talisman, or something mystical, you know, religious-like?"

"Well, maybe, a good luck piece, or some kind of mysterious religious piece. Who knows…maybe of foreign origin. It rather looks like something from Old England to me." She sat back. "So, it was just sitting there on the rock? Up there, in the middle of nowhere?" Angie nodded her head. "Yeah, and at this time of year, too! Bizarre, isn't it, Mrs. B?"

Mrs. Bundle looked at her, then at Cracker, then leaned back and pondered the situation. Cracker opened his mouth wide, meowed loudly, and hopped into her lap, sniffing at the large necklace.

Angie was on the edge of her seat. "I'd like to get to the bottom of it! It's driving Gumpy crazy, and Dad and Uncle both have their doubts about who might have left it, or how it got there, not to mention what's going on around here with things going missing."

She scratched her head in thought, then smiled at Mrs. Bundle. "It's a real mystery, isn't it? Wicked!"

Mrs. Bundle's face lit up. "Yes….it's quite…" she paused, "…fantastical!" She leaned back again and closed her eyes, then drew in a deep breath in quiet repose. She stroked Cracker's shiny black back as she pondered her next thought. Angie waited patiently for a minute.

Finally, exploding, she asked excitedly, "What?"

Mrs. Bundle opened her eyes, now twinkling brightly. She looked over at Cracker, who deftly flicked his tail in the air in gentle anticipation. Nodding at Cracker, she turned to Angie and smiled coyly. "My dear Angie, how would you like to join Cracker and me on an Adventure?"

Chapter 5

A–Hunting We Will Go

As she stepped off the farmhouse granite front stoop into the dooryard, Angie turned to Mrs. Bundle.

"Thanks again for the tea, Mrs. B. "

"You're welcome, my dear."

"Oh! Gumpy wants to know if you're still planning to come for Thanksgiving—he said to tell you he's making the coconut cream pie again this year…." She trailed off, enticing Mrs. Bundle. She knew how fond Mrs. Bundle was of her grandfather's celebrated pies, especially the cream pies.

Mrs. Bundle nodded, realizing Thanksgiving was next week. She hadn't done a thing to prepare, nor had she given it much thought.

"You know, girl, with the kids in their faraway places, I honestly hadn't thought much about my plans. My Lord, it's next Thursday, isn't it?"

(Mrs. Bundle's son Leslie, his wife Donna, and their son nine-year-old son Leslie, Jr., were in Japan where Leslie was in the diplomatic service. Her daughter Karen was somewhere off the Alaskan seaboard in the Bering Sea working for Greenpeace. Consequently, with no close family around, the thought of Thanksgiving dinner had been on the back burner for Mrs. Bundle.)

"Of course, I'll be there! I'll bring the usual favorites, all right?" She gave Angie a hug. "What would I do without you all? Bless you, you're a good girl. Now, are you all set with 'The Plan'?"

"Yes, Saturday morning, first thing. I'll be ready. Oh, I can't wait! I'll tell Gumpy, Dad, and Uncle about our exploring, and our plan for a hike out back, and that we'll keep them in the loop, but, I'm thinking we might want to keep the detective thing on the Q- T for now. You know how they like to horn in and be 'helpful'." She again made the little quote marks. "Plus, they might give you a hard time. They just think of you as Mrs. Bundle, next door neighbor. Anything new or different might kinda throw them for a loop. Not to say, they can also be stick-in-the-muds sometimes."

"Well, maybe they could use some shaking up, too." she laughed.

Angie nodded. "They've been doing the same things the same way forever! Geez, Gumpy's worn those same blasted overalls and same John Deere hat for as long as I can remember! And Uncle and Dad, they just keep plugging along on the farm, happy as two peas in a pod. Not much new or exciting happens when you're getting up milking every morning. So, I doubt they'll go hogwild about any detective work going on. How about we tell them if we end up finding out anything important?"

"Hmm. I don't like the idea of keeping anything from your father. But, you are right; they might feel the need to accompany us. We'll make sure we bring the cell phone with us. That way, if we run into anything unusual, we can give them a holler right away. Besides, what can we possibly find around here, in our little world? Right! Well! We've got a lot of work ahead of us! Between now and Saturday I'll get over to Mabel's at the Black Crow and see if she can shed any light on the pendant."

Mabel Weatherby ran the Black Crow Curio Shop, a tiny, hole-in-the-wall memorabilia and antique shop down the road in Woodstock. She and Mrs. Bundle had known each other for years, having gone to high school together. Later in life they had reconnected when Mrs. Bundle discovered her shop one day, and they both realized they shared in the joy and art of collecting memorabilia. Mabel's shop had grown over the years, and she had gained a reputation for honest trading within the network of local antique dealers.

Mabel, though slight in stature and unassuming in nature, knew her antiques and had been a wealth of knowledge over the decades to people (like Mrs. Bundle) whenever someone needed information about a collectible old item. Mrs. Bundle would bring an item in to Mabel and the shopowner always seemed to be able to ferret out the fact from the lore, identify most any old piece of jewelry or artifact, often sharing research information on the age or history of the piece, too. She was also a tremendous resource when it came to historical data.

"And I'll call Mrs. Northrup," Angie chimed in with her to-do list, "and Casey Juniper, and the Watkins and see if they've noticed anything strange up on Tattle Ridge."

Tattle Ridge was the neighboring high ground around the Bundle and Andersen parcels, and not too far from Old Man Boulder. Most of this expanse of beautiful Vermont hillcountry was tranquil and remote and the few hardy individuals who lived up on the Ridge were strong, private people who generally liked things to remain undisturbed. Angie knew the "hill people" and that land well, having spent her childhood years exploring, even spelunking the cave structure on the remote side of the ridge. In her own girlhood days, Mrs. Bundle and Althea had done the same thing in the same area. Mrs. Bundle felt a shiver of excitement and anticipation that she would soon be visiting that area again. Fun! Finally, some fun! Something to look forward to…

She sniffed the cold north air expectantly. "Well, they'll be frost on the pumpkin tonight! You best get going before you get a chill! Talk with you tomorrow and we'll tie up loose ends, luv. Later!"

"Back at ya!"

Chapter Six

The Swan Children

The next morning, Mrs. Bundle went out to the barn, slid the hefty barn door aside, and fired up her darling 1963 emerald green Volkswagen Beetle Sedan. The 40-horse engine chugged sluggishly in the cold north air, weakly wheezing and sputtering like a fragile *grande dame,* and then finally came to life with a happy hum. It sounded like the hum of a sewing machine, the new automotive 'heads' and muffler making her sing like a bird. Years ago, she had lovingly been nicknamed "JuneBug". Her curvy, trim body had always resided in the barn so there was absolutely not one spot of rust to be seen anywhere. She was just a great old Bug. The 2-door sedan had most all of its original parts, including the original roof rack above the sporty sunroof, and the diminutive Junebug still drove amazingly tight for having covered over 212,000 miles.

Luckily, Hudson's Garage had always serviced the vehicle; the oil had been changed religiously every 3000 miles. Royal Hudson, Jr., the unaffected proprietor, had tears in his eyes everytime he poignantly waved his oil-stained rag farewell to Mrs. Bundle and Junebug as they put-putted away from his modest establishment. The Beetle was like his special child, grown now, but always returning home for nourishment and friendly visits, and it was forever difficult to bid his child adieu.

"That darn Junie!" he'd say, wiping his eyes with his workrag as he shook his head in wonder. "She just keeps a-goin' and a-goin'."

There was no doubt that Junebug was one of Mrs. Bundle's most cherished collectibles, a relic of bygone eras, not to mention all the memories of many a carefree family outing. When the kids were young, they all would squeeze into the little Beetle, its roof rack securing picnic and sporting paraphernalia, and off they would go for an "Adventure". That had been Arthur's term, and the magical word meant going from a dull afternoon to instantly transformed fun for all of them.

"Who wants to go on an 'Adventure'?" he would ask, and they'd all go into a frenzied mode of enthusiastic emergency action, everyone scrambling around each and every which way to gather the necessary accoutrements for a fun day of being gloriously taxied around, sunroof open, by their adventuresome Junebug. She never failed them over hill and dale, up and down the back roads of Vermont, and into hidden and sometimes hard-to-access areas off the beaten path. It was always an adventure, to be sure.

Undeniably, the best part about Junebug was the original 8-track stereo player that had come customized with the car. Still intact, the unit played Mrs. Bundle's assorted library of tapes with precision and clarity, and the collection of hard-to-find, 8-track tapes had grown over the many years. This morning was no exception as she popped *Tom Jones Live in Las Vegas* into the cassette player.

"Let's roll!" she said merrily to no one in particular, backing the tiny Beetle into the driveway as the "The Voice's" lyrical bass tones of "*It's not unusual to be loved by anyone...*" bounded forth from the speakers.

Following Arthur's death, she had been advised by well-meaning folks to get a more reliable, newer car, one that would be more durable for the cold Vermont months. However, she was gently, but solidly, attached at the hip to her companion, the smooth leather seats comfortable in all the right places (having weathered many a bumpy back Vermont road) and the steering wheel molded to her fingers like a soft pliant glove. And whenever the natives saw the '63 bright green Beetle, they knew it was Mrs. Bundle and Junie burning up the roads of Pillson.

She crooned along with the seductive gravelly voice, *"But if I've found that you've changed at anytime, It's not unusual to find that I'm in love with you, whoa-oh-oh-oh- oho-o-o-..."* and she put-putted out of the yard.

Leaning on the jewelry counter, Mabel peered through her jeweler's loupe and studied the pendant in her steady hand.

"Well, it's Celtic. I know that for sure, from the design. And platinum, or platinum gold, dear, not silver, very nicely done, I might add. See the patina? That comes with age. The pattern is interesting. Celtic crosses surrounding what looks like three, no, make that four, swans' heads. And, I think the stones are real, precious or semi-precious, maybe even sapphire. Yes, if it is, I think it's pretty rare, that cornflower blue color, and this one…" she pointed gently, "is an emerald, then a ruby, I betcha, and yes….that's, maybe, a yellow diamond! Definitely not paste." She paused and looked up over her glasses at Mrs. Bundle.

"Real stones? And rare? And platinum, too! Really, Mabel! Go on, I'm captivated! What else can you tell me?"

"Okay," she peered again, "these swans' heads, here, yes…let's see…I've got a book right here at the shop that cross-references specific subject area and categories with Celtic jewelry…let's try that!"

She looked over her bifocals again, then nimbly hopped up onto the stepladder behind her. She reached long for a book on the top shelf.

Jumping down, she said, "Here we are, great resource book, *Celtic Jewelry and Design* by Oscar Delahanty." She sat down on the stool and opened to the back of the book. "Okay, let's look up swans and see what it has to say."

Thumbing through the index, she slid her pointer finger down the 'S' column as she read through, "'seal', 'stars', no," then suddenly jabbing excitedly, "here we are, 'Swans', pages 237-252. Yes, let's see....yes, here it is!" She rummaged through the thin pages until she found the section. Thumbing quickly through each page, she finally squealed in delight. She pushed the book triumphantly into Mrs. Bundle's view. "Oooh! Look here, Lettie!"

"Mabel, you amaze me! Why, those look almost identical to our piece!"

There, in front of Mrs. Bundle, were three pictures of various swan configurations with ornamentation remarkably similar to the pendant she held in her hand, but none as elaborate as the one on the counter. Mabel took the book back and began reading aloud:

Four Swan Design Jewelry of Ireland: usually in brooches, pendants, or watch fobs, popular and common in silver, legend-based on the folklore story of the *Children of Lir*

The Legend of the Children of Lir
The legend of the Children of Lir has been around in many versions for centuries and an essential part of Irish folklore. The story is varied, as with most legends, and the contrasting tales of events, names, and places are part of the mystery. The legend begins thousands of years ago in ancient Ireland when warlords ruled the country.

The ancient King Lir had four children: Fionnuala (the eldest, a daughter), Aodh or Aed (a son, Fionnuala's twin), and younger twin sons (Fiachra and Conn). Their mother had died at the last birth, and soon there was a new stepmother

Aoife, who never liked the four children. Very jealous, Aoife finally decided she must get rid of the children in order to have Lir's full love and attention. The next day she ordered her chariot to be readied and told Lir that she was taking the children to visit their grandfather.

Her real plan, though, was to have them killed. At the last moment, she backed down and banished them to a faraway land for 900 years, where they were transformed into swans with beautiful human singing voices as a final farewell favor from the Queen. The spell destined them to spend 300 years on Lake Derravaragh, 300 years on the Sea of Moyle and 300 years on Inis Glora. The legend goes on that the evil Queen said that their sentence would only be lifted when they heard the first bells of Christianity.

And so, their father found them in their swan bodies and was heartbroken that he could not take them home with him, nor could he break the spell. He vowed that their first 300 years would be spent in bliss, and he banished his wife Aoife into exile.

Over the years, people came from many lands to hear the beautiful singing and the wonderful stories told by the swans. The songs were calming and soothing, and everyone who heard the music would sleep soundly. The legend grew, and when the swans had to leave for the Sea of Moyle, they left their father behind not knowing they were never to see their father alive again.

The next 300 years on the Sea of Moyle, life was harsh for the Children of Lir. At one point, a fierce storm turned the sea violent and deadly. The brothers and sister swans were afraid they would be separated in the storm, so they agreed to meet at the legendary Rock of the Seals. Fionnuala, the oldest sister swan, waited there for her brothers, weeping, until finally they miraculously appeared and all were saved. After this, they vowed never to be separated again. Fionnuala would take care of her 3 brothers, always taking Aodh under her breast feathers, Conn under her right wing and Fiachra under her left wing.

The final 300 years of Aoife's curse were spent on Inis Glora where the most severe harshness was dealt them one hundred fold. They froze in the sea and suffered great pain. After this terrible time was spent, they finally made their way back to their father's home with great difficulty. To their sorrow their father was dead and nothing remained of their childhood home.

After a night, they traveled to Inis Gluaire and it was here that they first heard the Christian bells. They were elated. The spell was finally lifted, but sadly, the Children found themselves old and frail with death close at hand. Their one final wish was that they be baptized and buried together in the same way they had sheltered each other during their years of hardship with Aodh resting at the breast of his sister Fionnuala, and with Fiachra and Conn sheltered within her embrace. Their wish was respected with reverence.

The legend continues that when the Children of Lir departed life, people miraculously saw four beautiful children flying over the lake and going straight up to heaven. Today, the legend of the Children of Lir lives on in the beautiful jewelry that has been made in Ireland for centuries, and with the folklore which can be heard recounted by story tellers in Irish pubs scattered around the country. Also, it's a fascinating fact that swans are still considered protected birds in Ireland.

Mabel casually retrieved a vintage tatted hankie from her pocket and, sliding her butterfly glasses up onto her head, she dabbed at her eyes. "So, apparently, that's the legend surrounding this type of Lir jewelry, Lettie. Don't mind me, I always get wrapped up in my work!" She sniffed, cleared her throat, then set the text aside.

"Well, it truly is amazing to me what kind of story a simple piece of jewelry can tell! Rather tragic, isn't it? And very Celtic-romantic, wouldn't you say?" Mrs. Bundle found herself strangely touched by the tale, and she, too, sat silent for a moment. Neither of them was inclined to pass on melodrama if given the chance and they paused for a moment of brief introspection, each one processing the strange legend and its relationship to the piece of jewelry. Mabel was the first to move on, collecting herself daintily as she gave her thick hair, striated raven black and white, a quick shake, the glasses atop the mass defying gravity, staying locked in the same position. Her hands fluttered into and around her hairdo, fluffing it absentmindedly.

Mrs. Bundle said, "I'm thinking this particular piece has some Gaelic symbolism in its design. What do you think, Mabel?"

"Hmm, yes, most definitely. Let's take another look and see what we can come up with."

She picked up the heavy, patina-stained necklace and peered at it closely. "Okay, yes, see, that must be the big sister swan covering the brother and the twins in her breast and under her wings, like she's protecting them! And yes, see here? Those wavy squiggles must be the storm waves on the Sea of Moyle. And there's the bell!"

"Yes! For the bells of Christianity, when the spell was lifted?"

"Righto! And those Celtic crosses surround the swans, almost looks like the swans are imprisoned in a barrier or fencing of some sort, don't they?"

"Yes, I can see that…. Who do you suppose made this piece? Do you have any way of finding out how old it could be?" Mrs. Bundle asked excitedly.

"Well, let's see if there are any markings on the back." Mabel took the intricate medallion and turned it over. "Yes, here, take a look at this. There are markings, for sure. See that indented mark that looks like a…head of some sort? Here, let's look through the loupe. Where did I put that blasted thing?" She searched the jewelry counter in frustration until she found her important tool, then looked through its magnifying lens. "Aha! Yes, it looks like…uh-huh. That's a lion's head to be sure. See?" She turned the jeweler's loupe over to Mrs. Bundle so she could take a look, too.

Mrs. Bundle squinted at the indented markings. "Yes, I see it! And some other markings, too! Looks like some letters, I daresay. I think I can make out two letters…got it! '*I, period, I, period*'. And, there's a minute mark after it. Three sliver marks, one atop the other. Rather like a star." She sat back, reveling in the discovery, and looked expectantly at Mabel. "What do you suppose that means- 'I.I.' And the mark after it?"

"Yes, well dear, as I said, those are likely the identifying marks. The letters will tell us who made the piece, and hopefully, from those markings one can then research the age. We may even be able to find out what the value of the piece is. Sometimes it can be pretty interesting stuff. Do you want me to explore further?"

"Fantastical! Yes, let's pursue this, Mabel, if you don't mind. This is one component of a mystery of sorts that I'm involved in. I can't go into it now, but the more we can find out about the piece, the more it will help us find out what our next step will be."

Mabel put her index finger to her chin in thought. She knew Mrs. Bundle well enough to know she would share more information when the time was right. Meanwhile, she was willing to go with the flow.

"Righto, Lettie, no problem! You never know what we might come up with!" If an old friend asked a favor, it was good enough for her. She nodded and continued. "I'll make copies of the story for you. Would you like that? I'd like to keep the necklace here for a couple days so I can really study it. It'll go in the safe right there," she pointed below the counter. "And, you can be assured, mum's the word on this end! Let's just see what I can discover!"

―――

That evening, after Mrs. Bundle had finished reading the Children of Lir story over the phone to Angie, she sighed and asked her, "So, girl, what do you think of that?"

"Who would have thought the pendant could tell such a tragic story, Mrs. B?" She heard the excitement in Angie's voice. "But, really, now I'm really wondering how that piece of jewelry got up on the Boulder. That is really weird. Was it just dropped there from outer space? It just doesn't make sense. No one's up there at this time of year except maybe hunters, and we'd have heard about it if someone had a piece of jewelry go missing. I wonder how long it was there before Dad found it? Someone, somewhere must be wondering….and missing that piece."

Mrs. Bundle agreed. "Those are some of the same questions I have, too, luv…and hopefully, we can find out the answers somehow. What did you find out from the Ridge folks?"

"Well, nothing specific, only hints of something fishy going on. Casey says he hasn't noticed anything missing, other than a few canned goods and vegetables from his storage shed. He said he thought his Aunt Lucy had been by and had helped herself to his storeroom, which evidently she does on a regular basis. But, he wasn't sure about anything. Mrs. Northrup said she was of the mind that something queer was up. She has noticed things missing over the last couple weeks from her wash line. Wait a minute; let me get my list!" Rustling sounds were heard, then she resumed. " Here it is, yeah….heavy socks, one of Jasper's woolen hunting shirts, and a couple old towels. She confessed she thought the Clancy kids might be pilfering whatever they could get their hands on again, so she wasn't too concerned. But she did say if much more went missing she was going to talk to the Sheriff about it."

"Well, if it was the Clancy boys—not saying it is, mind you— we'll look into helping them out again. Those Clancy kids have had a hard time keeping things together," Mrs. Bundle added sympathetically, "what with their home situation and their Dad…" she trailed off.

They both uttered, "*Eh-huh*," acknowledging the other's unspoken thoughts.

Everyone knew the Clancy boys: Nicholas, Christopher, Anthony, Joseph, and Andrew, all named after their mother's favorite Patron Saints. A devout Catholic, Mary Clancy had done her best with, at the very least, a difficult situation. Over the years, the family had always had a troublesome time making ends meet, and had fallen on more austere times recently. This was especially true since late last summer when their father had been carted off to the Woodstock Regional Correctional Facility. Jesse Clancy had been caught red-handed poaching bears in the Northeast Kingdom, and his future did not appear too promising.

The boys' mother worked three jobs to make ends meet, and consequently, couldn't always keep an eye on their whereabouts, which caused an abundance of problems as the boys often found creative ways to make money. Creative meant often "finding" and selling anything that wasn't nailed down. They customarily worked as a slick team of five, collecting other people's belongings in an organized and systematic manner like a well-oiled machine.

After Jesse Clancy's arrest, the villagers had come together to try to help Mrs. Clancy and her family during their hardship. Mrs. Bundle was under the impression that, because of the intervention, the boys were all doing as well as could be expected at this point. Some of the local family men had volunteered to take each boy individually, as a loosely organized mentor network, to focus them on more positive ventures. Nick and Chris Clancy, the older two boys, were now working at Harper's Feed Store part-time after school and weekends. Anthony, the scholar of the group, had been given a part-time job working at the Pillsonville Library under the direction of Louis Montembeau, Head Librarian, so that the third Clancy boy's spare time was absorbed in reading about (rather than planning) escapades. The youngest two, Joey and Andrew, were now on a regimented after-school and weekend schedule of helping area farmers with simple chores. The wives made sure the boys were picked up, fed, homework and chores done, then delivered home safe and sound to Mary Clancy's little hut in the woods. The gentle male guidance, interspersed with motherly interaction, appeared to be working, and all the boys were now doing well in school and seemed stabilized. Hence, things seemed to be back on track while the Clancy clan awaited Jesse's trial.

Angie continued on with her accounting. "But, Mrs. B! The best scoop I got was from Esther Watkins! She definitely saw something very interesting last Tuesday. She was in the barn patting down her mare after her ride, as usual, and she heard a ruckus out back behind the tool shed. You know her big Lab, Corey, right? Kind of mean, if he doesn't know you? Well, Corey was barking up a storm and had chased someone all the way up the hill and into the woods behind the house. She ran out just in time to see a tall person in a long black coat—leather, she thought—disappear behind the stone wall. She didn't call Sheriff Will-O' 'cuz she knew he wasn't around this week, according to Weezy. She didn't think it was that important, especially since she had Corey to protect her. And," Angie's voice escalated as she passed along this last piece of information, "she says Flossie's been off her milk for weeks—which she says is very odd!" She drew the last word out, and Mrs. Bundle could almost see Angie arching her eyebrows.

It seems all of Pillson is aware that the Sheriff is away on his hunting trip this week, Mrs. Bundle thought, making her familiar clucking sounds. "Hmm. Well, it sounds like someone may be helping themselves to fresh milk and other necessities. And one person of unknown identity almost got his backside bit off by Corey! I'd say all in all we're making some progress, wouldn't you?"

"Sounds pretty fishy to me!"

"I'm going to email Althea before I go to bed and see if she can give us some of her wise intuition. I think it can be very effective, you know, to have an outside party involved, sort of to bounce things off?"

"Right. She can be our remote think tank." With delicious conspiracy, they laughed, then Angie asked, "What do you think we'll find out there in the williwags, Mrs. B?"

"Well, I'm not sure, really. All I know is, it all feels very strange. Something in my gut just tells me we need to pursue this."

"Weird! I feel the same way!"

"Well, luv, we've got a busy day ahead of us! Let's see what we our travels bring tomorrow."

"Can't wait! See you bright and early!"

And they said good night.

Chapter Seven

The Hike Begins

Saturday morning they met at 7:00 AM in their prearranged spot, the southeasterly corner of Mrs. Bundle's property. A gray granite marker indicated the boundary between Mrs. Bundle's land and Eva Brown's property to the south. This would be their point of beginning. Their plan was to walk the perimeter and beyond of the Andersen and Bundle properties, not an easy feat. Mrs. Bundle's property consisted of about 25 acres, most of which was woods and heavy undergrowth past the orchard, but Walter's expansive 50-plus acres went up hill and down dale, backing up to a section of Fuller Stream, the Bog, and the big ravine. It included a dense section of marshland that would require slogging through wet, saturated vegetation, thus requiring waterproof footgear. To accomplish their goal, they would have to walk up the southerly line of Mrs. Bundle's property, trek the combined back lines of both properties, then traverse down the northwesterly side of Walter's property. If time permitted, they would hike into the highland to Tattle Ridge and beyond over to Old Man Boulder, and then on to where the hidden caves were.

The sky was grayish, with a hazy sheen on the horizon. The weather forecast called for a light misting rain throughout the day hovering around freezing temperatures, so they all had dressed for inclement weather. And what a sight they were! Mrs. Bundle wore the oversized tweed hat, along with Arthur's worn red plaid hunting britches, her hefty black rubber muck boots, a warm winter parka, and a special "detective fanny pack" filled with items she had gathered together the evening before. The pack had been fun to arrange, and she had taken considerable time imagining what items she might need in an emergency scenario. It contained all her sleuthing essentials (or, what she imagined detectives might need to sleuth with), along with a myriad of possible "just-in-case" items for today.

In a large ziplock bag she had placed the following: matches in a waterproof tin, a couple small penlights, three air-activated hand warmers (usually used for skiers to keep their mittened hands and booted feet warm), a small baggie containing two teabags, a honey packet, some instant dry vegetable soup, and last but not least, a crisp ten dollar bill. As she had told Cracker the night before, "You just never know what you might need in an emergency, even on a backwoods hike to nowhere." The fanny pack also contained her reliable magnifying glass, a flask of brandy (for emergencies only), some dental twine, and Arthur's trusty Swiss military penknife. Not to be remiss, she also carried a can of Kitty Kaviar treats in her pocket for her indubitable feline partner's nourishment.

Angie, who appeared to be outfitted for any potential emergency, shivered excitedly in her L.L. Bean boots and cherry red, extreme gear jacket. In addition to her heavy outerwear, she wore three extra thermal layers underneath. Her rich chestnut hair was pulled back and hidden under her favorite knitted long-tail, multihued ski hat. She also bore a hefty backpack chock full with all the prearranged items she and Mrs. Bundle had discussed. The knapsack contained a 16' lightweight rope, three thermoses (hot water, milk, and cocoa), various dry snacks, digital camera, cell phone, and two 2-way radios, which had a range of up to two miles (Angie and her friends often used them to keep in touch when downhill skiing).

She handed one of the radios to Mrs. Bundle and, grinning from ear to ear, whispered excitedly, "Isn't this a blast?"

Bringing up the rear, of course, was Cracker. He stepped proudly, the misting rain glistening on his shiny cat nose. Mrs. Bundle had really outdone herself this time. She had spent the evening before sewing him a sturdy travel outfit, something fit for sleuthing in the Vermont fall climate. On that account and not to be outdone, he was decked out in the miniature Inverness cape Mrs. Bundle had crafted especially for him. Reminiscent of a very famous detective's coat, it was a brown plaid, collared slicker with a capelet attached under the neck band, all of which slipped snugly over his body and around his furry legs to neatly protect him from the elements. The collar had a small snap-in loop, fashioned to hold a mini-flashlight in place. An ardent fan of this legendary detective, Cracker had admired himself earlier that morning in the hall mirror before leaving, noting how splendidly Holmes-like he appeared. *Yes, I quite like this Sherlock look. All I need is the deerstalker cap and calabash pipe*, he mused in cat-thought.

They headed off up the hill and discussed their plan of action. Earlier, they had decided upon the outside boundary perimeter search of the two combined Bundle and Andersen properties, which would take the better part of the morning if done properly. Then, time permitting, they would head over to the back land property behind the higher ridge and reconnoiter back down the northernmost boundary back to the farms.

As they trudged up past the orchard and into the far meadow, a faint mixture of very light rain and sleet came down, not at all unusual for early morning weather this time of year. It had not yet snowed, even though Thanksgiving was right around the corner. The lay of the land was stark and cold, silhouetted browns and grays against a pale horizon. The open land up behind the farmhouse allowed for good views toward the distant mountain range. As the sun rose and gave some luster to the expansive range and forest, they plodded along, observing their surroundings with the renewed sense of their duties as "detectives". Something about the morning's tranquility induced them to whisper, and they quietly discussed the past mysterious happenings and let their imaginations run with what they might find today.

The three companions hiked resolutely, leaving the fields behind them, and now passing into the pine scented woods. This was the time of year when all the animals began to hunker down and start their survival process throughout the cold months. The air was stinging in the morning light, and the icy particles stuck to their clothes like frosty confetti. After a time they reached the back line of the property, bordered by a ravine of some 50' in depth. The natural boundary kept them on track as they turned west, parallel to the main road some 1200 or so feet away. They looked back down the expanse of frozen meadow they had just traveled, noting nothing out of the ordinary.

"Nothing of interest yet that I can see…" Mrs. Bundle shielded her hand over her eyes and looked down at the land they had just traversed.

"Do you suppose anything is happening up at Goochie?" Angie asked.

"If we had time, we could wander up that way, but we'll save that for warmer weather, I think." Angie was referring to Goochie Pond which, over many generations, had provided a plethora of outdoor sporting activities, including swimming, fishing, and ice fishing, and skating. If one traveled down the small path into the ravine and back up the steep hill, the pond could be found about a quarter mile further into the woods. With no roadway to the pond, it was only accessible, in any season, by a small footpath. A tiny body of water with a small sandy cove, the area was entirely pristine and undisturbed, the water untainted and the location serene. It was a wonderfully quintessential illustration of one of Vermont's last truly private spots, whose exact location was privy only to locals who also were smart enough not to let the word get out that the pond had the best trout fishing (not to mention skinny-dipping) around. One could find total solitude on the tiny pond. On the tree by the swimming hole was a handwritten primitive sign that read, *"No Flatlanders Allowed!"*, the Vermont term earmarked for tourists and out-of-staters.

"I bet that pond water is cold today!" Angie reflected as they continued on their way.

The ravine cliff's depth subsided as they walked along, until it eventually became a small gully, the bog creeping slowly in beneath their feet, the earth becoming wetter and wetter. As the mist continued, they slogged through the outside marsh fringe, eyes to the ground, looking for anything unusual. They approached the marshy interior, the vegetation wet and squishy under them, and suddenly they observed a bull moose in the distance. The dark animal was hazily chewing twigs, leaves, and a variety of plant life, perfectly blissful in his feasting. His enormous, massive head raised up and his snout pushed into the air. His feeding trance interrupted, he breathed in their scent and his nostrils flared. They stopped and stood perfectly motionless, lest they give themselves away. The moose looked toward them nonchalantly and turned his head slightly to the side. Knowing that not only the antlers but also the front feet and hind feet of the moose are potentially dangerous weapons which can take their toll on an unwilling adversary, the group took the circuitous route around the animal, watching him carefully. Slowly, they backed further into the marsh, leaving him to peacefully continue his watery meal. Their feet sloshed through the boggy ground beneath them—which was moist, cold, and very mushy.

The budding detectives had not yet discovered one piece of evidence of person, unusual circumstance, or strange sound, and Angie asked impatiently, "Do you think this is a waste of time for us to be out here, Mrs. B?"

"Well, if nothing else, we're getting a heck of a workout today, aren't we, luv? Besides, Cracker and I haven't been up this way for awhile, so it's an adventure in itself just to be exploring again, right, Cracker-cat?"

Cracker jumped up on a fallen mossy log and pranced down the length of it, his wool capelet fluttering in the wind. He dashed inside the rotted hollow opening to investigate the possibility of any live playthings. Finding nothing of great importance, he scampered along behind the two investigators, stealthily following their cautious suit of keenly observing everything in their midst.

About four hours now into their hike, the air started getting moister and the misty rain became more urgent with the higher elevation, turning into frosty sleet peppered with snow. Four lone ebony crows loitered in a circle nearby, huddled close together against the cold air as they pecked at some edible shreds on the dappled ground. They began to caw relentlessly at the newcomers. *Move on*, they squawked impatiently, *go on*. They rapped at the long-dead prey in front of them with detached curiosity. Meanwhile, their intelligent banter, unmatched in the bird world, seemed to mimic human sounds and words, encouraging the threesome to, Caaw! *Gaa—Go, go on, now! Gaaw!*

Mrs. Bundle looked up at the upset sky, wondering aloud if the inclement weather was a warning for them to turn back. If they went slightly south, they would travel by the old cemetery on the ridge, whose entombed inhabitants were from the late 1700's to early 1800's. (The Pillson Hill Cemetery had approximately fifty lonely headstones, a few of which still stood at attention like skinny forlorn soldiers, while others tilted sideways. Years before, the cemetery had been cordoned off by the Village Preservation Committee from the surrounding wild, untended growth, the burial ground neatly packaged inside an ornate wrought iron enclosure.)

Should they turn back now, which would bring them by the old cemetery and back out onto the Anderson north line? Or, should they go on and risk the chance that the weather would get worse?

"What do you think?" she asked her waiting partners, motioning to the wet atmosphere.

Angie shrugged her shoulders and said, "We're almost to Old Man Boulder, and then it won't be that far to the nearest cave." She looked at her watch, noting it was almost eleven o'clock. "Why don't we take a break at the Boulder, have our hot soup and cocoa, and then we can go on—only if the weather isn't too bad?"

It was obvious Angie wanted to proceed. They listened as the crows still squawked relentlessly. Mrs. Bundle ruminated; on the one hand, she was most excited about visiting the caves after so many years. On the other hand, she wanted to make sure they would be prudent in their search. She knew there might be risk involved and was determined not to put Angie or Cracker in any danger today. She also knew that the caves might just be the highlight of their exploration and that they could find something very important. She looked at Cracker.

Let's go, he cat-thought, *I'm ready for whatever comes our way.*

Weighing all the ramifications, she nodded at Angie.

"Sounds good!" she said, confident that among the three of them they could handle almost any situation. So, they headed north toward the last section of Tattle Ridge and their ultimate rocky destination.

They reached Old Man Boulder in forty minutes and sat their tired bodies under the huge, craggy rock for shelter.

The view of the distant low farmland and further removed mountain range was spectacular, skinny rivers snaking through the area like ribbon candy. Angie and Mrs. Bundle ate in silence as they negotiated cups, hot liquid, and thin saltines through their cumbersome gloves. Cracker blew out cold breath from his mini-mouth, ate a couple more Kitty Kaviar treats and polished them off with some of the warm cocoa from the thermos cap. Silently, they filled their bodies with new energy, knowing the inactivity would surely invite the coldness inside their layered garments. A light snow had started, the misty rain now morphing into a small snow squall, which they both expected would pass through quickly at this higher elevation. The wind was beginning to whip at their bodies, and Mrs. Bundle broke open a package of the air-activated handwarmers and handed them to Angie to put them into her mittens. Cracker stepped lightly from front paws to back. *Well, are we ready for the next lap, ladies?* He cat-thought, *If so, let's skedaddle!*

Once they passed over the rocky section of the Tattle Ridge range, the hiking became more intense. Mrs. Bundle was thrilled to have Angie as her partner, leading the way with deftness and maturity, and she reminisced in breathy spurts to Angie about her own travels in this area with Althea during a much earlier time period. Angie giggled through frosty lips as Mrs. Bundle related her childhood exploits to her through gasps of intense hiking, telling her about one particular time Allie and she got into a real pickle.

"You see, we didn't know the caves could go on for quite a distance, and when we finally got our bearings deep inside, we realized we had traveled down in quite a fair stretch. By the time we found our way out it was way past suppertime and don't think our mothers weren't upset! Holy Moley! We were not allowed back up here for quite some time."

"Well, you know, Mrs. B, as much time as I've spent up here, it's still very easy to get lost. Some of the caves go nowhere, and others intersect and end up in the same place. I think Billy and I found about five separate caves the summer he was here from NYC."

Angie always referred to it as "NYC" when she talked about Billy Witherspoon, who was Angie's friend, a boy who had visited the area through the Fresh Air Children's Program when Angie was ten years old. He had taken to the countrified area right away, even though he'd never been outside his own urban environment. He and Angie had immediately hit it off, and although he was two years older, he was a willing student with Angie's direction. They had spent the summer exploring the new rural world he had found as strange and wonderful. He also had become a welcome guest at Mrs. Bundle's farm from the first time Angie had brought him along for teatime.

He had truly loved his summer in Vermont and had always stayed in touch with his fresh air family, cultivating the friendships he had formed during that stay. Now, years later, he was finishing up his first semester of college, having received a full scholarship from Brandeis University where he was majoring in environmental studies. His love of the outside had stuck with him, and Angie and Mrs. Bundle always loved hearing from him.

"I miss seeing him, don't you?"

"Uh-huh!" Angie's breathing was heavier as she crashed through the final few feet of heavy forest toward the caves.

Where the boulders ended and the irregular, copious pines and evergreens were scattered again, Angie threaded her way in behind the thick trees until she came to a huge heavily-laden evergreen in front of an unmoving massive boulder. Its boughs touched the ground with the heavy weight of age, the now-freezing mixture of rain and snow, and intricate branches. She expertly scooted under and through the branches, saying cryptically, "Wait here. I'll be back in a minute!" and disappeared into the mountain of rock.

Mrs. Bundle and Cracker waited patiently, both moving from one foot to the other in the frosty air.

"It's getting pretty dang cold out, wouldn't you say, Cracker-Cat?"

Cracker curled himself around her legs, rubbing against the rough, red plaid wool pants. *Yeah, colder than the south side of the North Pole. Whose idea was this?* he cat-thought, his whiskers icy white with frost.

About five minutes passed, the both of them drinking in the quiet forest, and then the crackle of Mrs. Bundle's 2-way radio harshly broke the soundless air.

"*Mrs. B?*"

She drew the radio up to her mouth, "Angie, where are you?"

Angie's very low, whispered voice rasped through the radio, "Can you hear me?"

"Yes!"

"I'm headed back your (muffled)…" crackling noises impeded their hearing, "…get you and Cracker… (muffled)…found some interesting…(muffled) that…" loud popping and static radio sounds burst forth, "…been here…pretty recent…"

Angie's voice sounded somewhat labored, and Mrs. Bundle asked, "Are you okay?"

"10-4! Hold on."

Silence filled the air for another minute. Mrs. Bundle waited, then repeated anxiously, "Angie! Are you ok—"

She was interrupted as Angie's head popped out from under the branches and she pulled herself clear of the thick boughs and undergrowth. She inhaled deep breaths as she brushed herself off. She exhaled. "Whew! Everything's fine. But, wait'll you see what I found! C'mon! Are you ready?"

"Ready as we'll ever be. Let's go!" And with that, the three of them entered the cave.

Chapter 8
Singing from the Depths

As they extricated themselves from the barely three-foot circular portal, they turned on flashlights. The illumination created glossy images on the dark cave walls. Cracker's collar minilight was particularly eerie as he made his quick feline movements exploring the dark interior, the elongated images appearing ghoulishly larger and then smaller against the rock walls.

Angie stood still and pointed to a corner crevice about twenty feet or so just inside the entrance. There, in front of them, was clear evidence that certain individuals had visited, and could still possibly be occupying, the cave. Two pairs of shoes, neatly placed side by side with toes pointing toward the entrance were set there, almost as they would have been at the front foyer of a home! What was significant was the diminutive size of the footwear. One set looked like baby or doll shoes.

"Who do you suppose has been here, some Lilliputian people, or trolls from the dark side?" Angie whispered, trying to diffuse her apprehension as she giggled nervously.

"Fantastical!" was all Mrs. Bundle could say.

Cracker made a loud meowing sound—*C'mon guys!*—and both Angie and Mrs. Bundle jumped. Realizing how skittish they both were, they tried to calm down and familiarized themselves with their surroundings. Slowly, they raised their bodies up from their crouched positions, gingerly attempting to stand up. They moved bit by bit, carefully stepping very closely with each other until they both had their bearings. Cracker followed diligently behind. Once well inside the cave entrance, they had no trouble standing upright in the six-foot elevation. The inert mineral air, dank and clammy, met their nostrils as they methodically made their way in, winding gradually deeper into the darkness. About fifty or so feet inside, they arrived at a second natural stone landing area, which grew larger and higher with each watchful step they took.

"Here's where I stopped and turned back," Angie indicated, pointing at a small pile of debris. It was a jumble of everyday products, wasted and used now. In the heap was a collection of empty cans, consumed boxes of dry goods, and the like.

"Someone's been here, and it looks like it was relatively recent," Mrs. Bundle said in a low whisper.

Their vigilance was keen as they continued deeper into the underground chamber, and they moved in silence for another fifty feet or so until they all stopped abruptly, frozen.

"Listen!" Mrs. Bundle whispered. Cracker stopped mid-paw, head high and immobile, as they all listened incredulously to dulcet sounds coming from much deeper within the chasm.

It had begun as slight, faraway echoing musical sounds, liltingly sweet but distant. As they progressed further into the cave the resonant vibrations gave way to a youthful, sweet singing voice. It was a song of lament with foreign-sounding inflection, almost like a wail. Mesmerized by the sound, they stepped in slow methodical pace to the beat, closer and closer to the haunting ballad.

"Who is it?" Angie asked in an undertone, as they strained to listen to the lyrics.

My young love said to me "My mother won't mind,
And my father won't slight you for your lack of kind,"
As she turned away from me and this did say,
"It will not be long love, 'til our Wedding Day."

As they labored to hear the touching rendition, they continued to move quickly and silently, barely able to contain their suspenseful expectations.

"*Shhh*," Mrs. Bundle hissed, "stop a minute!" She gripped Angie's arm and held Cracker close to her. She whispered, "See the bend up there? That singing is coming from right around there, I suspect." Angie nodded. "When we round the corner and can see who it is, don't make a sound until we're able to assess things, okay? We don't know what or who else we'll find."

Angie nodded again in agreement. Cracker's mini-light wavered slightly in an up and down motion.

Oddly discernable was a youthful voice that they could distinctly hear now, quavering hauntingly, slightly faltering in the darkness. The beautiful voice was offset by a tortured soulfulness. It was a voice full of fear and pain, and the sounds tore at the listeners' heartstrings even before they could put a face to the rendition.

Using hand signals now, they stopped again quickly to regroup. Covering her mouth to barely be heard, Angie murmured, "It sounds like those English accents on TV! Or, kinda Irish!"

"Yes, just like the song I heard the other day, definitely Celtic," Mrs. Bundle whispered back excitedly. "No more words from this point on."

Sounding troubled and hesitating, the little voice raised its volume defiantly, singing freely and louder, as though challenging the blackness and the gloom of the cavern.

> *As she stepped away from me and she moved through the fair,*
> *And fondly I watched her move here and move there,*
> *And then she turned homeward with one star awake,*
> *Like the swan in the evening moves across the lake.*

The sweet voice trilled louder, trembling with vibrato, as they moved within visual range. They crept closer, only about thirty or so feet from their target. Turning off their flashlights, they labored against the wet cold wall boundaries. Like a precious silver bell tolling in the night, they were pulled like a magnet toward the mystery now just around the corner.

Last night I dreamt, my dead love came in,
So softly she came that her feet made no din,
As she laid her hand on me and this did say,
"It will not be long love, 'til our wedding day."

A sob escaped the lamenting voice, the voice cracked and croaked, and the song abruptly ended on an eerie note. It sent shivers down Mrs. Bundle's spine. *That has to be the most brilliantly sad little voice I've ever heard,* she thought.

Deliberately, they rounded the last corner and finally came upon the tiny minstrel in full view. What they saw left them speechless and gawking like rubes at a circus sideshow.

Sitting alone on the cold ledge in the eerie sheen of the cave's natural light, surrounded by various empty food containers and rabble with a blanket wrapped around her little legs, sat an impish girl figure rocking back and forth. Wild black curls escaped from beneath a shining hard hat, and her heart-shaped, stark white, freckled face was the canvas for a broad quivering mouth, tiny nose, and large, frightened dark eyes. Her arms were solidly wrapped around a smallish, rounded bundle on her lap. There was no light, save the last dying embers of a dwindling campfire.

There was a glint of shiny steel; something metallic-like was covering her head. Upon closer scrutiny and most absurdly out of place, they could see the waif was wearing what appeared to be a colander on her head. The pathetic appearance strangely gave the skewed, somewhat comical, impression of a helmet on a valiant medieval soldier.

Dirty, empty pans, bottles and other paraphernalia were her only friends. She was shivering; her teeth chattered like a rogue typewriter. This lonely figure sat against a background of these incredibly coarse, frugal living arrangements. Mrs. Bundle, Angie, and Cracker gaped in disbelief at the pitiful youngster in this most unusual setting. They were too astonished to speak, totally confounded and confused by what was before them. They were thinking the same thing: What was this child doing here—in a cave—miles from civilization or creature comforts?

As she came out of her singing trance, the urchin looked up and was startled to see three sets of ghoulish eyes staring at her through the darkness.

She opened her mouth but not one utterance came out. Wide and silent and struck with fear, she tried again, but...nothing. At that moment, before the three of them could speak or calm her, she threw her head back, opened her mouth once more, and let loose with a earsplitting scream.

Before they could reassure her they were harmless, she passed out cold on the ledge, the little bundle falling gently to her side, the silver colander crashing in loud echoes against the hard slab floor.

Chapter Nine
What Child Is This?

"It's a baby!" Angie cried, as they quickly surrounded the young girl and tried to revive her.

Mrs. Bundle, preoccupied with loosening the buttons around the neck of the oversized plaid shirt the waif wore, responded, "Well, no, luv, I'd say she's about seven or eight years old."

"No, Mrs. B, look here! I mean, it's a baby HERE!" She pointed to the bundle.

"Oh, Lord help us! Let's get some light…my land! You're right!"

Cracker had positioned his body at just the right angle and the penlight shown directly on the small, cloth-wrapped package. Swathed inside the bundle, the baby the girl-child had been clutching was just a mite of a thing, apparently calm and asleep throughout the entire ruckus. Now stirring just a bit to readjust inside its cocoon, he or she went back into a deep sleep.

"The girl's breathing fine, but we've probably scared her to death." Mrs. Bundle clucked, assessing the situation. The diminutive poppet's frame was tiny, very slight, yet solid. Her incredibly messy hair was short, about three inches in length, but the unruly black curls spiraled every which way, surrounding her face like a frizzy halo. *Whoa! I have a feeling this little ragamuffin's a handful,* Mrs. Bundle thought.

It was obvious the girl had been caring for herself, along with the baby, for a time, although it was hard to determine how long.

Dirty and unkempt, the child had a wild look about her, even in repose.

"We've got to get them to a warm place—ASAP," Mrs. Bundle directed.

"Where's their mother, Mrs. B?" Angie moved quickly, gathering up the surrounding warm clothing items and blankets.

"Lord knows how long they've been here or what their sad story is! From the looks of it, they're on their own. Yes, wrap her in that blanket, Angie, and I'll take the baby. Oh, *my Lord*, what a situation!"

They looked around quickly for warm articles to cover the children, and Mrs. Bundle placed an opened hand warmer packet inside the baby's blanket and another inside the old horse blanket that secured the girl. The girl was unconscious, her strength and fortitude visibly spent.

Luckily, Angie was able to get a signal with the cell phone at this high and remote elevation and reached her father through the crackling reception.

"*Dad!* We're up on the Ridge!" she shouted, hastily trying to enlighten him as best she could, through bits and spurts, the signal breaking up their communication. Through the mayhem of sound, Clay Andersen said that he and Uncle Carl would bring the tractor and wagon up to the North field, and that they would wait for them at the edge of the forest. It would be a daunting task for the trio to get down to the North field—a good three-quarters-of-a-mile south of them. The good thing was, it would all be mostly downhill. All agreed it would be fruitless to try to meet each other midway anywhere on the mountain as they might miss each other in the thick wood. With too much chance for error and a keen sense of urgency, it was mutually decided that this was their best bet.

"They'll be there to meet us, Mrs. B."

"Okay, we're all set… right, everything's going to be fine. If you can carry the girl, I'll carry the baby. Now don't worry. Cracker, lead the way so we can see where we're going," Mrs. Bundle urged. "Let's move quickly, now."

Organized, they moved expeditiously back out of the winding cavity toward the cave outlet. Mrs. Bundle gently galvanized the group as they headed back in the direction they had come. The going was laborious and dimly lit, but they plodded along as best they could, eventually arriving back at the entrance to the cave.

As they emerged from the opening, huge gusts of wind pushed them back, frigid sleet severely slapping their exposed faces. They wrapped their scarves tightly around their necks and face, exposing only their eyes to the elements. Angie draped the still-inanimate tiny girl-body over her shoulders, securing her arms and legs by holding them close to her own chest while the bulk of her torso rested on the backpack. Mrs. Bundle used the rope to secure the child a bit better, wrapping it loosely around Angie's waist. Mrs. Bundle felt confident that Angie was extremely fit and up to the task of carrying the petite package.

Mrs. Bundle had opened her own coat halfway, slipped the snuggling baby inside, placing the ends of her scarf over the top of the baby's head to shield it from the elements. Then, she cinched the fanny pack on the outside of her jacket waist area, securing it tightly underneath the baby's bottom, similar to a Snugli baby carrier. She buttoned up her coat as best she could.

She followed Angie into the gale. Cracker had done a fine job leading the way down the cave passageway, and now continued charging forward into the furious wind. His protective capelet flapped defiantly in the blustery mess—*Get out of my way!* he cat-yelled to the biting cold mess. *We're heading home and nothing shall stop us!*

Although they had been inside the cave for all of an hour, the weather had changed brutally in their absence, and snow and sleet now pelted their bodies like an arctic automatic machine gun. The freak storm was indicative of the old homespun saying, "If you want to know what the weather is in Vermont, just wait a minute." Everyone in these parts knew it could be snowing like crazy in the higher elevations and a bit further down the road it could just be spitting snow. (During the winter months, the Pillson villagers often joshed with the North Pillson Corners folk, teasing them endlessly about living in the "The Pillson Alps"—the upper atmosphere—where it snowed every day and the air was pure.)

Saving their strength, they moved in silence, trudging steadfastly down the rocky path. As they forged ahead over the rocks previously traversed and out of the wooded grove, the visibility was now near-impossible and the traveling quite laborious. At the highest point on the rocks the wind was merciless, whipping at their clothes, attempting to steal from them whatever energy it could.

They moved adroitly, taking the most direct route home—"as-the-crow-flies"—down the dense hills toward the winding and worn myriad of old trails below. Angie knew these trails like the back of her hand. At one time, Mrs. Bundle had known them, too, and their trek down was oddly still familiar to her. Mrs. Bundle was secure in Angie's knowledge of the trails—no doubt, she would be able to get them to safety. She also knew her Cracker-Cat would never let them down.

As they reached the lower elevation into the heavier tree growth, they spoke sparingly, making sure they stayed close together, heads down, fighting the harsh wind.

"Welcome to Vermont!" Angie joked, yelling into the harsh wind. "This is harder than Chinese algebra!" she said, trying to ease the tension with her Grandfather's axiom.

"Should have listened to the Almanac!" Mrs. Bundle heaved, her breath coming in bits and spurts. The combination of the high elevation, the grueling temperature and storm, and the baby's weight was growing heavy on her, and she blew the cold air in and out of her lungs. "Cat's Granny! It *did* call for unsettled weather the week before Thanksgiving." She drew in her breath and then, gaining a second wind, she continued on with relentless purpose.

A half-hour later they stopped to catch their breath and do a check on everyone's wellbeing. Mrs. Bundle was thankful for all the many hikes she had taken over the years in all kinds of inclement weather; she was holding up well, all things considered! *I'm pretty rugged—for a' mature' woman. There really is a lot of spunk left in this old girl,* she thought. Amazingly, the baby still slept soundly, and the girl appeared to be so worn out and exhausted she just hung limply on Angie's back, semi-conscious save for a deadened groan or whimper every once in awhile. Her low mumbles were feverish babble, none of which they could make out, and they comforted her as best they could, assuring her that soon they would all be safe and warm.

As they got closer to the three-quarter mark, they encouraged each other through the now-blizzard conditions. The icy cold was settling into their limbs, making it difficult to put one foot in front of the other. They resembled abominable snowmen as they pushed along, the large flakes of sugar snow literally attaching themselves to their clothes like frozen burrs. Cracker looked like a little round snow bunny, his coat now a heavy white furball.

"Keep going," they encouraged each other, "don't stop, we're almost there!" This became a mantra as they continued on, not being one hundred percent quite sure, because of the low visibility, that they were on the right path, but forging ahead as they headed down the dense hillside toward the open lowland area below.

"I'm not sure where we'll come out exactly…but it should be in North field." Angie fussed, wiping the thick snowflakes from her eyelids and brow while she adjusted her heavy load.

Then, out of nowhere, came a blatting, a sound not unlike a huge foghorn.

They heard a distant blast, again, and then again. Large, loud, flat, sounds came through, piercing the air, sharply slicing the thick condensation. Moving their frozen feet ahead step by step now, almost by instinct, the bellowing horn sound was like a solitary lifeline in the blizzard. It grew louder with each step, and finally, they distinctly heard the boisterous blaring—like a Roman centurion. It came directly from the field below. And now, they could hear deep shouts calling out their names!

"*Angie!* Mrs. Bundle! *Hel-looooo! Hey!* Down here!"

Angie's face lit up and she hastened her pace.

Bla-aatttt!! Bla-aattt!

"*It's them!*" she yelled over her shoulder to her relieved mate. "Holy cow! He could wake the living dead with that horn! I swear, I will never…" she labored under the load, moving as quickly as her boots would slog through the snow, "…ever complain to Uncle…ever again… about that dang *bugle!*"

Mrs. Bundle heaved a sigh of relief. "Just in the nick of time…" she mused wearily as they came into full view of the field.

There were the Andersen men in the pasture's far perimeter, diligently, anxiously, waiting by the tractor. With kids in tow, Mrs. Bundle, Angie, and Cracker broke through the last line of trees and finally, thankfully, were welcomed back into the warmth and safety of Walter Andersen's farm.

Chapter Ten

The Mystery Unfolds

"Why, she's nary bigger than a thimble!" Walter reflected after they got the children into the house and began to assess the situation. First, they had laid the little girl carefully on the old settee. Mrs. Bundle still held the baby in her arms as Walter continued inspecting the older child. "And there ain't an ounce of meat on her little skinny arm. Lookee here—she's scrawny as a naked plucked chicken! Better go fetch Doc Jackson, Carl. She'll come in a jiffy. No need to alarm the whole dang medical world durin' this storm."

Everyone was busy, moving like a well-oiled machine. Angie called Doc Jackson to let her know Carl was headed over. Carl brought the truck around to the back door and let the engine idle while he brought towels downstairs, then left. Clay retrieved a large plastic bag from the attic filled with Angie's baby clothes. First priority, they all agreed, was to make the children comfortable.

"They must be famished!" Mrs. Bundle exclaimed, and Walter went to the kitchen to heat some milk for the baby, giving a deft stir to the chicken soup bubbling in the big black cast iron pot on the stove. He cleared an area on the circa-1940's double ceramic sink. He laid a thick towel on the drainboard and yelled to Clay, "Git over here and take the young'un from Mrs. B and put it over here, son!"

Clay lay the baby down while Walter spouted on. "I daresay you all must be starvin'! Right I am! Yer both more stubborn 'n a pig on ice, ain't ya?" he admonished both his granddaughter and Mrs. Bundle, shaking his head as he rummaged in the lower cupboards under the sink. "What in hell's bells were you doin' way up there? And so long? And in this weather?" He continued searching, furiously yanking pots and pans out from the lower shelves. Triumphantly, he yelled, "*Got* it!" and surfaced with the aged container of Angie's old baby bottles, covers, and nipples, along with other baby dishes, spoons, and the like.

As they collectively and gently undressed the baby, "it" awoke with a start. Its lungs filled with howls, startled by the bright lights and all the surrounding big humans poking and prodding.

"Let's get the baby cleaned up first," Angie's Dad said. "Angie, draw the warm water for me, would you?" Angie filled the kitchen sink to half full as Clay comforted the child.

"*Shhh*, hush now, little one. No one's going to hurt you, calm down. That's right, hush now." His soothing voice seemed to have a calming effect, and the child's cries subsided.

"Angie, I'm surprised at you!" her father said sternly as he drew back the baby's diaper. "*Whoo-eee!* You stink like a barnyard animal, little one! That's okay, sweetie. We'll get you all cleaned up, good as new." He wiped the baby down and readied it for the inviting warmth of the tepid, clean bath water.

"The water's ready, Dad," Angie said.

"Yes, let's put the babe in slowly… Gently, now! Well, it's a baby girl we got here. Good Lord! This one has been on her own for awhile….Gaw!" He gently bathed the baby, speaking soothingly, "Well, all right, yes…you've had a struggle, haven't you little one? I bet you'd like to tell me all about it."

The baby cooed and pursed her lips, happily enjoying the warmth of the water, eyes now bright and alert. She babbled, making little primitive sounds as though trying her best to communicate. As Clay talked gently to her, she looked into his eyes. She uttered petite sounds, endeavoring to explain in beseeching "babyspeak" what she had been through. She was a beautiful baby: large blue eyes and long luscious lashes, a little rosebud mouth, and fragile golden-brown wisps of hair shooting out from her brow like little posy petals. She had rolls of baby fat around her chunky flailing legs, which sloshed water in every direction up and over the kitchen sink.

"Hang on, little one. We're almost done. You're a real corker, you are! There you go, now," soothed Clay as he drew her out of the sink, wrapped her in a clean warm towel and dried off her little body. He put on a fresh cloth diaper and pinned it in place and she cooed contentedly as he held her in one arm and grabbed a little yellow smocked baby nightie from the bag of clothes nearby. "Danged if you don't ever forget how to do this," he mused to himself. "This size looks just about right..." he guesstimated, holding it up for Angie's approval. Angie nodded, and they dressed the baby together, delighting in her perfect little hands and the clean baby smell she now possessed. The soft warm cotton johnnie against her soft baby skin made the little girl sigh contentedly. He carried her over to the rocking chair and sat down.

"Here, try this, son." Walter thrust a ready bottle at Clay.

"Time to settle down, little one," he chided gently, rocking her as she sucked happily on a warm bottle of whole cow's milk, the best milk she'd had in quite some time, he reckoned.

Meanwhile, Mrs. Bundle took her own heavy clothes off and was at work on her charge, gently undressing her and then rubbing the girl down with a towel to get the circulation working. "Her forehead's hot to the touch. She's got a temp, I'm pretty sure. She is just plain worn out, the little poppet!"

Cracker hovered nearby, sniffing the air and gently nudging the little girl. Mrs. Bundle looked her over from head to toe. Angie came into the den with a set of her own warm flannel pajamas, a pan of very warm water, and an unopened fresh cake of Ivory soap, along with a facecloth and towel draped over her arm.

"Let's wait until Doc Dottie gets here before we move her too much," Mrs. Bundle suggested, and just as she made this remark, the individual in question came through the door in a burst of contained energy—followed by an out-of-breath Carl.

Doctor Dorothy Jackson, or "Doc Dottie" as she was affectionately known in these parts, was an octogenarian retired physician who had settled in Pillson some twenty-odd years ago just down the road from the Andersen farm. Her younger sister, Josephine, had moved to Vermont during young adult life as the new physical education teacher two towns over, living alone until she, too, had retired forty years later. Doc Dot had visited her sister over the years, finally buying a gloriously rolling gentleman's farm high atop a mountain just outside Pillsonville. She and the sprightly sister had moved in together.

By now, most of the locals had forgotten that the Doc had been a Flatlander, a transplant from Connecticut to her final Vermont retreat. Presumably, she had planned on spending her remaining years quietly, without the pressures of a large urban doctor's practice. At first, she had retired to the quiet community and hung up her medical instruments with the firm intention to begin working on her gardening skills.

However, in the country there were always emergencies that popped up, and as time evolved, everyone knew they could call on Doc Dottie "in a pinch". And, although the years had taken a toll on her now-arthritic body and limbs, her mind was quick and agile. Bent over and deliberate in her movements, she gave the appearance of frailty and vulnerability, but that was just an illusion. She was all of five feet tall, but her constitution was three times in proportion. And, as Walter often said, "God help anyone who stands in that female's way!" Over sixty years of operating in predominantly a man's world had hardened her nature, and she was always ready for any situation. She had a brusqueness about her that initially was daunting, but her heart was as soft as putty and her eyes were all-knowing and caring. She spoke in staccato sentences, hastily evaluating the situation and efficiently directing all those around her, editorializing freely as she went about her duties. She used an economy of words that she had learned early in her career, knowing that often as not, time was of the essence.

"Carl's filled me in on the details. What he knows, anyway. Looks like you've got the baby settled, Clay. I'll take a look at her in a minute. It is a her, right?" Clay nodded. She turned to the kitchen. "Good. Walter, you've got the water going and hot food on the stove, too. Gaw! What on earth?" She surveyed the supine figure of the little girl, whose naked body was covered by a warm blanket. "Let's take a look at her first. Hmmm, very emaciated, wasting away, the poor thing. Up in the caves, you say? She's about eight years old. C'mon, honey, let the old doc listen to your heart." She pulled her up gently, placing the stethoscope on her bare little chest.

The child stirred, moaning as she tried to sit up in a half-stupor, then laid back in utter exhaustion, slipping into a deep slumber. Her breathing came in rough, deep rasps.

"Heart is…" Doc Jackson listened, then sat back. "…okay! Lungs, too! She's malnourished, but all limbs seem okay, no uncommon bruises, just tuckered out, it looks like, and feverish to the touch. I don't see any evidence of frostbite. Let me take her temp."

She placed the thermometer into the girl's mouth and glanced at Mrs. Bundle. "What *in tarnation* were you and Angie doing up there?" She squinted at the electronic thermometer—"Yuh—a good one—102—and we have to watch them both for a time for hypothermic symptoms. Overall, at this point, I think she needs total rest, some good hot food and plenty of it, and quiet! She needs sleep, and her body needs to recover. She stays right here for the time being!" She looked at the men; they nodded acquiescence.

Next, she checked the baby out methodically from head to toe, as everyone watched with nervous anticipation. She looked into her tiny ears with the otoscope, checking to see if she had an ear infection, or other ear issues. Finding nothing out of the ordinary, she turned to speak to the eager group.

"She's about 14 to 15 months old. A little small for her age—but overall appears to be in fine health. Must come from hardy stock. Definitely a serious situation. I don't really want to move either of them. They'll both stay here for the duration?"

Everyone said an emphatic "Yes!", and Cracker jumped up on the couch. He nuzzled the hand of the young sleeping girl, his rough tongue licking her still palm.

Folding her otoscope and other instruments neatly, the doctor deftly put them away in her tattered physician's satchel. "Feed them as much as you can, bathe the poor girl, and put them to bed. I'll call in the morning to see how they're doing—call me tonight at any time if things change in any way, you hear? Everyone's pretty tuckered out, right?" They all nodded in unison.

Doc Dot rested a gentle and experienced hand on the baby's sleeping head, quick eyes taking in everything in a final sweeping survey. She looked at Mrs. Bundle and Angie, and then at Cracker. "Lord help us! What's that get-up *he's* in?" she asked.

Cracker raised his hind end and flicked his tail in the doctor's direction.

She crowed, "He's drenched, too! Get that cat out of that sopping wet costume post haste. He'll catch a death. Gaw! What a sight you all are! You *all* get out of those freezing damp clothes and get some rest, y'hear?" Mrs. Bundle deftly removed Cracker's cape and penlight headgear.

Doc Dot did not suffer fools gladly, and they all nodded obediently, even Walter. "We'll deal with this tomorrow!" And with that, she turned on her heel and was out the door, with Carl following behind her.

The baby, blissfully happy with a contented look on her sleeping countenance, was settled in the same antique cradle Angie had been rocked in as a baby. Clay sat by the cradle, rocking and singing to the baby, marveling at the baby's soft features and labored breathing.

Angie and Mrs. Bundle bathed what seemed like a few weeks' worth of filth and grime from the child, gently rubbing her little body, but careful not to disturb her half-in, half-out consciousness. She mumbled words but made no sense, her eyes closed, nothing they could decipher. They fed her a few spoonfuls of the rich chicken soup, which she swallowed by reflex. Afterwards, they put the warm flannel garments on her little body. She fell into a dead sleep with Cracker's warm body purring at her side.

Carl returned from bringing Doc Dot home, and sat down behind Clay, leaning forward, totally enamored with the baby's gentle breathing. "She's a real pip!" was all he would say, and Clay would add, "Yup, a real pip," over and over.

Walter came in from the kitchen and reviewed the now-calm scene. "Geez *Lou-eeze*," he snorted. "Well, I'll be fit to be tied. Cat's granny, don't this beat all?" He shook his head and snapped, "I 'spect you're all starved! I'll get things ready in two shakes of a lamb's petootie!"

A bit later, they all sat around the parlor fireplace. The inviting flames caressed the dried logs, creating merry cracking noises. Angie and Mrs. Bundle ate on worn TV trays close to the fire. They devoured wonderful homemade chicken and rice soup with biscuits, along with cups and cups of warm tea and honey. Finally, after they couldn't eat another bite, they told the story of their trek through the woods and search of the cave. Cracker sat nearby, meowing occasionally, putting in his two cents worth.

"I guess we better spill the beans about the detecting, too." Mrs. Bundle admitted contritely. She proceeded to tell the men of her new career. Surprisingly, the three men listened without much reaction or comment, taking in this news as though this endeavor was not at all unusual for a retired woman in North Pillson Corners, Vermont.

Angie took over the narrative, filling in the details of the evidence of debris and paraphernalia they had found in the cave. "We wondered where their mother could be. They couldn't have ended up in that cave by themselves. And, judging by the collection of junk there, they probably haven't been on their own that long."

"Well, I'd say it's pretty lucky for these kids that you went up that way." Carl said.

"Uncle Carl! The music was what drew us in — it was beautiful. Gaw, that little girl can sing!" Angie said.

"I think it was her I heard the other day." Mrs. Bundle described the first time she'd heard the lyrical strains, the day she'd been out for her hike with Cracker and then, the second, the song of today. She tried to remember some of the words. "I think the first one said something about 'co-cannon in the little skillet pot', The second one was this lovely sad song about a girl at a fair."

"Yeah", Angie added, "something like this guy who has lost his true love going through the Fair." Everyone listened as they both further described what they remembered about the song.

Rather smarmy if you ask me, Cracker cat-thought although his cat musings fell on deaf ears.

Lastly, Mrs. Bundle and Angie told the men the full story of the Children of Lir pendant. Carl smoked his pipe and sat forward, listening carefully to the Irish folklore tale, nodding his head and rocking back and forth.

When they were finished, he was the first to speak. "Well, it all fits, to be sure. Those are Irish folksongs you heard. The first one you heard last week was '*Colcannon*'. It's a traditional Celtic song about nostalgic times in Ireland, like mothers making colcannon stew in the little skillet pot. Colcannon is an Irish cabbage."

They all looked quite amazed, not only at this wealth of knowledge but also at his understated delivery of this important information. He got up, went to the parlor across the hall to his extensive CD and album library. They watched as he rummaged around, then chose a CD and put it into the player. He came back in to them with the jacket of the Song for Ireland CD by

Mary Black, a well-known Irish songstress. "Here's the words," he said, handing the CD jacket, along with the lyrics, to Mrs. Bundle. They all listened to the song.

"That's it!" Mrs. Bundle cried.

They listened to the lilting happy sounds of the Irish singer, the folk song describing wonderful memories of Irish food and childhood.

"I knew I'd heard that song before!" Mrs. Bundle said, fondly remembering her trip to Ireland with Arthur.

Carl continued deliberately. "The other song you heard the little one singing in the cave sounds like '*She Moves Through the Fair*'." He went on, "It's another traditional Irish folk song, dating back hundreds of years." He went back into the parlor, and after a bit, he found that song on another Celtic album. They all listened to the lyrical strains intently.

Angie was the first to say, "Uh-huh! That's definitely the song she was singing. And she had the words and Irish accent down to a 'T'."

Mrs. Bundle agreed, "Her accent was very Irish-sounding, and her little voice was beautiful! My, you should have heard it! It was so sad and beautiful, and so true. Come to think of it, we've yet to hear her speak! She's been mumbling something, a lot of gibberish, but that's all. The poor thing fainted dead away as soon as she saw us." Pensive, she wondered aloud, "Here's a little girl in the middle of nowhere, singing Irish songs." She looked around the room at everyone, and shaking her head, said, "What a mystery!"

"Well, nothin' ain't going to get solved tonight, that's for sure!" Walter interjected.

Angie continued on excitedly. "Do you think this has anything to do with the necklace? That would be so weird! Because, the story of the pendant is based in Irish folklore, too. You know, the swans, and the Irish King, and all that?" Angie conjectured, looking around to see what everyone thought of this theory.

"Well, it tweren't like it grew legs and walked itself up there. And it was on Old Man Boulder, which ain't too far from the cave where you found 'em. Yep, you're right smart to think that through, Angie! That's why that girl's going to college! Good decipherin'!" Walter pointed importantly, smiling at his granddaughter. Truth be told, he (and his sons) couldn't help but be proud of her overall performance today in the face of such adversity.

"Who knows how much longer those poor kids would have survived, especially now that winter is kicking in?" Clay theorized, shivering at the thought of what spelunkers might have found in the spring. He ran his fingers through his thick yellow hair, pushing the strands away from his scalp. "Well, daughter, you've got yourself into a fine jumble. You too, Mrs. B," he nodded at her resignedly.

"And," he said, scratching his head in thought, "you can't blame a fool for what he doesn't know...I think you both know now you took on a bit more than you could handle, right?" They nodded as Cracker swished his tail saucily. "But here we are now," he paused, looking quite serious, "and the question is, where do we go from here?"

They all looked at him expectantly.

His face bore the faintest hint of playfulness as he watched them blandly. Then, in true Yankee fashion, his stoic face gave way, and he guffawed loudly. "Why....it's enough to jar your mother's onions!"

The homespun statement was meant to diffuse the tension in the room and it did. Tired laughter rang out.

"Let's sleep on it tonight and see what tomorrow brings." Mrs. Bundle suggested, politely stifling a yawn.

Chapter Eleven

Three Calls

It was close to 8:00 PM that evening when Mrs. Bundle finally arrived home, exhausted yet still exhilarated from her exciting adventure. The children were safe for now at the Andersens. Cracker had been adamant about staying close to the little girl's side, refusing to leave. *You go ahead,* he cat-thought, *someone needs to watch over the kids tonight.* Of course, Mrs. Bundle understood, happy to have his help in keeping a watchful eye.

She drew off her now-limp clothes, dropping her hat, mittens, scarf, boots, and the rest of her belongings on the woven floormat by the back door and went into the kitchen. She stirred the embers inside the wood cookstove, threw in some kindling, a piece of shredded newspaper and a couple pieces of split log, and lit the fire. Slamming the heavy door shut, she realized she could barely stand. She was exhausted!

She thumped down into the comfortable maple armchair rocker nearby. As she thought about the day's occurrences, she drifted into a dreamy state, asking questions of herself, trying to absorb what they had discovered. She had been formulating some ideas, and had something in the back of her mind. What was it? She started to doze as the residual warmth from the stove surrounded her tired body. She pulled her sore, aching limbs up from the cozy rocking chair and forced her feet to move slowly up the stairs toward her bedroom. Looking back, she noticed that the red message light of the answering machine on the hallway table was blinking like a beacon. *Blink, blink, blink, pause, blink, blink, blink....1,2,3* — three messages. *Oh,* she thought wearily, *I'm just too tuckered out to listen tonight.* She hazily found her way upstairs to her warm featherbed and the long-overdue rest.

In the morning, she awoke slowly, deliciously drinking in the thoughts of yesterday's adventure and wondering what lay ahead for those two dear children. Probably the State would have to step in, she fretted, already concerned for their welfare. She knew she didn't want to think about that possibility right now. She couldn't wait to head down to Walter's to check on the kids and find out which way they should proceed next. She knew she wanted to help find the youngsters' family, if possible. She wondered what the strange little girl would have to share in the way of information today. Hopefully, she would be able to disclose enough about who they were and how they had ended up in the cave for both she and the Andersens to help them. As she got out of bed, she looked outside. There, before her, was the aftermath of the yesterday's early season storm, the new fresh layer of the first snow of the year; about five inches had fallen all told. Mrs. Bundle realized they were all very lucky to have arrived home uninjured yesterday.

She went down the narrow back stairs, picking up the laundry and sorting out her things from yesterday, and shuffled into the kitchen. Sundays were usually spent leisurely, but Mrs. Bundle had a feeling today was going to be very busy. She stoked the embers in the woodstove's cast iron belly and got a good blazing fire going. After preparing her favorite Irish Breakfast tea and buttering a piece of toast, she pulled a battered white stepstool out from under the huge maple butcher cutting block.

Stepping up onto the second step, she reached for her grandmother's antique tin recipe filebox on the top shelf of her Hoosier cabinet. What had Cracker called it? She smiled; yes, this was her "High-tech Private Eye filing system". She stepped down and opened the box on the counter. She took out a fresh recipe card and sat down at the table.

Mrs. Bundle began by jotting down some notes about the recent discoveries, in hopes of organizing and consolidating her thoughts of last evening. The strings of this mystery were like a sea anemone's ethereal tentacles, gently unfolding and attaching to her mind, and she knew she worked best when she had everything organized, in order, and on paper. At the point she was done, she placed the card back in the box under "C" (for Children, of course). Then, she sat down in the hallway chair beside the answering machine and pushed the "play" button.

The first phone message was Althea's cheery voice. "Hi, honey, how are you? It's about 2 o'clock my time. I got your email and am wondering how your search went today. Hope you're back and nothing too weird happened. I've gone over all the 'clues' you gave me...love the info about the necklace, by the way. That was too cool! Sounds like you've really got a good mystery on your hands! Give me a call when you've got a minute. Things are beautiful here, but oh, not quite so interesting as in your little world. Talk to you soon!"

The second message was from Mabel at the Black Crow Curio Shop. "Hi, Lettie, it's Mabel. How are you? It's about 5:30 Saturday and I'm closing up shop and headed out the door, but I wanted you to know....I've done some research on the *you-know-what.*" Her voice lowered as she went on in somewhat conspiratorial tones, "I think you'll be quite interested in what I've found out. Or, what I *think* I've found out. Could be quite a pricey piece, but I won't go into the details on your machine. Give me a call or stop in when you get a minute. I'll be open tomorrow 'til 2! Later!"

Mrs. Bundle pushed the "stop" button and doodled big Irish shamrocks on the notepad beside the phone as she speculated about what new and exciting news might be forthcoming from Mabel's research of the Lir Pendant. Interesting, she thought pensively, *very interesting.*

She went on to the final message. Like an English bulldog's bark, a very proper British accent bounded forth in short, clipped words. "Darby Quicksilver here! I saw your ad in the local gazette and would like to discuss the possibility of employing you. I am in need of a professional in the matter of locating a certain person and items. Please give me a call at The Dark Horse Inn in Quechee where I have set up temporary residence. Ta, ta for now!"

Well, it never rains but it pours, Mrs. Bundle thought, sitting back and absorbing the last message. A new, legitimate case right away! *Oh, Lord,* she thought excitedly. And he was staying at the Inn in Quechee. "Hmmm," she wondered aloud. He must be here expressly to take care of his business.

Quechee was known as a quiet place just minutes from sophisticated Woodstock. She was familiar with The Dark Horse Inn in Quechee, as she and Arthur had visited the old-fashioned tavern housed in the Inn years ago. Of course, that was when it had been called "the old Dickens Inn". The Tavern attracted various locals from the Quechee, Woodstock, and West Lebanon area; it always had had a reputation for being a comfortable place to hang out and catch up on the latest goings-on. Tourists staying at the Inn had always been intrigued with the provincial flavor, delighting in observing a bit of the "local color".

More recently, though, it seemed the Inn had fallen on rough times. The last time she was up that way Mrs. Bundle had noticed its general disrepair. The grounds had looked neglected, the flowerbeds desperately needed manicuring, and the exterior sign had been hanging slightly off-kilter from its post. The humongous main building had a very tired-looking appearance, its vast life span uncomfortably conspicuous. The new owners "from away" had taken over the property a year or so before, renaming it The Dark Horse Inn.

Quechee was a very special place to Mrs. Bundle, primarily because it was where she and Arthur Bundle had met one evening at an outdoor party at the Quechee State Park. The small, charming community of Quechee, part of the town of Hartford, boasted one of Vermont's main attractions: The Quechee Gorge, also known as the "Grand Canyon of the East." The gigantic Quechee Gorge was formed after the ice age, the Ottauquechee River carving a huge swath through the Vermont hillsides. Nowadays, it was a major tourist attraction due to the massive 165' depth of the gorge from the top of the Quechee Bridge, which was just up the road from the village center. That steel bridge was a dramatic invention, massive metal girders spanning the remarkable depth beneath.

That first night they'd met, she and Arthur had walked all the way from the Gorge bridge to the Village, where they then sat under the quaint Quechee Village wooden covered bridge, talking for hours. Like many other Vermont villages, Quechee Village had once been a thriving mill town; it was settled in the 1760's when homesteaders built mills along the Ottauquechee River. The mills provided everything from lumber to cider, spurring economic growth in the growing area. To accommodate this growth, the smaller covered bridge was built in the village over the Ottauquechee River, where it still remained to this day.

She would never forget the night Arthur had proposed to her under the quaint bonnet of that village covered bridge many years ago. Ah, sweet memory! As she had gazed up at Arthur's illuminated face in the shadows, the full moon had sent slivers of flickering light through the latticed sides of the bridge, the shadows of the translucent water shimmering below. It had been a most romantic setting for such a special occasion, and she forever cherished the memory.

The Dark Horse Inn was located just 200 yards up from the covered bridge and less than a mile's drive from the Gorge. She sighed, bringing her thoughts back from the glorious past. *Here and now*, she reminded herself.

So, who might this new potential client be? Quite cosmopolitan, he sounded. She was already intrigued, and Cracker would be thrilled, she thought, chuckling to herself. She dialed up the Andersens.

Angie answered the phone, indicating the kids were just getting up, and all was well except for one troublesome issue.

"She refuses to talk," referring to the young girl, Angie said, "not a word! She won't say anything, just purses her lips, takes her thumb and pointer finger and puts them to her lips. Then she flips her fingers like she's locking them, and, don't you know, she throws away an imaginary key."

"Well, that's mystifying!"

"She's something else! Meanwhile, she's eating like there's no tomorrow—but she's still very weak. We've got her in bed and Doc Dot says she is to stay there for at least the next two days and is not to be moved. Her little body is skinny as a stringbean, and she's got a cough now, too. Doc said she would take full responsibility if anyone has a problem with us keeping the girls here—including the authorities. We're to follow those instructions, she said. She did say she has to notify the authorities sometime soon. Hopefully, it will be down the road. Dad and Uncle have already fallen in love with the baby, and she's the sweetest, happiest thing you'd ever want to see. Gumpy's out buying some disposable diapers, says he's too old to be changing cloth diapers. You can tell he's crazy about the kids, too. He just kind of looks at them and shakes his head. Oh, and Cracker won't leave their side. He's making sure they're not alone for a split second."

Mrs. Bundle told her about the message she'd received from Mabel. "I thought I'd head up to Woodstock later this morning to get the info about the pendant in person."

"Yes, we'll keep the kids occupied," Angie said. "More like they'll keep us busy! We've got it under control, though."

"By the way, how are you feeling today? Are you all right?"

Angie hooted. "Are you kidding? Yesterday was a total blast, Mrs. B!"

Mrs. Bundle sighed, "Yes, it was, wasn't it! We really had an Adventure, capital 'A'! Okay, kiddo—I'll be over when I get back from Woodstock," Mrs. Bundle assured her.

They rang off.

Her next call was to Mabel. It was just close to 9:30 AM and Mabel appeared not to be in yet. The phone rang and her answering machine came on. Mabel's chirpy voice proclaimed, "Black Crow Curio Shop, not in, leave a message at the beep!"

She left Mabel a message saying she'd stop in later to "get the scoop on the 'you-know-what'". She looked at the clock and decided it was late enough to call Althea. "Hey, girl, how are you?"

"Not as good as you!" came the ready response.

She spent the next fifteen minutes filling Althea in on all the particulars of their discovery yesterday amidst a number of "You-don't-say!"s from her friend. Then, she told her of the newest development—what would, hopefully, be the first paying case for the fledgling detective agency.

Althea was skeptical. "I think it's wonderful you found the children yesterday and all, but you and Angie could have been stranded up on the mountain with them if the weather had gotten any worse. Good grief, L! You always were a bit…impetuous. Please take care today. Don't go jumping in unless you know things are safe. And promise me you will let people know where you are, okay?"

Mrs. Bundle laughed resignedly. "Oh, Allie, you're right, I suspect. It is true—I can be…somewhat headstrong. You know me so well. I promise to call and let you know everything—especially what, if anything, transpires with this mysterious Mr. Darby Quicksilver. I'm going to try to meet with him today."

"If I were there with you, I would feel much better about all of this. We'd be doing all this together. I'm glad you have Angie and Cracker to help you, but these are adventures of growing magnitude, and I'm getting a little jealous." She became serious, "One word of caution, L. If you are going to meet a 'mysterious stranger'—I emphasize, stranger—someone you don't know anything about—you need to take care. I'm sure he's harmless, but...please use caution." She said these words deliberately and slowly. "If you make arrangements to meet with him today, where do you plan on getting together? Will it be at the Dark Horse Inn?"

"I'm not sure. I'll have to give that some thought..." Mrs. Bundle said, realizing that she valued the thoughts and opinions of her dear friend. Althea had been in some pretty dangerous spots herself in the past.

"What about a place like Bentley's? That would be a good spot. It's right out in the open. You could yell for help if you needed it."

Located in the center of Woodstock, Bentleys Restaurant was a busy, friendly, well known and well-lit eatery. Everyone in the area knew where Bentleys was located, right on the Woodstock town square opposite the Village Green. Bentleys Restaurant was locally run, low key, but strategically located in a highly visible area. Its massive street level windows framed the whole corner of Elm Street.

"Hey! Great idea! I'm going to try to reach him after we finish talking."

"Okay. So, tell me more about the kids." They discussed the children a bit longer, and then said their good-byes; Althea left her with, "Don't take any wooden nickels!"

Eagerly, Mrs. Bundle picked up the phone to call Mr. Quicksilver. His name and accent certainly sounded very enigmatic, unusual for this area and her experiences. Her fingers trembled slightly as she dialed the number for the Dark Horse Inn. "May I have Mr.

Darby Quicksilver's room?" she asked the clerk.

"Mr. Quicksilver is in the dining room." A nasal, thoroughly bored voice answered her. "Hold on just a minute."

Mrs. Bundle could hear the background sound system blaring Garth Brook's "I've Got Friends in Low Places". She waited patiently. About two minutes later, the decidedly English voice cut through the peripheral noise. "Quicksilver here!"

"Mr. Quicksilver, this is *B&C Detectives* returning your call. Mrs. Bundle at your service—how can we help you?"

"Mrs...ah, Bundle? I see. May I assume that *you* are the proprietor of the agency?" he queried expectantly.

Mrs. Bundle thought she heard a tentative tone in his voice. "Yes, I am. Em...specializing in discreet private investigating and research," she surprised herself by saying.

"I see. Ah-*ha!* I have a somewhat...hmm, sensitive situation that needs investigating," he hesitated.

Hearing uncertainty again in his voice, Mrs. Bundle offered the following. "Would you like to meet today to discuss your... situation? I could meet with you in Woodstock if that works for you."

I wonder if he thought I'd be a man, she surmised dryly. The designation B & C Detective company name had been chosen specifically so that their PI services could be offered without being gender specific. She had had some reservations, hadn't she (as had Cracker), about people's reaction to a woman of her generation in such an occupation and here was her first evidence that it could be a minor stumbling block.

"Poss-ibly. Do you...have an office in Woodstock?"

"Well, no, my office is, uh, somewhat mobile, you might say." Her voice was bright and hopeful. "I have other business to attend to in Woodstock later this morning, though, so I could easily meet you there." Mrs. Bundle's glibness under pressure surprised her. "How about Bentley's, say, around 2 PM if that would that acceptable?"

Thank you, Althea, she thought, *what would I do without you?*

"Yes, I'm quite familiar with the place. I'd be happy to meet you there. I'll be wearing a gray suit and a maroon muffler." he said matter-of-factly. "I'll look forward to our meeting, Mrs. Bundle." He gave her name a hint of emphasis, his uppercrust English accent dripping with—what did Mrs. Bundle sense—was that snobbery she heard in his voice? *Oh well,* she thought, *let's just see what this is all about.*

Mrs. Bundle called Althea once more before she left, mostly to reassure her that she would be fine. She agreed to call her later in the day, or at the latest by evening, after she'd returned from Woodstock and visited with the girls.

Althea said excitedly, "Things are heating up, L! You've got yourself one heck of a mystery already—with those two kids, that is. And, if all goes well, a new client and another mystery, to boot! Good luck!"

Chapter Twelve

Sunday Sleuthing in Woodstock

Moisture filled the air and the wind gusted in little mini-squalls as Mrs. Bundle headed down the busy avenue to Mabel's shop. Carrying her umbrella in one hand and her purse in the other, she didn't bother shielding herself from the misty, wintry drizzle during her brisk walk.

The tarnished bell over the door chinged merrily as Mrs. Bundle stepped inside the Black Crow Curio Shop. The interior was warm and cozy and, as usual, was chock full of interesting and unusual items. Mabel was already engaged with a customer, so Mrs. Bundle busied herself perusing the "new" old items in the shop that she hadn't yet seen.

Waving from across the room, Mabel greeted Mrs. Bundle with an excited air. "Hi Lettie, how are you?"

She was at the front counter waiting on a customer but excused herself politely, (indicating she'd be right back), and took Mrs. Bundle aside. Mabel Weatherby resembled an enthusiastic Scottie dog with her mop of disheveled gray-black hair and wide eager eyes. Her body seemed almost to quiver and wag good-naturedly like a little pooch ready to jump up and lap her face.

Mabel could barely contain her excitement as she whispered in a hushed, rapid voice, "I'm glad you decided to come in today! Let me take care of this customer and then we can go over what

I've discovered." She gave her a large accomplice wink and returned to finish up with the shopper. The patron was barely out the door when Mabel took Mrs. Bundle's arm eagerly and said, "We've got a good one here!" She went to the shop entrance and locked the door, turning the "Open" sign to read, "Back in ten minutes".

Slipping behind the counter, she took the Lir Pendant from the large safe under the shop counter and placed it on a worn piece of black velvet on the glass countertop, and then reached beside the cash register for a heavy tome. Written in large gold leaf lettering on the cover was *The History of Celtic Jewelry: 14th to 18th Centuries, Volume II, revised edition 1998,* by Sir Jeffrey Archer-Keating, Professor of Antiquities, Ashmolean Museum of Art and Archeology, University of Oxford, England.

"I borrowed this from a dealer friend I know over Hartford way. He does business exclusively in high-end European collectibles, precious stones, and antique jewelry," she said, raising her eyebrows knowingly. "I think we've found this particular Lir Pendant, and the information about it is quite remarkable!"

Mrs. Bundle waited expectantly, electrified.

Mabel opened to the bookmarked page, arranged the butterfly glasses draped around her neck onto her dainty nose, and read aloud to Mrs. Bundle:

Chapter 12

Silver Masters of the 18th Century in Ireland:
Children of Lir Pendant
Museum of London exhibit, fine jewelry of the 18th century Irish, Limerick, c. 1760, sterling silver, 4" diameter

Based on the Celtic Folklore of the story of the Four Swans with Christianity bell, a pendant with precious stones associated with corresponding symbolic meaning—emerald, signifying Christian hope; sapphire signifying heaven-bound; amethyst for martyrdom; and yellow diamond for eternity, set into the piece as the one visible eye of each of the four corresponding sibling swans.

Also etched into the piece is the ocean wave, symbolic of the Sea of Moyle and the Celtic knots and fences symbolic of their imprisonment and banishment by the wicked stepmother Queen Aoife. The Christianity bell in the bottom on the piece expresses the elation of the evil spell being lifted and the swans' final release at death to become four beautifully singing children.

This piece bears the mark of Joseph Johns, a Limerick silversmith who had a workshop on the main street of English town, now Mary Street. His mark of 'I.I.' on either side of the lion's head is also accompanied by 'Sterling' showing that the piece is of sterling standard.

Early in his career Johns became the darling of Dublin society, his intricate, legend-related designs delighting the English gentry who had adopted Ireland as their own. The British aristocracy flocked to his shop, preoccupied with his special designs and legend-oriented pieces. In later years and generations, the fashion for these pendants was followed by other designers, who created new designs and adapted old images of the classic Celtic Lir Swans design.

Its importance in history as an uncommon antiquity lies in the fact that the Johns Lir Pendant is the only virtually intact example of its kind and period—though there were two more of record that were known to have been made by Johns.

One of these, a solid platinum version signifying purity, was purported to have been a wedding gift to Charlotte of Mecklinburg-Strelitz, in 1761, upon her marriage to a devoted King George III, and which disappeared, along with other royal gems, during King George's derangement around 1810-1811. It held the usual Johns' 'l.l.' mark of identification, along with three lines etched atop each other to form a minute star pattern. There is no other concrete knowledge of the second piece.

Another rare piece of Johns' work, a "pap" or baby bowl, is in the Hunt Museum in Limerick City, Ireland and is considered a noteworthy relic from that period of time.

Estimated auction value of the Johns Lir silver pendants, brooches, fobs: can range in value from £10,000 to £30,000. Estimated value of any authentic platinum version mentioned above: possibly the £200,000 to £275,000 range.

Mrs. Bundle was flabbergasted. "Are you saying a piece of Johns work, like this necklace, could be worth," she stopped to catch her breath, "thousands of dollars?"

Mabel nodded enthusiastically, "Thousands and thousands! Maybe hundreds of thousands!"

"That can't be possible…whew! Wouldn't that be… unbelievable! Oh, my goodness. Oh, my!"

"Indeed! Isn't it exciting? Now, it could be a fake, or a reproduction—that happens all the time in this business. Someone with much better skills than me would really need to authenticate it. My experience in antiquities leads me to believe it's possible it could be the real McCoy. Obviously, it would have to be looked at by an expert in that distinct, specialized field."

"Yes, that makes sense."

"I'm not even going to ask you where you found it, bought it, or how you came by it, Lettie. But, it's very special! Mind you," she stopped, raising a cautioning finger, "I would advise that you secure it in *a very safe place*. And, look into insurance, to be sure!"

"Yes, I understand what you're saying. And, I agree with you. First and foremost, I think it would be wise to explore its authenticity before we get too excited." She blinked her eyes in disbelief. "Oh, this is truly...fantastical!"

"The email address of this Professor Archer-Keating at Oxford is in the reference section at the back of this book, along with his professional designations and other information. If we could contact him directly, I think there's a very good chance he could help verify its authenticity, at least initially. Possibly, we could accomplish this by taking photos of the pendant with my digital camera," Mabel offered, "and sending them over a secure Internet line to him. We do it all the time. If he gets back to us, we've hit a home run right off the bat—if it all pans out, that is."

"Yes, good thinking! That's a great idea, Mabel. Let's explore that."

Mabel opened the nearby drawer and took out a digital camera. She took some front and back photos of the medallion, angling the camera so that the pendant could be viewed from every vantage point.

"I'm thinking you might want to take the pendant with you, Lettie. I'm not sure I want the liability—if you know what I mean..."

"Yes, yes, of course, Mabel." Mrs. Bundle took the heavy pendant, wrapped it up in the soft tissue paper Mabel provided, and tucked it deeply into her purse. She knew the perfect place she would hide it when she got home. But for now, her purse wouldn't leave her side; that was for danged sure!

She pulled her checkbook from her purse and began to write Mabel a check for all her trouble to date, but the kind shop owner refused to take it. Mrs. Bundle insisted, and a tug-of-war ensued.

"This is what makes my business fun, Lettie! You've been a loyal customer over the years, so please...." she said, handing the check back to Mrs. Bundle. "I'll call you as soon as I know something. Meanwhile, sit tight."

"Right. We don't want to start a feeding frenzy." Thanking Mabel for all her help, she headed out into the misty precipitation.

Imagine, she thought to herself, *who would have ever thought she could be involved in such…intrigue?* She chuckled aloud, somewhat preoccupied. A few days before she had been bored and uninspired and now look! How things change!

Well, she mused, *what next?* She walked across the Village Green to the triangle of shops and eateries in the heart of Woodstock.

At 2 PM sharp Mrs. Bundle walked into Bentleys, located in the corner building known as The Cabot Block, and looked around to see anyone fitting Mr. Quicksilver's description of "gray suit and maroon muffler". There were four separate parties seated at the round wrought iron ice cream tables in the small luncheon area: three tables with two patrons and one table with a single. Focusing on the single, she observed a trim, refined-looking gentleman in a gray wool business suit sitting facing the entrance. He looked up at her and raised an eyebrow in question. A maroon scarf was folded neatly over the chair beside him. A large black umbrella also hung off the back of that chair, and gray kidskin gloves lay beside an upside-down coffee cup, thereby completing his neat, conservative ensemble. Walking confidently up to him, she offered her hand, and inquired, "Mr. Quicksilver? Mrs. Lettie Bundle. Nice to meet you!"

He rose immediately. "Mrs. Bundle. How do you do?" He offered to take her coat and held out her chair. She removed her coat and handed him the umbrella also, which he placed on the empty fourth chair beside her. He reached for her purse but she quickly drew it back. With slight surprise and light humor, he inquired wryly, "What is it, I ask, about ladies and their purses?"

She demurred, smiling, and held the purse tightly on her lap, meanwhile asking if he had been waiting long. While cursory light conversation about the weather and other innocuous topics ensued, Mrs. Bundle had a chance to look Mr. Darby Quicksilver over. He was a tall man, over 6'2" she reckoned, and his thin elegant hands and graceful features gave him a cultivated appearance. Abundant, shimmering silver hair topped his head; he resembled an imperious lion in a subtle, yet regal way.

His eyes (which Mrs. Bundle always believed were the true soul of a person showing one's innermost thoughts and feelings) were piercing, yet devilishly charming, a striking and intense malamute blue that were veiled by heavy, lazy lids. His tanned face was smooth shaven and very well cared for.

His overall looks exuded an image of good health and ample finances. He quite reminded her of the 1940's era actor Errol Flynn, very natty and almost quintessentially English-looking. *Yes,* she thought, *he's a very handsome man, even for someone in his senior years.* She bet he had had his share of the ladies in his life. He appeared to be around 65-ish, although he could have been much older. He spoke with an educated air, bordering on the superior, but appeared to hold this deftly in check with his very charming, well-groomed exterior. *Hmm, not to be entirely trusted,* Mrs. Bundle concluded shrewdly, falling back on her inner radar. *I think this is a man whose captivating ways and handsome appearance have opened many doors without so much as a second thought.*

They both ordered tea and blueberry scones, the waitress bringing their order swiftly and without fanfare.

"She's a very snappy table girl," Mrs. Bundle observed agreeably.

He nodded, buttering his scone delicately. "Yes, I concur. Very efficient." Taking a modest bite, he chewed, swallowed fastidiously, and pointed lightly at the scone. "Not quite as good as in my native England, but they will do in a pinch." Meticulously wiping his mouth with his napkin, he said, "Well now, tell me a little bit about yourself, Mrs. Bundle. Are you from the area originally?" She thought his brilliant smile was quite disarming.

As she gave him a thumbnail sketch of her years in North Pillson Corners, she realized he was assessing her, too, his eyes moving over her as though reviewing a document or taking a photo for later critiquing.

He asked innocently, "How did you come to be a detective? It seems to me—and please forgive me, I mean you no affront—you don't fit the typical profile."

She laughed. "Well, you see, that's exactly why it works so well." Her bravado surprised even her and was pure chutzpah in action. She continued on her high wire, the adrenaline kicking in. "Who would ever think," Mrs. Bundle paused dramatically and held up both hands in front of her, "that *I*," she placed special emphasis on 'I', "would be a private eye?"

They both laughed, although Mrs. Bundle's laugh was somewhat artificial as she sighed internally. Who knew she had such ability to fib under pressure! She crossed her feet, hoping this would relieve her guilt and prepare her for any future "fudging". On the one hand, she hadn't *really* been untruthful but on the other hand, she reasoned to herself, who would hire her if they knew she was green?

Moving right along, she asked, "So, how can I help you, Mr. Quicksilver?"

"Call me Darby," he said, with a gentle pat to her hand. "And, may I call you...Lettie?" He smiled attractively and gazed into her eyes.

"Oh, Mr. Quicksilver..." Noting this very subtle breach of professional demeanor on his part, she pulled her hand back gently and reached into her coat pocket. Ignoring his advances toward familiarity, she pulled out a small notepad and pen, sat up straight in her chair, and looked at him expectantly.

He cleared his throat and smiled wryly, seemingly unaffected by this subtle rejection. "Well, let's see. I have a somewhat sensitive matter I am embroiled in, one which I find I can no longer handle alone. It involves some missing items from my sister's very substantial estate. You see, she passed away in England last March, leaving a considerable legacy. The family is in hopes of resolving some," he paused carefully, "unpleasantness surrounding the… ah, how shall I say…*unlawful* distribution of her assets. Hence, my journey here to America."

He took a deep breath and looked directly into her eyes, his forehead creased in intense sincerity and concern. She nodded, her expression urging him to continue.

"It seems some of the more valuable items in her estate went missing directly after her passing. We have yet to recover a significant number of these valuable antiques that were," he coughed, choosing his words deliberately, "ahem…. removed…by a certain distant nephew. The person who we feel is responsible is no longer in Great Britain. His real name is Ashley Whitewick."

"His real name?"

"Yes. We believe he has been using aliases since his flight. Remarkably, we have reason to believe he has come to this area of New England—we've found evidence that he has made himself quite comfortable, in fact. We have followed his trail through some of the cheaper hostels in Vermont, but he has repeatedly slipped through our fingers every time we discover his whereabouts. Unfortunately for the estate, we believe that he has been systematically selling off the antiquities in question piece-by-piece. This, of course, is very distressing to the Quicksilver family. He keeps evading us, the scoundrel! And that is where you and your services, hopefully, will come into play…" he paused, taking a sip from his teacup, then wiped his lips lightly. "Our hope is to find him sooner than later—before he sells off the entire collection. We believe he is still here in the Woodstock area. To that end, I have been directed by the family to employ a professional post haste."

Mrs. Bundle nodded in understanding, "It sounds like a very

touchy situation. The most obvious question, though, from my perspective is…have you contacted the police? And if not, why?"

He shook his head vehemently, "Oh, no, no! No! This is a very, ah, delicate, matter, Mrs. Bundle. We would prefer not to have to involve the authorities. That is why we have decided to contact a private investigator such as yourself. The family would like to have this handled as quietly as possible and with discretion. We don't believe he is dangerous, just…misguided and in need of the family's help. We need someone like you to find him and notify us immediately of his whereabouts—at which point, we will take it from there."

"Might I ask what leads you to believe he is living here under an alias? Or that he has been trafficking the family's possessions?"

"As I said, we have come upon his whereabouts, unfortunately, after the fact. He has left a trail of items that he sold to various local art and antique dealers. Of course, these dealers say they were unaware that my nephew did not have the authority to sell the items. We have seen two of the articles in local shops."

Mrs. Bundle made some notes as he continued.

"One was an antique pocket watch belonging to my grandfather and namesake, the initials D.Q. inscribed on the gold fob. The other was a miniature oil painting dating back to early 18th century. Both were of considerable worth."

Mrs. Bundle made tiny clucking noises with her tongue. "What a shame. Were you able to retrieve them?"

"Regrettably, no. Neither proprietor was particularly forthcoming with information relative to their purchase of these items. Both shop owners gave varying descriptions of the peddler—my nephew—which leads us to believe one of two things. Either they were—as you say in America—'covering' for him, or he has been cleverly disguising himself. One described him as an elderly gentleman with a beard and glasses. The other indicated it was a younger man, very nondescript, who went by the name of Smythe. Of course, it will take a bit of work on the family's part to prove that these two pieces he sold belonged to my sister's estate. We will address that once we find him." He smiled, "So you see why it is imperative that we find him as soon as possible. We believe someone who is well connected in the area—someone like yourself—someone who has lived here a long time and knows the locals, is the best person to aid us at this point. Do you think you qualify?"

"Well, it all sounds very interesting. There's no doubt I am more than familiar with the area. As far as 'knowing the locals'; if I don't know them, I probably know someone who does!"

"May I ask what your fee would be, Mrs. Bundle?"

Luckily, Mrs. Bundle had researched this part of the investigative field in anticipation of her first real job, and she offered, "Well, we don't charge an arm and a leg in these parts, I can assure you. If we both agree we're a good fit and if I think I can help you, I would charge a $200 retainer fee, and my hourly wage is very reasonable—$30 an hour, not including expenses. I would charge you only when I'm 'on the clock' as they say. The fee does include detailed written reports as we progress."

"That sounds acceptable. If you are available, I'd like to get you on the case as soon as possible. In fact, I'd like you to take a look at this…"

Before she had time to respond or acknowledge acceptance, he reached inside the prim suit jacket's interior pocket and placed a photograph on the table directly in front of her.

"This is my nephew Ashley." He watched her face closely as she looked at the photo. A smiling, charming countenance looked back at her, ruddy complexion, jet-black curly hair; all in all, quite a good-looking young man. It was his eyes, though, that caught her attention. Bright blue, animated, friendly, and yes, very penetrating, cerulean blue eyes. Very handsome, she concluded.

Ashley Whitewick's upper body—from the waist up—was visible in the photo. He was attired in an off-white cable knit fisherman's sweater. Closely alongside him protruded another's shoulder, obviously another person whose image had been cut from the photo to his left. Mrs. Bundle adjusted her bifocals and scrutinized the image further. She could tell from the background that the picture had been taken outdoors, probably in the autumn months, as the leaves on the trees were deep variegated shades of greens, reds, yellows, and oranges. Other than that, there wasn't much else that was remarkably telling about the photo.

She looked up and couldn't help noticing Darby Quicksilver's keen gaze, as though he was waiting for a reaction.

"What do you think?" he asked, somewhat with an edge. His mouth was frozen in that charming smile and his malamute eyes revealed nothing.

She shook her head, moderately taken aback, and remarked frankly, "I can't say as I'd think he was dangerous if I met him on the streets, if that's what you're asking. My first impression is that he looks pretty benign, not at all nefarious. But, I suppose," she smiled, "that's often how criminals get away with things, isn't it? They learn how to….endear themselves, don't they? He does look," she studied the photo once more, "very *endearing*."

Mr. Quicksilver tapped his spoon agitatedly on the side of the coffee cup. "Yes, well I can tell you from experience that he is not endearing at all. He is a hooligan! The boy has a wicked, very unpleasant side to him. He's not to be trusted, I can assure you."

Noting the change in Mr. Quicksilver's demeanor, Mrs. Bundle was stymied. Why, he appeared to lose his cool momentarily. He recovered quickly, though, and smiled pleasantly once again.

Hmm, she wondered uncertainly, realizing she was facing a quandary. While she was excited about the initial details of this case, she remembered Althea's words of caution. On one hand, she was encouraged by the opportunity to sleuth, but on the other, there was something about this man that made her just a smidge uneasy. She decided she must have some time to consider the pros and cons before taking on this challenge.

Backpedaling expertly, she looked at Darby Quicksilver and, trying to muster as pleasant and professional tone as possible, said,

"Of course, I'll need to run the details of this case by my partner before I can commit to take this job."

Taken completely by surprise, Mr. Quicksilver exclaimed, "Oh? You have a partner?" Immediately removing the photo from her gaze, he carefully tucked it back inside his suit pocket.

"Yes, well, he's a bit of a *silent* partner, my Mr. Cracker is, mostly on a consulting basis but very much a participant in the business side. A numbers cruncher. Uh-huh—I'm the 'B' and he's the 'C' in *B and C Detectives!*" she laughed good-naturedly.

There I go again, she thought, *Oh my!* A mental image of her dapper cat came to her mind and she continued smoothly, "You see, I *must* run everything by him. Company rule. All our final decisions are made jointly, so..." she drifted off, looked at him expectantly, and shrugged.

He did not seem at all amused. "Well," he shook his head, "it is a bit unorthodox. My intention was to hire you today if all went well. However...if you must consult with your partner, you must. Please don't leave it too long, Mrs. Bundle. When will we hear back from you?"

"My partner will, uh...let me know...within the next few days," she paused and he watched her, his cool eyes glassing over with... was that irritation, she wondered? Or, she stared intently back... something more like anger?

He began to say something, but just at that moment, the "snappy table girl" brought their check. He was silent but his demeanor was unsettled.

"What?" Mrs. Bundle asked him as she wasted no time in swooping up the check first.

He closed his mouth, as though thinking better of it, and smiled charmingly, "Nothing, nothing, dear lady! It has been a pleasure meeting with you today!"

She withdrew a ten-dollar bill from her wallet against Mr. Quicksilver's protests, and placed both the check and the cash on the table. Quickly, she gathered her coat, purse, and umbrella, stood up, and used her professional voice again, "I'll be in touch, Mr. Quicksilver."

Without further fanfare, they shook hands cordially and she departed.

Once outside, Mrs. Bundle left Bentleys, crossed Central Street, walked about twenty feet, and then stopped outside the next store window, The Woodstock Pharmacy and Emporium, located beside The Cloverleaf Gift Shop. Looking into the front display window of the general store, she feigned interest in its holiday cornucopia display. *Whew!* She peered into the window, searching the reflection until she spied Mr. Quicksilver's thin figure exiting the restaurant.

She watched as he stood on the threshold, wrapped his scarf around his neck, and then casually put on his gloves, all the time gazing in her direction. Surprised, she realized he was simultaneously attempting to watch her retreat as she surreptitiously watched his! Even though her back was to him, he was within her view. It was evident he was watching her movements carefully, and she honestly wasn't sure why. *Oh,* she thought, *what would the clever Mary Russell do?* The female equal to the legendary Sherlock Holmes (one of Mrs. Bundle's favorite protagonists) would surely have had a clever plan in this same circumstance.

Not missing a beat, she boldly snapped her fingers in exaggeration—as though she had forgotten something—and hastily entered the busy Emporium. Briskly gaining entry, she immediately blended in with the many tourists inside. She positioned herself discreetly behind two animated customers. They were gushing, "*oohing and aahing*" over a Vermont cheese and pear wines display. Using them as a blind, she peered out through the frosted store display window to see if Quicksilver was still watching her. He, in turn, stood for a minute, hesitating, exposed to the corner's cold wind. He tightened the muffler around his neck and then, evidently assured she was absorbed in her harmless shopping task, he turned on his fashionable heel and walked east on Elm and around the corner to Central Street.

There's something that's just not right here, she concluded skeptically and, giving in to her intuitive and curious nature, decided to follow him. The busiest street in Woodstock was teeming with strolling shoppers frequenting all the small shops along the avenue. It was especially busy today, Sunday, and during this pre-holiday season. She was more than curious to know why he would be interested in her movements after their seemingly harmless meeting; certainly the groups of sightseers would be very good cover for her.

When he was a good fifty feet ahead of her, she adroitly left the shop and advanced gingerly behind him, making sure she kept a number of shoppers and pedestrians in between them.

Following well behind, she passed NT Ferro Jewelry Store on her right. She noticed he had picked up his pace, heading away from the center of town. The heart of the village consisted of a multitude of trendy shops interspersed with inns and quaint homes, and there was always a lot of pedestrian activity. As she passed the vintage clothing shop, Who Is Sylvia, across from High Street, she continued to discreetly shield herself.

Just in front of her, a spindly, teenage boy was negotiating three dogs on separate leashes: Cocker Spaniel, Lhasa Apso, and Dachshund. They looked like jumbled, flavored ice cream scoops on a banana split as they wove themselves and crisscrossed into each other, yapping and yelping as they dashed along. The cherub-faced adolescent teetered on the rough curb of the sidewalk, attempting to keep the leashes straight, and the general mayhem that ensued provided comic relief for the passerbys. Mrs. Bundle deftly overtook the commotion, stepping off the curb neatly as she kept her target in sight.

She followed along as best she could past Pane E Salute, the Italian bakery shop, but as Quicksilver abruptly turned left onto Bond Street, she lost sight of him and feared she would lose her quarry. The street was quiet, almost devoid of activity.

Ah, there he was! She could see him ahead, but realized he had stopped his brisk walking. Why, it appeared he no longer was alone! Darby Quicksilver was in earnest conversation with a strange-looking, sturdy, little man. Ducking into the shelter of a house's dense arborvitae-lined walkway, she was able to observe the interchange unexposed.

The other man was uncommonly dressed in a mustard-and-black-colored checkered suit; a black bowler hat was tipped to one side on his head. Although only about 5'8", he was powerfully built and his outrageous getup accentuated his stockiness. The snug, bright suit was just a dite too small for him, the pantlegs just clearing the top of his enormous, scuffed, pointed black boots. He nervously chewed on a stubby cigar while engaging in what appeared to be a very heated conversation with Mr. Quicksilver. The bantam figure looked like a little bruiser bulldog as he peered up at the towering Quicksilver. He gesticulated, using his cigar to make his point as he glared, frog eyes bulging, all the while bobbing and weaving like a used-up boxer.

He's not much in the looks department, Mrs. Bundle observed, noting wide teeth that looked like a half-eaten mealy corncob. *All in all, he seems quite a disagreeable fellow,* she thought, *shady and disreputable, not at all the type of company a man of Mr. Quicksilver's position would associate.* They continued their intense conversation, Quicksilver mostly listening, the other man animated and very intense. Clearly, this was a disagreement of some sort, Mrs. Bundle perceived. Both men couldn't have been further apart in looks or demeanor, she decided. Darby, with his tidy distinguished appearance, was the antithesis of this rough character's decidedly seedy and slippery-looking demeanor.

The two men were so absorbed in their conversation they were oblivious to anything around them. Trying to hear their conversation, Mrs. Bundle moved a tiny bit closer, cloistered behind a large arborvitae. Although their voices were raised in volume, she just wasn't close enough to hear anything of substance. *Dang*, she thought, *I'm missing some very important information.* Taking a risk of great magnitude, she eased her way apart from the large shrub.

She stopped short when they both turned toward a nearby beat-up, black, early-model Lincoln Continental. The vehicle had every appearance of being on its last legs. Long, low, and wide, it had been a luxurious car at one time, but now had the appearance of a huge dirty barge.

"Checkers" (the new name Mrs. Bundle had dubbed the rough character) walked around to the driver's side; the dirty window slid open. Barely discernable behind the wheel was a man, a cigarette dangling precariously from his ribbon tight mouth, his dark hair slicked back into a 1950's "duck's tail" style. He turned his weasel-like face toward Checkers, listening intently, body slumped, then nodded twice, taking direction from the funny-looking man. It was clear the chain of command was Quicksilver, then Checkers, then the slippery-looking ne'er-do-well behind the wheel.

As Mrs. Bundle got a better look, she gasped. Astonished, she realized she actually recognized the driver! Or, better said, she knew of him and his infamous local reputation. Trying to remember as she watched the interchange, she finally recalled his name. The pair's chauffeur—loosely termed in this instance—was a local known in the surrounding communities as "Dirty Dave".

His real name was David DeMont, and he had long before developed a reputation as an entity called trouble with a capital "T". Originally from up Northfield way, he had made a disreputable name for himself in the area. Swarthy in complexion with an unpleasant disposition all housed in a slender body, he was known as a loner and a troublemaker. He was seen often around town, slithering like a viper snake, seemingly proud of his reputation as a cheat of dangerously large proportions.

She recalled that he was also known to spend a good amount of time in the local taverns. She knew that over the years, through his chronic delinquency, he had developed a relationship with, and was a thorn in the side of, local law enforcement. Consequently, he had spent more than his share of time away in the slammer—that is, when the courts were able to catch up with him. Mrs. Bundle remembered one time seeing his name in the "Court Docket" section of the State Standard for petty larceny and bouncing checks and asking her good friend, Sheriff Will O'Malley, about him. All he had said was, "Lettie, that boy's never been the brightest bulb in the pack." In conclusion, she knew of Dave DeMont's cagey demeanor and questionable integrity to the extent that most law-abiding citizens, such as herself, tried to steer clear of him.

Knowing that his infamous reputation as a troublemaker and a hothead preceded him, Mrs. Bundle wondered what in the world the elegant Darby Quicksilver was doing in the same company with Dirty Dave DeMont?

She watched as Mr. Quicksilver looked nervously around him and then slid quickly into the back leather seat, almost as though watchful that he might be caught associating with these lower class individuals. Checkers sat in the front passenger side, barely able to peer over the front deck and long hood. The car wallowed away from the curb, creaking and lurching straight toward Mrs. Bundle and she quickly memorized the mud-covered white license plate: **VS4547.** Hmmm, not a green Vermont plate? That was strange. With the car heading her way, she couldn't discern the state of origin, although there was blue and yellow in the border of the plate. *Must be Checker's car,* she theorized.

Slipping quickly back into the nearest house's front walkway and opening her umbrella to shield her body, she anxiously held her breath and closed her eyes. *Oh, Lord, please don't let them see me,* she prayed. The dark, overly abused car lumbered along toward her and then, picking up speed, accelerated past her down the tree-lined street, leaving a stinky, noxious blue cloud in its wake as it disappeared around the corner.

Chapter Thirteen

The Children's Fate

When Mrs. Bundle arrived at the Andersen farm, the men were just coming in from tending the animals. Angie was playing with the baby on a blanket on the floor. The baby looked up, smiling and cooing. Struggling, she pulled herself up, grabbing the coffee table and stopping, one knee raised, to see if anyone was watching.

"Lookee how smart she is! I'll bet she'll be one of them child *prog-gidys!*" Walter exclaimed in a unique description of the child's genius. "And she's already learnt who's who!" He looked at the baby, and very slowly and deliberately, in painstaking baby talk, he cajoled, "Whee-eere's Ann-gie?"

The child looked around the room, pulling herself to her feet by holding onto the corner table, wobbled slightly. She held on tightly and then looked expectantly at Angie. She smiled broadly, a toothless, happy smile, and said, "Jeeeee!!!"

Everyone clapped and cheered, "Yeah!"

Clapping her hands in glee, she teetered on two unsteady feet, and then landed squarely on her backside, her thick diaper softening her fall and making a whoopee cushion "whoosh!" as she landed. Startled, she puckered up as if preparing to cry.

Angie cried, "Oh, sweetie!" and held out her arms to the little one. Suddenly, the baby giggled instead, which caused everyone to roar with laughter.

Walter picked her up, saying, "Give Gumpy a hug!" and she did just that. Angie gave her a quick peck on her little rosy cheek.

"Where's our other little friend?" Mrs. Bundle asked.

"Oh, she's upstairs in my room," Angie said. "She discovered my old toy chest, and she's been amusing herself up there for the last couple hours. She knows she has to stay in bed, doctor's orders, so she's got all the dolls and stuffed animals in bed with her and she's having a ball. Of course, she's still not talking to us yet, but she seems very happy at the moment. Doc Dot thinks she may be traumatized by what she's been through, or she may just not trust us…yet. She's taken a shine to Cracker, though, and he's at her beck and call. They're up there now together—as thick as thieves."

"She ain't spillin' the beans to nobody 'cept him," Walter said.

"Hmmm," Mrs. Bundle said, "Let me give it a try, okay?"

As Mrs. Bundle walked down the upstairs hallway toward Angie's bedroom, she could hear the youngster talking in low whispers, the gentle words impossible to discern. She stood outside the door momentarily, listening to the child's murmurs. She was heartened to hear the girl phrasing what sounded like sentences, although the little voice was husky, the rasping quality undoubtedly the result of the ordeal she'd survived. Presumably, the combination of the cold, damp cave chilling her to the bones and the trek down the mountain had completely exhausted the child. Mrs. Bundle clicked her tongue and smiled as she listened for a moment to the barely audible hoarse tones.

"Now, Miss Maypool, (mumble). Yes, you look so lovely in your gown (cough, cough). Aren't you beautiful? (Mumble) you are now." The soft, raspy voice had an odd lilting quality to it; Mrs. Bundle could scarcely hear the words. "Let's take a look at you! You say you'd like to go to the *Ball*? Well, yes, let's put on your glass slippers. Oh! The Prince is here! Oh, hurry now, he's waiting!"

Not wishing to further invade the little girl's private world, Mrs. Bundle quickly stuck her head around the corner. There sat the girl in bed in resplendent repose, her black curly head completely ensconced in a large floppy hat *a la* Queen Elizabeth-style, with a vividly sequined scarf wrapped flamboyantly several times around its brim.

Mrs. Bundle whispered, "My, my, how beautiful you look!"

The little girl looked startled and Mrs. Bundle added, "Hello, sweetheart, how are you feeling?"

The girl immediately ceased her whispered chatter and looked up suspiciously from her fantasy playing. She reached fearfully for the big doll beside her.

Amazingly, the doll's head jerked, then moved again. Slowly and as if by magic, the doll body raised itself up. There sat a resolute Cracker, imperturbably gazing back at Mrs. Bundle. He laid in the crook of the girl's arm, slack and apathetic, faintly recognizable in a lovely pale-blue doll's bonnet. His comeliness was unsurpassed as he played the role of the indomitable "Miss Maypool". His limp body had been stuffed into a very fancy doll-size evening gown complete with crinoline petticoats and silk doll stockings. Particularly fetching was the iridescent string of pearls wrapped around his furry neck. None the worse for wear, he languished in her arms, completely resigned in cheerful servitude to his charge.

Mrs. Bundle knew Cracker as no one else did. Frankly, she was quite surprised and delighted to see the level of tolerance he was employing.

She couldn't help but gush, "Oh, Cracker, you look ravishing!" and smiled innocently.

Cracker yawned, blinking twice. *Yeah, yeah. We're having a bit of harmless fun,* he cat-thought, *I've been getting her to open up, the poor kid. She's had it pretty rough. Besides, real cats don't have a problem showing their more feminine side.* He yawned again.

Mrs. Bundle sat on the edge of the bed and turned to the little girl. "It's so good to see you've perked up a bit, my dear. We were really quite worried about you yesterday."

The girl's wide dark eyes watched Mrs. Bundle with interest. Her cautious air was so endearing to Mrs. Bundle. What else has this child been through, she wondered?

Probing gently, not wanting to upset the little one, she said, "I understand you don't want to talk just yet. And, that's quite all right, dear. You can share you thoughts whenever you feel ready. By the way, I'm Mrs. Bundle. Do you remember anything about our adventure yesterday? I was there in the cave with you, as were Cracker and Angie. We had quite a time getting down from the mountain in the storm, didn't we?"

The little girl looked at her and shyly nodded her head.

"I want you to know we all want to help you and your little sister. Gumpy, Angie, Angie's father and uncle…everyone wants to help you. Me, too! But first, we want to make sure you get better. Does that sound okay?"

She nodded again and Cracker's rough tongue licked at her hand.

Mrs. Bundle smiled. "Do you like it here at the Andersen's?"

Another nod.

"Well, sweetheart, it would be very helpful to us if we knew your name…even just your first name, if you like." She chuckled gently. "We don't know what to call you, now do we? Say, I think I have an idea that might help!" The girl looked at her with interest. "See, I have a notepad here." Mrs. Bundle took her small notepad from her pocket, along with a pencil. "Do you know how to write, how to write words?"

Another nod, this time more animated.

"Could you write down just your first name? That way, you won't even have to speak one word and we would know what to call you. What do you think?"

The little girl sat in serious thought, her little brow furrowed. Nodding seriously, she picked up the pencil. On the blank page and in very large letters she painstakingly scrawled the letters: E—R—I—N.

"'E-r-i-, yes, that's an 'n', isn't it? Oh, your name is Erin? Why, that's a lovely name! Thank you so much for sharing that, Erin. Now, we don't want to tire you out." Mrs. Bundle touched the side of her nose in thought. "Oh, goodness! There's just one other thing... Let me ask you this, Erin, my girl. Do you suppose it would be all right for us to know your sister's name, too? She is your sister, isn't she?"

Erin nodded, and, for the first time, she smiled. It was a small smile, but nevertheless, it was apparent that she was enjoying this game of silence with Mrs. Bundle. "Okay, you write, I'll read... deal?"

She nodded, her little head bobbing up and down. The pencil went down to the pad once again, and she labored over the spelling. Carefully, and with a number of stops and starts, she wrote: A–I–N–E–E–N. She sighed deeply and handed the pad of paper over to Mrs. Bundle.

"Hmmm, that's not a name I'm familiar with! Let's see...*a-i-n-e-e-n*. I think that would be Ai-neen! Very unusual. Is that how you pronounce it: 'AA-Neen'?"

Erin nodded emphatically, then pulled Cracker closer to her, pushing her face deeply into his thick black coat. He licked her little hand, her best friend now.

That's enough for now, wouldn't you think, my dear? he cat-thought.

Mrs. Bundle smiled warmly. "You like Cracker, don't you Erin? You know, he's my special friend, too. In fact, usually he lives at my house, which is that farmhouse right over there. See?" She pointed through the curtained window. "Can you see the big white place up on the hill over there, through the window?" The little girl craned her neck and peered out the window. "Yes, up there. That's Cracker's and my house! That's where we live!" She smiled, her voice warm. "It's quite all right with me that he's spending time with you. If you'd like, he can stay right here with you for the time being. He's used to coming down here and visiting the Andersens all the time. And, when you get better, you can come up the road and visit us both at our house." She pointed again, confirming the location once more. "How would you like that? Would you like to come to visit, and maybe come for a tea party sometime soon when you're better?" Erin's eyes lit up. "Angie could bring you when she comes up." With Erin's affirmative nod, Mrs. Bundle continued, "Okay! So, we'll just keep things the way they are for the time being. You concentrate on getting better, and I'll concentrate on our first official Tea Party. This will be Cracker's home-away-from-home until everything gets more settled."

She smiled at Mrs. Bundle, her dark eyes shining. Then, she reached out gingerly and gently touched Mrs. Bundle's open palm. Emotion was trapped in Mrs. Bundle's throat and her hand closed over the little girl's. She whispered, "Good girl!"

We'll keep an eye on her, Cracker cat-thought.

Mrs. Bundle beamed at the both of them.

"Well, I'm off to take care of business. Have fun playing! And, Cracker-jacks," she kidded, "you be good! I'll see you both later!"

Mrs. Bundle walked into the parlor where all three Andersen men were seated.

"Well, what'd you squeeze out of her? Did you git her to spill the beans?" Walter asked.

She chuckled. "Well, in a way. It's a start, but I think we have the girls' names now, at least their first names." She shared the information.

Clay said with interest, "Aineen? Well, you don't say! It's a lovely name and it suits her! I never heard it before. Wonder what it means? Sounds kinda foreign."

The phone rang and Walter, who was close to the hallway phone, got up to answer it.

Carl took a book from the library wall, one of many from the weathered, old encyclopedia section. He searched through the resource book. Looking up, he said matter-of-factly, "It's a name originating in Ireland, means, '*bird*'."

"Interesting! Bird, you say…" Mrs. Bundle said.

"Yes, she's our little bird! Aren't you, sweetie?" Angie cried, smiling and looking down at Aineen. The baby sucked contentedly on the bottle that Angie held, her gorgeous doll-eyes getting as heavy as lead.

"You sweet little moppet." Mrs. Bundle smiled lovingly and lightly touched the child's warm brow.

Walter returned from the phone call, closed the parlor door, and spoke in a low, concerned tone. "We got trouble brewin'!" he said, shaking his head.

Everyone looked at him expectantly and he stage-whispered, "That was the Doc! She says she cain't hold off the law anymore and has to tell them about the kids and this whole *pre-dicker-ment* they was found in—'cuz she's a doctor. She don't want to, but she could lose her licensing. *Gaw!* Prob'ly somethin' to do with that *Hippycrudup* Oath them doctors have to take. Anyway, she says the 'Dee-partment of Hu-mane Services' has to come over here right off!" He scoffed, "Prob'ly tomorrow or the next day—with her. And, they're gonna wanta know where the dang mother is, and why them kids was left the way they was, all dirty and abandoned. She says there's a good chance the State might take the young-un's right then and there, put them into foster care, and we cain't do nothin' about it." He was running on, his voice very agitated, "Well, anybody knows me knows I'm stubborn as a mule! I kin dig in my heels, too!" He looked like a caged badger. Visibly shaken, he paused and put a calloused hand to his wide brow.

Clay stood up, also clearly upset, and Angie protested, "They can't do that, can they?"

Walter reached out to his granddaughter, "Now, Missy, don't you get yourself in a tither. You let us men and Mrs. B handle this! I'll tell you what—no one's takin' those two little peanuts out of this house unless they want to mess with the boys and me!" He stomped his foot soundly, "Yes, sir!" He clenched and unclenched his fists.

Mrs. Bundle spoke calmly, "Wait, now, Walter! Let's not put the cart before the horse here. Maybe there's a way the kids can stay here for awhile, at least until more is discovered about their situation. They're settled in and comfortable. They're obviously happy in their new and safer surroundings. Among the five of us," she looked around at Walter, Clay, Carl, and Angie, "we can more than provide for their needs."

They all nodded.

"And, it's Thanksgiving week coming up, for goodness sakes! Who would be cruel enough to rip them out of a secure environment at this time of year? Hopefully, we can convince the officials to let us keep the kids here at least through the holiday season. What do you think?"

They all agreed wholeheartedly and spent the next hour planning and deciding what they would need to do to ready themselves for the State's bureaucratic onslaught.

That evening, before Mrs. Bundle went to bed, she put into place three very important pieces of business.

First, she went to the parlor and moved the green, ribbon-striped-silk Queen Anne chair to the side. She rolled back the round braided rug from the living room floor. Then she knelt down and, feeling lightly with her fingers, touched a section of the hardwood floor. Carefully, she removed a well-matched, fused section of boards of about 1' by 2' rectangular. Under these floorboards was the old safe the original owner of the farmhouse had installed dating back to the 1830's. It hung from the rafter under the old partial foundation, inaccessible from the outside tight granite footings. Arthur and she had discovered the safe by chance one day when he was refinishing the floors. They had worked for many months trying to figure out the old lockset combination, until one day Mrs. Bundle tried the year they thought the house had been built— 1-8-3-4. The safe opened, and inside she and Arthur had found the original deed to the property, written in fine script and including all the land, outbuildings, ducks, geese, and sheep that Ebenezer Kangas had owned at the time he had conveyed the property to Silas Jenner.

She gently slipped the Lir Pendant into the soft, black velvet bag she'd found in her jewelry drawer upstairs, pulled the braided drawstring tight, and placed it in the safe. Carefully, she made sure the bag was securely wedged in between the few objects already encased in the strongbox. Closing the heavy safe door tight, she moved the tumbler around to mix up the combination once more, put the boards back in place, and drew the hefty braided rug back over the floor. She sat in the chair to catch her breath.

There, she thought, *we'll deal with this once things have settled down around here.* With all that was going on at the Andersens, she had not even had time to tell them about Mabel's opinion of the pendant's value. *Things will just have to wait until we get the kids' issues settled,* she decided.

She stood up, moved the chair back into its rightful spot, and looked around the room, making sure that all was the same as before. She sat quietly for a few minutes deep in thought, then withdrew her small notebook from her pocket.

As she contemplated whether or not she should take on today's offer of employment, she went over the notes of her conversation with Darby Quicksilver. Call it woman's intuition, or just a gut feeling; something, a kernel of doubt, gave her pause.

How much was real about Mr. Darby Quicksilver, and how much was façade, she wondered? More than anything, she was just plain confused by the day's events and seemed to keep coming back to the same conclusion; something was just not right with this picture. Although her potential client's story seemed credible, the consequent observation of him and his entourage did not give her a good feeling. She had no idea who Checkers was to Quicksilver—he might just be an acquaintance or someone he recently met in the area, but certainly it was clear to Mrs. Bundle that Darby Quicksilver did not appear to be making the best choices with whom he was associating.

Mrs. Bundle had always been a very good judge of character, and frankly, things just did not feel right when it came to the dapper-looking gentleman. She decided to follow her intuition. She would do some added research, after which she would make a decision as to whether or not she would choose to take on the job.

On that note, the second thing she did was to pick up the phone, dial up Mabel Weatherby, and make one more request of the dear woman.

Lastly, before she went to bed, her final essential deed was to sit down at the computer. First, she emailed Althea a complete update of today's activities. After that, the Internet research she did during that hour originated from just a hunch, really, that she might need some expertise in a particular area. Based purely upon conjecture, she brought up various search engine results and spent time brushing up on the skills she had learned a number of years ago. *You never know*, she thought, *this might just come in handy.*

Chapter Fourteen
Mrs. Bellows Arrives...

Mrs. Bundle stood in front of her mirror reviewing her ensemble, squirming this way and that with her plaid skirt, making sure the lines were straight and her blouse was neatly tucked in. She draped a blue cardigan over her shoulders and shivered.

I'm nervous, she thought surprisingly, realizing how important today really was. She pinned and then smoothed her thick braids in place, making sure everything was perfect as she put the final touches on her toilette.

It was Tuesday morning. Yesterday had passed very quickly as she and the Andersens had readied themselves for the Protective Services meeting.

She had spent the last two days bonding with the rescued children. And, what a joy they were! Erin and Aineen had easily settled into a routine, and Mrs. Bundle and the Andersen men anxiously discussed their combined strategy (out of Erin's earshot), trying to anticipate what the Department of Human Services outreach worker would be like and how they could convince her to leave the children there, in their care.

Doc Jackson had called Monday to let them know that she and the caseworker were scheduled to arrive at the Andersens later the next morning. Mrs. Bundle and the Andersens had worked feverishly to prepare, and they believed they were ready.

Monday, after school, Angie and Mrs. Bundle had made a shopping run to Rutland to buy clothing and personal items for the kids, and Walter and the boys had reshifted the upstairs living quarters, moving various furniture around to provide the girls with their own room and shiny new belongings. Angie was tickled to death to have the little girls in the next room over, and everyone was hopeful that all would go well.

Erin was much better: eating well, already looking healthier, her general coloring more robust. In fact, her growing appetite now far exceeded her little frame. She seemed to have a voluminous sweet tooth, and Angie had caught her twice now eating spoonfuls of sugar right out of the sugar bowl. Angie had gently chided her that her teeth would soon fall out if she continued on that course.

Although Erin continued her moratorium of silence, her innocent expressions and reactions spoke volumes, and she was able to communicate by pointing and gesticulating when she wanted something. It was becoming harder to tell the hardship her little body had been through and it was heartening to see she was now able to get up out of bed for short periods of time, although she tired quickly and napped often.

The baby was seemingly unscathed by the harrowing experience, eating well and constantly getting into things: poking, banging, turning and twisting everything within her reach. She was also a "scream" to watch, as Walter so aptly put it, as her discoveries often ended with her in a jumble on the floor, giggling and cooing. She was the pleasantest of babies and a joy to have in the home.

The adults were optimistic that the State would allow them to keep the children indefinitely, or, at the very least, through the holidays. They were also in hopes that all their preparation for the visit would not be in vain. In anticipation of that, plans were also being made for the following Thursday's festivities, Thanksgiving Day. As usually happens during this time of year, most people's business and other matters fell by the wayside during the busy short week while errands were run, baking was being completed, and all the final details were being executed for a wonderful holiday dinner. *One step at a time*, Mrs. Bundle thought as she pinched her cheeks and gave her mirror image a confident smile.

Mrs. Bundle headed down the long hill, wishing to arrive early at the Andersens to lend a hand before the meeting. Walter was the first to greet her in the back shed, closing the door behind him.

He took her coat and spoke in *sotto voce*. "Well now, Mrs. B, our little darlin' Erin is up, dressed, and *fit* to be tied!" He gave a low growl, "*Grrrrr*! She's like a wooly bear, that one is! Snatch me baldheaded, I ain't never seen the likes of it, not even with Angie! Whoo-*eee*! That little one's been downright peevish to everyone in the house! Flippin' that hair and *slammin'* that bedroom door! I told her she musta fell out of the grumpy tree and hit all the branches comin' down!"

"What on earth is the matter with her?" Mrs. Bundle asked.

"We reckon she musta overheered us at some juncture talkin' about them officials comin' over today. She ain't too cheerful, that's for certain."

"Oh, no," Mrs. Bundle said, "I was hoping we could discuss it this morning with her."

They went into the living room and there Erin sat. Rigid as a ruler in the overstuffed chair, she was dressed in her new clothes, a warm blanket over her lap. Cracker was sitting protectively at her feet. She looked adorable, her black curly hair neatly combed and graced with multi-colored butterfly hairclips, her new red-belted dress neatly starched and unsoiled, the patent leather mary-jane shoes shining like black beacons on her feet. Her lips were pursed and her eyes wide with panic. She looked at Mrs.

Bundle beseechingly, like a rabbit caught in a trap, straining to appear composed as she sat straight and tall in the chair.

Mrs. Bundle could see she was more than agitated and went over to the chair and rested on the wide armrest. She put her arm around her and Erin's eyes filled with tears.

"Now, Erin," she said kindly as she took the little girl's hand, "You know Gumpy, Angie, and all of us here are not going to let anything happen to you or Aineen today, do you hear?" She motioned to Walter and the boys, who'd entered the room and stood nervously nearby. "We're all on the same team and we need your help this morning." The little girl tried to focus. Mrs. Bundle went on, "There is a person coming over—in a few minutes, in fact—with Doc Dot. They want to see how you and the baby are doing. This special person coming with the Doc will be checking to see if you are eating right and are being taken care of properly, which you are! That person may ask you some questions, and you need to try your very best to understand that they are trying to help you, too." She took the little girl's hand in hers as Angie entered the room, having just put the baby down for her nap. "Now, we're all going to be here with you the whole time, so there is nothing to worry about, okay? You must try not to get upset."

Erin wiped at her misting eyes, and held her other hand out to Walter. The move was so touching Mrs. Bundle thought she heard a nearby sniffle from one of the boys. Taking her little hand, Walter smiled and tucked something into it. She reached back in surprise and opened her hand, her eyes alight as she saw the peppermint confection he had placed there.

"Geez, Pops, why do you have to give her candy this early?" Clay said, but he and Angie smiled fondly at the little urchin.

"Try not to get the sticky stuff on your party dress, okay?" Angie said. "And, honey, there's nothing to worry about, you just wait and see."

The doorbell rang with an ominous *brinnng*!

Carl said gently, "There they are now. I'll go."

He left the room, and Angie quickly ran upstairs for one more check on the napping Aineen. When Carl came back into the room, he was followed by Doc Jackson and a harried-looking woman well under five feet tall. She was a sight! The woman's dirty blonde hair was mussed from the wind or the job (one couldn't be sure), her glasses were set just off the bridge of her miniature round nose, and her overall petite appearance was one of being not yet finished, somewhat half-baked with everything slightly askew.

She was a rainbow of disorganized color. She looked like a little gnome in her oversized pale green casual suit. Her arms were laden with a heavy briefcase, a huge handbag that looked like it weighed half a ton (which made her appear even more reduced in size), and a tape recorder. Her heavy brown boots were unsnapped as though she had thrown them on "on the fly", her red sweater car coat wide open. To complete her ensemble she wore a multicolored lamb's wool knitted scarf, which was half-flung over her shoulders and reached all the way down to below her knees. Doc Dot first introduced her to everyone as "Belinda Bellows" and then introduced the group to her.

The troll-sized woman spoke for the first time, her high-pitched baby voice accentuating her miniature presence. "How do you do? Just call me Belinda, would you? I'm the Family Services caseworker that's been assigned by the State to look into this matter and determine what is in the children's best interest."

The same thought went through everyone's mind—how could anyone with that voice and stature be at all intimidating?

She continued, the sweet little voice reminiscent of the tiny woman at the circus, "As you know, the state has certain procedures in crisis intervention that they must follow when circumstances such as this occur." She smiled broadly as she spoke. "Our obligation is to make sure the children are protected in the best way we can provide and, as the assigned intake worker, I will be preparing a report to submit to my superiors."

Walter Anderson made a sound as though to comment, but the look Mrs. Bundle gave him stopped him cold. Angie rejoined the group and was introduced to the caseworker. Then, Angie stepped aside as Mrs. Bellows approached the little girl in the big chair.

"This must be Erin" Mrs. Bellows spoke softly, looking directly at Erin. It was clear that she was a woman with a sensitive nature. She trilled sweetly, "Hello, Erin. How are you?"

Erin stared at her, as if her body was made of stone, unmoving and resolute. Her face was expressionless, the wide eyes staring like little black coals in her pale, grave face. Her arms hung limply at her side save the tiniest twitch of her pinkie finger that tapped Walter's nearby hand ever so lightly.

The woman sat down in front of Erin, unraveling the cord from the tape recorder, explaining slowly as she plugged it into the nearby outlet. "This is a tape recorder, and I'll be speaking into the internal microphone, here." She showed Erin, obviously in hopes that the small machine would not intimidate the girl. "You can speak into it, too, if you'd like. I'm just going to leave it running while we talk, so that afterwards I'll be able to listen to everything we talked about. Is that okay with you?" She looked around the room, all eyes watching her in anticipation. Begrudgingly, Walter nodded.

She continued speaking to the silent group. "Also, at some point I may need to talk to Erin alone," she forewarned in her naturally sugar baby voice. She received a collective nod back.

Erin's legs fidgeted underneath the blanket, her shiny shoes peeping out and silently dancing in mid-air, and everyone waited, hardly breathing, while the caseworker readied herself. Assuredly, Mrs. Bellow's demeanor was non-threatening, her baby voice strangely comforting and encouraging as she began.

"Erin, I understand you don't really like to talk just yet. Is that so?"

Silence.

"Well, I was wondering if we could spend some time just getting to know each other this morning. If we could, I'd like to talk with you about why you and your sister were living up in the cave on Tattle Ridge."

Erin stared unflinchingly and continued to keep her prim lips tightly squeezed into one thin line, which strangely looked like a rubber band stretched to its max, ready to snap any minute.

Not meeting with success with this approach, the woman gently tried once more.

"It's important that you try to communicate with us, Erin, so that we can help you. Do you understand that?"

No answer. Erin squirmed in the chair, her eyes looking as wild as a caged cheetah.

"She don't like to talk!" Gumpy bellowed, unable to stop himself.

Four people looked at him and commanded, "*Shhhhhhh!!!*"

Mrs. Bellows apologized, "Please, Mr. Andersen, I don't want to have to ask you to leave…"

Clay said, "She's just trying to do her job, Pops! And we want to help Erin, too."

Belinda Bellows continued, her calm professional manner unshaken, "Well, that's all right, Mr. Andersen. Now, Erin, let's see. How old are you?"

Erin slowly lifted her hands, silently counting, and held up eight fingers.

"Eight years old! My, what a big girl you are! And you were taking care of your sister weren't you, I understand—from what Doc Dot told me?" Erin shook her head no.

"No, you weren't taking care of her? I see." Mrs. Bellows made a notation in her notebook. "Erin, have you ever been to school before?"

Erin nodded yes, her dark eyes sparking slightly.

"Do you like school?"

Another nod.

"What grade are you in?"

Erin shrugged her shoulders and looked up helplessly at Gumpy.

Walter reassuringly tapped Erin's arm. "That's okay, missy." He looked at Mrs. Bellows. "*Lookee* here, Mrs. Caseworker. I can tell, she don't know how to solve that out." He sniffed and then cleared his throat impatiently. "How many of them dang questions have you got there, anyway?" he asked, looking over the woman's shoulder in an attempt to see her notes.

Mrs. Bellows continued in her tiny voice, politely ignoring Walter, her eyes on Erin. "Okay, let's talk about your sister. Her name is Aineen, right? That's a very pretty name. We'd like to make sure she's okay, too. Doc Dot says she's doing fine." Erin looked her deeply, squarely in the eyes as Mrs. Bellows went on, "Tell me, Erin, how did you and Aineen come to be living in the cave?"

Silence. Not a motion or word was going to pass through those taut, rubber band lips—of that Mrs. Bundle was sure, as she observed this skilled social worker falling flat in her attempts to obtain any information from this unwilling youth.

Mrs. Bellows delicately leaned forward. "Erin, this is very important. We need to know how you got there. If you can't talk to me here, it may require me taking you to meet with someone else—a doctor. And, we want to try to find your mother, if we can. Can you tell us, please, Erin, where your mother is?"

This, apparently, was the last straw in Erin's discipline, the final question that caused the effect, although it surely was not the effect Mrs. Bellows had expected or wanted.

Erin finally….let go. Taking in a huge breath, she opened her mouth wide and, in complete replication of the diminutive caseworker's surname, Erin bellowed so loudly it shook the rafters.

"WHAAAAA!" Her face turned as red as the nearby fireplace bricks, her voice possessed as she let loose with an earsplitting wail so powerful the group almost jumped out of their skins. Her lungs built up a head of steam, and she bleated out another clamorous bellow. Huge crocodile tears began to stream down Erin's face, a face that was unpleasantly corkscrewed into a mass of angst, terror, and raw emotion.

"WWWWEEEEEEAHHHH." She wailed. Her little body was like a stiff, unyielding ramrod, shafting upward with the force and sound of a Space Shuttle at full throttle, with the caterwaul at optimum warp speed. All in all, the vision was no longer that of a pleasant little doll dressed for a party; in fact, it was just the opposite effect—not a very pretty sight at all.

Mrs. Bundle stood by calmly, ironically noting that the banshee sounds were as darkly humorous as they were terrifying. It was almost like being in the middle of an "out of body" experience, the likes of which you knew was unfolding in front of your eyes, yet you were powerless to control. In particular, she couldn't help noting the remarkable length and amplification of each yowl, one loud roar after another, ostensibly defying normal breathing logic.

Cracker, who was the closest to Erin, was duly impressed with the high-pitched sounds she was emitting. *Whoo-eeee! Howling like that is quite remarkable*, he cat-thought admirably.

Walter, on the other hand, was not at all delighted. Covering his ears, he yelled to Mrs. Bellows, "*Jeesum-jee hassafrats*! There, now you've gone and done it! Why in tarnation are you peskerin' her? Ain't it obvious she don't know where her mother is, otherwise the womin'd be here mindin' her?"

Mrs. Bellows looked at him helplessly and mouthed something (which no one could hear above the clamor), her professional demeanor shaken.

The child's wailing persevered, bleats and braying of agonizing persistence and piercing clarity with no apparent indication of letting up. Clay was the first to recover, adrenaline pumping and in full gear as he quickly reached for the howling girl and attempted to comfort and silence her all at the same time. But his fatherly instincts failed as she continued unchecked. For the next thirty seconds there were no words, just unadulterated noise and clatter reverberated from Erin's overly-huge and incredibly further-expanding mouth; shrieking and howling the likes of which would put the most ardent coyote to shame. Now on a roll, it was clear Erin was fully engaged, 100% committed to the clamorous distress she was creating.

In the midst of this bedlam, Mrs. Bellows continued to appear startled and a bit confused. Her mouth appeared to still be forming words, although nothing could be heard above the din. No amount of shushing and hushing from the others seemed to abate the racket; Erin's little innocent frame was now apparently inhabited by this alien being.

"*Gaw*, she'll wake the livin' dead!" Walter shouted, "*Somebody do somethin'!*" He looked desperately, pleadingly, at Mrs. Bundle.

Mrs. Bundle moved quickly and sat down once again on the arm of Erin's chair. Carefully and deliberately, she whispered something into Erin's ear. As if by magic, Erin stopped midair—just a millisecond—to listen, curious. She opened her mouth again and the howls continued—but with much less intensity as her ears continued listening to Mrs. Bundle.

Mrs. Bundle kept whispering, repeating the words in gentle hushed tones while she stroked Erin's rigid back. Eyes blinking, Erin's howling dwindled to a moan and then, finally, whimpers.

Cracker jumped into her lap, and the lament diminished to sniffles as he gently nudged her side. She clutched him to her, holding him as though he was her dearest and only friend in the world. She began to weep softly into his soft ebony fur as though her heart would break. Mrs. Bundle continued her encouraging whispered words. The group stood by helplessly offering comfort as the little waif gradually calmed down.

Although she had not yet spoken one word, Erin's emotional reaction to Mrs. Bellow's questions had spoken volumes. What terrible misfortune had occurred to elicit such unbridled emotion from this little girl?

Mrs. Bellows cleared her throat, set down her pen, and motioned to the Doctor. They stepped into the hallway, earnest in conversation, and then went upstairs, presumably to evaluate Aineen and the living arrangements. No more than five minutes later they rejoined the group.

Erin now sat in Mrs. Bundle's lap, a tired heap of soggy tears, her eyes half-closed as she appeared to be on her way to sleep. Angie stood protectively nearby, poised for the caseworker's final word. Carl had put a soothing Brahms recording on the stereo, and the dulcet sounds wafted through the room like a melodious tranquilizer.

Everyone turned expectant eyes toward Mrs. Bellows as she reentered the room. She motioned them to gather round her.

Speaking softly, just out of Erin's hearing, she said, "It is obvious to me that Erin has been traumatized by her experiences, whatever they may be. At this point the reality is we know very little about the girls, whom they belong to, or even where they came from. Our initial inquiries, locally, intrastate, and interstate have come up blank, and even a search of the national computer bank of missing children has yielded no matches. It seems no one—that we can determine, as yet—has reported children of their description missing, lost, or abandoned. And, we have no idea who the mother and father are, or even where the girls came from." She smiled wanly. "It is my position that it is premature to speculate on these matters. It is also not apparent why the children appear to have been abandoned." She paused, "Therefore, I believe I have determined the right course of action, notwithstanding it being a temporary course of action, at best."

Everyone waited with bated breath for her to continue.

"It is my professional opinion that it would be in the children's best interest that they not to be moved at this time. I need to talk to my superiors regarding intervention by professionals other than myself whom we may need to involve to help Erin open up. Doctor Jackson concurs with my opinion and has agreed to sponsor and oversee the children in an official capacity while this is in process." She looked at the doctor, who nodded back silently.

Mrs. Bellows turned to Walter. "From what I have observed, you seem to have a nice way with Erin, Mr. Andersen. As the senior head of household, you would be responsible for the welfare of the daily activities of the children." She looked around the room, nodding, "The home is clean, and the environment healthy, in my opinion, to more than adequately take care of these two young ones. I don't think it would be wise to disrupt the children once more, until at least we have more history. Therefore, Doc Dot will also make formal application with Protective Services on your behalf so that you can continue as primary caregivers for the children indefinitely—that is, until we have a more defined action plan. Erin appears to feel safe and secure in this environment, so for the time being I will recommend that they both be left here." She finished her monologue and looked around the room expectantly.

Happy nods flourished across the room as she continued, "Meanwhile, we can explore the other options, including placing them in more permanent foster care if necessary. I will come back in two week's time to reevaluate the situation. Hopefully, by then we will have garnered more information about the girls' family. By the way, Mrs. Bundle, I will need you to give a written account of your discovery of the girls, and Mr. Andersen, you will need to fill out these forms. Does this meet with your approval?"

Walter fairly leapt into the air like a gazelle. "You just give me them papers." He snatched them from her and cried, "don't mind doin' that at all, Miss Beloo!"

Carl reached down and scooped up Erin and said, "C'mon little Missy, you're staying right here with Gumpy and all the rest of the Andersen clan!" He picked up the limp doll form and carried her gently upstairs. Cracker followed behind, cat-thinking most encouraging thoughts as they disappeared up the steps.

———⟨∞⟩———

Later, they sat at the old round oak kitchen table—Walter, Angie, Carl, Mrs. Bundle, and Clay—discussing the day's events and their future plan of action. Although they knew it was going to be a huge undertaking to care for the girls, no one seemed to mind. Everybody was excited and agreed it was the best game plan, at this point. Angie had already begun her Thanksgiving holiday break from school, and everyone, including Mrs. Bundle, agreed to pitch in to make sure the girls were looked after. In addition, there was a huge resource of friends, neighbors, and church that would come forward to help, if necessary, once they knew what was going on.

"I'm not worried about anything," Carl said, then looked pensive as he turned to Mrs. Bundle. "But I do have a question for you."

She looked at him expectantly, "Uh-huh?"

"What in the *heck* did you say to Erin to get her to stop that wailing?" They all chimed in, chuckling as they recalled the dramatic scene.

Mrs. Bundle cleared her throat and said very slowly, "'*Bi ciuin, m'as e' do thoil e'*.'"

Blank stares and silence met the woman's gaze. She smiled.

"*Bee-koo-in, massa da*—whatzit?" Walter cried. "Gaw! I never heerd sech a thing. Sounds like gobbledy giblit to me."

"Yes, I said to Erin, '*Bi ciuin, m'as e' do thiol e'*.' Along with, of course, '*leanbh, stad, deas girseach*'."

Carl looked at Mrs. Bundle, his eyes dancing with intelligence. He was the only one who seemed to understand this puzzle of foreign-sounding mysterious words. He nodded appreciatively and said, "Very clever, Mrs. B. Well done!"

She looked around at them and then replied, "Yes, Carl, you understand, don't you?"

"Well, not the words so much, but definitely the language. It's Irish."

"Yes, it's Gaelic. In Gaelic tongue. What I said simply means: *'Be quiet, please child. Stop, nice girl.'* I had a feeling she would understand, so I just kept repeating it over and over."

She let her words sink in. Finally, everyone realized the significance of her words. It was as though light bulbs illuminated the room.

She beamed at them and explained, "I had a hunch, you see. And, as it turns out, I was right. The other night, I brushed up on the language that Arthur and I grew so fond of when we traveled to Ireland. I thought it might come in handy at some point because, you see, we have two little *Irish* girls in our care. I don't know how, and I don't know why, but I think it's all very *fantastical*—don't you?"

Chapter 15
Thanksgiving Gifts

Oh, how Mrs. Bundle always loved the hustle and bustle of preparing Thanksgiving dinner! As she strolled down the familiar hill, she pushed the newly fallen snow in front of her, each boot step spraying the delicate powdery mixture into the crisp air, creating an ethereal ivory shower. She carried an overly large picnic basket, chock-full to the brim with goodies for today's festivities. Carefully contained inside were plump calamati olives and luscious Manzanilla green olives mixed with cream cheese and pimentos and stuffed into shoots of celery. There was also her prized jellied cranberry salad, and other wondrous delights.

She had baked super-duper double chocolate-chip cookies, and was carefully transporting the makings for a raspberry trifle, which she would put together once she arrived at the Andersens. Cracker followed behind her, deftly jumping into each yielding impression her boot made, careful not to mess the white collar and the black bowtie Mrs. Bundle had fastened around his neck for this special occasion.

"My, Cracker-cat, you look splendid in your festive attire. What do you think the lovely Miss Maypool and her court would think of you today?" she teased.

You're very humorous, he cat-thought. He'd already been over to see Erin and the baby earlier that morning after having spent the first night away from them since they had arrived at the Andersen's.

He had to admit that he had become very enamored with those lasses. Erin and he had their own way of communicating, and he was in hopes she'd be able to open up to the rest of the folks sometime soon. And, when she did, well…he ran ahead of Mrs. Bundle, then flipped his body sideways and slid into her path. She stopped and looked at him expectantly.

"Did I forget something?" she asked.

Ahem! I hope you remembered my special treat! Cracker knew Mrs. Bundle had baked his favorite cat dessert, a scrumptious kitty cookie concoction dusted with catnip. Oh, truly indeed, did he love those! Like most of his cat contemporaries, Cracker prided himself on being quite a *bon vivante*, and reveled in these special times when fine food and good company came together as one, relishing that perfect dining experience.

She tapped the basket and nodded, smiling.

It was right around 11 AM and there was a lot to do before the abundant sit-down affair scheduled, at Walter's directive, for "Three PM sharp! Right on the keester!"

It had become a tradition for the Andersens and Mrs. Bundle to share this festive meal, especially since Arthur's passing. Bringing back some of the memories of past festivities produced a smile on her lips. Let's see, there would be the Parker House dinner rolls, a tradition that made Mrs. Bundle's mouth water now as she envisioned the divine experience of her first bite into the buttery sweet, warm roll.

Everyone would be helping in his or her own way in the preparation of this ultimate meal. There would be savory squash with maple syrup, sage dressing with rich chestnuts, marvelous cranberries in relishes and fruitbreads, and gobs and gobs of mashed potatoes. Mashed potatoes that kept coming and coming, with hot steaming gravy that erupted and overflowed your plate like an irrepressible volcano.

This year Walter had made more pies than ever: apple, blueberry, mince, custard, coconut cream (her favorite), chocolate cream, and a new addition this year, key lime. Yum, yum! The mixed aromas filled her senses as she walked through the door. Cracker skittered past Mrs. Bundle and went looking for the girls *Yes, these were aromas of family and home,* she thought contentedly. This year would be a very special Thanksgiving, particularly with the two new additions to this already-extended family.

As usual, the Andersen household was a happy but chaotic scene, and everyone was bustling around, busy with his or her respective tasks. The sight of Erin, sleeves rolled up to her elbows and covered with flour, good-naturedly helping Angie with the Parker House dinner roll dough, was a pleasure for Mrs. Bundle to see. Erin's wild dark curls were covered with a bright green, very familiar-looking John Deere baseball cap, the oversized bill turned backwards. Barely clearing her powdery white eyebrows, Walter's cap on Erin's head reminded Mrs. Bundle of one of the locals at Bette's Lunch and Breakfast.

Aineen sat nearby Erin in the old-fashioned wooden highchair, a towel wrapped loosely around, then pinned, at the nape of her neck as to provide a makeshift bib. Every bit of exposed hair, face, arms, and hands was totally covered in flour as she played with a piece of dough on the tray in front of her. She looked like a fluffy white snowball as the flour fell like a mini-blizzard, forming a three-foot circumference on the floor around her chair. She patted, poked, slapped and tapped her doughy mixture with abandon while she giggled. She punched her thumb squarely into the middle of the round soft dough. Squealing with childish delight, she inverted her fist with the dough still attached. The dough hung precariously in mid-air and then, with a thump, fell onto the tray in front of her.

Angie looked up from her task and grinned. "Erin, look who's here! Hi, Mrs. B! We're just getting ready to set the rolls aside to rise. We've been waiting for you, though. We need you to help us make the blueberry scones, too."

"Good morning, girls! Blueberry scones, too? Oh, my!" Erin smiled up at her through the haze of dusty flour.

She gave them all a quick kiss on the cheek. "We're going to have such fun today! I talked to the kids this morning and they send their love to you, Angie, and everyone. Can you believe they're both working today? And Leslie said he'd be working tomorrow, too." Using the biscuit cutter, she began cutting the rounds of soft dough, then let Erin take over. "He, Donna, and Les are going to be in Japan at least through the next two years. As he said, it's been a wonderful experience but they sure miss the U.S. a lot, especially at this time of year."

"Les," (Mrs. Bundle's nickname for her grandson, Leslie, Jr.) "said he wants to come for a visit this summer." She got out the blueberries and started sorting through them. "I must admit I especially miss him. Lord, he'll be a grown boy before we know it!" She sighed. "Karen called right after Leslie. She was in the middle of preparing turkey for *twenty* people on the boat. Twenty! She said her Greenpeace friends are patrolling an area off the Alaskan coast. Thank goodness for cell phones—what would we do without them! She wanted to know how everyone in Pillson is doing."

She helped Angie slice the top of the rolls, making the defining mark that signified these were real Parker House rolls.

Angie said, "So the both of them have their own thing going on, right?"

"Uh-huh." She looked down at Erin, who was sitting there ready to burst, all ears, but still, true to form, not uttering a sound.

Mrs. Bundle nodded back, "Well, that's all my news. Oh, no, wait a minute! I almost forgot. Don't you know, Althea sent me an email last night telling me that she has a 'big surprise' for me. Said not to even bother trying to find out, I'd find out for sure tomorrow. What do you suppose that could be about?"

Erin's voice was mute, but her face held much expression as she looked eagerly at Mrs. Bundle. *It won't be long before she speaks*, Mrs. Bundle thought, as Erin opened her mouth and then closed it tightly. Her curiosity was getting the better of her and she looked like a horned toad ready to explode. Mrs. Bundle could almost read her mind; she imagined the little girl was thinking; *who were all these people that Mrs. Bundle was going on about?*

Angie leaned over and confided to Erin, "Althea is Mrs. B's best friend from when they were young girls, Erin. They've been friends forever. She lives in California now. They have nicknames for each other; Mrs. B calls her Allie and she calls her L."

The two girls giggled together.

Angie said, "Hey, Mrs. B. I'll bet she sent you some kind of Thanksgiving surprise, maybe flowers or something like that! What do you think, Erin?"

Erin nodded, thrilled to be included in the conversation. Mrs. Bundle took the pan of rolls sitting in front of Erin and, noticing a large object hanging from her neck, asked, "Why Erin, what is that?"

Erin gave Mrs. Bundle a huge smile, puffed up her chest, and proudly pointed to the object. Hanging on brown jute packaging string was a roughly carved wooden whistle. Erin's demeanor had become happy and carefree in the last two days, with only momentary spurts of worry clouding her young face. A smile peeked through and she took a deep breath and blew her whistle. Her cheeks puffed like a blowfish as the high-pitched whistle pierced the air. She carried on for a few seconds, puffing and blowing, then giggling, then puffing and blowing. Aineen shrieked, her voice filled with gurgling giggles each time her sister's noisemaker created the shrill sounds.

The loud squeals finally drew a good-natured, "Erin! Didn't I tell you to stop blowin' on that *blasted* thing every dang minute!" Walter cried, busy mashing turnip by the kitchen stove. "*Goldarn* that Carl! I'm goin' to throttle him for givin' you that tooter!"

Erin sniggered, her nose crinkling and her chest heaving. The mirthful game that had evolved with Gumpy was a fun charade and she liked to hear him yell. Meanwhile, the entertainment factor was off the hook for Aineen, who threw her head back and squealed with delight, pounding her fat little fists on the tray.

The next half-hour went by quickly as the girls and Mrs. Bundle prepared the scones and then the raspberry trifle. Mrs. Bundle entertained them throughout this process with stories of when she and Althea were young girls, detailing how brave, yet foolhardy, they had been as youngsters.

"You never knew what that girl would do," she chuckled, speaking of Althea as though she were still a young girl in pigtails. "She always had a lot of gumption!" She looked intriguingly at Erin. "Just like you, Erin, as a matter of fact!" She patted Angie's shoulder, "And just like our Angie, too! We'll just wait and see what kind of 'surprise' Althea Swain has in store for me."

There was still plenty of time before the big sit-down dinner. So, a fair amount of snacking and nibbling began and a multitude of scrumptious "finger foods" begged to be tasted before the big feast. Snacks like Mrs. Bundle's olive-stuffed celery, and Carl's specialty, clam dip with peppercorn crackers, along with Angie's favorite, sardines in mustard sauce on saltines (with a touch of horseradish just to "give it a little kick", as she said). Erin turned her nose up at this special concoction, but was eager to try the stuffed celery. She made big smacking and crunching sounds as she ate, clearly enjoying every bite as she polished off the culinary treat, unabashedly licking her fingers clean.

She bent down and handed Cracker one of his special treats, his favorite liver cookies. He meowed loudly between wonderfully deliberate, delicate bites. *These are the best!* He cat-thought. *Nothing finer than good food, good company… what more could you ask for? It's turning out to be a momentous day!*

Around 2 o'clock, as the final preparations were being readied, everyone was socializing in the kitchen and open parlor while Aineen played loudly with the pots and pans on the kitchen floor. She pulled the mismatched lids, containers, utensils, and kettles from underneath the cupboards, each new piece bringing delighted giggles. It was as though she was unearthing the most special treasures of the world. She held a wooden spoon tightly in her grip, the picture complete as she pounded away on the side of a pot like the town crier, totally absorbed in her clanging and banging.

"Mmmm, that turkey smells wonderful!" Mrs. Bundle breathed in the comforting smells of the deliciously slow-basting bird. "Walter, do you want me to put these desserts out now?" she asked as she slathered the freshly whipped cream on her magnificent raspberry trifle.

"Yep! Right over on the *boo-fay* next to the pies, if you can find the room. Hey, there, Erin, how 'bout helpin' Gumpy mash the 'taters? I don't know about you, but I'm gettin' so hungry I could eat the north end of a southbound skunk!"

Erin giggled, then jumped up on the chair beside Gumpy, knowing it was quite an honor to be considered old enough to help with this monumental task. He placed the huge pot in front of her on the counter.

"Here, let me add them secret *ingreedyants*, would you?" She watched in awe, waiting. Walter poured in buttermilk, added a stick of butter, and lastly, an egg.

"There you go, girl, now *go at it!*"

The pot of cooked potatoes was massive; inside were enough of the root vegetables to feed an army. Erin, sleeves rolled up, wielded the potato masher like a professional. The old-fashioned masher slowly pushed the potatoes down, squashing them and molding them into fluffy starchy pillows. When she was finished, the pot cover was restored and a warm towel was placed on top to keep everything warm until dinner.

Clay, who was stoking the fireplace embers, asked Carl if he'd mind going out to the shed to get some more wood.

"Not at all, brother," Carl replied, grabbing his heavy work gloves and disappearing out the door.

Mrs. Bundle sat down beside the fire. "There's nothing more comforting than watching those warm reds and yellows dance around the logs. I just love a nice warm fire."

Clay nodded, lighting his pipe and drawing on the rich tobacco. "Right, as they say, *finest kind*!" He threw his spent match into the fire. "Say, Mrs. B, did you find out any more about that necklace we found up on Old Man Boulder?"

"Oh, yes! Well, with all the hoopla that's been going on I haven't had a chance to tell any of you the news. Actually, I planned to tell you all today… about what Mabel Wetherby believes we have. But, I thought we'd wait until after dinner when we're all sitting around relaxing." She winced and smiled apologetically, "Sorry to sound so cryptic, Clay—it's just that I'd like to tell everyone about it at once." She fingered the pocket of her denim skirt absentmindedly, "My gosh! So much has happened in the last few days."

"Jeesum crow, you can say that again! We've been right out straight! And, course I'm agreeable! Great idea. Let's wait until after dinner when things are quiet and our bellies are full." He chuckled as he sat down beside her on the couch. "I'll tell you what! You know Angie has really enjoyed all the excitement this past week. Your detecting operation really turned our world upside down and then some! All in less than one week!" His pale eyes softened, "Funny, it almost seems as though something was missing here, now that the girls have joined us. You know, like they always…" he hesitated. "All I can say is," with great care, he tried to express his true feelings, "well, the truth is, Mrs. B, they're really great little girls, and funny as all get-out, too! And it's good for Angie to have some other kids around—girls, that is. It's been hard for her, being the only girl, with no mother." He blushed deeply, lowered his eyes and his voice was choked with emotion, his gaze lost in deep reflection. This was a subject he had never discussed with Mrs. Bundle in all the years she had known him, and she waited patiently for him to recover. When his thoughts returned to the here-and-now, he smiled at her and said, "Well! Hopefully, someday soon we'll hear Erin talk. Better yet, Carl will get out his guitar and we'll get her to sing us one of those Irish ballads like you say she was singing in the cave."

"You know, Clay, someday soon—I think when things settle down—we're going to get some answers about a lot of things. But, for now, I suspect we just have to be patient and just let things fall into place as they most certainly w—" she stopped abruptly.

Her words were interrupted by a huge commotion outside the house, somewhere near the back woodshed area. Everyone was startled into silence, including Walter, at what sounded like a scuffle. Then, within earshot came a crash, garbled noises and banging, and at least two very loud, agitated voices.

Carl's voice rang out with something that sounded like, "*Come here!* Blast it, don't even think about it, you hear me? Put that down, you snake in the grass!" And then, another voice could be heard, muffled and deep, yelling "*Stop!*" Finally, there was an ungodly man's scream and a huge bang!

Meanwhile, Walter and Clay had gone running toward the ruckus. Just as they reached the back kitchen door, it blew wide open. A huge gust of wind and bluster was followed by a furious Carl. He was holding a struggling, grubby young man by the scruff of the neck. By all appearances, he was an older boy; Mrs. Bundle guesstimated his age to be in his late teens.

"Jeezum-*jee-hassafrats!*" Walter yelled, "What in tarnation is goin' on?"

"Look what I found skulking out behind the back shed! Getting ready to steal us blind! I knew it! I knew we'd find the thief before too long!" Carl declared as the rough-looking young man squirmed under his hold. The darkly handsome culprit was tall, probably all of six feet and then some, but the man-sized musculature was contradicted by his very young-looking face.

"*Jack!*" Erin, to everyone's shock, jumped up from her chair and, gloriously finding her voice at this moment, screamed at the top of her lungs. "*Oh bràthair!* You came!" It was a sweet, lilting Irish voice, "You *found* us! Uncle Carl! Ach! You let go of him *right now!*" She stomped her foot in protest as her strong Irish brogue range out.

Carl looked fit to be tied and hung onto the boy in total confusion.

"Oh, Jack we missed you so!" She reached for the boy but Walter held onto her protectively. She struggled and said, "*Sguir!* Stop! Sure, and I knew you'd come! Angie! *Mrs. B! Gumpy, please!*" She pleaded, looking at each of them, "Please, please make Uncle Carl let him go, won't you now?"

Angie spoke up, "It's okay, Erin, no one's going to hurt him." She eyed the devilishly attractive boy suspiciously. "I've never seen him around here. Who *are* you?"

Carl loosened his hold, letting go of the boy's arms. Everyone stared at the newcomer in astonishment as he extended his worn out arms out to the young girl.

Erin reached his side in a split second, hugging him around the waist and crying, "Oh, Jack! Ach, you're here, you're really here!" He held her tight to him, his head down.

Finally, she turned to the group, and her rhythmic voice shook excitedly as she said, "Everyone! This would be our dear brother, Jack!" The brother in question stood stone still.

Walter dropped bottom-first into the nearby rocking chair and, for once, was speechless.

Carl kept a firm hand on Jack's shoulder as Clay stood within inches, both of them not ready to let down their guard. Everyone in the room was tense. Should they be angry or happy that the boy was here? Why would they welcome this stranger with open arms? One thing was certain; the young chap had a lot of explaining to do.

Mrs. Bundle assessed his appearance. The disheveled fellow wore tattered, very mucky clothes. It was a mishmash of garments, all of which had seen better days, a colorful hodgepodge outfit apparently designed to contend primarily with the frigid weather—definitely not with fashion. The motley array of his rumpled garb was almost scary: bright red hunting cap, green plaid wool jacket over at least three visible layers of other colorful undergarments. He also wore a pair of very familiar-looking yellow deerskin gloves, along with heavily soled mountain boots of an astronomical size (obviously too large for the impoverished boy's feet). A thin layer of icy precipitation rested upon his generous eyebrows, and melting water dripped off his nose, giving an overall dismal appearance.

His flushed face exhibited a myriad of emotion: anger, hurt, distrust, disbelief, and shock. This was a face in pure agony. More than anything, his wild eyes were what caught her attention. The cerulean blue brilliance set against his ruddy Irish-looking good looks were traffic-stopping. Black frozen hair stuck out every which way underneath his Sad Sack woolen hat and beneath it, under all the dirt and grime, his chiseled fine features seemed to, nevertheless, reflect integrity Those beautiful eyes were bright and angry right now, and he spoke up curtly, words that were hard to understand behind the strong Irish accent.

"Aye, my name would be Jack O'Rahilly Corrigan, and they would be *my sisters*." He motioned boldly toward the two girls. "I'd be obliged if you would let go of me, mate, so that I can take them out of your way and home with *me* right now! They're rightfully mine, aren't they now?" He was defiant, bravely standing his ground and, not waiting for an answer, enjoined his sister, "C'mere, Erin, lass. Get your coat. *Laithreach bonn!*"

Erin cried, "Jack, oh Jack. We missed you so much! Oh, I'm so glad you're here!" Erin clung to him, her little limbs holding on for dear life.

"Do as I say, child, would you now?"

Walter stood up and put a light hand on Erin's shoulder. "Ahem! Sorry to say, youngblood, that ain't gonna happen, not yet anyway." The boy's chin jutted out defensively as Walter continued, "Now, you jest hang on a peachy minute. Don't get your britches in a bunch." The boy struggled to understand the elderly man. "We're having a shindig here today and seems to me, you've got some solvin' out to do before you go anywhere with anywho. Gaw! You look like you're nigh ready to keel over! Heck, you're as skinny as a rail fence!" He looked squarely at the young man, eye-to-eye, "Now, sit down, son. Take a load off yer feet and calm down." He motioned to his sons and said calmly, "Let's all take a couple-three and relax."

Walter's voice of quiet authority seemed to work magic. Seconds passed, and then the young chap reached for the kitchen counter, as though stricken. Unable to stand any longer and without a sound, he collapsed into a nearby straight back chair.

They watched as his jacket fell below his shoulders, revealing a miserably lean upper body with no extra fat to spare. His body looked well built and muscular but acutely emaciated beneath his layered clothing. It was evident to all that this was a boy who had recently been through some very hard times.

His eyes were glazed, almost feverish, and he looked completely done in. Removing the gloves, he put his head into his rough, red hands, seemingly disoriented.

He attempted to focus twice, shook his head as though to clear his thoughts, then looked up and whispered, "Surely, I'm not here to cause any trouble. Em...could I have a bit of water, sir? *Ach! Ta tineas cinn orm!*"

"Hell's bells! Yes, boy, of course, you must be drier 'n a cork leg!"

Angie handed him a glass of water. He thanked her, avoiding eye contact. He took a long drink, his hand visibly trembling. Drops of water fell onto his lap. Erin reached to help him.

As Mrs. Bundle watched this scene, her mind was racing. Things were moving too quickly, and her brain was a muddle of scenes vaguely familiar.

All at once she realized what she was seeing. She gasped quietly, clutching her hands to her chest. "Oh, my Lord!" she exclaimed under her breath. It was…his eyes. The same eyes, bright, sky blue, that beautiful blue! Looking carefully, she noticed the only difference was that, now, they were ringed with the dark sockets in his head, presumably from exhaustion and a great deal of stress.

She realized that there, before her, unbelievably, was…yes, the young man in the photograph! Incredibly, it was the boy from the photo, the photo that Darby Quicksilver had shown her. Absolutely, for sure, this boy was a dead ringer for—what was his name? Yes, Ashley Whitewick, the bad nephew. The one that was stealing the Quicksilver family blind.

Oh…my… gosh, she thought.

"Fantastical!" was all that she could whisper.

Chapter Sixteen

Jack

After Jack had had a chance to catch his breath, warm his tired physique by the kitchen woodstove fire, and have a warm drink, he appeared ready to talk. He held Erin in his lap and hugged her protectively to him, almost as though he dared not let go. Aineen played merrily at his feet, and he bent over to kiss the wispy brown curls atop her head. All could see that this young man loved his sisters dearly. Walter finally cleared his throat and asked in a gentle, coaxing tone, "So, Master Corrigan, could you please tell us how in God's green earth you ended up here in the willywags?"

The young man looked around the room, cleared his throat, and pulled out a worn, dirty envelope from deep within an inside pocket. They all leaned forward to see what he had removed, anxious but quiet, waiting for him to speak. When the words came, they were halting and painful. The room was as quiet as a Catholic confessional booth. His strong Irish brogue was evident; as it was somewhat difficult to understand without attending closely, they all strained to hear his next words.

"I've been running....ever since we got here... and...I reckon I can't run anymore. Right, and I'm just knackered. My sisters and I have been... alone in this country for the last two months. *A Dhia Dhilis!*"

They all looked on in wonderment. Jack's hands shook as he opened the papers. It looked like a letter, thin frail pages of neatly written, even penmanship were visible. Resignedly looking around the room, he laid the letter in his lap and attempted to explain.

"We are orphans. And us, truly, just off the boat from Ireland." He took a deep breath. Then, in a rush of pain-filled words he blurted out, "Both parents died within the last year." He made the Catholic sign-of-the-cross quickly on his chest.

Angie clutched her hand to her throat. "Dead?"

"Well don't that just eat my lunch!" Walter proclaimed softly.

"Our parents were part of a group of musicians in our country called the Travellers." Jack continued. "Em, do y' know what they are, the Travellers, *Giofog*?"

He looked around the room defensively, his eyes dark and angry. They all shook their heads.

"Well, now, let me tell you! The Travellers are a group that are seen as *problems* in our dear Ireland, rather than as people. They are a minority group with their own language and social customs. They are denied even their most basic rights and are even refused entry into shops and cafes and the like throughout the land. They are often segregated into separate classes in school, and are banned from almost every pub in the country." His eyes were bitter, his face pinched tight as a corkscrew as he continued his narrative. "Not so long ago, Irish Travellers were referred to as 'Tinkers'—because their occupations were through history, often as not, tinsmiths. Some Travellers, like the group me parents belonged, relied on making music for their livelihood, singing the many traditional ballads and songs of Ireland. Legend has it that they are the descendants of traveling bards, d'you know?" He pressed on, his voice a tired monotone as he tried to explain, "Aye, but the real story of Ireland's traveling people are often the street beggars, which is something our own dear group would never stoop to. The begging and the suspicion that attaches itself to the likes of such wandering folk as our lot have made the Travellers a very unpopular minority in Ireland. Little has changed in Ireland for hundreds of years in the world of the Travellers. You could say, couldn't you now, that it's quite a cross to bear. Bein' looked at as common gypsies and nomads?"

"So, you're one of these Travellers?" Clay asked.

"Right, we *were*. Sure, and it's been a hard road, being part of it, but I'm proud to say our own dear family lived a happy life." He patted Erin and she smiled; the look they gave each other was of remembrances of happier times.

"But why are you here in Verm—?" Mrs. Bundle began, and Jack held up a weak hand.

"Truly," he said, shyly, "I think that if I can show you this," he held up the papers, "and well, mum, maybe read it to you all….it will answer a lot of questions you might have." He said earnestly, clutching the worn document, "*Na fírinne*—the truth!"

He looked around the room hopefully, and everyone nodded.

Clay said, "Go ahead, let's hear it!"

Jack ever-so-softly began reading the fine cursive script.

To My Son, Jack

My Dearest Boy,

You are reading this letter now because you know I'm no longer here to care for you and the wee ones. There are some important things I need to explain to prepare you for the tough road ahead. Over the years, times have been hard and the way we have had to live has often caused our family great pain.

As the firstborn, you were witness to the many times our family of Travellers was treated badly. Truth be told, as kind as the Travellers family was to us over the years, they were never the kin you were born into.

Aye, my descendants are from the clan O'Rahilly, or as they were known in ancient times, Ó Raghailligh. The name came from Ragheallach meaning "gregarious race", from the great-grandson of Maolmordha! Our ancestors were thought to be kinsmen of the great

O'Conor kings of Connacht through Maolmordha, and our family
O'Rahilly, comes from County Cavan, or the Lake Country, of Ireland.

As you know, lad, I grew up in the little hamlet of Ballyhaise, a village
in existence since the early 17th century a mere fifty miles from Dublin.
My beautiful County Cavan was a place of rolling hills and lakes and
picture perfect to my memory.

In Ballyhaise, my parents ran the local pub, The Singing Swans, and
my memories of my youth are carefree and wonderful. Your grandfather
(me Da) was a boisterous fellow, name of Kelley. Aye, he never gave me
mother anything but love and fun. His only surviving family member,
a younger brother called Ian, left Ballyhaise at the tender age of 14,
just after World War II. Me father said he yearned to go to Derry to
find excitement and join the Sinn Fein party of resistance against the
English. Word came back to Ballyhaise that he had somehow become
involved in the deaths of some English soldiers and so he was spirited
away by the Brotherhood across the ocean to America. I can remember
me father said he heard from him only once after that, a correspondence
that was smuggled into Ireland to him and which told of the wonders
and beauty of America. After that, Ian was never heard from again, and
Da was left with no kin save me dear Ma, who he loved to his death.

My parents would perform while they worked, singing together at
the little Singing Swans Pub—and a merrier place to stop over would
be hard to find. I grew up harmonizing with them to our ancient Irish
ballads, performing with them on our harps and flutes. Rightly so, me
own brood have inherited that gift of song, and you with your special
talent too, Jack, of picking up and making wonderful music with
any instrument. Whether it be singing, or playing a flute, a harp, or
concertina, you have a natural ability to make people's hearts soar, lad,
just as your Grandmother Aineen did before you.

When I was 16, me Ma came to me as I come to you now, and gave
me this treasured heirloom, along with its story. She, too, was dying, and
wanted me to know about our heritage. She wanted me to know the story
of the swans so that I could continue the family legacy, the legacy of the
special medallion you're holding in your hand.

Over the years I have told you and Erin the legend many times. She insisted that our family's heritage was intertwined with the legend, and that her parents named her Aineen—aye, 'bird' in Gaelic—because of their belief in that heritage. The legend and the reality are woven together as one. In your hand is a piece of your ancestry, a piece from many former generations long before you and I existed.

This heirloom has been passed down from parent to oldest sibling from one to the next. God willing, you will pass it down to your firstborn someday, too. I haven't a clue how it came into our clan, or for that matter, what the piece is worth in modern-day currency. To me, it is worth its weight in gold many, many times over. It is our kinsman bond to our forebears. This piece has been held in the hands of O'Rahillys for hundreds of years. It is now yours, at least for the while. Their blood flows through your veins, my son, and I trust you will always wear the name Jack O'Rahilly Corrigan nobly, wherever you go.

My mother handed this medallion to me shortly before she died, leaving my father lonely and heartbroken. As time progressed, his remorse grew. He was unable to continue working. Ach! He couldn't seem to function without his 'darlin' Aineen'. The Pub became a place of mourning, no longer cheerful, no more singing, and the business fell off to nothing. Less than a year later, me poor Da passed away in his sleep.

I was alone in the world and a young girl of 17 when I first laid eyes on your father. He was a handsome lad, wasn't he now, full of fun and high of spirit! When Frank Corrigan came through Ballyhaise as part of the Travellers performing group, I fell in love with his independent mind, his beautiful singing voice, and the freedom he could offer me. I had nothing left in Ballyhaise. We shared a kindred spirit from the start.

He was an orphan, without knowledge of his ancestry. When he came of age at 16, he was turned out of the orphanage. He drifted for awhile, then shortly thereafter was taken in by the Travellers. So, when we met, it was as though we were both starting our lives fresh and new—together.

Your dear father proposed to me on the banks of the Ammalee River on that beautiful summer day and a promising world opened for me outside of Ballyhaise. I packed one satchel and left town with him and the troupe the following week, never looking back—never to return to the tragic village of my youth.

Our singing voices complemented our lives together like one glorious sound, and all was wonderful as we created our own family. And, until a few months ago, our life together was most wonderful, loving, and exciting. It didn't matter where we lived or that we were poor; we always had each other.

Your father and I wanted a family so much! I blessed the day the doctor told me I was going to have twins. And when you survived that difficult birth and your dear sister lay stillborn—already dead inside my womb—I knew that you must be a special gift from God. You were destined to survive, Jack. I was reminded of those other children in our legend who survived—Fionnuala and Aed who were firstborn twins. It was your fate to be nurtured, and then, later, to care for our two wee ones when you grew older. Of that I am sure, Jack.

You know, God makes the choices and we accept all the twists and roundabouts that life brings. Your father was a bit of a "seanchai", wasn't he now? The storyteller and soothsayer in him, it was for sure. Aye, I think somehow he knew he wasn't long for our world. And when he was killed it was hard for all of us to go on. To be taken from us in his prime, so unfair to you children! Ach, and me heart broken in two!

You've taken care of us all, lad, in the midst of our tragedies. What with me being sick and Aineen just a babe, and three mouths to feed... but we have survived, thanks to you and our God above. Sure, and I know it's been a struggle, son.

So. We've always talked about the green hills of Ireland, treasuring its beauty as we traveled the countryside. We've journeyed through the boroughs and counties of Ireland, through Armagh and Donegal, to Sligo and Kildare, Tipperary, Cork and back. We have admired the many natural shades of brilliant green that are spread over the landscape of the beautiful mountains, hills, lakes, rivers, valleys, woods and forests of our Ireland.

Yes, lad, our life has been a trial. But, my hope for you and the children, now that neither your father nor I can be there for you, is that *you find a new life in a new place—free from the bigotry of the Travellers label. It is a cruel brand—A legacy I cannot leave for you and the girls, Jack! I want, more than anything, for you to have a place you can truly call 'home'. Now is the time for you and the girls to make that change, a change to a better life.*

There is a faraway place in America I have heard of, no…dreamed of over the years. It is called "Vermont". From what I have read, it is very much like our beautiful Ireland in so many ways. "Green Mountains" is what the name means, doesn't it now? Rich forests and bright green pastures, much still undisturbed and exquisite. Ah, what a grand place it must be!

I want you to take the children to Vermont—far away from Ireland— where, God-willing, you will no longer be viewed as cast-offs. When we had naught but each other to depend on, this fine dream kept me going and I know it can come true for you, too, if you believe it will.

Steady on, son—I know this will be the hardest thing you ever do.

Take the last of our meager savings here, and go to this place of peace and tranquility. I have taken measures to see that this can be accomplished.

That is my dying wish. Aye, surely when I close my eyes, I can see you there now. I pray that you will make a better life for you and the girls.

One other thing, Jack. Always hold your head high. Be proud of your family. Keep the girls safe and close to you…

Jack stopped reading, his voice cracking, unable to go on. Walter cleared his throat, and Carl pulled his red bandanna handkerchief from his back pocket and blew his nose loudly.

Clay said, "It's all right, son, go on with your letter."

Jack continued reading, his eyes misty and his voice coarse.

When times are tough, and you are lonely and unsure, hold this close to your heart. I will be with you. I am as close to you as that family pendant is to your breast.

Think kindly on your mother and father, Jack. Someday, you will treat

your own children with respect and love and they will never fail you, as
you have never failed us, dear lad.

Me Da used to say, 'May you have warm words on a cold evening,
a full moon on a dark night, and the road downhill all the way to your
door.'

Share our songs with the world. Gently, carry this heritage in your
hands to a new life. God gave me the most wonderful lad in the world. I
love you, and Erin, and the babby with all my heart and soul, and will
wait for you in Heaven.

Your loving Ma,
Maire O'Rahilly Kelley Corrigan

The young man stopped reading and looked up, his face laced
with tragedy and grief.He spat out the words, "She died a cruel
death, the cancer taking her quickly from us. Aye, the Friends
of St. Luke's Hospital—for paupers like us—provided for her
care until she passed away." He sniffed slightly. "At first, I was
afraid to think about this huge task she'd given me, this last dying
wish. Although we'd been with the Travellers all our life, I knew
we must go." He shrugged his shoulders. "I knew I must go on.
Teaghlaigh—Family!"

Walter said, "Comin' all the way from Ireland to Vermont!
How'd you do it, son?"

"Aye, and well you should wonder! She didn't miss a trick, did
me Mum? C'mere now, in the envelope she had included our
visas, a sum of money, and three tickets for passage to America
on the Seabourn Cruise Line—fourth class. There was…" he
paused, the renewed pain clearly showing on his countenance,
"also a final written note scrawled in me mother's last feeble
handwriting." He raised his eyes in thought, having committed
to memory her last message. "'*All is in order. I have booked the*
voyage for the three of you. Stay safe. Trust no one. Remember, I
want a different life for you. Good Luck, lad. Ma.'"

The room was a vacuum of silent empathy. Jack exhaled slowly, as though relieving himself of a huge weight. The group as a whole was deadly quiet, absorbing the recent trauma and emotion of the last hour in their own manner. Erin sat close to Jack, innocent tears quietly streaming like clear rivulets down her cheeks.

He continued his monologue.

"Our poor Ma died in late August. We buried her with my Da, who'd been killed by a gee-eyed lush cabbie seven months earlier. That was just after the Government had relocated us as part of their program to get Travellers off the roads and into permanent housing. Here we were in Dublin with no family stuck in a sorry flat with no support. So, we said our farewells and made our final plans. *The Seabourn Pride* arrived in Dublin on the 10th, where we embarked. Aye, we slipped through the cracks with the authorities, to be sure; no one seemed to question our voyage minus parents."

"You traveled across the ocean alone?" Angie asked.

"Aye. When we left port I was still mourning the passing of our dear Ma. The three of us stayed in one small cabin for the majority of our passage, and altogether the trip was uneventful. People were very helpful but kept their distance. Right, we stayed to ourselves as much as possible and did not bring any undue attention. Surely, there were a couple of strange occurrences, but there's a tale to be told another time. Finally, we arrived in New York on September 24th."

He took another sip of the tepid water, looking around at the solemn group. He shook his head dejectedly. "Ach! Since then, we've had nothing but bad luck! It's as though the black cloud of the divil descended and settled over us from the minute we reached America." He bowed his head as though ashamed. "We lost our luggage and near all our belongings the first day we arrived in New York."

Mrs. Bundle clicked her tongue in despair. What terrible misfortune!

As though determined to spew out all the pent-up emotion, Jack said hurriedly, "Aye, we cleared Customs and took the shuttle to Amtrak for the next leg of our journey—to the *magical promised land.*" Scorn filled his voice and he clenched his fists, "On the shuttle bus there was this priest—really, I should say, a man dressed in priest's clothing. He asked if we were new to the States. He said his parish was located in New York and that he was just returning from a holy group pilgrimage to Lourdes. His kind smile would have melted butter, now, wouldn't it! Surely, I had no reason to disbelieve him, did I now?"

"Most people *would* trust a priest," Mrs. Bundle said, trying to console him.

"What a daft fool I was! He befriended us at great length, even offered to take us to a small eatery across from the station while we waited for the train. He seemed very compassionate and caring, sure and he did, and he listened with interest as I told him where we were bound." He paused, shaking his head, regrouping his thoughts; the room was spellbound.

"He was especially keen on our destination, assuring us that there were Catholic resources in Rutland that could offer us help and wouldn't he be glad to refer us once we arrived? Then, with the kindest of gestures, he welcomed us to come to the church rectory and wait until we left for Vermont later that evening." He looked at them all beseechingly, "You must understand, in Ireland a priest's integrity is never to be questioned." They nodded, and he went on. "Of course, this all sounded wonderful to me, and I jumped at the chance for a respite before our next long journey. He helped me put all our belongings into a large locker at the Amtrak terminal, save a small bag with things for the babby— nappies and the like—that I carried, and then he hailed us a cab. He gave the cabby the destination address and a $20 bill, saying he would follow along after he had checked in with the Bishop's office."

Erin piped up, *"Is minic aingeal ar an Diabhal fein!"*

"Right you are, lass—" he explained, "it's a Gaelic saying, *'There's often the look of an angel on the devil himself!'*—to be sure, now! So, as we traveled through the winding, confusing city streets of New York, I began wondering if something wasn't a bit off kilter. *Cén fáth?* Why, I asked myself? Don't you know, the streets started looking rougher and rougher. Em, the cabby finally stopped and there, in front of us, was a burned-out tenement building, all boarded up and deserted. The priest was a phony beggar! How thick could I be—and me not knowing that he'd nicked all our belongings and rumbled us good!" Jack stopped and wiped his eyes, angrily smacking one fist into the other. "The cabby took pity on us and returned us to the Amtrak terminal without a fee—we were lucky on that, to be sure. When we opened our locker, it was empty of all our worldly possessions. He'd nicked everything! A local scam artist who swindled us out of everything we owned! The only thing I had left was around my neck. Aye, that precious heirloom of me mother's, tucked safely inside me shirt." He gave a cynical, tense grin, "And, if I hadn't tucked our cash inside me sock, he would have left us penniless, too. The rogue!"

"Did you go to the police?" Clay asked.

"Nay, nay! That would have been a fool's errand, wouldn't it now? My experience as a Traveller told me to keep our heads low, to not ask anyone for anything. *An dtuigeann tu?* Understand? So, in the end, we decided to take the very next train north to Rutland, didn't we? I'll take the blame for it all, you'll be sure to know. But, aye, how was I to know it would be one disaster after another? When we arrived, no one wanted to hire a foreign lad. I've not yet been to university. There's a lot of hard work I'm willing to do, just turning eighteen and all, but you have to have a work visa. 'Where's your green card, kid?' is what they kept asking me. 'You got to have a green card to work!'"

"It's been a nightmare. Finally, I heard of a job near here that would suit me. I saw an advert from this sheep farmer in Tyson who needed a hired hand, lodgings included. So I rung him up and, lo and behold, he said get myself over there and he would hire me! *Ach!*" He paused to shake his head once more. "Right, and we used most all of our money getting over to his farm. When we arrived at his doorstep, he saw the two young lasses and, without blinking, the bloody beggar sent us down the road. He wouldn't even consider taking the three of us in, even for just the night." His voice took on a gruffness as he imitated the farmer, "'*I advertised for farm help, not a family, you nitwit!*' And he slammed the door in our face—that's what he did, didn't he now? What was I to do? Of course, I was beside myself. Here, in the middle of nowhere with no food, no money, no lodgings. The only good thing was the girls. This little one has been wonderful through it all." He gave Erin a quick hug and lightly kissed her wet cheek. She drew closer to his body and her little hand gently, maternally patted his shoulder.

"*Hmphhh!*" Walter Andersen croaked, "Well, I'll be horsewhipped with a feather! That sure as naught sounds like old man Hattersley, don't it, boys? Granville! Ain't that his name, son? Cantankerous and ornery—all rolled together into a nasty nugget… and, they say he's tighter 'n the bark on a tree!"

Carl nodded affirmatively. Clay said, "Sounds pret-near right on, Pops."

"Since then, it's been mostly hand-to-mouth," Jack glumly continued. "I've tried to keep things going, but winter was on the way and everything went downhill quickly. We ran out of all the money fast. Since then, I've scrounged for whatever food or lodging I could find: in barns, under trees, whatever. I searched the hills looking for temporary shelter. And I reckon I did what I had to do to feed the kids and survive. *Fuar!* The cold!! That's how we ended up in the caves."

He drew in a deep, long breath, as though gearing up for the words to come. "We've lived in worse, haven't we now, with the Travellers? Holed up in that dirty, cold cave, fending for ourselves.

And me trying me best to provide, scavenging for food. Then, last week, the worst of it, I lost the dearest treasure, a family heirloom my mother entrusted to me!" He slapped the letter down hard on his knee in utter frustration. "Ach! I don't know, I must have laid it down on the rock and forgot it in my troubles. I was so low; everything seemed so hopeless. *Ta tuirse orm*—so tired! When I went back later on, it was gone. Right, and I looked everywhere. Sure, and that was the blackest day for me and the girls. Truly, I near gave up."

"Good God, son, didn't you know people would help you?" Clay asked incredulously. "You really, honestly didn't need to go through all of this on your own, son! Why, I ask, did you?"

"Well, me Ma said not to trust anyone, and she was right, wasn't she now? After we were fooled the first time, and turned away cold the second, I really couldn't risk it. Here I was in a new country, almost like, well, being on a different planet as far as that goes. Ah well, so I borrowed things to stay alive, didn't I?" He looked directly at Walter Andersen. "And, sir, on my own Mother's grave, I make a promise to you, here and now. I intend to pay everyone back for everything I've taken." He pulled out a very weather beaten, little black notebook from his jacket, and opened it to what appeared to be quite a detailed list.

He passed the book to Walter, who adjusted his spectacles and began to read the list aloud, "...hmmm, lookee here....'*Tan gloves from white farmhouse on the knoll, blanket from red house on ridge, sieve from Andersen property...*'" he looked at Jack quizzically. "Sieve? What sieve?" His eyes grew wide, "Oh! You mean that old *colly-ander?*"

Confused with the term, Jack shook his head. Then, understanding, he cried, "Aye! The collander."

Erin piped up, "*Aye!* That was for me!"

Jack said, "—because she was so afraid of the bats flying around in the cave, she said she needed 'a helmet', didn't she now?"

Walter gave a snort and continued reading, "'*ham from Andersen farm, starter fluid and matches from Oleo Farm on Grasshopper...*'"

"Right! See, there!" Jack pointed, "em, see now, I listed the date I borrowed things, so I wouldn't forget. Sure, and if I knew the owner's name I listed that, too! Can you see, now?" His voice rose in his defense, "I wager that I'll pay everyone back, aye, I will! I've a strong back and a willing spirit, and I intend to work off every penny borrowed."

"Scratch me baldheaded," Walter said. "I betcha you will, too. But, lookee here, Jack O'Rahilly Corrigan," he put special emphasis on each of the boy's given name, "you've underestimated the goodness of folk in these here parts. We're hardy people, but we ain't hardhearted! The Good Lord didn't make us all a bunch of danged mean-spirited fools! He's got His ways of workin' things out, y'hear?"

Mrs. Bundle sat back and looked keenly at Jack, scrutinizing his face, not sure she was ready yet to accept his story until all the pieces fit to her satisfaction.

"I have a question for you, Jack. May I ask what led you to leave the children alone in the cave?"

Jack looked at her, his eyes misting over uncontrollably. "Yes, mum, and I'll tell you. We had been living in the caves for quite some time, don't you know. We were in a desperate state. I was at my wit's end; you can believe that for sure! No food, no nappies for Aineen, the weather turning fair freezing, and I knew I had to do something to get us out of this mess I'd gotten us into." He rubbed at his forehead, agitated.

"I left at four that morning, Saturday it was, and dark and cold! After I got the kids situated in the cave with a good fire going, I told Erin I had to go out and find us some food, and try to find some work so I could get us a better place to stay. She knew I'd be back. I told her I was going the back way over Tyson Road into Ludlow. What with winter and ski season, I figured I could find something there, maybe at the Mountain, anything in fact," he said, referring to the local ski resort at Okemo Mountain. "I assured her, *promised her*, I'd return by nightfall at the latest, and that it was her job to be a big girl and take care of Aineen as best she could. I'd made a decision I couldn't come back until I had provisions and God willing, some money to move us closer to town and into better lodgings.

"It was my last chance!" he said, entreating them to understand his dilemma. "Y'see now, I made her promise me she wouldn't leave the cave, and that if she heard anything or saw anyone she wouldn't speak or make a sound. I left her with a blazing fire and plenty of wood stacked nearby to keep her and the babby warm. She had candles, and plenty of covers, and I thought they both would be safe. Sure, and it was the hardest thing I've ever had to do! I told her to sing to Aineen, and keep singing if she got afraid. Aye, she begged me to stay, the poor lass, but I knew I had to go or we'd die in the cave."

"So you left them before dawn." Mrs. Bundle said.

"Aye, after I got to Ludlow I went door-to-door, asking the shop owners if they had any work, anything at all. Late that morning, I finally got lucky when I got a job cleaning an estate office. I think the owner took pity on me, sad and needy as I looked, and said he could pay me cash at the end of the day.

"I began at noon when the office closed, vacuuming and sweeping the premises, all in good order. As late afternoon came I'd finished washing and waxing the floors, cleaned the offices, kitchen, and bathroom, and was just finishing up. The owner paid me well, more than I deserved, and said he had been on hard times himself years before—before his business became successful. Right! And I could have the job weekly if I wanted it, he said, couldn't I now? I was elated when I left—money, and a job!"

"I went outside and the first snow was coming down hard. I was worried to death how the girls were doing. Aye, truth be told, I was near sick. I quickly purchased a bag of supplies and hitched a ride back—the winds were blustering, the snow streakin' across the road. By the time I got to the ridge it was around five. It took me two hours to get from the dirt road up the highland to the caves, the snow was coming down so hard! I couldn't see where I was going. By the time I got there, it was long after dark. Ach! They were gone! Right, I was beside meself, you can be sure! The fire was out, and there was no trace of where they'd disappeared to, no tracks that I could see or find. I near passed out in panic. Jaysus! I went out searching but was forced back inside. All I could think was they were in the storm, freezing to death! Bloody hell!"

He stopped to take a breath, then cried desperately, "I was near frozen meself, wasn't I? Crazy from the fear—like a vice around me neck!" He implored, "How did you ever find them? Or, did they find you? And, when? Did Erin leave the cave with the babby?" he queried, hesitating, and looking around.

Mrs. Bundle replied, "We found them. Alone. In the cave."

"Ach! I've searched for them every day! Without a trace, they'd vanished. I…almost couldn't go on."

He looked up in awe at Mrs. Bundle. "How did you find our cave?"

"Well, last week people in the area started noticing things missing. After we started comparing notes, it was clear to us that there were some strange goings-on in our little neighborhood of North Pillson Corners. Things seemed to be going missing with no real valid explanation. And, a stranger had been spotted in the area, which always raises a red flag here in these parts—because everyone knows everyone."

"Did you know about us, then?"

"Enough to wonder what was going on. So, Angie, Cracker," she pointed to the sleek black cat in his bowtie finery, "and I decided to go on a search, a fact-finding mission, you might say; mostly, an adventure of sorts, to see what we could discover."

Jack looked at the Angie, and then at Cracker. He wasn't sure why a cat would accompany them on their search into the highland, and shook his head in disbelief.

Aye, my Irish mate, Cracker cat-thought grandly, *you haven't heard about our incredible detective skills yet.*

"We really had no idea what we would find, Jack, if anything. So, early Saturday morning we combed the area looking for clues, trekking over many miles and ending up past Old Man Boulder around the cave area. We had no idea we'd find two hungry, tired little girls. Imagine our surprise when we heard Erin's little voice singing, literally wafting through the cave. When we discovered the two, Erin was distraught with fear, and they were both very cold. Erin had come down with a slight fever as well. It appeared to us that they'd been abandoned. We had to act and act quickly."

"Sweet *Jaysus*! I'll be thanking you 'til my dying day for getting them to warm shelter." Jack crossed himself again, then shook his head sadly. "I've never seen the likes of this. I honestly never thought anyone would come near those caves. I can't believe it, but I know now you probably saved them. Aye, that you did!"

Erin piped up, her small chin quivering, "I fell asleep, Jack...I got a chill and I couldn't keep the fire going. We were perishing cold. But I held onto Aineen, like you told me to, *bràthair.*"

"It's all right, lass. You did a grand job. I've been looking for you all week, haven't I now?" He comforted her and hugged her to him.

Angie continued the story. "When we found the girls, they were so chilled we bundled them up and between us, carried them down the mountain in the blizzard. By the time we got to the back pasture, there was already six inches of snow on the ground. My Dad and Uncle Carl brought the tractor and wagon out into the north field to find us. Luckily, they were there to carry us all back to the house. Lucky, because the storm became so intense on the mountain. If it had been later, we might not have been able to find our way down!"

Clay took over, "Since that night, we've been getting the kids back to being healthy, and we've been trying to find out where in heck they came from. It didn't help that Erin wouldn't talk. She wouldn't breathe a word."

Carl reiterated, "Yup, she's quite a riggin', isn't she! She wouldn't say boo to no one about nothing." He touched her head gently, smiling.

Jack watched this simple display of affection for his sister. A smile jerked tautly at the corners of his mouth. "Em, well now. Little did I know the moppet would take me so literally and not speak a word to anyone, right!' He tapped her head. "Aye, she's been a real brick through all this, and I'm proud of you, I am, lass!" He kissed her gently on her cheek.

She smiled and said proudly, "I promised you Jack, didn't I now? I wanted to tell Gumpy all about us, and tell Angie, too! But I promised not to talk to anyone!"

"Aye, that's a miracle unto itself as gabby a lass as you are!"

She lowered her voice and whispered deliberately, "Em…I told Cracker but he promised not to tell. Aye, what a grand cat he is, Jack! He's my best, best friend, aren't you now, Cracker-cat?"

Cracker sidled up and rubbed his body against Jack's leg, and Jack gave a gruff chuckle, "Yes, well, that's a fine thing, Erin, for sure." He turned to the group, "She's always partial to most any animal—strays, pets, horses." Erin motioned down at Cracker, and Jack said, "Aye. Thanks, mate, for taking care of my wee sister."

Not a problem, Cracker purred back, majestically raising his head high.

Carl cleared his throat. "Seems the only crime here is you letting your pride get the best of you, Jack. You know, with you so down on your luck, there would have been plenty of our community around here willing to help—if we'd known about it."

Jack nodded his head reluctantly. "Aye, you could be right on that…"

Erin interrupted, "Oh, Jack! Mrs. Bundle knows our Gaelic tongue, truly she does! Sure, and I'll wager she's magical powers about her! She's going to have me to her home for a tea party, too, aren't you, Mrs. B?" She radiated a huge smile at Mrs. Bundle. It was the first time Mrs. Bundle saw pure joy on the young girl's face.

The girl continued talking, gaining momentum now after having stored up her sentences for a very long time. "And Uncle Carl, he made me my beautiful whistle, see?" She held it up for him to view. "And Gumpy gives me lots of sweets…" The floodgates were open now and Erin was out of the gate, prepared to talk Jack's ear off. She told him about Mrs. Bundle whispering words in her ear, and Miss Maypool going to the Ball, and how today she had helped baked Parker House rolls and scones with Angie and Mrs. Bundle, and helped Gumpy mash the potatoes, too! Hurrying to the end of her monologue, she said, "And now I'm not going to have to go with *'That Lady!'*" She made a sweeping, triumphant motion with her tiny arm, pointing in the direction toward the front door.

Oh, no, Mrs. Bundle thought.

"What's that, what d'ya mean, luv? Go with who? What lady?" Jack drew back into himself, running his hands through his rich, dark, but overlong, unkempt hair (tresses that hadn't seen a barber's clippers in many months). His worried face had new anxiety written all over it at this latest piece of information. He repeated, "*What* lady?"

Clay cleared his throat uncomfortably while Walter jumped up, "Well, now! I daresay we've had just about enough conversatin', at least for now." He placed his hands on his hips and proclaimed, "Who wants turkey?" The nervous tension in the room was released like a huge bowling ball hitting a perfect strike.

Erin gave an excited, "*Yay! Turkey!*" Aineen clapped her hands at the laughter.

Mrs. Bundle took Jack's arm gently. "Walter's right, Jack. We can talk about all these other things later. Let's sit down and have our Thanksgiving dinner. It seems we all have a lot to be thankful for, wouldn't you say?"

"Right, mum."

She pointed to the beautifully decorated table: the antique chandelier above the sparkling silverware and china table settings, ready to be bountifully laden, waiting for everyone to sit down and enjoy. "Welcome, Jack."

Everyone took her lead and joined in. "Yes, welcome Jack, c'mon young man…"

Carl pulled out a chair at the table and motioned for Jack to sit down. Gingerly walking, as though in a trance, he finally sat down at the table.

"Sure, and I don't know. I…..well, it's true that I am feeling…a bit peckish." He begrudgingly shared this information. "Me head feels like its splitting wide open from the worry."

Angie put an extra place setting down in front of him, and Erin asked, "Can I sit beside you, Jack?"

He smiled at her, his eyes wet, "And who else would be beside me except the likes of you, a sweet colleen in all her finery? Look at you! Aye, now, you sit right here."

Mrs. Bundle placed Aineen into Jack's arms. He looked as though he might cry. The baby lay quietly in Jack's lap, her head resting in the crook of his arm as he held her close. He whispered softly into her ear, "Ach! And would you look at you now, my sweet one. *Milsean Aineen*…." he whispered, then bit his lip, unable to speak.

Clay said in a hushed tone, "Don't you worry about anything, Jack. We'll work it all out together."

As they all prepared to eat, the movement from the kitchen to the dining table was fast and furious. As if by magic, the dining table was transformed into a feast of enchanting proportions. The aromas were wonderful; the rich bouquet of deep red cranberry sauce, colorful vegetables and mashed potatoes, thick dark gravy, freshly baked rolls and pies, and glorious roasted turkey, all the smells of Thanksgiving fragrantly wafted through the air.

Just as they all sat down, Angie put her hand to her head, "Oh! Wait, Mrs. B! We've got one more piece of business we need to tell Jack about before we celebrate, don't we?"

Everyone, including Jack, looked expectantly at Mrs. Bundle.

"What in tarnation? I'm hungry!" Walter grumbled good-naturedly, as he honed the two large carving knives against each other.

"You know," Angie urged, "*THE PENDANT.*"

Jack looked up, startled. "Pendant? What d'you mean, now? Are you telling me...you know something....about where me dear ma's necklace is?" Everyone turned to Mrs. Bundle.

Clay said, "It's your turn, Mrs. B!"

Jack asked, "Did you find it, Mum? A necklace, large, and round?" He motioned. "Right, and that would be a miracle from God! *Ach!* Don't be playin' with me, now. Where is it, d' you know?"

His hopeful eyes begged for answers from Mrs. Bundle.

Making a decision based upon a lifetime of experience, she reached into her skirt pocket. Carefully, she withdrew a black velvet pouch—the very same she had placed in the safe days before—and, handing it to Jack, said simply, "Yes. Angie and I know. We all know about it, in fact. Here it is. Your pendant."

In disbelief, Jack opened the pouch quickly, his hands shaking, and the glorious necklace tumbled out onto the table with a resounding clunk. The precious gemstone eyes of the swans glittered in the bright prisms of the hanging chandelier's light.

Everyone gasped at its simple beauty.

He clutched the talisman up and held it to his breast. Unable to contain his emotion any longer, he broke down. "Oh, Ma, Ma!" he whispered, covering his eyes. Everyone comforted him as best they could.

"It's going to be all right now, Jack." Mrs. Bundle said, knowing what no one apart from her (not even Jack, apparently) knew. All that could wait for another time. Clearly, the pendant's intrinsic worth was all that this boy cared about.

When he could speak again, Jack looked up said, simply, "A *bhui le*. Thank you."

And, with that, they all sat down to dinner. After giving thanks, a wonderfully magnificent meal filled with much love, goodwill, and unbelievably delicious home-cooked fare was consumed in great quantity by all.

Chapter Seventeen

Trust

Afterward, it was decided that Jack would come back to Mrs. Bundle's house and stay with her, at least for the next few days, until things were sorted out. She had a lot of extra room, and the Andersen house was chock full at this point. There were so many unanswered questions, too, and Mrs. Bundle felt that she would need some time with Jack alone to sort through the challenges they now faced. Although he was reluctant to leave the girls, he finally agreed, sensing that his family was now secure, that these people had their best interests at heart.

"They'll be right down the hill," Mrs. Bundle assured him, "you can see the Andersen farm from my front parlor!"

Later, they sat alone together in that same friendly, warm parlor, exhausted and full from the food and the afternoon's events. It was then that Mrs. Bundle slowly and methodically told him all the information she had learned about the Children of Lir Pendant.

She concluded with, "Of course, it's all based upon the information in Mabel Weatherby's resource book, Jack—a long shot, at best. But I think it's a pretty good chance that you have, at the very least, a very old and very valuable piece in your hand. Possibly worth a large deal of money—more than you know. And, more valuable than you may be able to handle right now, if it is the real McCoy."

Jack was dumbstruck. "Ach, no way! I can't get my head around it! Sure, and my dear Mother had no idea. Little did she know the value is worth 'pure gold', isn't it now?"

Mrs. Bundle sat silently, letting Jack's mind sift through the startling information. She contemplated the other matter, obviously important to her. She wasn't sure she should share it with him. Better to wait awhile on that, she concluded.

She paused, weighing her thoughts, then spoke, "Jack, my dear husband Arthur used to always say I was the best judge of character he ever knew. In fact, what he used to say exactly was," she smiled, imitating Arthur's deep voice, "'Letitia, my dear, you have the nose of a bloodhound, the ears of a barn owl, and the heart of a baby koala! One might say you're smarter than the average bear when it comes to figuring out what people are about!'"

He smiled shyly—a long overdue reaction for him—and she continued, "I'd like to take a giant leap of faith. What I want to say is…I trust you, Jack." She nodded confidently, "Yes! And, I think you are of good character, too. You are a decent boy—no, a decent *man*," she corrected herself, "who I believe *I* can rely on."

"Right, of that you can be sure, Mrs. Bundle. I'll not do you wrong."

"Okay. So—help me move this chair, would you?"

His eyes were wide with surprise.

She smiled, lowering her voice to a whisper, "We have to put the Lir pendant back in its hiding place, wouldn't you agree?"

She motioned toward the large Queen Anne chair, and he helped her move it, pushing it off the rug and to the far side of the room, blindly following her direction.

As she pulled back the braided rug, he watched, unsure of exactly what was happening. She yanked the rug and he helped her finish rolling it back, revealing the oak floorboards beneath. She put her finger to her lips (indicating "secret"), removed the wooden floorboards section, and then showed him the strongbox concealed below. He whistled low and watched with wide, innocent eyes.

"See?" she noted furtively, "there's a secret compartment here with a combination lock tumbler and everything! Only a very few know of it…and now, you will be one of those very few!"

"*Jaysus*, Mary and Joseph!" He pushed his long hair back. He stammered, "St-stop the lights—I won't tell a soul! On the holy rosary, Mrs. Bundle, I won't—you can count on me."

"Good! Jack, I will hold you in my deepest confidence. I will trust you. By the way, you can call me Mrs. B. That's what Angie's called me since she was a youngster."

He nodded silently, uncomfortable with his newfound position of secrecy and trust but relying on his intuition about this newfound friend.

Together, they placed the Lir Pendant into the safe. He didn't ask why, he just followed her lead. Just so, their solemn pact was created; Mrs. Bundle trusting that Jack would keep the safe's location secret and Jack trusting that she knew best and that this would be the best place for the pendant, at least for now.

They pulled the rug back over the floor, placed the chair into its previous location, and looked at each other, differently now, more as comrades. They spontaneously shook hands very solemnly, their gazes held each other in serious promise. Then, they both broke out in nervous laughter.

Mrs. Bundle yawned loudly and shook her braided head. "We have so much to talk about, Jack! The pendant, the girls, and other matters, too. However, you've been through a lot, and I daresay we're both very, very tired. Enough for now, all right? We can talk tomorrow."

"Aye! Right, and I'm wrecked for sure." Jack said, his eyes heavy with fatigue.

"You know the saying," she smiled at him as they turned to walk upstairs, "'tomorrow is a new day!'" A truer proverb could not have been uttered in a more innocent way.

Nonetheless, in another location miles away, a deadly sinister plan was being formulated—a plan that would alter the course of their lives not only tomorrow, but for the rest of their days together...

⸺⸺

The next morning, after they'd had breakfast (of which Jack heartily consumed copious amounts of sausages, eggs, home fries, biscuits, jam and coffee), they sat enjoying the peace and quiet of the farm, and recollecting yesterday's events.

The physical change in Jack was quite remarkable. He had taken a long, hot shower, and was scrubbed clean, hair combed and in place. His thick curls were tamed now, his face shiny and newly shaven, and his ruddy Irish complexion had taken on new color and looked invigorated. A good night's sleep (probably the first he had had in months) had done wonders, and he looked relaxed and happy. His features were striking, his intense blue eyes deep and handsome, and he smiled as he sat back full of food and peaceful in spirit.

Mrs. Bundle had raided Leslie's bureau of old clothes and had come up with an oversized University of Vermont hooded gray sweatshirt, clean underclothes, and boot-cut jeans. The faded jeans were large for him and he wore them slung loosely around his hips. Thick, heavy wool socks completed his relaxed look.

"Ach! I've never seen the likes of it! Sure, and those were the best bangers and chips I've had in too many days to mention!" He smiled awkwardly. "Em…Thank you, Mrs. *B*."

He placed special emphasis on the last word, his silent acknowledgement of their new friendship. Then, they eagerly called to check on the girls. Jack caught up on the morning's activities with Erin and then Mrs. Bundle got on the extension and asked Angie if she could come over and join them right away.

"I need you to brainstorm with us, Angie! There's a lot going on here besides just the kids and the necklace. Can you get away?"

"Sure, as soon as the kids are situated, I'll scoot up there. I'll bring Cracker back up with me, too, okay?"

"Yes, if Erin doesn't mind...I miss my poor Crackerjacks!"

Angie arrived fifteen minutes later, Cracker prancing in closely behind her. She breezed into the kitchen, her rich chestnut-streaked ponytail flying; golden-flecked eyes like green marcasite sparkled against her light olive skin. She was an extraordinary burst of total energy, not unlike a cyclone. "Good morning, everyone!" she proclaimed as she bounded into the kitchen with Cracker not far behind. When her eyes finally rested on Jack, she stopped dead in her tracks.

"Wow, *you* sure look different!" she smiled, adding, "For the better."

His face, initially troubled at her exclamation, changed immediately. He relaxed, and they both laughed.

"What's going on?" She drew the trusty lacrosse ball out of her pocket and lazily tossed it into the air. She expertly caught it up and, slipping it through her fingers, threw it into the air again, higher and faster this time.

Jack focused on her actions immediately. "D'you play?" he asked.

"I do. Yeah, a bit."

Angie's modesty allowed Mrs. Bundle to add, "Angie is an All-American in lacrosse at her high school. She'll probably play college lacrosse after she graduates next year."

The icy formal air thawed as Jack's interest was sparked.

"The sport's become popular in Dublin, hasn't it? Most of the blokes who play on the World Lacrosse Team in Ireland are from the states—didya know that? But, there are a few of our lads on the national team that can make up the difference in a pinch. One fellow was a mate of mine—Dickie Gilligin."

So the conversation went and the three of them chinwagged with modest familiarity, almost as though they'd known each other longer than just a day.

They sat around the kitchen table with Cracker lying at Mrs. Bundle's feet and Angie finished telling Jack the most recent stories about his sisters' antics, including all the latest happenings of that morning. It seemed Erin had been deemed healthy enough to go outside for the first time later in the morning, and she was greatly excited about the prospect of helping "Gumpy and the boys" feed the cows and chickens.

"She asked Gumpy if she could count the chickens, all 100-odd of them! He told her if she could get them all to stand stone still while she counted them, then more power to her! Oh, yeah, and she wants to learn how to ride the horses! Dad's already told her she can have Blender," she said. "You know…." she looked at Jack, who returned a quizzical stare. "Blender's covered with lots of colors, you know, grays, and blacks, whites, and beige, like when you put a bunch of things into the blender and hit the button?"

"Oh, aye!"

She giggled. "Erin saw him through the window and fell in love with him. All she's talking about this morning is Blender this, and Blender that. 'Blender's going to by my horse, don't you know' she keeps saying."

Jack's look was uncertain, "Em…right, now. She's a city girl, aye. She's not been atop a horse before."

Angie's face softened, "Don't worry. He's the gentlest pony we have on the farm. We'll keep an eye on her. Geez, I learned how to ride when I was her age."

Jack nodded shyly, taking in her easy unaffected nature (not to mention her good looks). She spoke with animation, heedless of his sidelong stares. She told him about her father and uncle's role as farmers and what it meant on a daily basis to live on a working farm.

As Angie finished, Mrs. Bundle drew in a deep breath and looked around the table expectantly, her eyes finally resting on Jack. "Well, Jack, here we are. Angie has been in on this mystery from the beginning. I wanted her to be here, and of course, we must include Cracker, also."

Jack looked at Mrs. Bundle wryly, not sure where she was going with this. Cracker sat nonchalantly on the floor beside him, scratching at the rug with his long talons.

That's right, Jack me'boy, Cracker cat-thought, *I'm the silent partner. Without me, they'd likely still be wandering around all over creation.*

Mrs. Bundle resumed, "In any case, the one question I have for you, Jack, before we go any further, is," she paused dramatically, drawing in her breath and then releasing it slowly with the query, "who is Darby Quicksilver?"

Jack stared at Mrs. Bundle blankly. She watched him with interest, unblinking.

"*Gabh mo leithscéal?*" Jack was thrown by her question. "Sorry, mum. Pardon me?" he repeated in English. "What was that name again?"

"Do you know why someone here, in Vermont, would have a photograph of you? A man named *Darby Quicksilver?*" she asked pointedly.

"A photo? Of me? Sure, I'm gobsmacked—I have no idea! I'm sorry but, aye, you've lost me, you have. I'm in the dark here."

She was silent.

He cried out, pushing his chair back, "What kind of blarney is this?"

Angie said, "Who is this guy Quicksilver, Mrs. B?"

"Sure, and I *don't* know what you're playing at here!" Jack said. "C'mere now, could you let me in on what's going on?" Jack looked at Mrs. Bundle squarely, suspicion and distrust clouding his brow.

Mrs. Bundle drew in another deep breath, smoothed her apron with her hands, and then nodding assuredly, put out a calming hand. "I'm sorry, Jack! Really, I am!" He shifted in his chair as though ready for flight. "I had to ask—to gauge your reaction. I apologize for upsetting you. It's quite obvious to me that you have no idea there is someone out there—someone quite mysterious, in fact—who is looking for you!"

He opened his mouth, astonished. "Right! Looking for *me*, are they?" he finally squeaked out angrily. "*Jaysus*! I've never heard the likes of such….. That's bullocks! No one even knows us! Who, would you tell me now, would be looking for me?"

Angie twisted one of the windblown tendrils that framed her face. "This is so confusing, Mrs. B! Who is it? What's going on?"

After Mrs. Bundle told them about her meeting with Darby Quicksilver and the photograph of Jack, she then told them about her further sleuthing activities, how she followed Quicksilver, leading her to the discovery of his association with Checkers and Dirty Dave DeMont.

Jack looked as though he'd been hit with a brick. He slumped back into his chair, totally deflated. "*Janey* Mack! I honestly haven't a clue as to who this Darby fellow is. I can tell you he's no mate of mine. What in the world can this be about?"

Just then, there was a quick knock at the back shed door and Mrs. Bundle moved to answer it; simultaneously, the phone rang. "Angie, will you get that, luv? Just take a message." she said, pulling her sweater around her shoulders as she left the kitchen.

"Nicholas, what a surprise!" As she opened the door, Mrs. Bundle was astonished to see Jesse Clancy's oldest son on her doorstep. "What brings you to our neck of the woods?"

There stood Nick Clancy, tall and handsome, cold, frosty air fanning from his lips. He had on a long-sleeved tee shirt over which he wore the bright green golf shirt with the *Harper's Feed Store* logo on the pocket.

"Come in, *quick*, you'll catch a death of cold!" she chided, wondering why kids these days were compelled to go out in the freezing cold without a jacket! He stepped inside the back room.

What a fine-looking boy he had turned out to be! Sandy curls were trimmed into a short and neat haircut; his light eyebrows were naturally refined, shaped perfectly to frame light azure eyes. Square-cut jaw and dimpled chin complimented the high cheekbones and his handsome, enthusiastic features exhibited a good-natured interior. He had a brawny build; his shoulders were broad and strong like his father's and he held himself with quiet assurance.

"Hey, Mrs. Bundle! Can't stay but a minute. I'm on break from the store."

Mrs. Bundle ushered him in, "Come in, come in. I have someone I'd like you to meet."

As Nick Clancy entered the kitchen, he looked surprised to see Angie there.

"Hey, Angie, what's up?" His usual confident nature seemed thrown off kilter just a bit, and two flushed pink spots appeared like magic on his cheeks.

Why, it's almost as though...yes, he's smitten with the girl, Mrs. Bundle observed.

"Hey Nick, what's up with you?" Angie greeted him back, her friendly, indifferent nature seemingly oblivious to his affectionate gaze.

"Not much—" he stopped when he saw Jack.

Mrs. Bundle made the formal introduction. "Nick, this is a friend of Angie's and mine—he's new to the area. Meet Jack O'Rahilly Corrigan." Jack stood up, nodded, and they shook hands, looking each other over.

"Yeah, I heard over at the store this morning that there were some new kids staying at the Andersens," Nick said. "You must be one of 'em. Pleased to meet you."

Jack responded politely, "Right, I am. Cheers, lad."

He shrugged good-naturedly and turned to Mrs. Bundle. "Mrs. Bundle, Dad called this morning from Woodstock Regional. He wants to know if you can come in to see him during visiting hours this afternoon. It'd have to be sometime between one and three."

Mrs. Bundle knew Jesse Clancy was currently being held in the Woodstock Regional Correctional Facility and still awaiting his trial on charges of poaching bear up north. "He wants to see *me*?" she questioned, not sure why Jesse would need to talk with her.

"Yeah, he just told me to get to you right away, something was up and he needed to talk with you." He eyed the biscuits on the table with the experienced eye of one known never to turn down food if it was offered, especially good food; being from a large family of five boys also prohibited shyness of any type on that subject, too. Mrs. Bundle pushed the plate toward him and he took a biscuit, nodding thanks.

"Do you have time to stay and eat a meal? I've got eggs, and sausage—" she asked politely.

"No, no, wish I could but I gotta get back to Harper's. You know, the day after Thanksgiving, busiest shopping day of the year! We've been swamped! Everybody and his brother have been in. *Gaw*! It's crazy!"

Mrs. Bundle put together a plate of sausages, biscuits, and jam, covered it with tin foil, and handed it to him as he headed out the door, reminding him he was welcome to come over anytime. He thanked her and asked, "So, you'll go over and see him? It sounded kinda important."

"Of course I will. Today, just as he's asked."

"Great, thanks!" Then he stopped, turned, and said to Jack, "Dude, do you like to fish?"

Jack looked startled, "Em, right, and surely I do, now! Aye! Haven't been in a donkey's year, though."

"We've got a secret fishing hole, my brothers and I. Best fishing around these parts. All kinds of trout, perch, don't you know. We'll take you over there sometime, if you want." The corners of his mouth upturned into a faint grin, amused. He added, "Even if you do talk kind of funny, like a foreigner."

Jack tentatively smiled back at the gentle teasing. "Ah, do I? We'll see who talks the best with a fishing line in their hand,

won't we now? I'd like to take you up on it. Em, really I would."
They both smiled affably, and he added, "Aye, thanks, mate!"

"Okay, see you around, then."

"Yeah, see you around. May your lines be tight, lad!"

Nick nodded, the universal fisherman's bond having been created.

Nick then looked at Angie, suddenly fumbling with his "to-go" plate, and smiled shyly. "Later, Angie. Hey! You gonna be around for the Christmas Dance? There's a group of us going..."

"Of course! Sounds like fun—just give me a call. Later, Nick."

After seeing him out, Mrs. Bundle came back and sat back down at the table.

"Well, that's all very interesting. I can't imagine why Jesse Clancy would want me to visit him at prison, especially today. It must be important."

Mrs. Bundle and Angie gave Jack a thumbnail sketch of the circumstances of Jesse Clancy's incarceration.

"Back to our business at hand." Mrs. Bundle concluded, "I think it would be important for us to go up to White River Junction today and pay a visit to Sheriff O'Malley. I think we need to bring him up to speed on everything that's happened so far."

The mention of the word "Sheriff" had caused Jack's body to stiffen and his face to go rock hard.

"Now, Jack, really, don't be concerned," she reassured him. "He is an old family friend, and a fair and decent man. I think he needs to know what all has occurred here in North Pillson Corners—and the fact that someone is out there presumably looking for you under false pretenses. We have no idea why this Quicksilver fellow would represent that you are his nephew when you're not. Or, why he'd make up what I'm inclined to think was such a ludicrous story! It's all very mysterious. Somehow, I sense some potential danger there, too. Would you both agree?"

"No doubt, Mrs. B." Angie said.

Jack resignedly nodded his head in acknowledgement. "Aye, I guess you're right."

"Good! On our way back from White River Junction, we can visit the Woodstock Prison to see what's up with Jesse Clancy. All right, Jack?"

"Aye, you said I need to trust you and I'll do my best on that score, Mrs. B."

"Oh! Wait, I almost forgot!" Angie exclaimed. "Guess who that was on the phone?"

"Don't tell me it was Mr. Quicksilver…."

"No! Mabel Weatherby! Here, I wrote it all down. She said she was getting back to you about your discussion the other evening. The message was," as she read from the notepad, "*'Tell Lettie that I spoke with that Professor in England and it is 'highly likely' it is authentic! He wants to speak to you.'* Also, she said to tell you," (she continued reading from her notes), "*'None of the antique dealers in the Woodstock area have purchased any of those items you asked about, or anything even similar'.* And, she said, '*Make sure! Tell her I checked with everyone—no stone unturned!'*"

Mrs. Bundle sat back, stunned, "Congratulations, Jack. Can you believe it?"

He didn't look as happy as she thought he would or should be; in fact, he looked furious. "What about the other part? About the antique dealers?"

"Well, now! That resolves a big piece of this puzzle, Jack. This information confirms that Quicksilver was less than truthful—In fact, I daresay he was lying through his pearly white teeth, which in turn corroborates your story. It also tells us that scoundrel can't be believed about anything he says or does, now or in the future. Which means," she clapped her hands, "we're making progress!"

Jack reacted by pounding his fist on the table in frustration. "It's too brutal, isn't it? Have you ever seen the likes of this? Whoever this Quicksilver chancer is, he's been playing you *and me* about, and I don't take that lightly, mind you. I can't get my head around it, but sure and I'm certain it's foul play." His Irish temper flared and he said threateningly, "I want him. That rotten beggar should be tarred and feathered for the lying and deceit he's put out there for all to hear about me. I haven't got the foggiest what this is about, but I'm going to get it all sorted out in the end, to be sure. I'll not rest until I've found that *bloody* bloke!" His chest was bursting at the seams from his anger, and he stood up, shaking his fist, and cried out, "May the *divil* cut his head off, make a day's work of his *neck*, and then swallow him sideways!"

Angie burst out laughing. "Hey, calm down!"

His face was beet red with anger, but he paused and she urged, "Really, take a break here! We're on your side."

He sat down again, chagrined. "Just so long as you believe me, Mrs. B—that's important to me."

She said, "Yes, of course I do, Jack."

He hesitated, then added uncertainly, "Aye. Right. And, you too, Angie? Do you believe me?"

She smiled enchantingly, tossed her pony tail, and said mischievously, "Aye, mate, I do!"

Chapter Eighteen

Meeting with the Law

Sheriff Will O'Malley leaned back in his chair, his huge bulk tipping the seat backward precariously to almost the point of no return. His once-athletic, now-rotund body teetered on the soft brown leather chair on caster wheels, like gooey marshmallow on a hot fudge sundae concocted to seep and ooze over the dish's lip.

Everything about the sheriff was Big, from his ample frame to his booming voice. His oversized presence dominated most rooms, people often hearing him first before seeing him. And, for all his massive girth, powerful voice and strong enforcement of the law, he was also known for the many kindnesses he had bestowed on the less fortunate and of the gentle soul behind the voluminous voice.

He had been listening astutely for the last half-hour, interrupting only briefly to ask a question here and there, while Mrs. Bundle and Jack started at the beginning of their saga and told him everything. His sharp eyes followed Jack's every movement and expression as the young man, albeit reluctantly, enlightened him about the life he had led with his parents and the Travellers in Ireland, recounted his mother's dying wishes and the subsequent downward spiral of events that had led to his recent pitiful situation and the loss of the Lir Pendant.

Then, Mrs. Bundle told him about her new sleuthing endeavors, including how it came to be that she and Angie had found Jack's sisters in the cave. She shared with him her encounter with the mysterious Mr. Quicksilver, together with being shown the photograph and observing the strange interaction between her potential client and the two strange characters, Checkers and Dirty Dave DeMont. (She noticed astutely that the Sheriff's interest seemed to perk up when the latter's name was mentioned.) She told him about Jack's arrival yesterday in time for the Andersen Thanksgiving celebration and her subsequent decision to welcome him into her home.

Finally, they both told the Sheriff about the latest discovery today; specifically, that the family necklace could have substantial monetary value as an antiquity.

"So, where is this family necklace?" he asked.

Jack squirmed in his seat and looked anxiously at Mrs. Bundle.

"Umm…it's in a safe place, Sheriff," Mrs. Bundle offered, "a place where Jack feels comfortable storing it until everything shakes out."

"Huh!" was all he spat out. He loudly cleared his throat and sat dangerously further back in his worn work saddle while picking up a pencil from his cluttered desk, a feat of balance he was evidently quite accomplished at performing.

When he spoke, his words came forth in his typically bold and vigorous fashion.

"Well, you've got yourself quite a yarn there, Lettie." She winced under this strong statement. "You know, if you and I didn't go back as far as we do, I'd think you were making this all up. On the other hand, I've always had a lot of respect for you. You did a fine job raising your kids, you got a nice place over there at the Corners, you've been a great contributor to the community—you know what I'm sayin'. But, that being said, I've got to ask…" he sat bold upright, massive torso front and center, and blasted her, "what the *heck* are you thinking?"

She opened her mouth the speak, but he stopped her, rubbing the sparse hairs atop his balding head before holding up pudgy fingers, one at a time and tapping the eraser end of the pencil against each of them individually for emphasis. "Number one," (tap!), "meeting strangers and traipsing around Woodstock, then two," (tap, tap!), "hiding behind trees—add to that spying on people," (tap, tap, tap!) "and then, all this....this subterfuge!" A miniscule speck of spit left his lips and went sailing through the air. "What the *heck*? Think you're playing a game? Being a detective? What are you doing, Lettie? You can't realize the seriousness of this—that you could get yourself in a heap of trouble, if you're not very careful. You *do* know that, right?"

Mrs. Bundle sat back primly. She straightened her skirt and placed a gentle but firm hand on the desk in front of her. "Well, Sheriff, granted I didn't think things would happen so quickly. And granted, this is a new vocation for me, but—" she stopped, pausing deliberately, "this new job is one that I want you to know I intend taking very seriously. I must add, with all due respect, Sheriff, that I'm not 'playing at' being a detective. I am one—or, I'm going to be one! I just need to get my feet wet—which I already have done, to some degree!" She held up her hand and daintily counted off on her fingers, "One, I researched the necklace and the strange happening in the Corners which, two, led us to our hike up to Old Man Boulder. And, three, we did find the children, didn't we, Angie and I? That call from Quicksilver came in for my services legitimately—*four*—from my advertisement, in fact, the very first day it went into the Standard."

Pushing air past his upper lip in frustration, the Sheriff countered, "Lettie, I'm just saying you *might* want to explore the fact that it takes years to become a good detective—and there's a lot of training on top of that. And, I know it's not essential here—as yet, that is—but in most states, you must have a license to be in the surveillance field and do what you *think* you're doing."

"Well, I admit it started as a bit of a lark, but....it seems to be developing quite nicely, doesn't it—especially this mystery surrounding the English fellow. And his possible connection to Jack."

"I'll grant you that." he said begrudgingly, raising a quizzical eyebrow. "And you say you're sure you saw him with Dave DeMont?" She nodded resolutely and he said, "A very nasty character. We've got our eye on him—that's all I can say. Can't imagine why he'd be connected in any way to this Brit, but I'll give you a word of warning. Dave DeMont is trouble with a capital 'T'! You need to steer way clear of him, do y'hear?"

She said emphatically, "Yes, of course. I want nothing to do with him. And, I've already decided Quicksilver's story has a lot of holes. Especially, because of the lies he told about looking for his nephew. So, I'm not interested in meeting up with him again, either, unless we have the law involved in that, too." She sat back and he turned his full attention to Jack.

"And *you*, I must admit, are another piece of work. Have you used that head on your shoulders for thinking?" Jack blinked and Will O'Malley shook his large head, pointed his chubby index finger at the boy but directing his comments to Mrs. Bundle, "*This* one's got himself into a world of trouble in a very short amount of time! How do you know you can trust him, Lettie?"

"I just know I can. Call it women's intuition."

He jerked his chair back and eyeballed his victim. "You're dang lucky the Andersens and Mrs. Bundle here have seen fit to take you in, my friend. To come to this country by yourself, with two little ones in tow! How long exactly did you say you've been in the U.S.?"

"Em, well, since late-September, sir." Jack paused, started to speak, and then thought better of it, not sure of what else to say and knowing it was his turn to listen now.

The Sheriff stared at Jack with penetrating, experienced eyes, orbs that seemed to drill a searing hole through the boy's thick gray sweatshirt and into his inner chest. Rather than sinking down deeper in his chair (which is what he really felt like doing), Jack sat straight up and took the onslaught full force.

"It's not that I don't believe you," the Sheriff continued, furrowing his deep brow, "but you have to admit, your story is pretty bizarre, even for my jaded ears. And, mind you, I've heard just about every story there is. All this stuff about Travellers and coming to America without parents, getting fleeced of everything in New York—the whole lot of it is pretty strange! Something just doesn't add up here. I'm not sure we've got the whole story. Where'd you say your mother's family was from?" he asked Jack abruptly.

"County Cavan, sir."

"Well you know, I'm an O'Malley from Clare!" He shifted his bulk, pulling his body upright, and looked menacingly at the young man. "You must be familiar with that name, you being Irish and all. We come from hardy stock, the O'Malley Clan of Clare Island. I'm proud to say my father was first generation Irish-American—fought his way here!" He puffed his huge chest and raised his booming voice even louder. "Legend says my ancestral O'Malley's of Clare were powerful warriors, very wise and," he glared, eyes now ignited and fiery red, "not known to put up with a lot of malarkey! Did you know that now, son?" he said, the faint hint of the Irish lilt in his voice, along with the curl of his lip that showed unreadable emotion brewing underneath.

He glared, waiting for Jack to respond, tapping the soft eraser end of the pencil on the desk. Mrs. Bundle wondered just who would flinch first.

Still sitting upright, Jack also raised his voice just a tad. "Right!" Not mincing words, he said, "Sure, and I wouldn't want to mess with you or any of your clan, sir." He squared his shoulders and placed his large hands resignedly in the air, palms up. "Em, swear to God! May I never hear the cuckoo nor the corncrake *ever* again if I'm lying to you! Sure, and I've told you the truth and all I know!" He looked unflinchingly at the Sheriff.

The Sheriff glared back, the two locked in a testosterone stalemate.

Then, a guffaw, like a boisterous bucking bull charging out of the bronco pen, escaped from the elder's voluminous lips. "The *cuckoo* nor the *corncrake*? Billy be damned!" His laughter shook the teetering chair to the max. "You got more brass than Carter's got liver pills, haven't you, Corrigan? You're what we—in these parts—call a scrapper!" He slapped the desk, rattling everything in its deafening wake.

Jack shrugged, bewildered, and the Sheriff continued, "Well, now, son…I'd be the first to say truth is stranger than fiction, especially around here! Heck, I never heard such a tale, but I'll put my dollar on it all being true!" He wiped his tired eyes. "And, if it is true, you've had quite a time these last couple months. But, you're in good hands now," he gave a sidelong look at his old friend, who was smiling, "and that's where I want you to stay put for the near future, d'you hear?"

The boy nodded silently.

"I think we understand each other." He turned back to Mrs. Bundle, "This will be one for the book, Lettie—the one I'm going to write when I retire." The release of tension was tremendous. Sheriff Will O' sat back again in his comfy throne. Mrs. Bundle gave Jack an encouraging glance and his body slackened a bit, relaxing, to some extent.

The Sheriff now became quite serious and thoughtful. "I must admit, I agree with Walter's theory about Hattersley." Sheriff Will O' pointed his chunky finger in the air for emphasis, once again raising his voice to loftier decibels. "What kind of a mean so-and-so turns away a penniless boy with two little ones? Tyson's lousy with Hattersleys—that whole Hattersley clan's always been a miserable bunch. And, always in trouble for something or other, the lot of them!"

"Yes, I've heard," Mrs. Bundle agreed. "Don't most all of them live on Buzzard Hollow Road?"

"Yup! Scalawags, on the whole. Y'know, I grew up just over the hill from there—off Grist Mill Lane—a mile or so down the road. The old guy, Granville Hattersley—the one who runs the sheep farm—was always a nasty son-of-a—" he took a deep breath, his chair rattling unsteadily, "—biscuit! I can just imagine him sending the boy off without so much as a thank-you-very-much. Unbelievable!"

"We couldn't comprehend someone in these parts doing that either, Will. He must be a very mean man."

Rubbing his strong chin, the Sheriff added resolutely, "Oh, he is! Seems I remember he had a much younger sister by the father's second marriage. Tormented the hell out of her. Lucy was her name," his brow wrinkled as he searched his memory. "She wasn't half bad—our age—seemed pretty nice. By all rights, she was the only good apple in the barrel. But," he smiled wryly, summarizing, "then she married into a bad lot up Northfield way, had a couple-three more marriages after that, to my memory. Kind of sad, really."

Mrs. Bundle added, "Yes! I remember her vaguely. Can't say I remember any of the others, really. I only know *of* them. And what I know, I don't want to know more."

He shrugged his large shoulders. "Anyway, what's done is done."

"So," she straightened up, all businesslike, "where do we go from here? How should we handle Quicksilver?"

"Well, first of all, this is not a '*we*'. This is a '*me* and my department'. *You* will sit tight and let us do our work. I'll make some inquiries," admonished the Sheriff. "Not that I don't think you might be able to handle it on some level, Lettie," he softened his voice a bit, "but, please, leave this to the authorities. For all we know, those men—Quicksilver and the Checkers fellow—may be very dangerous characters, too. As they say, 'water seeks its own level'."

He picked up the phone and asked the deputy in the outside office to come in. Hanging up, he said, "We'll check them out, of that you can be sure. And, we'll run a check on this license plate number you took down."

"*Oh!*" she started, "I haven't had time to fully research it, mind you, but I did find out—when I went online, that is—I'm pretty sure it's a Pennsylvania plate."

He held up the yellow slip of paper that Mrs. Bundle had provided for him, on which was scribbled the recorded license number of the beat-up Lincoln.

"You say the plate was white, with a blue stripe on top and a yellow on the bottom? Yeah, you're probably right—again! Good work," he said begrudgingly. "Okay, we'll get a line on that." He knitted his brow once more, then cleared his throat. "Meanwhile," he looked directly at his friend, "you stay out of trouble, y'hear? Just sit tight—the both of you—for the next few days, is what I'm saying. Arthur—God rest his soul—would never forgive me if I let anything happen to you. And, I'm too near retirement now to have things go haywire." A thin smile appeared. "You can take over my turf next year when I turn in my badge for a fishing pole."

"Oh, *pshaw!*" Mrs. Bundle teased, "You retire? I'll believe that when I see it. Really, you needn't worry about me, Sheriff. I can assure you I have no intention of getting into trouble," she countered, smiling sweetly at him.

He lifted his huge frame and stood up, rolling his eyes toward the ceiling.

"Famous last words…" he muttered as he walked them to the door.

Chapter Nineteen

The Dark Horse

Mrs. Bundle and Jack were both deep in thought, the rural drive pleasantly restful as they headed west on Route 4 toward Woodstock and the correctional facility; the country scene was so idyllic, so simple and unfettered. Lost in their private thoughts, they sat in mutual silence, both contemplating their respective next moves. For some strange reason, they were unusually comfortable being with each other within the close confines of the little VW's limited space. So comfortable, in fact, that they could sit in silence and ruminate on their recent happenings without awkwardness. The Mamas and the Papas filled the air, the quality of the 8-track player superb, as they listened to the melodious strains of "California Dreamin'." Mrs. Bundle hummed along, deep in thought, to the lyrics, *"All the leaves are brown...and the sky is gray.."*

All that had occurred recently had thrown their day-to-day lifestyles into this completely topsy-turvy existence. They both knew this. It was as though these events had now drawn them together into a kind of makeshift alliance; a lifeline linking them to their respective realities. What was real and what wasn't? They both wondered, instinctively choosing to depend on each other for their truth at this moment. They were confidantes, colleagues of sorts, in this crazy business that had taken over both their lives.

As Junebug puttered along, Mrs. Bundle was the first to break the silence. She looked at Jack intently and reached over to turn the volume down the tape. "Well, Jack, I'm quite interested to know…what did you think of our Sheriff O'Malley?"

Jack emitted a low whistle and shook his head; curls wobbling like errant corkscrews. "Well now, Mrs. B, I wouldn't want to mess with him. That's for certain! He's, *em*, quite a large man, isn't he now? C'mere, and I'll wager he's a straight shooter if ever there was one!"

"Of that you can be sure!"

His eyebrows knitted together in puzzlement. "As far as this whole mess goes, well…. everything's in swings and roundabouts, isn't it, Mrs. B? What I'm saying is, it all makes not a whit of sense to me. Am I daft, or what? It's…all bolloxed up!" He raised his voice (and his eyebrows) in utter frustration. "Ach! I'm just a simple lad from Ireland! How did I get involved in all of this?" His striking blue eyes were filled with skepticism. "It's all so… overwhelming, along with this news about me family necklace, too. Frankly, it makes me head spin. Your Sheriff O'Malley must think I'm an *ee-jit!*"

"Ee-jit?"

"An ee-jit—a fool—daft!"

"Oh, *idiot!*"

"Right! And me with no clue as to what the *divil's* going on! It's bloody crazy!"

Mrs. Bundle chuckled, "Well, if you're daft, move over, I'm right in the thick of it with you!"

He shook his head in doubt. "Well, I've never seen the likes of these shenanigans! What are they playing at? And why?"

She searched his face like a cartographer charting a map, seeing the pain this was causing the young man. "You know, Jack, one thing I've learned over my many years in this world is that things always—*always*—have a way of sorting themselves out. They do, you know."

These simple words seemed to relax his worried expression a tiny bit, so she continued on. "We've made a lot of headway this morning, I think. The Sheriff is in the loop now and that is comforting to know. We can trust that he will protect our safety. I guarantee nothing bad will happen on his beat. He's been protecting this county forever!"

He nodded, "Aye, I can tell that."

"Say! We've got some time before I go see Jesse. Would you like to take a drive by the Dark Horse Inn? It's only a couple miles out of our way in Quechee Village. I don't think there's any harm in our checking things out—from afar, that is. Who knows? Maybe we'll see that old Lincoln there, in the parking lot."

"Right! Surely, I'd like to find that divil Quicksilver and wring his whiney neck for causing you all that trouble, lying and such."

"Well, we promised the Sheriff we'd lay low, remember now."

"Aye, and I should just forget the lying he did about me flockin' his family antiques, should I now? The bloody fool spreading his blather, c'mere!"

"Well, maybe not forget, just put it on hold for a bit."

As they drove into Quechee Village, they disappeared under the quaint wooden bonnet of the Quechee Covered Bridge, then emerged on the other side and came to a stop at the Main Street intersection.

"See the huge rock formations in the Ottaquechee, Jack? It used to be very quiet here, years ago. Not the tourist magnet it is today. In fact, in that section of the river—over there? That's where my friends and I used to hang out," she smiled, "years ago, now—in the summer!"

"Aye, looks a fair amount colder today, doesn't it now?"

She slowed Junebug to a snail's pace, pointing out the mill buildings now transformed into trendy shops and eateries, streamlined to meet the needs of the tourist and flatlander populace that inhabited the town. Nearby, the frigid river water cascaded across the bulbous, ice-covered rocks into a myriad of rivulets over the Dam, providing the Mill's restaurant patrons with a timeless winter scene to view.

Taking a left up the hilly street that ran northward along the river, Mrs. Bundle drove slowly by the Parker House Inn on their left (which fronted on the banks of the Ottaquechee), and then past the Quechee Village Deli and General Store.

At this point, she pulled off to the side of the road and pointed just past the two buildings up the hill on the right. There, set up on a small, but impressive knoll, was The Dark Horse Inn and Tavern. The early-1800's brick colonial was grand in size, its presence dominated by two sets of massive twin chimneys and a large Victorian wraparound front porch, added on in the latter 1800's. There was a smaller, attached clapboarded ell about 20' x 40' in size that housed The Tavern section. Overgrown, unruly pines and rangy evergreens stretched out on either side of the building, partially hiding the massive attached barn looming like an overgrown ancient mastodon at the rear of the property. The front yard was primarily comprised of the knoll, thick with foliage and untidy bushes with a gravel parking lot below, which was empty save for one car, a dirty brown station wagon.

Overall, the antique structure was huge, appearing even larger because of the full front porch running the length of the main building. This long-neglected appendage was definitely askew to the naked eye, and the occasional missing railing spindle (looking like broken teeth in an overused comb) further exacerbated its dilapidated appearance. Two solitary rocking chairs, looking abused and dejected—especially at this time of year—swayed in the wintry wind.

"Looks kind of run-down, would you say?" Jack said. "Aye, and the whole place needs a paint job, surely it does."

"Yes! The last couple years I've noticed the Inn has gotten rather seedy-looking. I'm not sure what's been going on here. You know how you hear things…" she trailed off. "New owners from out-of-state. Lots of 'comings and goings' at the Inn, is what they say."

"So, this is where he's staying, aye? Looks deserted." His eyes studied the building, as though logging its finer points. "Right, now. Not the kind of place for a proper English gentleman, is it?" Jack said cynically.

"True. And I think the 'local color' comes out later in the day. The Tavern is a busy place at night, from what I hear. At least, it always has been. As I say, I'm not sure how much business they actually do here—especially, since it's become so shabby."

"*Jaysus!*" Jack exclaimed, "That old barn out back is huge! And abandoned, too, wouldn't it be now? I'll wager no one spends much time out there."

"Huh! I never really noticed it before—just kind of blends in with the rest of the property, really. You're right, though, it's in pitiful shape."

"Aye," Jack said gruffly, "I've seen enough." Under his breath, he growled, "*Leòcach madra!*" He spat as though he had a mouthful of dirt.

"What was that?"

"Sorry, mum. Nothin' for the likes of your ears."

Suspecting he had uttered a couple very timely curse words, she revved the little engine and said, "Okay. So! On to see Jesse Clancy!"

Ten minutes later they were driving into Woodstock proper.

Mrs. Bundle drove into the Maplefields Market parking lot and said, "How about if we grab a bite to eat? You could stay here and have lunch while I visit with Jesse at the jail. I shouldn't be long. They only allow visitors a few minutes with the prisoners."

Jack nodded agreeably, "Sounds fine, mum. I'll just wait 'til you're done."

The jail was located directly next door to Maplefields. In spite of the fact that Woodstock was considered a very posh village, the

Woodstock Correctional Facility was planted right in the heart of the town, comfortably surrounded by lovely old homes and quaint shops. To the unassuming tourist, one could barely discern that this structure was actually a place of incarceration; the village had kept their prison's visibility to a minimum by utilizing discreet signage, well-placed trees and fencing, and high shrubs.

Built in 1936, the jail was a small facility, obsolete in this day and age, with only about twenty 5' by 8' cells housed in the institutional brick building. Originally, there had been an 'A' and 'B' cell block where prisoners, ranging in crimes from misdemeanors to felonies and murder, had stayed. In the old days there was also a maximum security holding area sequestered on the first floor, configured to house only the worst of offenders. Primarily used as a County Jail holding facility since 1969, most of the current inmates were detainees waiting for their trials to begin. Occasionally, local DUI offenders, domestic or restraint lawbreakers, or lighter offense criminals and the like were brought in; their stay was usually short-lived until they slept it off, settled down, or were bailed out.

Woodstock Correctional Facility was Vermont's oldest jail, and the building showed severe evidence of its age and disintegration. Scheduled to close for good the following month, the prison's usefulness as a facility for hardened criminals (or any other offender, for that matter) was outmoded. The new $28 million Southern State Correctional Facility under construction in nearby Springfield, with its state-of-the-art electronic security coverage, beds to accommodate 350 inmates, and future expansion potential, was targeted to open next fall. Jesse Clancy had the dubious distinction of being one of the last prisoners to occupy the old jail before its doors closed. After the closing, the building would be totally renovated to accommodate the Sheriff and County offices, along with the new Probate Court.

Mrs. Bundle walked up the wide granite steps leading to the visitor's entrance, signed in with the circumspect guard standing at the door, and took a seat in the small anteroom. The length of her wait was based upon the visitors who had signed in before her, and she observed only one party: a young woman with a small, neatly dressed child. Other than that, the anteroom was vacant. *Good, the wait shouldn't be long,* she thought. Knowing her time with Jesse would be limited to five to ten minutes max, she tried to anticipate Jesse's need to see her in hopes of facilitating things. *More than likely,* she thought, *I'm here to help him with the boys, his wife, Mary, or his trial, which I'm glad to do.* She could see through the Lexon glass security booth window into the visiting room where other inmates were conversing with their visitors, and she waited patiently until it was her turn to go inside.

Chapter Twenty

Jesse's Tale at the Jail

"We're in a pickle, Miz Bundle!" Jesse Clancy sat opposite Mrs. Bundle at the stark prison table, his huge head tucked into his massive neck, his long unruly locks of hair pulled back into a rough-and-tumble ponytail. There were two other couples at other tables, all deeply engrossed in their own conversations. The oversized room was desolate and barren, with only a handful of meager chairs and two tables dotting the room like tumbleweeds in a stark desert landscape. A prison guard stood at the door, keenly watching everyone's moves.

Looking around skeptically, Mrs. Bundle was convinced it was going to take a lot of state renovation funds to bring the prison back to an acceptable level as office space.

Mrs. Bundle could feel Jesse's barely-contained uneasiness. She smiled and leaned eagerly toward him in the hard metal chair, conscious that she was precluded from greeting him with a handshake.

"We are?"

He put one beefy hand surreptitiously over his mouth to veil his speech and nodding, spoke in a gruff undertone. "Yuh. How's the world treatin' you? I'm sure glad you could come 'cuz there's something real fishy goin' on, Miz Bundle."

Jesse looked none the worse for wear for having been incarcerated these last two months. His oversized friendly features matched his mammoth body; large, brown eyes abundant with laugh lines were framed with huge furry eyebrows and a full robust mouth bursting forth in a perpetual smile. His body was brawny and muscular; the orange prison uniform strained around his barrel chest. His overall look was reminiscent of a mountain man, a very powerful and strong hunter, a throwback, not of today's workaday world. Nobody messed with Jesse. That was evident by the sheer size of his body. Anyone, including Mrs. Bundle, could see where his five boys got their good looks and tremendous, healthy bone structure.

The why's, whatzit's, and how's of Jesse Clancy's arrest were known by all the locals, and he had resignedly accepted his fate for having been caught. The bear-poaching charges had stuck like chewing gum to a chair; he'd been unwilling to come clean with the district attorney about anyone else's involvement, refusing to give up the names of the loosely organized poaching ring near the Canadian Border that he had been associated with. That said, there was a fair amount of local sympathy for the well-liked native Vermonter.

So, here he sat, awaiting his trial. Charges were pending which could, upon conviction, result in significant jail time and fines and restitution for the wildlife he'd allegedly killed. Sadly, it appeared likely that he would be convicted, especially because he did not have the legal support or monetary resources to get him off. And with the jail's closing next month, it was likely that he would be shipped off all the way up north to Chittenden to await his trial, which was not yet even on the docket. With months of uncertainty ahead, his situation appeared bleak. At any rate, it was clear that he would *not* be home for Christmas—that appeared certain.

"You look well. How goes the battle, Jesse?" Mrs. Bundle asked.

"Heck, *I'm* fine! Well, as fine as can be expected, Miz Bundle, but it's you I'm worried about. Like I said, somethin' fishy's goin' on and believe it or not, I think you're right smack dab in the thick of it!"

"Me?"

Continuing his low murmuring, he said, "Yup! I've got somethin' to tell you, but we gotta keep it on the *Q-T*, absolutely positively!"

"You have my full attention. The guard said we only have a short time—ten minutes max. What's up, Jesse?"

"Well, y'know, these walls are flimsy inside here. You hear things about what's goin' on out there..." He leaned even closer, whispering hoarsely. "Okay. You know about the bunch of break-ins in the county, right?"

Mrs. Bundle followed suit, whispering back. "Break-ins? You mean the recent house thefts?"

"Uh-huh."

"Yes, it's been in the papers, lots of stolen antiques, even furniture. From what the papers say, it appears to be a very organized ring of professionals."

He leaned even closer, their faces almost touching, his voice barely audible, "Right! Did ya ever hear of Dirty Dave DeMont?"

Mrs. Bundle sat back in her chair, somewhat taken aback. "Yes...I know who he is. I actually saw him a few days ago—before Thanksgiving, in Woodstock. Why?"

"He was inside here last night, got arrested on a misdemeanor. Seems he got tanked up yesterday on the holiday and then got into a chewin' match with one of the good ol' boys at the local tavern. Fightin' over money or some such thing, enough so they both got carted off to the hoozcow to dry out. By the time they got here, they were the best of buddies again—you know how that goes. Nevertheless and so on, when they brought them in late last night, they put him and the other loser in the cell right beside me. *Jeesum*, it's like sleepin' with sardines in a tin here, don't you know! *Gaw*! What a racket he put up! Hootin' and a-hollerin' and drunker 'n a skunk! Geez Lou-*eeze*, I didn't get a wink of sleep all night!"

He stopped and unceremoniously pulled on his nose, soundly cleared his passages with a deafening *Honk!*, and then continued, "Dang dry air in here! Does a number on your sinuses! It ain't like bein' out in the wide open spaces, that's for sure! In any event, he finally settled down early this morning as his jag wore off. But truth be told, I'd already overheard plenty—and what I heard made my ears stand on end! His tongue was loosy-goosey, being liquored up and all. Braggin' to the guy to beat the band, then when he passed out, talking to himself mostly, muttering all these bits and pieces. All enough to make me sit up and take notice, if you know what I mean." He lowered his voice to an almost indiscernible level.

She nodded encouragingly, "Yes….?"

"Seems he's deep involved in some thievin' activity; I'm pretty sure it's this fencin' ring!" he rasped. "All those antiques from all those ritzy houses around Woodstock and the like, right? Bigtime operation. Heck, Miz Bundle! I heard him outright admit to being totally in the thick of it, right up to his grubby elbows. Nasty business, I tell you what!" He raised his bushy brown eyebrows, soundly making his point, and Mrs. Bundle nodded, motioning to him to go on.

"Anyways, here's the worst of it! Some of the rest I heard was about you—yeah, that's right! I overheard him talkin' about 'old lady Bundle's property'—" he coughed delicately. "Uhh, sorry, Mrs. Bundle, that's his words, not mine. And, you're the only Bundle I know in these parts. I heard somethin' about 'we'll set her straight Saturday night'—I'm *pretty* sure that's what he was goin' on about—something about 'charming antiques'. That's all I got, but it was pret-near plenty—enough to make me worry about your safety—especially after hearin' all the other stuff about him bein' involved in the fencin' ring. I don't know if you got any, but I'd be gettin' rid of anything like antiques, dear to you or not, that could be stolen in the next few days."

"Are you sure you heard him say *my* name?"

"Most definitely. The ninny! In the early hours, he was still going at it. They couldn't shut him up! Yellin' about how his attorney'd have him out of here in less than a day and, don't you know, by God he did. The fool was gone by breakfast! That's why I had to get to you today."

His eyebrows came alive like fuzzy caterpillars on a twig; they churned and knitted together to form one dense, long, centipede line of worry.

"I heard plenty more, too, but that's neither here nor there to do with you and I don't like being a rat! Bottom line is, I'd never forgive myself if anything happened to you. You've been great with my boys, especially recently—with all this," he looked around at his confining walls, "and you know they mean the...well...they mean *everything* to me."

"Yes, I know, Jesse. And I can understand why you'd be concerned about what you heard. It's strange that he'd be interested in my house, I'm sure I don't know why... Jesse, listen to me. You must know...I'm going to have to talk to the Sheriff about this."

As he protested, she leaned forward. "Don't worry. I won't compromise what you've told me, and if you choose to share more of what you heard with the authorities at some point, that is up to you. In fact, this may help you in the long run. Please trust me to handle this, Jesse. I'll take charge on my end, you can believe that."

He winced, then said "Guess I gotta, at this point. The whole things sounds too peculiar, Miz Bundle. Somethin's in the air. I got a nose for this stuff. What's going on? Do you have any idea?" Jesse's sharp tracking and hunting senses seemed to have picked up on her concern.

"Nothing that I can put my finger on yet, Jesse, but I'm getting closer. By the way," she smiled, changing the subject, "you'll be interested to know I've started my own detective business."

"Huh?" Jesse gulped back a laugh. "Well, slap me with a salami! No kiddin', Miz Bundle! You, one of them private eyes! Just like on TV. How'd you come up with that?"

"Oh, needed a change of pace, more excitement, basically. And believe me, things have been changing like a kaleidoscope for me ever since I started this new venture."

"Two minutes!" bellowed the guard impatiently.

As their time quickly wound down, Mrs. Bundle asked, "So, how goes your case here, Jesse?"

He spread his massive hands palm-up on the table: imperfect, callused, powerful hands. "Hey, I got caught. No doubt, I knew what I was doin'. Used to be you could make a livin' for your family huntin' and fishin'—and not be penalized. Too much regulation now, that's the problem! Did'ya know there's over two hundred bear sightin's alone, right around here every year? Dang, I got traps I can't even use now, the way the laws are! Ain't right the way things are today, but… that's a hard lesson. I know when I done wrong with the law, and I'll pay the piper."

She nodded empathetically.

He gave her a wry smile and said, "Don't get me wrong—and don't I hate a bellyacher—but it's just too bad my kids have to see me this way. Can't help but screw them up and I'm ashamed of that, pure and simple. It's all my fault, no one else to blame! Mary's a saint to have put up with me. Dumber than a pound of rocks, that's what I am. They've all been sufferin' for my stupidity. I know I ain't the best role model for my boys, but I always put a roof over their heads and food on the table. And they're the best dang kids any father could have—you better believe it! You see how big my Nick is now? Ain't he a fine young man?"

She nodded and smiled, "Absolutely!"

He stopped to take a deep breath. "Whew! I guess when—and if—I get out of the slammer," he pondered, his half-smile ripe with chagrin, "I'll be lookin' for a *real* job."

After her meeting with Jesse, Mrs. Bundle concluded it would be best to keep the substance of their conversation confidential (not wanting to cause alarm), at least until she had a chance to talk to Sheriff Will O'. Both she and Jack were subdued on the way home; he seemed as distracted and distant as she was, and she chalked it up to them both being tired with lots on their minds. She dropped Jack off at the Andersens to visit with his sisters, agreeing that they'd catch up later at supper. Then, she headed up the hill to her farm.

Chapter Twenty-One

Where to begin? At the beginning.

As she hung up the phone, she pondered the heavy information she'd received this afternoon from Jesse Clancy. She had just tried to reach Sheriff Will O' to fill him in, but with no success. She left a brief message with his deputy, recounting the rumored possibility of another antique heist in "her neck of the woods" scheduled for "sometime this weekend", and asked that Sheriff O'Malley get back to her as soon as possible.

"I know he'll want to talk with you about this asap, ma'am." his deputy assured her. "I'll give him your message as soon as he gets in. You should hear back from him as soon as he's clear, for sure."

As always, whenever Mrs. Bundle was confused, troubled, upset, or just needed peace and quiet, she felt the need to take one of her hikes across the tranquil fields and woods. Quickly grabbing her coat and leaving Cracker soundly snoozing by the fire, she trudged along the gravel lane, pushing the stout boot soles firmly into the frozen ground.

She felt as though her head would burst with all the information her brain had taken in during the last few days. What a week it had been! The pieces of the puzzle were coming together, yet she still didn't have all the answers. All the threads of the intricate conundrum intersected like a difficult geometry equation; however, the pieces didn't touch or connect—yet. It was as though the fragments of fact were all on different levels or planes awaiting proper arrangement.

Only too well now, she understood why this detecting process was so arduous; why, in her mystery books, the diminutive detective Miss Marple, for instance, had to completely think through every aspect of each crime's challenge! Yes, and why Amelia Peabody, with all her wisdom, couldn't get to the bottom of things right off the bat! Here Mrs. Bundle was, in the thick of a mystery, and she hadn't a clue how to get to the heart of the matter. She made small clucking noises with her tongue, deep in thought.

She thought about the Children of Lir pendant and its story, mumbling incoherently to herself, "Let's see...four *singing* swans, the singing Corrigans, singing, *singing*, lost in the Sea of Moyle, banished by the evil queen, the sad king...a cruel, harsh world..." Fleetingly, her mind then moved on to Mary O'Rahilly's heart-wrenching letter. *Oh, that miserable farmer, Hattersley, turning those poor kids away! How cruel this world could be*, she thought.

Kicking up the snow in front of her, her mind segued to the odd little Checkers man figure, his pudgy fingers jabbing away at Darby Quicksilver. He had such a look of cruelty about him. And that weasel Dirty Dave DeMont, what was his business with those two men? All of a sudden, she was furious. How dare he discuss her? And what "charming antiques" was he talking about? How dare he talk about her home, and invade her *privacy*?

She stopped dead in her tracks. Something pulled at her that she just couldn't grasp. It was right...there. Murmuring words to herself that sounded nonsensical, she resumed her hike. She went through various theories, one thought after another popping into her mind, meanwhile remembering snippets of this past week's conversations. Everything kept flying around inside her head, an annoying whirlwind of buzzing facts and thoughts like the most vexatious mosquito refusing to give up until it pricked the flesh.

Lucy Hattersley, Granville Hattersley's step-sister, popped into her consciousness. Why on earth was *she* invading her thoughts at this moment? Sheriff Will O' seemed to feel sorry for the girl and how she was treated back then. She tried to push her memory back to many years before, trying to remember anything she could about Lucy. *Kind of a simple girl, black-haired and round-shouldered ("slouching" is what her mother used to call it), and painfully shy. Rather a fly-on-the-wall type, if you will.* She scrunched her forehead, trying to remember what Lucy looked like and then it hit her. *Wait just a minute,* she thought, *was there…could there be a connection? Possibly, a coincidence…or more?*

She shook her muddled head free of all the buzzing inside. *Oh, this is so frustrating,* she thought querulously. *If only Althea were here to bounce things off!*

Her mind snapped forward to Erin Corrigan's sweet Irish ballad singing, so innocent and clear, and then jerked agitatively back to the big tome in Mabel Weatherby's shop. What was it called? *Yes, that was it. The History Of Celtic Jewelry: 14th to 18th Century.*

Concentrate, she told herself. She went over and over in her mind the information contained in the book. She ruminated over every detail: the history, the legend, the Irish silversmith Johns—*darling of the English gentry,* she remembered, the pendant's symbolic meaning, reviewing it all, step by step. *Oh! Oh dear! Yes,* she thought with interest, *now, that's reasonable…that make sense.*

She clapped her mittened hands together for warmth. *Don't get ahead of yourself, Letitia,* her darling Arthur would say if he were here, *slo-ow down.* She could hear his voice now. Calmness and order. *Organize your thoughts,* he would chide, *and take a deep breath.*

She looked around at the countryside, taking in the Four Corners, the covered bridge, her little world here in North Pillson Corners. *How did all of this mystery, this web of intrigue, come here to her?*

Look outside the box, Letitia, the calming voice urged once more inside her head. *Try to look at your little world from the outside, as though looking in,* she heard as clear as though he was right beside her and they were conversing aloud.

Her mind cleared and one question bounded to the forefront. *Why was Darby Quicksilver in the Woodstock area?* Better yet, why did he call *her?* She realized, by now, it must have had something—everything—to do with Jack. There was, now, a direct connection.

Trusting her instinct, she started her thought process again from one crucial premise.

"Go with the basics," she heard herself say aloud.

She started at the beginning again, walking deliberately, laboring up the snowy backland, her heels digging in with each hardy step.

First, there was the decision to become a detective and then, the discovery the necklace. Or, was it the other way around? They both were so intertwined, weren't they? The hike, the children, the Bentleys meeting, Jack's eyes, Quicksilver's smile—so, so charming, so smooth, so disarmingly dishonest….the necklace.

Slowly, she began to see the logic (fuzzy at first), then finally, much clearer as all the pieces started to fit. *Yes,* she thought, *it could be just that. So downright…elementary.* But, she had to admit, so truly unusual that it all intersected here, in her little world.

As the late afternoon sky turned to shadowy gray, the air had become dismal and she looked at her watch.

Four o'clock already! Faint sleet had begun to slightly obscure her vision. She shivered as showers of sharp icy pieces of rain began to fall.

Determinedly, she changed her direction and headed back toward home, still reflecting over the finer points of her reasoning. Yes, her mind's lightbulb was fully illuminated now. By the time she arrived back at the farm, she had it all figured out. That is to say, she had *most* of it all figured out. The rest of the diabolical particulars were, ominously, soon to follow.

Chapter Twenty-Two
Danger at the Farm

Anxious to share her developing thoughts, she went straight through the farmhouse's front door and, not even bothering to switch on any light, went directly to her front parlor phone. She wanted to call Jack and Angie right away to tell them what she had finally pieced together. And, she desperately needed to talk to Sheriff O'Malley. Especially now. She reached excitedly to dial the number.

A chilling voice erupted from the far corner of the room. Its harshness broke the privacy of her thoughts like the crack of a whip, stopping her completely; the phone's handset jumped in midair as she nearly lost control.

"Put the phone *down*, Mrs. *Bundle*."

She jerked back, the cold words like frigid, splashing water hurled against her face. "Lord! You startled me!" she cried, instantly realizing who that distinctive voice belonged to.

Sitting in the corner of the darkened room was the motionless outlined figure of Darby Quicksilver. Feigning friendly surprise, Mrs. Bundle exclaimed, "Why, is that you, Mr. Quicksilver?" She swallowed, gesturing toward the door, "I see you've let yourself in. Why on earth are you sitting here, in the dark?"

In a matter of seconds, she took it all in. Peering at him, her eyes gradually becoming accustomed to the dimness, she observed that his appearance was slightly altered from her visit with him at

Bentleys. Although his abundant silvery hair was neatly trimmed, it was now slicked back, flatter and less elegant in style, and yes, Mrs. Bundle observed, was that a moustache? He now had two pencil-thin, severe stripes above his upper lip. This new addition gave him a more forbidding, sinister look. Such a small change to effect what end, she wondered? Both hair and moustache seemed to be a shade darker in color, more ashen gray than silver, which slightly, but successfully, modified his pristine appearance.

Even more apparent, though, was the way he was dressed. His attire had changed dramatically from his dapper representation the previous Sunday. Now, a long, dark leather raincoat draped his shoulders; underneath he wore a heavy black turtleneck sweater and black cargo pants. The pants were tucked into what appeared to be heavy field combat boots; a utilitarian look that altered his overall appearance tremendously, likening him more to a clandestine operative or sinister spy than an English gentleman. Was this the real man coming out now? She was afraid to believe it was.

She looked around the room, quickly surveying her possibilities for a hasty way out.

His voice streamed forth as fluid and icy smooth as liquid mercury—like quicksilver, he said, "Why, indeed? Very good. Yes, well done, Mrs. B." A cynical snigger reverberated in his throat. "That *is* what the people closest to you call you, isn't it, Mrs. B? Here, in your little, insignificant world?" He placed special emphasis on the last three words as he motioned lazily and flicked his haughty, oiled mane back, every strand of hair unnaturally in place.

Who on earth had he been talking to? Mrs. Bundle was shocked to hear him use a similar characterization to the phrase she had employed in her mind's exercise minutes before: *Her little world.* A strange coincidence? He had her pegged as a simple woman, dull, if you will; she hoped he couldn't read her thoughts as she stood there before him.

This Darby Quicksilver (or whatever his real name truly was) was not anything close to what he had represented himself to be the other day. His refined accent had changed, ever so slightly; his voice had a ragged, less-cultured edge to it. Although subtle, the inflection in his voice was now more common, yes, more Cockney-sounding. He was much less the sophisticated, upper-crust, privileged persona he had shown to her in the restaurant. She understood she was seeing the real man now and it alarmed her.

She continued her guise of nonchalance, recognizing that the danger was genuine and that she was in a heap of trouble. "I'm really not sure what you mean, Mr. Quicksilver. I'm surprised you've seen fit to make yourself comfortable into my home, as unfamiliar as we both are with each other. Where did you park your car?" she asked offhandedly; she'd not seen any evidence of a vehicle when she had come up the driveway.

When he laughed without explanation, she steeled herself. It was an evil laugh, full of spikes and nails. Drawing herself up to full height, she hoped her false bravado would buy her the time she would need.

"I'd like to ask you, as a gentleman, to leave, right now." Her voice quavered just a hair as she considered the truth; the game was up and only trouble could lie ahead for her at this point.

It was as though a whip had been cracked. The once-charming gentleman now bared his bright white teeth and snarled. The words came across the few feet separating them like sharp barbs, "You *stupid* cow! You truly must have a nodding acquaintance with reality." Her head snapped back as he growled at her like an angry Pit Bull, "How could you ever think we'd be daft enough to believe you could be a detective?" He laughed cruelly. "You really thought you could put the slap on us, didn't you? Put us off for a few days, right? All that rigmarole at Bentleys—all for naught! What a pitiful joke. Alfie was right, wasn't he? It *was* a total waste of time." Only his hands moved as he spoke, and she noticed he was holding something.

Mrs. Bundle could hear rumbling sounds and heavy footsteps in the rooms above; there appeared to be quite a racket going on upstairs.

"What's going on? Who else is here? In *my* home?" Suddenly panic-stricken, she looked around as she realized, *where's Cracker?*

Smiling wickedly, he smirked, "Ah, yes. That's just our Alfie, isn't it? My valued assistant."

"What is he doing upstairs?"

He laughed again, eyes slit, mouth shaped quite roughly. "He's looking for something very special, Mrs. B, and I think you know what that special something is! In fact, we think you've hidden it right here somewhere..." he snarled in a most menacing way.

She moved quickly toward the doorway leading into the kitchen, but he was faster.

Like a lynx, he jumped up from the chair to the door, blocking her exit. At this close range, she saw what he'd been holding in his hand.

For goodness sake, she thought, *that's a real gun....a pistol!*

He pointed the forbidding barrel directly at her face. She froze, knowing too well that, at this point, he was in charge of her destiny.

"You and I have some unfinished business, Mrs. Bundle. Sit down, please." His insincere politeness was shrouded in a bullying tone, and she eased back into the nearby chair, the exact chair, in fact, that was innocuously positioned over the precious safe. He perched on the corner chair; cat-like, ready to pounce once again, if necessary.

She knew what he had come for. With all her heart and soul, she knew that it was the necklace he wanted.

Just then, footsteps could be heard on the back porch. The back door slammed, its usual reaction to the familiar hand of the often-welcomed visitor. Footsteps hurried down the hallway, past the kitchen. *Oh no,* Mrs. Bundle thought, *tea time!* She knew who it could only be. *Please, please don't come in!* She opened her mouth to give warning, but she was too late.

Assumingly unaware, Angie poked her head around the parlor room doorway but stopped abruptly when she saw Mrs. Bundle's troubled face.

"Hey, Mrs. B…it's only me." She looked around the room, " Are you okay? I didn't see any of your lights on and we've got troub—" She stopped dead in her tracks when she saw Quicksilver's shadowy frame, motionless in the chair. "Oh! *Uh*… you've got company!" Then, sensing danger, she said tentatively, "What's…going on?"

Mrs. Bundle motioned her away and cried, "Angie, *run!*"

But it was too late. In that split-second, as Angie turned to sprint toward the exit (heeding Mrs. Bundle's urgent warning) a man had come blasting down the stairs like a powerful wind shear. He stopped her cold, grabbing onto her tightly.

A chill ran down Mrs. Bundle's back at the sight of the man. It was Checkers; this must be "Alfie."

"*Oi!* And who's this bird?" the little man snarled in an evil, gravelly accent, his powerfully built arms holding Angie, vise-like. His face was so close to the girl's she could smell his breath, which reeked of cigar smoke. He sneered, revealing crooked, gapped teeth which were especially yellow. He was dressed in his strange checkered suit and bowler hat (now tipped precariously to one side on his head). Mrs. Bundle noted that the only change in his outfit was that he now wore a heavy, dark blue, sailor jacket, commonly known as a "pea coat", over the suit. Black leather half gloves revealing gnarled and strong knuckles completed his sinister ensemble, his thick, grubby, blue-collar-worker digits poking through the leather. The stale used stub of a cigar end still hung precariously, adorning the corner of his mouth like a crusty outgrowth.

Angie recoiled, repulsed by his crude demeanor and putrid smell. He eyeballed her salaciously, his arms tightening their grip on her like an evil anaconda. She struggled, her hands flailing under his clutches, trying to twist free.

"Let's see how tough you really are, luv! Here! Give us a proper kiss!" He laughed lewdly and gave her a bruising rough buss on the lips. She recoiled, and spit in his face, the saliva splashing into his eyes.

Cracker appeared in front of him, having skipped through his legs down the stairway. He moved quickly in and out between the man's legs, zigzagging back and forth, while Alfie continued his solid hold on Angie, his face mottled scarlet in anger.

Leave her alone! Cracker cat-thought. He rubbed and churned his body against the man, then reached a stalwart paw up and dug his sharp talons deep into the little man's leg.

"*Ow! Oi!* Get off, you blasted, bloody cat!" Alfie yelped, his grasp loosening a bit.

This gave Angie the break she needed, and she reacted quickly. "You *perv!*" she yelled, bringing her knee up between his legs.

Alfie was faster, though, and deflected the move, roughly shoving her knee aside. He was really angry now. "*Nobody* spits in my face, ya rotten little beggar!" With full brutal force, as though she was a ragdoll, he threw her savagely against the wall. Pictures and knick-knacks went flying cyclone-fashion; the air was electrified with intense violence.

Mrs. Bundle shouted, "Leave her alone!" but it was too late.

As though in slow motion, Mrs. Bundle watched in horror as Angie's head hit the doorjamb with a loud smack. The force of the impact was vicious and she slowly slipped down the wall to the floor, half-conscious. Her loosened hair cascaded over her face, and she bravely tried to get up once, then groaned pitifully and went silent. Her body fell to the floor, completely slack.

Mrs. Bundle rose again, in an effort to help her, but Quicksilver pointed the gun at her chest and said, "*Sit down*, Mrs. Bundle!" She sat, helpless, her eyes filling with tears.

"Tie her up," he said to Alfie, motioning with disinterest to the limp form on the floor. "We'll deal with her later."

Alfie drew some lightweight cord and a roll of duct tape from his pocket and stepped forward toward Angie's still form. However Cracker (clever cat that he was) had stealthily wedged himself in between the man's ankles, making it impossible for Alfie to take a step. Cracker's body was like a steel rod, as immobile as granite, and Alfie tripped, stumbling over Cracker and losing his balance. He ended up in a heap on the floor.

"*Bloody beast!*" he barked menacingly and righted himself. He looked around until he saw his target. Without hesitating, he drew back his heavy boot and kicked out at the gutsy cat.

Mrs. Bundle thought Cracker would dodge the blow, but the boot caught him off guard. It hit squarely and with such intensity that the poor animal shot out like a missile, helplessly sailing three feet into the air. Mrs. Bundle watched, horrified to imagine what blow's power had done to Cracker's small furry body.

Clearly, the impact was of deadly force—it knocked Cracker for a loop. His forelegs splayed as he sailed through the air. Passing by Mrs. Bundle with great force, the fuzzy projectile traveled like a demonic cyclone another five feet, bouncing off the rock maple end table abutting the couch and then careening through the doorway into the kitchen. Descending slowly like weighted matter, Cracker finally landed with a sad '*thump!*' first, against the rocking chair and then crumbled like a soft, fragile cookie onto the linoleum floor.

"*Cracker!*" Mrs. Bundle screamed, horrified. His body had cruised airborne more than six or seven feet in total. Now, he lay on the cold and unforgiving linoleum, near the familiar rocking chair he claimed as his most comfortable spot on so many happier occasions. His crash rocked the chair gently; she watched her fanny pack swinging lazily off the ladderback.

Poor Cracker lay stone still on the floor.

The criminal's ire was relentless as Alfie kicked the nearby stairway wall nonstop, causing a huge hole, meanwhile spewing profanity after profanity at the now-inanimate Cracker. His stodgy body heaved, then recoiled as he kicked the wall again and again.

Finally, he stopped. Unpredictably satiated, he laughed, a depraved and guttural chortle possessed only by twisted, sick human beings.

Mrs. Bundle looked on in horror, unable to speak, and he turned, slowly, until his evil gaze found her. He growled, "You ain't gonna be worth tuppence when the boss gets through with you!" Motioning toward the silent Quicksilver, he snarled, "You'll be worse off than that bloody cat!"

He bent over Angie, ugly and sweating, and finished tying her wrists and ankles in tight secure knots.

You cruel, cruel man, Mrs. Bundle thought, beside herself. She sat by powerless, unable to do a thing. Everything had happened so quickly.

Now, though, she went into action. She grabbed for the poker by the fireplace, and got as far as raising her fist before she was nimbly relieved of the weapon by Alfie. He snatched the poker from her hand and threw her roughly back into the chair.

"Let's top 'em tonight!" Alfie said gleefully, hauling back his gloved hand to smack her, but Quicksilver motioned to him quietly and Alfie reluctantly lowered his clenched fist.

"Oh, Angie, are you all right, girl?" she whispered to the unmoving body below her. She turned her anger toward Quicksilver. "If you've hurt her…. Oh, my poor cat! You've killed him!" she cried out.

"You moany old prune!" Alfie snarled, raising his fist again.

"Shut your face, Alfie." Speaking slowly and deliberately, Quicksilver turned toward Mrs. Bundle. "Calm down. If you do everything I say, and I mean everything, nothing more will happen to you and your happy little group. I promise." He smiled that cruel, disarming smile, and she didn't believe a word she said.

Quicksilver motioned to Alfie. "Go search the rest of the house."

Alfie wavered a bit, no doubt craving more violence, but Quicksilver said firmly and definitively, "*Now!*"

Alfie turned quickly and left the room.

Quicksilver turned his full attention to Mrs. Bundle. "Now, Mrs. Bundle, let's talk. Listen to me carefully and don't muck us about. We know you have it. Where is the necklace?"

She looked him squarely in the eye. "So, that *is* what you're after! When you put on that act at Bentleys, I knew something was off the mark." Trying to buy valuable time, she continued, "I always like to know who I'm talking to. May I ask, please, what is your real name?" She played this delicate cat-and-mouse game as bravely as she could, knowing that her only hope was to keep him engaged to keep herself and the others alive.

He sat back, surprised. "You rumbled us faster than I thought you would. You're a clever old cow, aren't you? My real name, you ask? If I told you that…" his mouth curled downward sarcastically, "then I'd have to kill you, wouldn't I? Maybe if we had time for a cuppa and a cozy chat, we could talk about it. However, I'm afraid right now, all I need is that charming necklace currently in your possession." His magnetism had turned quickly to menace. "We've wasted enough time in this godforsaken place—two months of pure hell up here in bloody freezing cold 'God's Country'! I know you've got it here somewhere—or, it's with him. That nosy Black Crow woman was a little too chatty for her own good."

"You haven't hurt her, too, have you?" Thoughts were running rampant in her mind. *Poor Mabel! What had she told them and under what circumstances? Should I give up the Necklace now,* she thought, *or wait?*

She felt very strange, knowing her captor would be amazed if he only knew…knew that the necklace was in the safe, directly under the chair in which she now sat. Suddenly, she felt a hint of inward control. She could not, at all costs, give it up to him— it was her only leverage, at this point. If she did give it up, the consequences would be dire for them all.

"It's not here." She said hurriedly, "I know all about the Joseph Johns necklace. And I know why you want it." She caught his mildly surprised look and continued, "Let's see, there's the one on display at the Museum of London and then, there's the one you want so desperately. You want it because it's very valuable. And, the other one? Do you already have it?" She conjured up a terse smile, "My land! It must be a very cunning individual, so driven as to send you all over creation, to the ends of the earth. To here, in Vermont! Really, it must be worth a fortune to whoever is employing you—especially if the necklace you want is the one linked to good Queen Charlotte. You're working for someone very…powerful, aren't you? Shall I call him your 'benefactor'?"

At her words, his face changed slightly, his eyes imperceptibly blinked. He didn't say a word.

Noting a further chance to stall, she continued, "What kind of avaricious individual sends you all over creation just for one simple antique necklace? It must be greed. The act of obtaining such a grand possession. A real coup for a collector?" She looked him with intelligent eyes and took a stab. "He *does* have the other necklace, doesn't he?" she asked.

Amiably, he replied, "We can make this easy or very difficult Mrs. Bundle, your choice." He sighed, "Aye, then, I'll give you a little nibble, enough to satisfy your need for chitchat. You're spot on. My illustrious employer—or benefactor, as you say—is a very powerful man." He appeared to relish flaunting his association to the mysterious personage. "Not that it matters a whit, at this point, but he owns most of London, aye, in one form or another. He also happens to have a lovely fascination, an obsession, if you will, for *certain* antiquities. He's very…discriminating."

His voice had become a tad pretentious as he emphasized each word, (as though speaking to someone far beneath him). "Of course, this makes *me* very happy, as I am the recipient, monetarily, of his obsessions. His penchant for antique Celtic originals keeps me and Alfie in the clover. And, we enjoy that relationship, to say the least. You will learn, Mrs. Bundle, that it's a sad day for anyone who gets in his way. He will do anything, pay anything, to get what he wants. And, Alfie and me, well, we are happy to oblige. It's all very...*simple*." He threw back his handsome head and laughed. "Ah, yes! This piece—a simple necklace—is something he has wanted for a very long time. And," his laughter halted abruptly, "you can be assured that we are more than willing to do whatever it takes to secure it for him."

She began to speak but he snarled, still smiling, "So, pack it in, Mrs. Bundle! Let's not waste any more time. Just tell me where it is or, better yet, where that miserable excuse for an Irishman is, so our business can be completed. We know he's shown his pretty mug around here; we'll find him, too, you can be sure." His words softened, and he spoke ever-so-pleasantly, almost cajoling her now as one would ask for an extra piece of chocolate cake, "So, come on, luv, give it up. Where is he, and where is our necklace?"

Knowing her strength was to keep him talking, to find out as much as she could, she continued to engage him, to bait him. "If you give me your assurance, I think I can help you. I have no interest in seeing my friends and family in danger. Things are very peaceful here. We're a closely knit community—mostly locals—and we like to keep it that way. Speaking of locals, though, I just have to know—" she conjured up her best "Gertie the Gossip" persona, "—it *had* to be Dave DeMont who told you Jack Corrigan was here in this area. Am I right? You see, I figured it out. His mother's a Hattersley." she said matter-of-factly as she tapped her temple. "Haven't seen her in decades, but she's the younger stepsister of the old farmer Hattersley—in Tyson. Dirty Dave has that same look about him as his mother, all her mannerisms." (Her own mother's term of "slouching" came back into her thoughts.)

Her deduction seemed to catch him by surprise; he shifted slightly. "You *are* pretty clever for an old bird." (Mrs. Bundle was too busy trying to save her life to take offense to his comment;

she stored it mentally, thinking, *Why, I'm probably a tad younger than you, truth be told!*)

He chuckled maliciously. "You want the tale and so, I'll tell it to you. Yeah, well, the old sheep farmer turned Jack away without knowing, didn't he? We happened by chance on Dirty Dave—at the Tavern, of course. Bit dodgy, he is, but he's become a right old mate, helping us with the ins and outs. He's got his own game going, clever bloke," he smiled. "Over a couple gay and friskys he told us about the Irish lad with two little ones who had shown up on his uncle's doorstep—calls him the 'mean old buzzard'! He was laughing about this poor sod who was looking for a job! Down on his luck, no money. When we expressed interest, DeMont said he thought they were still in the area. His uncle said they'd last been seen in North Pillson Corners and did we want his help? So, we bided our time, tried to flush him out." he scoffed, shaking his head. "Driving these miserable back roads, miles and miles, all for naught. Then, when we saw your advert, we figured it would bring us closer to finding the kid. You know," he laughed wickedly, recounting in a simpering voice her modest newspaper ad word-for-word, "'B & C Detectives, *at your service: no job too big or too small, North Pillson Corners.*' A bit of a stroke of luck for us, yeah, if we can work it right, is what we thought. We hire you, you know everything that's going on in this pea town, end of story. However, your antennae was up—I could tell."

She nodded obligingly. "And I'll wager you were the kind Father, too, weren't you? Or should I say, the fake priest that met the boy and his sisters when they arrived from Ireland?" she asked.

"Ah, brilliant, Mrs. Bundle! I see the boy's been talking. Awright, yeah, you've got it all figured, don't you?" He smiled arrogantly. "We'd have had the necklace in a heartbeat if we'd known he had it on *him* and not in his baggage! A minor slip up," he scoffed, shaking his head. "And here we'd kept track of him all the way from Dublin! Prior to his leaving Ireland, we'd been hot on the trail following a lead from one of our underground sources. He'd told us about a singing Traveller family named Corrigan and a woman named Mary who wore this large antique swan necklace. Just that! We were pretty sure we had it then, weren't we?"

Tipping the gun slightly downward, he made a small flipping motion with his other hand, then snapped his fingers. "Right. It all should have been a piece of cake! We would have just rumbled her and moved on. By the time we got to Dublin, we'd just missed the melancholy scene! Poor bird had gone and died. We found out Corrigan had headed to America just the day before, so we flew to New York and waited patiently. We almost left it too late, didn't we now?" His eyes darkened and his voice became even harder: businesslike, expeditious. "Money not being an issue with our precious Mr. Benefactor, though, we figured we'd get it all sorted it all out in the end!" He laughed. "We always do, luv. So, off we went to meet and greet them when they arrived in The Big Apple."

"And then you had to follow him here." She desperately wanted him to continue, to keep talking.

Alfie's boots could be heard tramping down the hallway, and he came slogging back into the room, clearing out everything in his path.

"Right! It's not to be found, boss. I've looked high and low, haven't I? Every nook and cranny. Blimey! I say it's naff to stick around! DeMont screwed things up by getting pinched last night! He'd better do is part, or else—too right! Let's get this job done and put paid to. There's too many blokes involved in the soup now and those farmers down over the hill will be nosing around anytime soon." He glared rudely at Mrs. Bundle.

She met his gaze without flinching, asking herself, *What is he talking about—about DeMont screwing things up? Was their plan to come to her house tomorrow night thwarted by his drunken babbling the night before?*

Alfie leaned ominously into her personal space, shaking his bully fist at her. "Quit *gawping* at me, you pitiful cow! Get stroppy with me and I'll show you what's what!"

His face was so close Mrs. Bundle could see his stained, sand-colored teeth widely clenched on the stubby tobacco remnant, in addition to the shining gold dental crown over his upper left incisor. The stench caused her to recoil, but she continued to stare him down.

He drew his countenance even closer to her, uncomfortably almost touching her cheek. His breath was hot and stinky. He grabbed her left arm roughly and pulled hard. "I am *that* fed up with you, you moany old prune! Blimey! Now, you tell me or else I give you what for! *Where's the bloody necklace?*" Mrs Bundle yelped in pain as he drew her arm roughly behind her back and twisted it sadistically. Her chin quivered uncontrollably, but her eyes remained clear.

"You're both…mad." she uttered, her voice filled with pain. "I can't give you…what I don't have. And Jack Corrigan is long gone! We haven't the faintest notion where he's off to, and good riddance," she lied. "He's left us, spooked by something or someone. That's all I know." At all costs, she must protect him.

Alfie pushed her roughly, the vigor of his shove rattling her teeth. She winced in pain.

"Leave her be for now, Alf. It's naff to try to get it out of her. Go on, check on the girl."

Alfie leaned over Angie, examining her to see if she was at all aware; she lay inert. "You know, I think I could *really* fancy you!" he whispered sleazily in her ear, pushing her golden chestnut hair back from her forehead. She made no motion, and Mrs. Bundle thought how fortunate it was that Angie was unaware of this mental torture.

A cell phone's jingle shattered the hushed room, causing Mrs. Bundle to start. Quicksilver calmly pulled the instrument from his inside coat pocket. "Aye…You've got *him*? Well done, mate!

Where was he? *Hmm*, right, that does complicate things. Where are you now?" Silence, then, "Does he have it on him?" Another pause and then, "So, that's what the bloody blighter says, is it? Promise him anything you want. Aye, we'll be there shortly!"

He hung up, motioning to Alfie, who leaned over. Quicksilver whispered a few short sentences to his cohort. Then, he turned toward Mrs. Bundle, and stood up, stretching with exaggerated laziness.

"It seems we don't need you any longer, Mrs. Bundle. Our mutual friend, 'Dirty Dave', as you locals so fondly refer to him, has our dear Irish boy with him." His brilliantly false smile and irritating voice grated on Mrs. Bundle's eyes and ears. "Evidently, he's told the boy we are here with you and he is quite upset. It seems DeMont has been forced to immobilize him. Shame, it is." He sneered, watching her wince.

Alfie grunted. "What about the—?"

The other man held up his hand in silence and smiled at his partner. "He's ours now; that's all that matters."

So cruel! Like pulling the wings off a fly, this man takes joy in the power he has over his prey, she thought.

Smirking, he joked, "Seems he was snooping around the Inn. Not too clever a bloke, is he? Thick as two short planks, right, Alf?"

"Too right! Nosey Parker, that lad." They shared their inside joke like two rowdy school-chums.

He motioned condescendingly toward Mrs. Bundle. "Tie her up and let's be off, Alf, before all the world and his wife gets wind of us."

"Right, mate. Now the game's up, we better do it up proper. They know too much."

They gave each other a quick nod and Alfie went into motion.

The game *was* up, Mrs. Bundle realized with trepidation, and she begged, "Please don't hurt Jack! He doesn't have the necklace! I know where it is!" She had underestimated Jack's ability to handle their side trip to the Inn, and she felt terribly, terribly responsible.

"It's no use, Mrs. Bundle. We know, now, who has the prize; and he's in no position to negotiate, is he now?"

Alfie dragged her through the kitchen doorway and tied her up in short order, making sure her hands and legs were secured with duct tape. Then, as she watched in horror, Alfie dragged Angie's slack body into the kitchen, turned the heavy wooden captain's chair on its side, and bound and fastened her into it like a butterfly in a cocoon. He wound the duct tape around her arms and legs so that she was restrained from any movement by the chair's side armrests and footrests, the angle of her prone body so bent that it prevented her from any action.

Through all this, Quicksilver appeared singularly calm, his cold gray-blue eyes betraying a detached, unbalanced state. He turned to Mrs. Bundle and watching her squirm, slowly switched on the oven dial of the gas stove. She heard the swoosh, the sound of gas vapors rushing into the lines. To her horror, there was no familiar poof! It didn't ignite.

Oh, no! she thought unbelievably, *he is going to kill us!* It wouldn't take long before the deadly gases would send Angie and her into senselessness, then slowly take their breath away, killing them. And, at the first hint of a spark, the house would surely blow.

Quicksilver rubbed his slender, impeccably clean hands together, as though this repeated dry washing would purify them. "We're going to say good-bye to Jack in our own special way, but not before we get what we want. He'll be hanging high shortly, if he's not already."

"Yeah, hanging high, right guv'!" Alfie chortled, busying himself with his knots, "high and not so dry, he'll be! Aye, gorgeous! And shocking, yeah!" They both laughed, delighting in the conspiracy of their sick inside joke, some secret game plan already in the making.

Alfie looked around at the devastated rooms. Mrs. Bundle's furniture was turned topsy-turvy, her possessions were strewn everywhere. He smirked, "The place could use a bit of spit and polish, couldn't it, guv'?"

Quicksilver gave Alf a conclusive nod and ordered, "Go get the car, Alf. Leave it—I'll take care of the rest here."

Alfie departed, the door banging unforgivingly behind him.

Quicksilver began opening kitchen drawers right and left, searching for something. He banged and clattered, pushing items to and fro.

Mrs. Bundle continued to plead with the villain. "You must know you won't be able to get away with this. Please, I beg you, don't hurt Jack. He's just a boy..."

Her words fell on deaf ears. She wondered, *if* he had the necklace that was ensconced in the hidden strongbox below, would he spare either Jack or them? Her instincts told her no. The necklace was their only salvation at this point...whatever salvation they had. She could not, would not—even at this late juncture—give it up.

Quicksilver shook the drawers as he rifled through their contents, his body agitated. In his haste to find whatever he was looking for, he was unaware that a small piece of paper, jostled gently, fell from his leather jacket pocket. It drifted to the floor beside Mrs. Bundle. She carefully watched him as he continued rummaging, oblivious. She deliberately inched her way toward the paper. He was heedless of her action and, finally, she was close enough.

She stretched her neck and was able to get more than a passing glance. The thin, bent paper, approximately 3"x4" in size, had a colorful image facing upward. Yes, she observed, it *was* a photograph, or at least a portion of one; it appeared to be ripped or cut on one side.

Time stood still as she strained her eyes to see exactly what it was. Determined, she squinted until she could make out a woman's massive amount of peppery black, curly hair, beautiful and full. She looked closer, her eyes stretching to see, the growing twilight making it nearly impossible. She focused, concentrating on nothing else. She must see! It was then that she saw *It*.

The shiny object stood out against the lovely woman's neck and breast, the backdrop of her white sweater showcasing the exquisitely large medallion. The Lir pendant! The woman's face was striking, vibrant and happy in the photograph; her right shoulder was not visible. Apparently, the photograph had been cut clean through, leaving only this remaining section of the picture.

She looked closer. There was a familiarity in the woman's face, a look that Mrs. Bundle knew. A pair of incredible, azure blue, penetrating eyes stared back at her. In an instant, she realized she was now looking at the other half of the photo she had been shown at Bentleys. The one of Jack. This was, undoubtedly, Jack's mother, Maire O'Railly Corrigan, unmistakably during happier days when she had been a healthy woman.

Breathing a triumphant, "Ah, yes! This will do just fine!" Quicksilver drew out a ball of heavy, fishing line from the drawer.

Opening the oven door, he turned diabolically toward her. Resolute on his final deed, he grabbed her by her shoulders and pulled her over to the gas cook stove, her left arm aching under his rough handling.

As she protested and wriggled in his clutches, he worked quickly, deftly tying her already-bound hands to the oven door handle, then looping the twine once again around the lower broiler door handle. This action prevented the oven door from closing completely, also causing the noxious fumes to impact her directly.

She struggled, entreating, trying to reason with him on any level, "You must understand this is wrong, Darby. Please rethink this, I beg of you."

Without warning, he suddenly lost his British cool. Hauling back his long, grand hand, he slapped her viciously across the face. The smack resounded with mercenary precision. *Fwap!* Especially brutal was the cruel dent the large ornate ring he wore left as it hit the woman, square on the left side of her jaw. The shock and force of the assault left her speechless.

Quickly, silently, he drew his face intimately close to her's, his lips so near she could feel his breath on her burning cheek. He whispered through hard, clenched teeth, "It's *game over*, Mrs. B." His voice was emotionless; his eyes were like dead and barren caverns, unreadable.

The welts he'd left on her face were bright red; four nasty, crimson, finger-shaped indentations scarred her pallid cheek. The inside of her mouth was cut like so many ribbons, and a little trickle of blood oozed gently from the corner of her mouth. The braids at the back of her head, usually neatly coiled, were now loosened unsymmetrical piles. A hairpin escaped innocently from one of the thick plaits and fell to her shoulder, then plinked as it hit the hard linoleum floor.

Mrs. Bundle realized the brutal truth about this man. It was no longer about the necklace—had it ever been? He loved the sadistic game of winning. Ultimately, it was about power. She swallowed queasily, fully understanding that Darby Quicksilver had tired of his quarry. His only goal now was to get to Jack, to control and command him, and to do whatever was necessary to force him to relinquish the necklace.

Looking at the scene with a sick, domineering smile on his face, he backed away, his job finished. He paused in the open doorway. His smile was perverse as he put his fingertips together, steeple-style.

"*Poof!*" he whispered, motioning, his fingers wafting into the air, his loathsome voice nauseatingly soft.

The rising moon silhouetted his figure as wild bits of silver sleet shone behind him in the headlights of the waiting car.

"Bright night, Mrs. B!" He cooed flippantly, his charming, twisted smile revealing white Cheshire Cat teeth.

He gave her a little farewell salute, then abruptly turned and disappeared fleetingly into the darkness. The door slammed behind him with a foreboding whack, like a coffin cover's final closing.

Chapter Twenty-Three
Fighting for Their Lives

Mrs. Bundle sat on the floor, wrists and ankles bound, her hands helplessly tethered to the gas stove. The wake of Quicksilver's exit still reverberated in the quiet room.

In the silence, she could hear the freezing rain tapping against the nearby windowpane. Angie lay motionless on the floor a couple feet away, secured to the captain's chair and immobilized further by the taut duct tape bindings. Mrs. Bundle could see the girl's pale face in the moon's luminescence, still and without emotion.

"My Lord, Angie! Angie girl, can you hear me? Wake up, luv. Are you okay? Oh, dear Lord! Help us! What have I gotten you into?"

Mrs. Bundle struggled helplessly, trussed and bound as tightly as she was.

She whispered again, "Can you hear me, Angie?" She was unable to move her wrists, so securely attached to the gas oven were they that her blood supply was significantly cut off to her fingers. Numbness had already started to set in, and she knew she would have to act quickly. She pushed her feet toward the girl and gently jiggled her.

Angie slowly opened one eye and then cautiously opened the other, wrinkling her nose in pain. Adjusting her eyes and blinking, she smiled wanly at Mrs. Bundle. She blinked again, looking past Mrs. Bundle, straining to see out the window to the darkened yard.

She whispered weakly, "Are you sure they're gone?"

"Oh, Angie! Yes, they've left. Are you okay, my girl?"

"I'm all right, Mrs. B. My head hurts pretty bad; I've been in and out. I heard most everything, though. They've got Jack, don't they?"

"Yes, I fear so."

"It's my fault!" she moaned, her voice full of pain. She tried to move but was unsuccessful, shackled as she was. "We've got to get out of here!" She gasped. "Oh my gosh—Jack. He went to the Dark Horse Inn. He was so mad this afternoon. I told him not to go, especially alone, but he wouldn't listen. Said he had to do it."

"Angie!"

"He made me promise. I let him take the truck! He was so dang stubborn!" She struggled unsuccessfully with her rope and tape constraints while she went on, her breath tight. "He said, 'Tell Mrs. B I've got something I need to sort out on my own'. *Gaw*, what a mess!" She looked closer at Mrs. Bundle, and cried, "Oh! Your face, Mrs. B!"

"It's all right, Angie. Slow down, girl, and let's think. We've got a lot to contend with here, right now. Don't you worry though; we're going to get through this." She made sharp clucking sounds with her tongue. "I should have figured this all out much sooner. It was right there in front of me the whole time." She shifted her weight on the hard floor and tried to not breathe in the noxious odor. "Right now, though, we've got to get the gas under control. If we don't, well….we're in a heap of trouble here."

Angie nodded, her eyes searching the room frantically.

"If I could just… get closer to that dial." Mrs. Bundle said, leaning forward. Each time she tried to reach for the dial, the tied-off door hindered her movements, making it a very frustrating exercise. Quicksilver had rigged it as a torturous, impossible feat for her to lift her tied hands up anywhere near the gas dial without drawing the oven door with her. It was maddening; she tried to stretch her hands toward the dial only to be thwarted by this infinitesimally minor, but crucially significant, distance. She was so close to turning off the dial, so cruelly close. Angie watched her anxiously.

"I just...can't seem...to reach it. *Drat!*" Mrs. Bundle huffed, out of breath as she struggled to lean back in a more comfortable position. The smell of gas pervading the room was more evident now, and she knew it wouldn't take long before the dangerous fumes would overcome them both. Facing the reality of the situation, she determined it was just physically impossible. She desperately tried to clear her mind.

The hallway phone rang shrilly, breaking the silence, and they both jumped. Angie bucked her body and tried to flip herself upright. Lashed to the captain's chair as she was, with her body totally immobile, made this a hopeless action. "I can't even move, Mrs. B!" she cried disconcertingly over the phone's ringing.

"Oh, *Lord!*" Mrs. Bundle yelled.

After four rings, the answering machine kicked on, the beep following Mrs. Bundle's pleasant voice to *"feel free to leave a detailed message."*

They heard the familiar voice of Sheriff Will O'Malley boom through the silence.

"Hi Lettie, it's Will—it's going on five-thirty. I got your message and I need to speak with you post haste. There are new developments. I'm going into a meeting shortly, but give me a call back as soon as you get this and I'll get to you as soon I can. And, stay put!"

He hung up, and sheer frustration mirrored both their faces.

"Stay put!" Mrs. Bundle cried out. "*Stay put?*"

"*Ooh!* C'mon! I can't believe this!" Looking at the kitchen counter, Angie took a huge breath. "You know, Mrs. B...if we had a knife, I could cut us free. My fingers aren't confined, just tied behind me. A knife, or scissors, something sharp! I could do it, I know!" Angie wiggled her fingers and vainly struggled in the direction of the kitchen counter.

"Hold on, Angie. Look, *there*! My fanny pack! Right there, hanging on the back of the rocking chair! Arthur's penknife is inside! Can you reach it or somehow get to it?"

Angie was a few feet, maybe three or four, from the fanny pack. It dangled heavily off the chair's backside and was precariously skewed, out of sync from Cracker's unfortunate slam into the chair. He lay below the chair, unmoving, silent. The bag seemed inclined to drop to the floor if given the right momentum.

With all her strength Angie forced her whole body into the air, chair and all. The energy caused a whoosh of air and the floor reverberated beneath them as she and the chair smashed into the hard base. The nearby rocking chair moved just a hair, then slowly, faintly, rocked back and forth, taking on a life of its own. The fanny pack swayed unsteadily.

She repeated the action, silent, concentrating. The chair rocked with more intensity.

Cracker lay motionless nearby, his small damaged body inert. Lunging upward with all her might, Angie made one more attempt to move the fanny pack off the back of the chair.

Suddenly, as if by magical force, the rocking motion bent the chair back far enough and the pack fell gently to the floor with a soft thud. It almost hit Cracker as it landed, clearing him by just inches.

Angie stretched her toes out to the max, but couldn't reach the pack. She wiggled and threw her body as much as she could in an attempt to secure any portion of the fanny pack and bring it closer to her, but to no avail. The chair she was lashed to was just too heavy for her to make any cooperative movement. She struggled, so confined to the captain's chair that she could only clap both feet together and make grabbing motions with her toes toward the pack. Mrs. Bundle offered words of encouragement.

"You've almost got it, girl." She coughed, and said breathlessly, "I've got Arthur's penknife in that pack, and we're going to get it, one way or another. You can *do* it, luv."

Neither female would give up; Mrs. Bundle urging her on as Angie continued for what seemed like an interminable period of time. Finally, Angie lay back exhausted, her energy spent.

"I know I can do it, Mrs. B. Give me a minute to rest and I'll get back on it." Her words were labored as her head lay on the floor, face dewy with exertion, her hair fanning out around her like a golden sunburst. She was totally out of breath and the air was becoming overpowering.

"Angie, we're going to get out of here. I have no doubt! Take a minute and regroup." The gas whooshed from the oven, and both women, affected by the fumes, were slowing down, tiring...

Suddenly, they were startled to hear a rustle. They turned toward the sudden, slight sound alongside the still-rocking chair

Angie said softly, "Mrs. B—Cracker's alive." As she spoke, the cat's head stirred, moving just slightly.

Mrs. Bundle's eyes welled up with tears, and she whispered, "*Cracker-cat*, you poor, poor thing. Oh *dear*! I'm here, Cracker."

Cracker stirred again, raising his head just a hair. Sticky wet, garish, red-caked blood covered the one tiny ear that pointed upward.

Slowly and deliberately, the indomitable cat pushed his paw forward, propelling the fanny pack barely an inch ahead. His paw jerked, as though in spasm, the sides of his damaged body heaving. With a great deal of effort, he pushed the pack another two inches, slowly, toward Angie's waiting feet.

This action, although excruciating to watch, made all the difference. Angie deftly secured the pack between the soles of her boots and pulled it toward her, all in one quick motion.

Mrs. Bundle cried, "Good *job*, Cracker! You've done it. You precious, sweet cat." Sadly, her gentle words fell on deaf ears as the prodigious cat exhaled, emitted a large, ominous cat groan, and then lay perfectly still.

Fearing the worst for her dear C-Cat, Mrs. Bundle held back the tears as she worked together with Angie. Kicking off the rubber muck boots she still wore from her trek across the fields, she used her stockinged feet to hold the fanny pack still for Angie.

Angie's nimble fingers unzipped the fanny pack and she shook out the contents. Out fell lock picks, the two penlights, dental floss, some fishing line with a hook, and finally- the handy dandy pen knife, which consisted of thirteen tools: carving blade, saw, Phillips screwdriver, slotted screwdriver, hole puncher, wire stripper, nail remover, file, pen, fork, tweezers, an ear pick, and… a cutting blade!

In short order, Angie had opened the cutting blade and cut through the duct tape on her hands. Then, she worked at the rope around her wrists. Minutes later, she cried, "Got it!" After that, the going was quicker as she cut through the tape around her legs, freeing herself.

Mrs. Bundle's voice was weak as she said, "Good…good."

"Be right there, Mrs. B!" Angie shook the circulation back into her limbs and, rising to her knees, turned off the gas and threw open the nearby kitchen window. Clean, fresh air rushed in. Then, choosing a larger knife from the kitchen counter, she hastily cut Mrs. Bundle loose. Mrs. Bundle lay back on the floor for a minute, catching her breath and trying to clear the dull, drowsy thoughts from her mind. She shook her white cold hands until the blood reentered her veins, rubbing her wrists briskly, shaking them back to well being.

As they both massaged the feeling back into their extremities, they discussed their plan of action.

"We've got to call Will!" exclaimed Mrs. Bundle breathlessly, and then looked with anguish across the kitchen floor at the still body under the rocking chair.

Angie asked breathlessly, "Is he…?"

Mrs. Bundle crawled toward Cracker and touched his fragile paw ever so lightly. She placed her face down close to his body, and listened. At first there was nothing, then she gave a surprised gasp. "He's alive!" His breathing was barely discernable; his heartbeat faint but there, to be sure. "We're going to get you help, Cracker-Cat. You hang in there, you hear me?"

She had whispered these words of encouragement intensely; now, she turned to Angie with renewed strength. "Angie, there's no time to waste. We'll call the Sheriff, but I'm pretty sure I know where they're headed and I don't want to lose precious time. Hopefully, I can get to Jack before it's too late." She looked at the clock, and stood up. "Jack was protecting *us* by telling them he has the necklace! He doesn't have it. It's here. So, I have to find Jack while you get your father..."

Angie interrupted her. "No way! Not alone, Mrs. B! I'm in. I'm going. We can call first, but we've *got* to find him. We've got to go!"

It was apparent to Mrs. Bundle that there was no use arguing with the girl. "The necklace, then." Mrs. Bundle said. Angie looked at her questioningly, and Mrs. Bundle said, "In the parlor. Help me, would you?"

Angie hastily gathered up the contents of the fanny pack and handed it to Mrs. Bundle. "We may need this. I have my cell phone, too."

They rushed back into the room where the violence had begun. Angie helped her move the big chair, and they quickly pulled back the parlor rug. As Angie watched, eyes wide, Mrs. Bundle nimbly opened the floor safe. She reached inside and pulled out the velvet bag. They quickly pulled the rug back over the floor and then rushed into the hallway.

They both stopped short as they heard footsteps on the back porch.

"Oh, my God!" whispered Angie, her face shiny with perspiration in the darkness. "They're back! What do we do?"

"Hide, quick! Behind the couch!" Mrs. Bundle picked up the iron poker from the floor and gripped it firmly in her hand. This time she wouldn't miss, she resolved, as she stood there frozen, ready to strike a resounding blow the moment the first sorry head appeared.

She raised the poker above her head and heard the back door open slowly. Measured footsteps, followed by much quicker footsteps, could be heard coming down the hallway.

They were silent. Slowly, the parlor door was pushed opened, and a mature woman's voice called out, "L? *L*! Where *are* you? Hell-*oooo*!"

Mrs. Bundle lowered the poker; it dropped to the floor with a thud. She knew that friendly, unwavering voice anywhere.

Not believing it could really be her, she cried out, "*Allie*!! Oh, my *Lord*, Althea Swain, you are a sight for sore eyes! What on earth are you doing here?" She threw her arms around her best friend. "My word, what a godsend!"

Angie jumped up from her hiding place behind the chair and ran to Althea. "Oh, my gosh! Althea!" They group-hugged, all laughing and crying together.

Stepping back, Althea exclaimed, "Good grief! What is going on, L? Is that gas I smell? What—? What have you got yourself into?" She quickly took in her surroundings.

Mrs. Bundle said, "Allie, you're really here?"

"I'm here to surprise you. The *surprise*…I told you I had a surprise? Well, it's me! Here I am!" They nodded, hugging once again. "This place is a wreck! Angie…will someone tell me— what's going on? Who's been here? Everything's been trashed!"

Mrs. Bundle cleared her raspy throat. "Oh, we're in the middle of a bit of a crisis, Allie—with no time to explain—but thank God, you're here to help us." Mrs. Bundle sounded calmer than the situation seemed to warrant. "You see, we've got to get to Jack before they kill him!"

"Jack who?"

"Jack, the Irish brother to the two little girls we found!"

"They have a brother?"

"Allie, listen closely. This boy's in grave danger right now. I need you to help take care of things here and we don't have time to dally! Angie and I have *got* to get over to Quechee right away. We need to find Jack before it's too late! They're going to kill him; I have no doubt of that. And, that could be minutes away if they don't get what they want. Can you take care of the crisis here?"

Althea nodded uncertainly. Friendship in an emergency was unwavering, and she nodded again, more resolutely, bent on following Mrs. Bundle's instructions.

"Okay. First, go down to the Andersens and tell them we had to go to Quechee. Tell them—this is important—tell them we know who fleeced Jack in New York City and the same madman is here, in Vermont, and that Jack is in danger."

"*Here?*"

"Yes! He's been here, yes! At my *house*! It's Quicksilver!"

"The English guy?"

"Yes! He and Checkers just left! Call Sheriff Will O' and tell him it's the necklace they're after. They want the Lir necklace. Tell Will that three men have kidnapped Jack, and they are armed and dangerous and are somewhere in the Gorge. Tell him to meet us there. Quechee Gorge, Allie, do you understand?"

Althea's emergency skills as a nurse were evident as she focused on the crisis at hand, absorbing all the information and retaining the facts that she would need to convey.

"Don't worry, L, yes, I can handle it. Good grief! You and Angie are going alone?"

"Yes, we can't wait another minute. Can you do it? We've got Angie's cell phone and we'll be in touch. We'll try to stay put until the Sheriff comes, but if need be, we'll try to locate Jack first, if we can. Oh! And poor Cracker...please get help for Cracker! He's been badly injured. He's on the kitchen floor; shouldn't be moved. That nasty man kicked him clear across the room! Call Doc Reardon!" Althea turned to leave. "Yes, go, *go!*"

They rushed out of the house in their respective opposite directions: Althea back into her rental car and down the long hill toward the Andersen farm, and Angie and Mrs. Bundle off to Quechee in the Beetle.

As their cars rumbled away from the property, no one heard the phone, ringing incessantly, inside the house. On the other end of the line was Sheriff Will O'Malley, now with a sense of extreme urgency as he tried to reach Mrs. Bundle from his county offices in White River Junction. Not receiving any response, he paused. He would have preferred to talk to her before, but…

His mind moved quickly to the task at hand. Decisively, he hung up the phone. He turned and walked into one of the most momentous meetings in his career as Sheriff of Windsor County.

Chapter Twenty-Four
Deep, Deep, Trouble

When Jack had arrived at the Inn, his intention was to merely poke around, stay low, and see what, if anything, he could discover. It had irked him, to no end, being the victim in this strange affair. He had wanted to find Quicksilver, get a lock on him, and gain some control, if possible.

He parked Angie's truck up the street in the Quechee Deli parking lot and then had walked nonchalantly up the hill, past the three buildings, to the Dark Horse Inn. He skirted the large gravel parking lot off to the side (filled now with a half dozen cars) and unobtrusively ambled past the front entrance of the Tavern. The old black bomber car Mrs. Bundle had described to him was nowhere to be seen. Reconnoitering the perimeter of the property, he looked up at the windows of the Inn, intent on seeing if *he* was being observed. It appeared deserted, the activity nonexistent at mid-afternoon.

Head low, he ducked around behind a small, attached woodshed beside the Tavern, where he could observe the comings and goings temporarily without being discovered. Upon close inspection, Jack's previous opinion was reinforced that the Inn, massive and old as Methuselah, had clearly seen better days and was in a shambles. The front brick façade was faded and worn with varicolored dark chinks of masonry missing from its enormous foundation. Although the average passerby might consider the general condition quaint, Jack's cursory and up-close survey told the sadder, truer story.

The building was literally falling apart. The chimneys were old and needed repointing, windows desperately wanted painting and reglazing, and the pine clapboards on both sides and back of the building were old and as dingy as a washboard. The huge old barn, which had caught Jack's attention earlier in the afternoon, extended off the back of the building and was, from a cursory glance, dilapidated. However, that building's piers and timbers were ancient but sturdy, having stood the test of time and neglect far better than the main building. *It just looks like a bloody wreck*, Jack thought, *aye, though, I'll wager it's solid as a rock inside.*

Jack stepped further behind the woodshed as a young couple walked out of the Tavern door into the grubby parking lot. Both wobbled precariously back and forth in a crisscross pattern, stabilizing their weight with each other's bodies. Obviously well-oiled, they paused in the middle of the parking lot, kissed passionately, and then moved toward two vehicles parked side by side. As they weaved their inebriated way through the near-empty lot, they boisterously discussed the pros and cons of their next destination. Their heated discussion contained a plethora of casual expletives, mostly punctuating their limited vocabulary like condiments on a basic burger as they argued about who should drive and where they should go for their next beverage.

The girl's long and frizzy, 1970's-style shagcut hair was wildly blowing in the wind as she yelled, "*Geez*, Frankie, I didn't know the freakin' time was so late! I got kids at home waitin' for me!"

He yelled a not-so-nice response about her "old man" finding out where they were, then barked, "Get in the *freakin'* car, b—!", and she shrugged and laid a huge, wet kiss on him right there for all of Queechee to see. After that display, they hopped into the dusty, cinnamon red customized Camaro and sped out of the parking lot, wheels spinning and dust flying.

That left four cars in the parking lot: the dirty dark brown station wagon (probably her's, Jack deduced), a truck with a Vermont license plate, a blue minivan with Massachusetts plates, and a pea-green Chevy Impala that had seen better days.

Jack crept over and tried to peer into the small window of the Tavern's door, but the dirty opening was streaked with years of caked-on cigarette smoke and grime, and he couldn't see a thing.

As he reconnoitered around to the back side of the building, he almost ran into a worn-out, little man dressed in a filthy white T-shirt, old jeans, and a dirty wet apron. The male was casually smoking a cigarette, just steps away from the back entrance's open doorway. Although he was probably all of forty years old, his used and abused body showed the wear and tear of a sixty-year-old man. His hands were red and swollen, the hands of a laborer. Jack presumed him to be the Tavern's kitchen help. Certainly they didn't bring this man out front to deal with the Inn's guests, dressed as he was. His sparse dishwater-gray hair was spiked at the top of his head into little tines, like the prongs of a fork, and his ears hung dangerously long, which likened his appearance to a very sad, dejected hound dog.

The fellow nodded once silently, sucking on the cigarette through the corner of his mouth, as though it was the last smoke he'd ever have. Balanced securely, it was tucked into the gaping empty spot where an upper left cuspid should have been but wasn't; this expansive tooth vacancy provided enough oxygen to sail through in limitless proportions. By the looks of him, Jack speculated this fellow probably liked to accompany this nasty habit with a good double shot of cheap Scotch on occasion, too.

Jack nodded back and, in his best replication of an American Yankee accent, said, "How's it goin'?"

The man, eager and ready to talk to anyone who was a welcoming warm body, answered through his already busy lips, "Yeah, how's it goin'?" He paused, sizing Jack up. "You from around here?"

Jack nodded, gesturing in a northward direction, "Yeah, just moved in up the road. You?"

"Yup. Lived here all my life. *Native* boy." He smiled, his near-toothless grin showing more empty slots.

"Must be busy, working here at the Inn?" Jack engaged him, attempting to keep his words to a minimum.

"Yuh, lots of tourists and Flatlanders. Drive you crazy. You ain't one of them, are ya?"

"No *way*."

"So. What you doin' down here at the Tavern?" The dishwasher's brain slowly churned, trying to put together why Jack or anyone would be out back in his territory, this no-man's land, the "Off-limits to guests" area. This was *his* private domain, his exclusive den, and he *just* might resent having a kid like this invade his personal space. He sized up the boy; trying to determine where he fit into the social hierarchy of the multitude above his own predestined station in life, or possibly, the few that he could "lord it over" below him.

Jack lowered his head and sighed. "I need some work. Lookin' for a job. Know if they got anything here?"

He puffed up his chest. "Well now, you could talk to Smitty. He runs the kitchen. But he ain't around right now." He paused, eyeballing Jack. "Said he'd be back in an hour, had to go pick somethin' up."

Jack, knowing he was taking a big risk, tentatively asked, "Got a question for you, mate. You ever seen this Englishman around here—you know, the one who's staying here? He's real tall." Jack motioned his hand to around 6' 2" height.

"Oh, yeah, I seen him. He's been stayin' here awhile. Hangs around with that other little foreigner-guy. Weird-lookin' dude." He squinted at Jack. "What about him?"

Jack wondered if he'd be better off leaving it for now, but forged ahead, thinking quickly.

"Well, I ran into him up the road the other day. The English guy had a flat tire, and I helped him get it right. He tipped me for helping him. Said he was staying here. Said if he could help me out to give him a shout." Jack shrugged. "I thought he might be able to help me get a job here."

The other man seemed to buy it, nodding. "Yuh, he stays here. Usually is out most of the day. I seen him in here at night." He decided this kid was worthy of his help. "Want me to go in and see if he's around?"

"No! Naw, that's okay, I'll go around to the front. I guess I can ask for him at the front desk. Thanks anyway." He started backing away, but the man followed him, throwing the cold cigarette butt into the gravel path beside the back screen door, an area already grossly littered with used butts and, obviously, his private ashtray.

"Wasn't you wantin' to talk to Smitty when he gets back?"

"Yeah, but can't wait that long, gotta go, but thanks, man, I'll stop back tomorrow."

The man coughed, shivering in his short sleeve shirt and headed back toward the kitchen. "Suit yourself." He wiped his hands on his filthy apron, then spit on the ground as he turned to go back inside.

Jack turned and walked away, too, giving the man the impression he was walking toward the front entrance. As soon as he heard the slam of the back kitchen door, he quickly stepped to the side, flattening himself against the clapboards. Hastily, he ran the few feet between the shed and the back building and hid inside the alcove breezeway between the Inn and the old barn.

His heart was pounding and he was sweating. *Close, Jack, very close,* he thought. *Steady on.* He wasn't sure if the guy had believed his story, much less his sad excuse for an American accent. But, knowing his window of opportunity was limited, he tried to collect himself quickly.

Now, c'mere, lad, let's see what else you can find out. As he stepped out over the large icy puddle in front of him, he had to detour around the corner to the huge barn area. Funny, he observed looking up, all the windows on the first floor of the barn were securely boarded up, and it appeared there was no ready access to the huge storage area.

The barnboarded structure itself was massive: three full floors, the exterior dull gray in color, a tilted steeple at the top, the weather vane long gone. All in all, the slightly askew building looked like a huge tumor sapping the strength of the smaller, slightly healthier Inn.

Amazed at the building's sheer size, he counted the windows, five on each floor, fifteen total, just on this one side of the building. Although the barn windows were covered over on the first floor, the second floor windows, for the most part, were intact with all the original windowpanes. He edged along the exterior wall, staying close to the building. Believing he was unseen by anyone looking out the Inn's windows as he blended into the building, he tried looking between the chinks in the old barn planking to see inside. All he saw was darkness. The barn's side entry double door, about thirty feet further down along the exterior wall, had a larger-than-normal padlock on it. *No chance of hiding in there*, Jack thought.

He needed a vantage place, one where he could watch the parking lot from afar for the eventual return of the banger black Lincoln. Searching for an area that might double as a safe observation point and a place to hide, he took notice of the large, heavy metal gutter on the barn. It ran the length of the third level, save for one piece, which had broken off and hung down two floors to about four feet above the ground. It rested prone against the barn, like a ladder. If the drainpipe were strong enough, he could shimmy up the ten-odd feet of pipe and then hoist himself up to the barn's second level of windows. And, if he could get inside the abandoned structure, he would have a perfect view of the parking lot, undisturbed.

The second level window directly above the pipe was large, and, eyeing it reflectively, he thought it should provide him easy entry into the building. It seemed like a good plan and, after testing his weight, he swiftly pulled himself up the pipe. At that point, he was confident the pipe would hold him and shimmied up it quickly. He then grabbed onto the window frame, and pushed. The window slid up with a groan and his strong arms pulled the rest of his frame easily up and over the sill into the dim room.

The sun was beginning to fade as he fell to the floor with a crash. He dusted himself off, and peered out through the edge of the old vertical sash, carefully perusing the outside to see if anyone was present to observe his misdeed. Everything seemed as quiet and peaceful as before.

He turned around to get his bearings and stopped short. It was a huge room, spanning the full length of the second floor. Massive columns supported the large space. Amazingly, the room was chock full, densely inhabited by looming shadows. He adjusted his eyes to the unlit space.

Everywhere Jack looked there were household furnishings; the room was jam-packed with furniture and accessories of every variety, mostly antiques. A lot of it looked very expensive, even to Jack's inexperienced eye. Everything was neatly divided into sections, very systematic and organized for such an unlikely place.

Jack walked down the aisles of furnishings, perplexed. *What was this*, he wondered, *some kind of storage space for a furniture store?*

Everything was clean and neat. Although old, there wasn't dust or grime on the items, as one would expect. *What the devil?* Artwork, colorful Majolica, English-looking porcelain, Chinese pottery; it was a treasure trove. *Blimey*, Jack thought, *this was like hitting the leprechaun's pot of gold! Or, a fox on someone's fishing hook, to be sure.*

As he turned beside the doublewide stairway accessing this level of the barn, he froze, listening. *Swoosh!* What was that?

He thought he'd heard something move. He half-turned, backing up, and brushed against a tall figure. He jumped, startled and ready for a fight with fists raised. Then, he realized he had backed into a standing full suit of medieval knight's armor, helmet and all; a stationary cavalier in full regalia at the top of the stairs standing silent guard over this huge cache of treasures.

Taking a few quick steps, Jack hid behind a large antique armoire and waited, holding his breath. He listened for more sounds, anything. All he heard was the creaking timbers of the building as the wind whistled through the exposed cracks and crannies. Nothing and no one appeared, and Jack stood silently for a number of minutes, waiting. *Ach! Probably just a barn rat or the like,* he concluded.

He exhaled slowly through clenched teeth. As he continued to observe his surroundings, he wondered about all these valuables in this unlikely, out-of-the-way, place. *Aye, right, something he could discuss with Mrs. B — not for him to worry about now.* Jack quickly sprinted back across the room to the window he had entered. He was here on his own mission; he wanted Darby Quicksilver.

His eyes searched the parking lot, then he gasped in alarm. He would have known that car anywhere. *No! How could he have missed him in those few minutes!* Taken aback, he was horrified to see the infamous black bomber with white plates, vacant. *Oh, gory, they're back! Jaysus, they must be inside the Inn.*

The beginning of dusk was setting in.

He was going to get a look at the men, especially Quicksilver, one way or another. Right away. He decided he had to risk going out through the same window that he had come in. Holding onto the window jamb with both hands, he lifted the sash. He put one leg over the sill. Looking down, he readied himself for the fall below.

There was a soft thud behind him and a quick shoe scuff to his rear against the hard floor, too swift a movement for him to react more than fleetingly.

He tried to extricate his foot from the window opening and

catch his balance as he turned his shoulders toward the threatening sound.

The quick, powerful blow landed squarely on his head. He never knew what hit him as he slumped to the floor.

Jack's head hurt and he stirred uncomfortably in the utter darkness. He couldn't move his arms; somehow they had been cinched behind him, and he was anchored down so that any movement was inhibited. The strong, rank odor of old rubber and dirty oil filled his nostrils and he choked as the fumes polluted his lungs. Barely able to breathe, he realized he was muzzled, a soft cloth fabric of some sort had been shoved into his mouth.

Stifling the intense gagging reflex, Jack tried to move his aching body and found his hands and feet were secured tightly together behind him. He was bound hostage-style, precluding any real movement. As he came out of his hazy stupor, he realized he had been unconscious, and he tried to put things together. *What the divil was going on? Where was I before this?* He strained his memory and tried to concentrate, but focusing was difficult as his head pounded fiercely with the worst headache he'd ever experienced.

He opened his eyes; the only vision he had was a blur of dark shapes, squigglys and ethereal stars parading in front of him. He literally could see nothing but blackness. *Right*, he regrouped mentally; *I'm in total darkness…and confined to a very tight space.* It was as black as death's door in this tiny space. He tried to calm himself, shifting uncomfortably in the gloom.

He lifted his head and hit it squarely, with a resounding bang, on a metal-sounding flat surface. *Ow!* he winced, his stomach turning over as he rested his head back down again onto the bottom surface. *Think, Jack,* he told himself. *Steady on, mate, and think!*

Taking a deep, purposeful breath and then another, he lay motionless for a number of minutes, resting his mind as he floated in and out of a dream-like state. He could hear a monotonous rhythm, a thumping every half-second or so, and its repetitious beat lulled him into a dangerous stupor.

He wasn't sure how long he was in limbo, but after a time he jerked involuntarily, his head becoming clear as he realized where he must be. He was inside the trunk of a car—yes, and they were traveling over a very bumpy, seemingly remote road. There were no other sounds save the steady rhythm of the car's own wheels. No vehicles passed them nor any followed behind them. As he listened to the tires thumping over the gravel, the past came back to him, gradually and indistinctly at first, then with more clarity as he put the pieces together.

Oh, what a bloody fool I've been, he thought to himself.

It all came slowly into focus as he remembered his exploits since he'd left Angie at the Andersen farm. She had told him it was unwise to go to the Dark Horse Inn, especially alone. *Ach!* He'd been compelled to find this Darby Quicksilver, the snake, and see what he was up to. Little did he expect to find himself in the predicament he was now faced with.

Oh, why, lad? Why didn't he listen to the Sheriff and Mrs. Bundle and stay put? And poor Angie, the lass must be worried sick about him. He quickly went over the latest events in his mind, trying to unravel what had brought him to this miserable state of affairs. He could hear a faint rumbling above the pounding in his head, and the gentle vibrations became loud bumping noises with jarring impacts to his body. They were on a much rougher, more isolated road now, and narrower, too, he conjectured as he heard the sounds of low tree branches and bushes violently brushing the vehicle's sides.

Finally, with a sharp suddenness, the car jerked to a stop. Presumably, they had reached their destination. The trunk opened unexpectedly and a blast of cold air entered the small space. Adjusting his eyes, Jack came face-to-face with a scruffy, dirty male reeking of stale alcohol, a man unknown to him (but not to the locals) who sneered in a sharp weasel voice, "Wakey, wakey! Time to rock 'n roll, punk."

Instinctively, Jack knew this was going to be pure hell.

Chapter Twenty-Five

The Race to Save Jack

Once they got on the road, they realized the speedy trip over to Quechee might be just a tad problematic. The roads were as slick as sliding over greasy, bubbly bacon, which made the going very difficult for the little car. The air inside the small space was filled with nervous tension, so electrified as to create sparks, as they traveled across the back roads.

Angie and Mrs. Bundle knew they were racing against a sinister clock, desperately trying to find Jack before it was too late. The diminutive VW chugged with great purpose up the slippery mountain on Church Hill Road past the Kedron Valley Inn, its tenacious tires obstinately churning their way slowly up, up, occasionally skidding precariously on the uneven gravel road. This shortcut, known by the locals as the "back way" to Woodstock, eliminated a much longer stretch of road. The down side was that, on the whole, this was a very dark and remote ride at night—somewhat daunting, particularly if one threw this time of year and the current freezing precipitation into the mix.

"Come on, Junebug. Don't let us down now, girl." Mrs. Bundle gently cajoled. The miniature car, dwarfed by the formidable giant hanging oak trees towering like sentinels along the dark unlit road, obstinately continued on. Fearlessly toiling upward into the highest section of the small mountain, the persistent little Bug's headlights illuminated the road in front of them as the sleet and snow persisted, wetter and heavier now that they were near the peak.

Big, sugar snowflakes hit the windshield like soft gobs of melting cotton candy to the extent that the trek was further complicated by the obstructed view. The windshield wipers clicked and clattered, doggedly zipping back and forth, back and forth, providing a limited view ahead.

"Holy *cow*, it's darker 'n a deep pocket!" Angie, in her nervous distraction, used one of her grandfather's favorite sayings. Shadowy dark images played around them like ghoulish apparitions; elongated, then flattened, their reflections against the windshield played tricks on the eye.

At last, with the gears grinding and the engine straining, Mrs. Bundle downshifted, and Junebug heaved, as though in tremendous relief. They had reached the summit and laboriously began the arduous decline. The winter tires dug into the icy pea gravel like a dog's toenails on a slippery scatter rug as they skittered and slithered down the other side of the mountain.

"There we go, Junie-girl, *good* for you." Mrs. Bundle's hands clutched the steering wheel, her knuckles taut, as she navigated the hairpin twists and turns.

Finally, the steep grade of the road leveled off. She soothed, "There now, we're pretty much through the worst of it, I'd say." Junebug sailed agreeably down the rest of the hill and Mrs. Bundle relaxed her hold.

Angie had tried repeatedly to reach her father and the Sheriff's office on the cell phone. Coverage was always spotty in this area and now, cell phone function appeared to be nonexistent at the moment. There was the usual disconcerting lit-up "searching" signal on the cell phone face, actively seeking a tower. Then, the flashing "R" indicating 'roaming' was present, albeit with a very weak signal. However, just as she tried to make contact, the signal 'call lost' would flash on and off, appearing on the little screen like a bad omen. They both knew from experience that, at some point, if one had luck on their side, the tower signal would light up and a call could be made, though often with very rough reception.

In this remote section of the countryside between large mountains, hills, and valleys, Angie grew impatient as she waited, once more, for the little tower icon to appear in the display window of her cell phone. The freezing rain tapped steadily on the window, unrelentingly, further creating a sense of urgency.

Her ponytail bobbed up and down in agitation as she fretted, and her long lashes fluttered. She anguished over their predicament. "I can't reach anyone, can't get through! Hopefully, Althea has gotten the Sheriff, right? Once we get closer to town, I should be able to get a signal." The bump on her forehead near her temple was bright red and had expanded to the size of a walnut.

"How is your head? That's a nasty knot you've got there, luv."

"I'm fine. Don't you worry about me —" A succession of queer little beeping sounds, then three short bursts and a long trill pierced the thick air. "Oh, no!" Angie exclaimed, thoroughly disconcerted. "It can't be!"

"Heavens, what's wrong now?"

"Mrs. B. that's the warning beep — my cell phone. The battery's low." Angie's comely face wore the signs of fatigue and frustration. " Gaw! I should have charged it today!" Her voice was filled with disappointment and her eyelashes seemed to moisten a bit.

Mrs. Bundle's voice was calm, once more the fortifying influence. "Angie, listen. We're in this together. I trust we can find Jack and if we do, keep ourselves out of harm's way as best we can before the police arrive." Angie nodded. "Now, let's think smart, Angie. We can trust that the Sheriff is being notified as we speak — we can rely on Althea for that, to be sure. And, we need to save your cell's battery power, so I think it's best to turn the phone off." She watched as the girl reluctantly pressed the "off" button. "Good girl. Now, here's the plan. We'll try to reach the Sheriff and your Dad when we get closer to the Gorge. We can use the phone sparingly then, only when and if we need to."

They came down the hill by the quaint stone Episcopal Church and reached the Village Green of Woodstock. The town center was serene, the quiet homes lining the streets like churchgoers waiting expectantly in their pews. There were very few cars on the road now, mostly due to the wintry mix accumulating on the roads but more likely, the typical tranquility that ensues the evening after Thanksgiving.

"The town's deader 'n a doornail. Nobody's around," Angie commented ruefully.

They hastened on, intent on their mission, and in a few minutes were turning into the deserted parking lot at the Quechee Gorge Bridge. There was no sign of the black Lincoln. As they drove through the parking area, the desolate scene was ominous, too quiet.

"Am I wrong about this?" Mrs. Bundle fretted, knitting her brow. "I'm sure—I'd bet anything, in fact—that their comments about 'hanging high' and 'gorgeous' had something to do with the bridge, or the Gorge—they're bringing their evil here or around the Falls somewhere. I feel it."

"I hope you're right. So, what do we do now?"

"We go looking. Before it's too late."

Chapter Twenty-Six

Bring on the Cavalry

The large commercial clock on the wall ticked loudly as Sheriff Will O'Malley stood silently poised at the front of the room facing the Special Joint Task Force.

Seated in front of him were State Police officers, local law enforcement representing the area towns of Woodstock, Norwich, and Hartford, sheriff deputies, and two Federal Bureau of Investigation agents who stood to the left of him, quietly observing the gathering assemblage. Silent and stone-faced, these two men were nondescript carbon copies of each other in demeanor and dress, sporting identical jet-black-rimmed, slightly darkened glasses and equally dark gray suits.

The hands of the clock urgently pointed at six PM sharp.

The Sheriff, in his official role as investigative ombudsman and liaison coordinator, rapped on the table, getting everyone's immediate attention, and the din respectfully subsided.

"Listen up, everyone!" his huge voice boomed out into the silence. "Welcome to you all, and thank you for coming together so quickly, courtesy of the county Sheriff's office." Low chuckles filled the room. "Through our joint cooperation, the investigative resources have been gathered here tonight." He paused and made a sweeping motion with his hand across the room, "This pool, representing local, county, state, and federal law enforcement agencies will investigate and, hopefully, solve the outstanding two case detailed in your handout. Our emergency Joint Task Force, composed of FBI Special Agents, state police, the county Sheriff's Department, and local detectives and police officers from the surrounding areas, has been formed to locate the alleged felons specific to two outstanding cases." He peered out at the small but intense group.

"The handout you were given as you came in is fresh off the press and should bring you up to date. I don't need to go over all the salient points of what exactly has occurred and why we're all here, but I will go over a couple things before you head out." He looked around at the eager men and women, then flipped open to page two of his notes. "If you haven't met them already, please welcome Special Agents Crisp and Harmon from the FBI Philadelphia Division."

The two gentlemen nodded, their faces betraying little emotion save a look of determination and keen judgement.

"They are here primarily in the interest of locating suspect David Michael DeMont, a/k/a Dirty Dave DeMont, who I'll address in a sec. They have also been assigned to follow-up on information I received late this afternoon out of Great Britain. That information is significant to our primary objective tonight, so I'd like to address that first. Gentlemen, *and ladies,*" he paused, placing special emphasis to acknowledge the female law enforcement in the room, "as all this developed today, we realized it had the makings of felonious activities spanning two continents, so I would urge everyone involved to, above all, use the utmost caution and discretion tonight—there are the international ramifications here that we must consider. And, make no mistake, we are dealing with some pretty unsavory criminals." Referring to his notes, he continued, "As we have learned, two suspects with dummy English passports entered this country in early September via Aer Lingus out of Dublin. They have been representing themselves as visitors, innocent tourists if you will, in the Quechee-Woodstock area. This afternoon, when our office contacted New Scotland Yard and Interpol, they provided us with new information regarding these two Brits. Prior to that, a cursory investigation by local authorities had turned up nothing. However, it was suspected that these two men were trouble and possibly had records. Consequently, we thought they might be in the international crime computer system." He flipped to the next page of notes. "Primarily, nothing came up on any combination of 'Darby Quicksilver', which didn't really surprise us. But, through a local private investigator, Lettie Bundle, I learned today that this suspect had made mention of another name in reference to a person he said he wanted her to find on his behalf. Told a phony story about a missing nephew, one 'Ashley Whitewick'. We asked the British authorities to input that name for us."

He gave the group a cynical grin. "Don't you know, we hit the proverbial nail on the head."

The group's low murmurs reinforced his satisfaction as he continued, "We're pretty sure this Quicksilver character is an imposter named Terrington Askew Whitewick," he paused, his words deliberate as he placed special emphasis on the surname, "also known in underworld circles as T.A. Whitewick. As you can see from your notes, he's quite familiar to British authorities, and a nasty piece of work at that. He's been linked to various white-collar crimes throughout the British Isles and Northern Europe and is purported to have been involved in a number of very high-profile thefts—one of the most significant crimes he's linked to was that 'London Tube Station Affair'." Low murmurings met this statement. "Right. If you remember, in that heist a thief inserted himself in the Palace as a palace secretary and walked away with over a million dollars in stolen jewels, all historically significant. Some of the Queen Mother's treasured pieces went missing in that robbery; it was all kept very quiet. He's fallen through the cracks repeatedly. Likes disguises—he's reincarnated himself into this 'Darby Quicksilver' alias in Quechee." He held up two fingers, "One, he seems to have a sizeable ego, and two, he seems to have unlimited funds."

Agent Crisp interrupted, "Excuse me, Sheriff. Any idea where's he getting his money? Have we got a paper trail here?"

The Sheriff shook his head. "If there is one, we can't find it. Seems to have lots of cash. He's also got this sidekick named Alfie Wilden who entered this country with him. It seems Interpol has been loosely monitoring them both for months now, but lost track of them. Whitewick and Wilden—real name Alfred Chexwidden—are here, in our County, and we want to know why. I'm going to put my reputation on the line and say these men are who we think they are." He leaned forward, placing his ample hands on the table, then tilted his large body frontward into its center gravity and balanced like a fulcrum. "If so, we've got our hands full. Chexwidden has an arrest sheet a mile long: assault, domestic abuse, five years in London's Wandsworth Prison for a Heathrow Airport armed heist that went bad. Do not underestimate either of these men. They are dangerous characters. Which brings me to the here and now and how these two are directly connected to David DeMont—who we need to find tonight, the sooner the better!"

The men and women rustled in their seats, eager to get out into the field and take on the job at hand.

"I want to make sure we're all on the same page on this one. Seems the three have gotten cozy; they've been seen about Woodstock together. We also have more substantiating information on DeMont that came in late this afternoon. This office has had him under a veil of suspicion the last couple weeks in connection with the rash of late-night burglaries throughout this area; specifically, fine antiques. We believe he is heavily involved in this elaborate fencing ring, not only in this state, but also throughout New England and down the Eastern Seaboard. Pennsylvania State Police have just notified us that they believe he is their suspect—wanted there for a variety of crimes including receiving stolen goods. If he is, that's transport theft across state lines—hence, our friends here, from the FBI. A vehicle currently in his possession with PA license plates—referenced in your paperwork—is stolen. We also had word late today another heist may be imminent—planned for sometime this weekend. Up North Pillson Corners way."

He stood straight, stretching his six-foot-plus frame to his full height, and folded his big arms at his chest, apparently winding down his monologue.

"This is where you local departments come in. You've been instrumental in obtaining some great tips that now lead us to believe we're hot on their heels. We've gotten numerous tips on the fencing operation's headquarters and where they have been stashing the contraband, and who is involved." He pinched his forefinger and thumb together. "We're this close to making arrests in this case but," he paused, "we do not want to compromise this investigation on any level—or the evidence we've collected—while we pursue both this and Whitewick's motives. We believe they are connected cases in some way. Thing is," he cleared his throat and coughed lightly, "as of early this morning, we no longer have an immediate location on Dave DeMont. Seems he was released on his own recognizance from Woodstock Correctional and disappeared."

The group collectively groaned, and Sheriff O'Malley shook his head. "Yeah, we really missed the boat on this one. Evidently, he was picked up last night on a misdemeanor, and, subsequently, bail was magically posted early this morning before this all came to the forefront. Bottom line, we need to contain him. We've lost him once but we don't want it to happen again. Our job tonight is to find him and get him under surveillance. If all goes according to plan, we will implement our task force sting and have that whole crowd in custody before the weekend is over if—"

Suddenly, he was interrupted by a commotion at the door. He looked over, completing his sentence, "all goes according to plan.

The two Brits—"

A deputy strode into the room and whispered urgently into the Sheriff's ear. The earth stood still for a millisecond. O'Malley's demeanor changed dramatically, his lips became pursed firmly together, and he passed his hand over the sparse gray hairs on the crown of his large, powerful head. Some of the color left his robust face.

When his words came, they were quick, decisive, and very grave in tone.

"Well, I guess things are heating up here much quicker than we thought. Listen carefully. We've got a hostage situation in progress in Quechee. The three suspects—DeMont, Whitewick, and Chexwidden—are all directly involved. Allegedly, they have kidnapped a young man I met earlier today named Jack Corrigan. In the last few hours, they tried to murder Lettie Bundle, the private investigator I referred to previously, along with a teenage neighbor of hers, Angie Andersen, holding them at gunpoint at the Bundle residence in North Pillson Corners and then leaving them to die by gassing them. At this point, I'm told Mrs. Bundle somehow freed herself and is en route to Quechee Gorge and has requested that we join her there posthaste."

He swore an unintelligible profanity under his breath, then continued, his face flushed back to a beet red. The group erupted with emotion.

"You heard me correctly. A message has been received via dispatch that Mrs. Bundle and Angie Andersen are headed to the Quechee Gorge Bridge site as we speak, where they believe Jack Corrigan has been taken. Now we know what Whitewick is really after—evidently, he wants an antique necklace Corrigan had or has in his possession."

The group as a whole started moving into action, adrenaline pumping as they checked their weapons and weighed the unfolding scenario. Several looked anxiously at the big clock on the wall, ticking away.

Sheriff Will O'Malley enjoined the group hastily, "Things could get very nasty here, officers. Stay off your radios and monitor for a possible Code Three. We mobilize immediately. Let's go!"

Chapter Twenty-Seven
Where is Jack?

Moments passed as Mrs. Bundle surveyed the perimeter of the parking lot, pensively scanning it for anything unusual, any sense of where Jack could be. She nodded. "Uh-huh. I feel it in my bones. They're nearby..."

They parked the car, discreetly hiding the little Beetle in an unlit far corner of the parking lot, then walked the full length of the empty lot to the bridge. Cautiously, they peered up the road, their way illuminated by the street lamps high above. Exposed as they were, they moved swiftly and silently. The Quechee Gorge bridge was huge, the oldest standing steel arch bridge in Vermont. Built back in 1911, it had replaced the wooden truss railroad bridge that had been used since 1875 and was the engineering feat of its day.

They streaked across the 285' span. Just as they reached the other side of the bridge, they felt a rumbling under their feet, that of a car coming from the north—and not too far away. Fearing that it might be the evil trio and not wanting to be discovered, they stepped off the bridge, crossed the concrete walkway, and quickly blended into the overgrown brown winter brush.

Just before the car rounded the corner and came into view, they ducked down under the north side of the bridge and waited, out of breath, in the cold darkness.

Although both of them had visited this natural phenomenon on numerous occasions, it was still intimidating to look down from their hiding spot at the impressive 165-foot-deep gorge known as the 'Grand Canyon of the East' and see Vermont's most spectacular natural wonder. From their perch, so high over the dramatic Ottaquechee River, they could see the distant shimmer of the night's natural light bouncing off the angry rolling current below. They hung onto each other as they peered down, not trusting the sturdy chain link fence holding them back from the rocky edge, preventing them from slipping down into the abyss.

They could hear the rushing Mill Pond Falls, located 300-400 yards further up the river. The darkness and brutal cold penetrated their senses and reached greedily through the multiple layers of their clothing. The tick, tick, ticking sound of ice-cold sleet rapped incessantly against the metal bridge span above them. They stood perfectly still as a minivan slowly came into view through the metal slats above them, harmlessly crossed the bridge without stopping, and continued on its way.

In the silence, they peered out from underneath the bridge, straining their eyes to get accustomed to the resultant darkness around them.

"Do you *see* anything?" Angie's voice echoed in the cavernous void. She pulled her cell phone from her pocket.

"Not a whit," Mrs. Bundle whispered, shivering in the cold.

The only sound they heard was the distant rushing water; all else was quiet.

"I'm going to try to get Dad again." Her icy fingers hit the speed-dial button.

At that same moment, a grotesque sound pierced the air. It was a chilling, stifled scream, animal-like, and full of unmitigated terror. It sounded like the wail of a fox, the cry adult foxes often use when in heat or as a substitute for fighting. The sound startled them and the cell phone slipped like butter from Angie's hand, falling to the ground.

"No!" she said breathlessly. Grabbing for it and missing, she watched it as it hit the frozen earth. They gasped as it bounced once, slipped randomly through the chain link fence, then clattered down, down, into the brink below.

Directly behind the first outcry came another, louder and more urgent this time, agonizing, filling the air with terror.

"What on earth—? Is that…a human voice?" Mrs. Bundle choked out the words, dreading to know the answer. Quickly reaching into the fanny pack and retrieving the two penlights, she whispered, "It's Jack!"

Angie grabbed for one, turned it on, and said, "So much for the phone, and so much for waiting! It's bad! We've got to find him."

"I'm right behind you, Angie. Go!"

Pulling themselves up the banking, they came out onto the road, knowing they must act. They ran down the Dewey Mills Road along the breakdown lane, their steps tracking the deep canyon of the Ottaquechee River in a parallel fashion.

"It came from that direction!" Like a flash, Angie was off at a run, and Mrs. Bundle followed as quickly as she could behind her, the small flashlight beaming through the patchy fog and falling sleet.

"Be careful. It's really slick in spots." Angie whispered loudly over her shoulder, "Come over here," she pointed to the gravel section, "it's not as slippery!" She pressed on ahead. "I don't see any cars—nothing! It's so remote here! Do you suppose they could be on the walking trail somewhere?"

"It's possible, but, how would they have gotten in there?"

The Quechee Gorge Walking Trail, part of the State Park, bordered the Dewey Mills Road and followed the river for miles. In the summer months, it was a popular hike that provided scenic rest stops and spectacular views of the Gorge, the Ottaquechee, and the Falls. Deserted, covered with snow, and with the intrusion of darkness, the trail's access, at this time of year, was unlikely.

They continued on the main road another hundred yards and then stopped to listen once more. This section of the road was remote and dark, without the benefit of residences or street lamps. The commercial, tourist-geared businesses further up on the main highway were all closed for the season. The area was as isolated as being plunked down in the middle of backcountry.

The world stopped as they listened intently, but the only sound they heard was the icy hard precipitation accumulating on the already-wet pavement.

Precious seconds passed. "*Where are they?*" Desperation filled Angie's voice, there was a wild look in her eye. Her face was aglow with nervous agitation in the penlight's faint glimmer. She turned to go.

"Stop, girl. *Shhh.*"

Not a sound.

They stood in their lonely spot, then slowly turned about, straining to hear. It was hard to hide their level of distress from each other. The air was deathly still.

"They must be here. But where?" Mrs. Bundle whispered, distraught and out of breath. They stood quietly, drawing in large breaths of cold, white air. "We can't give up...yet."

Once more, but more slowly this time, they turned together, rotating in a complete circle; listening intently, their hearts beat wildly below the silence. Their senses were fine-tuned now; their eyes acute to observe anything at all, anything out of the ordinary.

Finally, with hint of success, Angie whispered excitedly, "Look! Over there, Mrs. B!"

About fifty feet away was the familiar wooden, rustic "Overlook Point" arrow sign. It peeped through the bushes and winter shrubbery that densely lined the road. The State Park sign was an indicator for tourists and hikers alike, designed to lead sightseers to one of the most popular rustic summer settings, one which provided a spectacular vista of the Gorge and the Mill Pond Falls. And, one of the highest. Alfie's cryptic words, "hanging high!" came back to Mrs. Bundle.

"The *Overlook!*" They both said simultaneously.

Angie broke through the thin layer of crusted snow, sprinting onto the rough trail, and Mrs. Bundle followed closely behind. Stealthily, like Indians traveling a worn path centuries before, they made their way toward the site.

They cautiously crept along, moving quickly, bodies low. They painstakingly felt their way through the brush until they intersected with the rough gravel tote road, now covered with snow, along the river. This same road provided access for the Park utility vehicles to the Overlook site during the summer months.

They stopped, grabbing at each other. There, in front of them, was the foreboding dirty-black back fin—the rear fender of the Lincoln—peeking out from the overgrown brush. The remainder of the vehicle had been neatly hidden beneath a mammoth pine tree. A menacing red parking light flickered like an ominous cobra's eye in the darkness.

Just then, another garbled, suppressed scream pierced the silence; this time much closer, much more urgent. It *was* a human voice, they realized, unbearably strained, consumed with raw emotion, terror, and pain. As they crept closer and stooped down behind the car for a better view, they feared the worse. With Angie in the forefront and Mrs. Bundle directly behind, they adjusted their eyes to the incredible scene in front of them.

They could clearly distinguish the three criminals within the proximity of the car's headlights, which bore into the darkness, shining like a beacon out across the vast Gorge toward the distant, opposite cliff side. Dirty Dave DeMont leaned against the car's front fender; his skulking back toward them, his body slouched idly near the driver's side. Terrington Askew Whitewick and his cohort, Alfred Chexwidden, were standing within a few paces of each other at the farthest edge of the rocky Overlook. Unprotected by a chain link fence, this area's huge boulders and rough tree line prohibited the average hiker from entering near the notably dangerous zone, an area clearly marked with stern signs stating

"*Off Limits! Stay back!*". Whitewick and Chexwidden had ignored the warnings and appeared to be thoroughly engrossed in their actions.

Both Mrs. Bundle and Angie gripped each other in horror at the scene. It was like a queer stage, a diabolical theatrical set, so unreal in its presentation that one found it hard to fathom the incredible and staggering cruelty they were witnessing. Not more than thirty feet away, they could distinguish the naked silhouette of a man hanging from the sturdy limb of a tree. *Jack!*

He was upside-down; his arms swinging limply in the breeze like an aberrant pendulum. A heavily-knotted rope shackled his tethered ankles. He had been hoisted up and over the strapping gnarled limb of the massive maple tree that jutted out like a biceped arm about twenty feet over the Gorge. Hanging precariously over the jagged crevasse, his upended, slackened body swung to and fro in the frigid wind.

"Oh, my Lord, help us." Mrs. Bundle whispered hoarsely. In an instant, she took it all in.

The rope holding him was bulky, and the strength of all three men must have been required to lift his body, pull him up, onto, and then out to the further end of the branch, presumably by swinging him over the precipice with the leveraged rope. The end of the thickly-twined cable was wrapped around the enormous tree trunk, fashioned in place with a huge slipknot. Alarmingly, Mrs. Bundle noted that just a tight yank on the end of the rope would release the knot and send Jack quickly sliding down into the Gorge to his death.

As they watched, aghast, a low, muffled moan escaped from the boy's loosely bound mouth. "*Arrgh….*" Faint, shivering words escaped that sounded like, "Jaysus! Bl-bloody hell, (mumble) blokes…leave off, w-w-will ya?" Mumbling in a stupor of jumbled confusion, he was obviously spent and in a great deal of pain.

Far, far below, the gyrating, angry rapids swirled ominously into the rocky crevasse. Across the wide expanse, huge quantities of water cascaded over the lofty Mill Pond Falls, providing a treacherous backdrop for the tense scene. Jack's life was in the balance, his fate morbidly sealed by his captors.

Angie stared in disbelief. Barely above a peep, she whispered, "They've got his legs hog-tied! And they took his clothes!" What they both could discern was that he was unclad, save boxer shorts. His whole body was shuddering uncontrollably in the freezing cold air, and little icicles had formed like stalagmites on his head, nose, and chin. His appendages were silver gray in the night's light, covered in a shiny crusted shell of ice and snow. Barely conscious, and, at this point, more likely near delirium in his distress, it was apparent the weather conditions had already taken their toll.

They watched helplessly as Alfie reach up to Jack with a long shiny wand or stick of some sort, clutched tightly in his hand. Jack's arms flailed defensively, and they heard DeMont laugh savagely from his post. The instrument briefly touched Jack's bare chest, but the impact was like a miniature flash of lightening and Jack screamed, the same agonizing screech they had heard moments before. As the sparks flew, his body jerked with the impact of the shock and his face contorted in pain. The harmful tool gleamed menacingly in the pale night light, appearing almost to glow against the sheen of the cascading falls across the river.

Anyone who grew up in farm country knew what it was.

Mrs. Bundle was incensed. "They're using a cattle prod on him!"The device was a questionable instrument to use on animals. Undeniably, it was pure torture on a human being; the human skin's thickness was significantly more sensitive to the cattle prod's angry shock. Administered to a thick-skinned animal, it produced a minor surprise shock; the same shock given to a man was amplified tenfold. Although developed by a well-meaning veterinarian long ago, the yard-long, heavy electric prod was undeniably a severe weapon in the wrong hands. And these were the wrong hands.

Angie whispered, "They're torturing him. Where are the cops?" Wild with anger, she started to rise, but Mrs. Bundle quickly pulled her back.

"Wait, Angie!" Where indeed, were the police, she wondered desperately?

Upon closer scrutiny, they could see the cruel evidence that the cattle prod's mark had already left on Jack's body. In a numerous places on his legs, arms, and chest area, quarter-sized welts stood out like ugly medallions on his ashen, exposed skin.

The burns were vicious red spots, like hideous fleshy raspberries; an oozing blackish discharge was already seeping from some of his wounds. The weather conditions provided an extra boost of pain and suffering, moist air increasing the cattle prod's efficiency.

A short distance away, Whitewick spoke, "Right, mate," his voice a dispassionate monotone. "Now. You've played us enough. One last chance."

He raised the gun and pointed it at the head of Jack Corrigan. "Where's the bloody necklace?"

No time left; Jack's clock was nearing its expiration. Committed at the highest level of evil, Whitewick seemed menacingly undeterred from his ultimate goal.

Knowing innately that they had only seconds to act, Angie and Mrs. Bundle whispered briefly, conferring with efficiency, saving their speech.

Then, accompanied by courage and bravado she didn't know she possessed, Mrs. Bundle defiantly stood up in full view, stepping out and away from Angie's hiding spot.

"*Stop!*" The one word powerfully escaped her mouth.

She held the penlight upward at chest level, boldly illuminating her own stern expression in the eerie darkness. The men turned to face her, temporarily startled, as though viewing an apparition.

Stalwartly, she declared, "Stop, immediately! I have what you want—the necklace! Right *here!*"

She held her right arm high in the air, flinging her full fist back as though ready to hurl a pitch into the darkness. Desperately clutching the velvet bag in her hand, she threatened defiantly, "Believe that I will throw it into the Gorge....if you don't release Jack!"

"*Blimey!* You?" Alfie recovered his voice first. "What do you think you're playing at now, you meddlesome...?" He took a menacing step toward her, unaware that Angie was preparing for battle just outside his peripheral view. Angie had moved furtively, calculating her position, knowing her approach would be just to his rear in his blind spot. If her strategy worked, he would be outflanked, and the surprise attack could hold him at bay — hopefully, until help arrived.

"*Shoot her!*" Alfie cried to Whitewick, who was already raising his gun unwaveringly in Mrs. Bundle's direction.

Just as DeMont yelled "Watch out!", Angie rushed at Alfie, successfully taking him completely off guard as she jumped "Monky-Brushwein-style" onto his broad, dwarf back! His bowler hat flipped off his head and rolled haphazardly across the pathway as she attacked him with all her strength.

At the same time, Mrs. Bundle moved quickly, strategically positioning herself on the far side of the ensuing scuffle and effectively compromising Whitewick's aim at her. The cattle prod clattered to the ground as Angie pummeled Alfie's exposed head and ears with every bit of energy she could assemble, showing him no mercy. He howled with rage as he tried to grab onto a piece of her and throw her off his back. He snorted and lunged, but she held on in the best demonstration Mrs. Bundle had ever seen of a cowgirl on a bucking bronco.

Conscious that time was short, Mrs. Bundle drew back her arm, the golden arm that had won the State girl's softball championship in high school. She took a huge breath. *Desperate situations called for desperate measures,* she thought. Contemplating her next movement and fully realizing it was their only chance, she thought she heard the faint sound of sirens in the distance.

Thank God, they're coming! she thought, relieved. *If we can just hold on...* "Hold him, Angie!" she yelled.

Angie's valiant efforts provided the necessary diversion as Alfie continued to try to wrest her off his back. Whitewick swore repeatedly at his failed attempts to aim accurately, unable to fire his pistol at either Angie or Mrs. Bundle without shooting Alfie. Dirty Dave slithered close by and endeavored to get near the pair, but his efforts were thwarted by the flurry of wild activity of arms punching and legs kicking in all directions.

The next sequence of events occurred as though in slow motion. All of a sudden, Angie, taking Alfie completely by surprise, nimbly extricated herself, unraveling her body from him and pushing off his back. She vaulted far out of his reach, clearing his body by a good three feet. Recovering her balance immediately, she stood up and ran into the darkness.

Concurrently, Mrs. Bundle let loose, throwing the jewelry bag high in the air! It sailed slowly, deliberately high, up, up, and then leisurely arched down toward the watery brink.

Both Brits howled as they saw the bag sail through the air, their desperate cries ringing out in the night's stillness. Chexwidden was the closest to the airborne bag, and he screamed, "*No-o-o!*" as he saw its inevitable course.

It was headed straight for the cliff's edge.

"*Grab it!*" Whitewick bellowed to his underling, his speech unnatural, distended and stretched, like the scene in front of him, as he watched helplessly, much too far away to reach for it himself.

Mrs. Bundle held her breath. She could hear cars screeching to a halt. *We need a miracle,* she thought desperately.

Distracted by the questionable destination of the precious necklace, Alfie roared, his arms outstretched, reaching, and then reaching further for the medallion. As the velvet-clad treasure lazily cruised through the air and continued over the edge of the cliff, he hurled himself after it with greedy abandon, his avaricious hands reaching, straining for the bag. His body leaned over the rocky ledge in mid-air, his fingers *oh-so-close* to catching…the… *prize*. Sweat poured off his determined face; he was thoroughly, utterly, bent on winning.

Out of nowhere, incredibly, another's hand materialized!

It was Jack's, shooting out resolutely, gloriously rising out of the darkness like a phoenix from the ashes, lifted defiantly from his topsy-turvy position. Ostensibly from nowhere, he swung his battered body out and grabbed for the fragile bag, too.

The two men's eyes met in fierce visual combat as Jack's unyielding, damaged fingers closed first over the lightweight tasseled strings of the bag.

He grunted in pain. Pushing through his suffering with amazing fortitude, he gave a defiant roar, "*Argggghhhh!*" As if gaining a tremendous life force, he yanked the precious sack triumphantly away from and out of Alfie's reach.

The little bag's strings swung desperately in Jack's frozen fingertips as his beat-up body swayed pathetically in the wet wind. A section of the platinum chain slithered out of the bag's opening and sparkled in the moonlight.

"You wretched beggar…*Grrrr!* Give it here!" Alfie's face was purple with despicable rage and murderous purpose and he clutched at the bag, trying to extract it from Jack's hand.

With phenomenal intention, the strings and the chain were secured in Jack's hand, seeming to magically intertwine themselves around his stiff, impaired fingers. He shouted at Chexwidden, "*Your soul.to the divil!*"

Alfred Chexwidden tried to recover, tried to secure his footing at the edge of the precipice, but he tripped slightly. His feet fumbled around the knotty roots that projected out and around the base of the tree. He snatched for a nearby branch above him and missed; his balance was now in jeopardy, his eyes desperate.

Too late! He realized his fatal blunder; that of avariciousness superseding good old common sense.

Quietly and without fanfare, he hung momentarily, defying this strange mid-air gravity as though time was standing still, and then, he just disappeared from sight.

One final wild and desperate scream of terror could be heard throughout the valley, following him downward as he fell the 100-odd feet to the bottom of the gorge.

They could hear shouting now, loud commands, and the shrill barking of a dog.

"They're *coming*, do you hear them?" Mrs. Bundle yelled at the two remaining men.

Dave DeMont turned suddenly on his heel and dashed down the path like a jackrabbit headed for the exit hole, leaving Whitewick to handle the residual effects of their deeds.

But all was not over as he pointed his handgun directly at Mrs. Bundle.

"I should have killed you at the house with my own bare hands." His cruel eyes told her the whole story, his intentions very clear. His face held a strange, indifferent smile: poised, secure, deadly.

"Mrs. B! *Watch out!*" Angie yelled from the shadows.

As he cocked the gun and began to pull the trigger, a loud hollow thud suddenly resounded from his breast like a small explosion, arresting his actions.

A startled expression replaced the previously detached look on his countenance. Now, it held open-eyed astonishment. Coming to grips for the first time with the realization that his world of entitlement and intimidation might possibly be compromised, he uttered, "*Wh*—?"

He tried to speak but there was no air for him to breathe, for Angie had reached into her pocket and, removing her ever-present lacrosse ball, had hurled it at Terrington Askew Whitewick with deadly force. With the precision of a sharpshooter, she'd let loose the solid rubber, two-inch round weapon, knowing this little ball could be hurled at eighty miles an hour full force with a lacrosse stick. She had practiced this action hundreds of time before to improve her accuracy; even a moderate blow without the stick could be incapacitating if aimed correctly.

The hard white ball's target was true, striking its victim squarely in the chest. His lungs became debilitated bellows and the oxygen was sucked out. Whitewick grabbed at his heavy turtleneck collar for air, gasping for breath, his body recoiling in involuntary submission. Helplessly dropping to his knees, he gulped for air, but not before the gun discharged as it tumbled loosely to the ground. *Bang!*

He fell prostrate beside it.

The gun's report had been blinding. Going off at such close range, it sounded like a cannon, echoing loudly throughout the Gorge. Its force threw Mrs. Bundle harshly backward three feet and she lost her balance. Her spine slammed brutally into the hard base of the huge maple tree where Jack hung helplessly. The combination of deafening sound and flashing light made her lightheaded, and she lay momentarily stunned, trying desperately to recover.

She tried unsuccessfully to right herself. "Is everyone okay? Angie, where are you, girl?"

She couldn't see anything through the enveloping darkness.

Angie was at her side in an instant. "I'm okay, Mrs. B. They're coming. I can hear them." The gun's firing was a magnet for the police; a multitude of dark figures crashed through the growth and rushed toward them. "There they are!" Her voice held relief; her body was trembling. "*Help!*" she shouted desperately, "*We're here!*"

"I'm okay, luv. You....were so brave."

Mrs. Bundle put her hands to the ground to get up but felt a sharp pain. She lay back against the tree trunk, breathing laboriously. Reaching a heavy hand up to her chest, she felt a sticky wetness; warm and faintly familiar-smelling. Somewhat lightheaded, she looked down in mild surprise. *Why, I can't have been shot,* she thought, slowly losing her sense of logic as the night sky became darker still. Gracious, she hadn't felt a thing.

Men's shouts and the dog's barking finally reached them; rescue sounds bombarded her from every direction.

"Lettie?" Will O'Malley's booming voice sounded out through the thicket. "Lettie, are you there?"

Mrs. Bundle could hear more commotion, wavy, flashing lights striating the sky like air raid beacons and crackling police radios sounding very far off.

"We're all right," she whispered to no one in particular, "It's over, thank goodness. Please, can you help the boy…?"

"They've got him, he's fine," Angie cried, tilting Mrs. Bundle back in a vain attempt to help her catch her breath. Someone else reached out and broke her fall as her upper torso helplessly slipped off the tree trunk onto the cold ground. Distant, fuzzy voices, a flurry of movement….she couldn't make out a thing through the suffocating darkness around her.

"Will… is that you? Why all this infernal….racket?" she asked, and then drifted into unconsciousness.

Chapter Twenty-Eight

The Downfall of Dirty Dave

From The Rutland Daily News four days later:

Federal Fugitive Arrested
on White River Junction Train

Police surrounded the southbound Amtrak Vermonter train early Sunday morning and arrested a federal fugitive who they say was fleeing to New Jersey or unknown points south. David Michael DeMont of Norwich, the suspected felon in more than 15 crimes involving interstate vehicle theft, forgery, breaking and entering, credit card and identity theft, and attempted murder is now in custody, according to Colonel Henry S. Barker of the Vermont State Police.

Since Friday night, DeMont has been the subject of an all-out manhunt. It was suspected that DeMont, known in the area as a chronic offender, would be on the train because he bought a ticket with a stolen credit card found at a private residence that was believed to have been ransacked by him late Friday night in Woodstock. DeMont was in flight from the police, having narrowly escaped the authorities at the Dark Horse Inn and Tavern in Quechee Village on Friday night for a second time following a bizarre incident linked to the attempted murder of a local North Pillson Corners woman at the Quechee Gorge State Park Overlook site. That incident has left one alleged felon dead and one male victim injured and in serious condition. The female victim, Mrs. Letitia Bundle, is in critical condition at the Dartmouth-Hitchcock Medical Center in Lebanon, New Hampshire. Hospital authorities would not comment further on her condition.

Police in White River Junction had just minutes to prepare when word reached them at 7:15 that morning that a man believed to be DeMont was leaving the area on the Amtrak train. A Joint Task Force comprised of state, county, and local police and the FBI rushed to the site. In addition, escape officers with their search dogs set themselves up all around the Depot, on stand-by in case tracking became necessary.

"We had been working with the FBI and the Windsor County Sheriff's Department in this investigation," State Police Detective Ryan LeLorme said, "and that morning we got a tip that the card had been used. We entered the train undercover and asked the conductors if they had anybody who met his description. Head Conductor Simon Lemminton said, 'Yep, he's in the back car.' I went down and, after we determined he was our man, I approached him and asked for ID. He was traveling under an assumed name. Meanwhile, the other officers entered the car and evacuated the passengers. I asked him to come off the train; when he realized he didn't have a chance, he complied without incident and he was placed under arrest as a fugitive. He was carrying two concealed weapons, which we confiscated at that time."

DeMont's lawyer, Ronald Stoplespring, principal solicitor for Criminal Defense Attorneys of Burlington, said the charges were an "overreaction". "Some of these charges appear to stem from the recent hysteria of home thefts in the Woodstock area. Once I have a chance to go over all the evidence with my client, I'm sure his name will be cleared of all wrongdoing," Stoplespring said this morning.

DeMont has been "under suspicion" for the rash of area antique-related burglaries for quite some time, according to LeLorme. Search warrants were obtained and entry was made into a barn at the Dark Horse Inn in Quechee. It has been purported a large cache of the stolen antiques and other items have been found. Similar home thefts have occurred in nearby Manchester and Weston, all cases that have now been linked to DeMont and a network of criminals believed to span states as far away as Pennsylvania.

When contacted, Detective Jonathan Slayer of Wellington Township Police Department in Pennsylvania said, "We have charges pending against DeMont and there are six other counties that may also have various warrants out for his arrest. It seems he has been a very busy fellow. There's car theft involved, stolen credit cards and stolen goods, thousands of dollars."

Vermont State Police Captain Carla Mastrantino said, "We recovered more than 30 credit cards from a guest room where he had been staying at the Dark Horse Inn. We have confirmed who his contacts are in the area and where he has been fencing the items of value stolen during these burglaries. We have obtained more search warrants, and arrests are happening as we speak. Mr. DeMont has also been charged with attempted murder."

DeMont was being held in the Woodstock Correctional Center without bail pending an arraignment scheduled for this coming Thursday in Windsor County District Court.

In the attempted murder case, two other perpetrators were allegedly involved, one falling to his death into the 100-foot gorge at the Overlook Falls site and the other apprehended and being arraigned tomorrow. That man, identified only as T.A. Whitewick, no known address, is also wanted for questioning by the British authorities and is being held without bail at an undisclosed location. He is under 24-hour guard, according to authorities.

There has been a combined, ongoing effort at all law enforcement levels to contain both DeMont and Whitewick since their illegal activities became apparent Friday, according to Windsor County Sheriff William J. O'Malley. "The pieces began to fit together and we had to move quickly."

Authorities in Pennsylvania and Vermont are now working together to consolidate all of the outstanding charges against DeMont into a single district attorney's office that will coordinate them. FBI agents in Burlington and Philadelphia said the Federal Bureau of Investigation's interest in DeMont was largely in seeing him apprehended because he had fled across state lines.

Sheriff O'Malley had these shining words for the Joint Task Force involved in DeMont's and Whitewick's apprehension. "Here is just another excellent example of what can occur when law enforcement teamwork, manpower, and perseverance come together in a concerted effort. We are proud to have been a part of this operation and we look forward to seeing the alleged criminals involved in these related cases prosecuted to the fullest extent of the law."

Chapter Twenty-Nine
The Heroes

Everyone sat, anxiously waiting, in the darkened, somber room. The tension could have been sliced with a dull knife as they all tried to bear the excruciating silence.

Finally, above, a stirring was heard; deliberate footsteps, slow as a funeral march, cautiously descending each step, one at a time.

There was a torturous pause; they all waited desperately for the next step. When it came, tentative and light, they all sighed with relief. Each step downward sounded closer, closer; no one dared move an inch. The oxygen in the room hung suspended, as still as a stifling summer afternoon; not one person made one sound.

At last, the familiar, silver-brown braided head came slowly around the corner into view and everyone exhaled noisily. Lights were thrown on and boisterous, raucous shouts range out.

"*Surprise!* Merry Christmas! Surprise!"

Mrs. Bundle's astonished face lit up—nearly as bright as the nearby Christmas tree—and she surveyed all the familiar faces in this eclectic gathering. "Well!" was all she could say. "Well, *well!*"

She leaned gently on Jack Corrigan's arm, her opposite shoulder snugly wrapped in a light blue sling, and she looked only somewhat the worse for wear. Her face was thinner and quite colorless except for the two pale, rosy spots above her cheekbones. Her features were more defined, somewhat sharper with the loss of weight. But her comely eyes glistened, showing the indomitable and positive spirit behind them. Greeting the happy group, she beamed expansively, a brilliantly huge smile illuminating her face.

"Oh, *my*, what a surprise!" she whispered, truly at a loss for words. "Oh, how special! And, all for *me*?"

Erin came first to her, stepping out in front of the group, so filled with excitement she could barely contain herself. Her body rocked and jumped like a quivering bowl of Jello. "Here now, Mrs. B, we've got your chair all ready for you. See, isn't it grand? Aye, sit down and try it, would you now!"

There was her old comfortable wicker rocking chair at the place of honor in front of the tree and trimmed with a festive rainbow of curlicue ribbons. Tied to the back was a plump, bright yellow, smiley-face balloon, which bounced, buoyant and carefree, along the ceiling.

Erin continued, her lilting voice precise and very businesslike as she, the designated Mistress of Ceremonies, said, "Right there, Mrs. B, and you'll be very comfortable, I'll wager. Aye, and I'd like it if I could help you when you open your presents. Could I please, mum?" Now that Erin had found her voice, she had fully embraced the gift of gab and had no problem articulating directives or desires.

Mrs. Bundle affectionately nodded her acceptance and said, "Of course, dear."

As she eased herself into the abundant wicker chair, helping hands gently guided her navigation until she was settled and comfortable. Clay Andersen placed a small pillow behind her neck and she sat back, fatigued yet blissful from the labored efforts of her first trip downstairs since coming home. Even though she looked a bit wan from her harrowing brush with death over last few, arduous weeks, she was definitely on the mend now and very grateful to be alive.

"Thank you. Thank you all. It's so nice to have everyone here today." She looked around at her extended "family", and thought, *surely, this is going to be a day to remember!*

Present and in fine spirits were: Angie and the Andersen men, Jack, Erin, and Aineen, Doc Dot and her sister, Josephine, Mabel Weatherby, Sheriff Will O' (in an unofficial capacity), and, last but not least, Althea Swain.

Her dear friend, still here after all these weeks, had refused to go back to California, insisting rather that she must stay and oversee Mrs. Bundle's recuperative process. Having Allie's healing skills at her side had been just what the doctor ordered, not to mention the joy of having so much quality time to catch up with her old chum, which was the perfect elixir for Mrs. Bundle, helping to restore her spirits and mend her body.

The copiously trimmed Christmas tree, decorated especially for Mrs. Bundle, hung heavy with candy canes, dark brown gingerbread men, popcorn strings laced with cranberries, and twinkling multi-colored lights.

Carl placed Mrs. Bundle's antique tin star at the top of the tree while everyone clapped. Little Aineen laughed and struggled on unsure feet to reach the brilliant lights.

"No, lass, c'mere! Open this package," Jack said, and thus began the pleasant activity of opening gifts.

There were gifts for everyone and, as they all sat together opening gifts, Mrs. Bundle could not help but reflect on the past month as she watched. *Yes*, she thought, *things always have a wonderful way of working out.* She smiled as she viewed the scene, thinking about the here and now, and tying up all the loose ends nicely in her mind...

───ༀ───

Something good always comes from something bad, Mrs. Bundle acknowledged, another one of her mother's age-old sayings hitting home. Many things had occurred after she had been shot. Some had transpired prior to her release from the hospital; others occurred after her discharge to convalesce at home.

First of all, Vermont's Department of Human Services had determined that, because Jack had turned eighteen the past September, he was deemed to be an adult in the eyes of the law, thereby being in full control of his sisters. In her last report, Mrs. Bellows had recommended no action be taken against Jack. She suggested that the girls still remain in the Andersens' care with Jack continuing to stay at Mrs. Bundle's, until such time that he was able to provide for them on his own. The Andersens had wholeheartedly agreed to this proposal—as had Jack. *Splendid plan*, she thought, realizing how close they all had become.

Jack, even though severely injured himself, was determined to help her get better as quickly as possible. He had brought the girls over to visit every day while she was recuperating. His kindness and patience knew no bounds, it seemed; his experiences had taken him far beyond his eighteen years. Now that he had begun to feel a true sense of home and family again, he had become less serious, more open and willing to accept the kindnesses of the Andersens, Mrs. Bundle, and of Pillson.

The fireball, Erin, had been enrolled at the Pillsonville Elementary School. After having been tested, she was placed in the third grade and had assimilated easily into the school curriculum.

"Like a duck paddlin' in a pond!" Walter had boasted to anyone who would listen.

Erin loved coming home on the bus each day and showing Gumpy her daily lessons. Usually, he took time out from the chores to go over her papers with her, make her a snack, and then she would help him and the boys outside as his "official farmhand", directing and cajoling the chickens and geese until dinnertime. Clay and Carl were helpful in the evening with her homework, as was Jack, when he had time.

After he'd recovered, Jack's day had become very full with everyday activities. Some of it was spent working on the farm with the Andersens, who had taken special notice of Jack's hardworking and diligent manner and were helping him make restitution for the items he had borrowed while the girls and he were homeless. He had signed up for evening college classes through the local community college services, to commence in January. In addition, Royal Hudson, Jr., had offered him a part-time job at Hudson's Garage which he had gladly accepted.

Aineen continued to thrive with all the attention heaped on her from such a large and loving group of people. Mrs. Bundle watched as Aineen gleefully played with the discarded gift-wrapping. Although her gifts of stuffed animals, toys, and dolls had been plentiful, she was having the best time throwing the multi-patterned festive wrapping paper up in the air, then giggling as it fell down around her. An errant bow from one of the packages had somehow found its way to the top of her head and stuck there like a sweet orange persimmon on her wispy curls.

So, Mrs. Bundle thought happily, *everyone seems to have settled into a very nice, normal routine.*

Doc Dot had contacted their state senator to help the Corrigans get through the mire of immigration paperwork. Being of Irish origin with no survivors (but with sponsorship), had led to the Immigration Service putting the Corrigan file "on hold pending a review in six months."

After they were provided the proper legal representation, a major development occurred. Because they had become victims of a serious crime, their attorney applied for a special exception call the U Visa, which provided interim relief and lawful status for victims in their circumstance. Jack's testimony against Dirty Dave and T. A. Whitewick would solidify this process and was something he was very willing to do. As a result, they would be allowed to stay in the country and eventually become citizens, if they so chose. Jack had also been granted an immigrant visa petition and was issued a temporary green card.

Consequently, Mrs. Bundle thought as she watched the merry scene, *that piece of business is on its way to being taken care of, too.*

Angie and Jack had become steadfast friends the last few weeks. Since the harrowing exploits that had fatefully brought them together, they had bonded. Along with a strong will to live, the pure spunk and bravery of both had created a connection between them. It was evident that Jack thought Angie was a pretty special individual and his shy respect toward her was very endearing. *That the sun rises and sets with that girl, in his eyes, is pretty clear to me,* she thought.

Angie, in turn, had a special regard toward Jack's welfare. Taking particular pride in introducing him to her friends and others in the community had made certain he had been welcomed by all. Her manner around him was easy and caring, and she delighted in kidding him, egging him on good-naturedly to tell his stories about what life had been like for him in Ireland, helping him remember the good times he had had.

Of course, once they heard him, everyone loved Jack's singing; he had even gotten up and performed at the local Seedhouse Café the last two Friday nights with a very warm reception. When Jack opened his mouth, pure, deep, resonant sounds filled the air with enchanting soulfulness, and he was already becoming known in the small community as "that *Irish* boy who can sing."

During their daily visits, Erin and Jack had sung their Irish ballads to Mrs. Bundle many times and their harmonizing qualities were remarkable.

"Like larks on the wing…" she would tell them after each performance. They sang their beautiful Irish ballads, songs that now had names. "She Moves Through the Fair" was one of Mrs. Bundle's favorites, as was "Colcannon" and "Leaboy's Lassie." Jack's rendition of "Danny Boy" was enough to make even the hardest human being's eyes well up.

Carl had found a used Celtic flute for Jack. Also, for Jack's Christmas present from the Andersens and Mrs. Bundle, he had ordered a Celtic harp from one of his music catalogs. Today, it had been a pleasure to see Jack open this gift with a startled, then elated, look on his genuinely happy face. He had thanked everyone heartily, "Aye, mates, much appreciated. *Go raibh maith agat!* Aye, thank you!"

Not surprisingly, Nicholas Clancy and Jack had become "mates," their common interest in fly-fishing and lure tying becoming the springboard for a blossoming friendship. They had already gone ice fishing up at Goochie Pond and were planning fly-fishing adventures as soon as the weather allowed in the spring.

Then, of course, Mrs. Bundle remembered, *there was Jesse.* In her eyes, Mrs. Bundle believed Jesse Clancy was a good man of poor judgment who had been caught in a bad situation. She had hoped it would help his case if he came forward voluntarily with the DeMont information—along with other important information he'd overheard. In point of fact, he had decided to give state's evidence in the DeMont affair, and that testimony contributed to the arrest of a number of suspects involved in the fencing ring; to date, a federal grand jury had indicted 29 people. It had pleased her greatly last week when the favorable news came that Jesse Clancy had accepted a plea bargain. Jesse's sentence ordered him to do 250 hours of community service, which he had already begun.

Even better news was that some smart official in charge of Jesse's probation had put Jesse's knowledge of the land to use, matching his outdoor skills with the appropriate community service and had placed him with the State Park division. There was talk that they might even hire him as a winter guide. If all went well, Jesse Clancy might end up a bona fide employee of the State of Vermont working under the supervision of the Superintendent of the State Park Division. *Wouldn't that be something,* Mrs. Bundle thought, smiling. All this good news was like balm to her spirit. He was with his family for Christmas, too. *Oh, how wonderful it is when things work out*, she thought.

Mrs. Bundle's thoughts turned to the Lir pendant and she shivered. She couldn't believe the web of intrigue and deceit that had been brought to bear by a seemingly innocent piece of jewelry. She still thought of him as *Darby Quicksilver*, even though she knew his real name now. As that brilliant smile flashed in front of her, she winced slightly.

The memory of that cold night brought a flash of anger to her mind. Days later, after she had awoken, Mrs. Bundle learned from Angie how the ball's blow had knocked the wind out of Whitewick so effectively that he awoke to find himself in handcuffs. Evidently, the Andersen men arrived at the Gorge directly behind the rush of police. Clay Andersen had had to be physically restrained when he reached one of the men responsible for harming his daughter.

As Mrs. Bundle sat and enjoyed her party, Whitewick sat in prison without bail, a long list of serious offenses precluding his departure anytime soon. In true "survival of the fittest" philosophy, Mrs. Bundle knew in her heart that Chexwidden's death, unfortunate as it was, had been unavoidable. *Oh, how I wish he could have been prosecuted and made to suffer, along with Quicksilver, for his offenses*, she thought.

She sighed, realizing that, even after all that had occurred, she still believed in the goodness of men, even through her brush at death's door. *Honestly*, she marveled, *all this subterfuge and evildoing for a necklace!*

Yes, the necklace. Erin was wearing it now. She looked over at the little girl, the Children of Lir pendant dangling from her tiny neck and showcasing the pretty chintz dress she wore as she played. Earlier, she had told Mrs. Bundle proudly, "Aye, Jack said I could wear Ma's necklace for this special occasion today!" The bejeweled swan eyes glittered and flashed as she moved in the prismatic festive lighting. Mrs. Bundle was hard-pressed to decide who sparkled more, the beautifully healthy child or the lovely necklace.

Walter had asked Jack—after all the trauma was behind them, "Ain't none of our business, son, but, we *was* wonderin'.....are you fixin' to peddle it for all the cash?"

Jack's brow had creased in careful thought. Then he'd shook his head vehemently. "Not now, nor probably ever, sir. With respect to my dear ma, her family, and our ancestors, that necklace is part of our heritage, right, and it will stay where it is, with us."

Walter now boasted to anyone who would listen that Jack's story was "jist like out of one of those Horatio Algebra books." *God bless him and his Walterisms*, she chuckled to herself.

Her own children came into her thoughts and she smiled lovingly. Immediately upon hearing of their mother's grave injuries, Leslie and Karen had come from their great distances of Japan and Alaska. As she regained consciousness days after the shooting, they were sitting anxiously by her hospital bed. She learned of the seriousness of her injuries from them. The bullet had nicked her heart and she had also suffered a collapsed lung. Although the blood loss had been profuse at the scene and her life had hung in the balance for five days, she had rallied as she heard their voices through her hazy consciousness. *Oh, wasn't it wonderful*, she thought pleasantly, *to finally wake up and see their faces!*

Both had now returned to their jobs and families—at her insistence. And, when Mrs. Bundle had finally been well enough to leave the hospital, Althea had assured them that her nurse's training more than equipped her to take care of their mother. Mrs. Bundle smiled tenderly as she looked over at the special Christmas gifts they had sent to her. The lovely, old, silver-plated tea set Karen said she had found in a quaint curio shop in Anchorage was just perfect, and Leslie's beautiful floral arrangement (along with a heartfelt note) with all her favorite blossoms was.... *beautiful!*

Which brought her now to…yes, poor Cracker. Finally, the last blessing bestowed on her today. Mrs. Bundle looked over, eyes shimmering, at the undisputed Hero of the Day. Miraculously, her sweet P-Cat had survived! Her dear Cracker-Cat purred contentedly while he watched the festivities from a very special seat. By now, everyone knew about Cracker.

The previous Tuesday, Walter had spent all morning in West Lebanon painstakingly searching for just the right present befitting the powers of such a special cat. He had finally purchased the largest, puffiest, most luxuriously comfortable cat pillow he could find. Now, there sat Cracker, relishing all the attention, regally surveying the festivities like a monarch with his court.

He watched his mistress and she smiled at him. His whiskers quivered, remembering that day. After his sad treatment at the hands of the cruel Alfred Chexwidden, Cracker had been near death. Sam Reardon, the Vet from South Woodstock, made an emergency trip that night to Mrs. Bundle's house to evaluate Cracker's extensive injuries. Luckily, he had not been moved and, when the doctor arrived, he was barely breathing.

Cracker had suffered greatly; four of his ribs had been crushed, along with a broken hip and significant internal bleeding, all of which contributed to an uncertain prognosis as his life hung in the balance. But, true to cat form, he had pulled through, using up numbers three and four of his proverbial cat lives.

Mrs. Bundle closed her eyes and, for the next few minutes, dozed off contentedly while Cracker contemplated his current Superstar status.

Today, Cracker was not to be outdone. *Wasn't this his finest hour?* Cracker's attire was understated, yet elegant. Angie had known just the garment suited for him for such a glorious occasion.

As he lay there comfortable and unabashedly preening in his finery, he purred with satisfaction. Admittedly, the vintage red velvet (trimmed with *fake* fur, mind you) smoking jacket fit his present state of convalescence to a "T", yet made the proper fashion statement. His bandages peeked through the loosely wrapped robe, the last set of dressings he would have to endure before Doc Reardon removed them next week.

Deep in cat-thought (and aided by his favorite present, a special order of fragrant catnip courtesy of Mabel Weatherby) he appeared thoroughly delighted with himself. Cracker looked the picture of a meticulous, singular cat as he stretched gingerly. *I might even be up to trying one of the special liver lover cookie treats,* he cat-thought, eyeing them on the dainty, small silver tray Angie had placed on the pillow beside him.

He reflected on his newly gained celebrity.

"Did you hear about the Bundle Cat?" was the question on everyone's lips after Angie had shared the amazing story of his uncanny ability, at near-death, to move the fanny pack.

He stretched his body tentatively, once again reliving the precious moment in his mind's eye. Yes, why, even *he* had to admit what a grand cat he was!

Chapter Thirty
Christmas in Kilarney

The room looked as though a confetti bomb had hit it. Festive paper resting everywhere, presents merrily strewn around the room, scattered paper plates and party hats mixed in for good measure —*what a wonderfully glorious mess*, thought Mrs. Bundle as she awoke, contentedly surveying the area. Children's peals of laughter could be heard coming from the next room where a blindfolded Gumpy was vainly trying to pin the tail on the donkey.

"How about another sugar cookie?" Clay asked, quietly coming to sit beside her.

She sighed deeply, "No, thank you, Clay. I'm so stuffed! Too many cream puffs!"

He reached over and patted her hand affectionately. "You've done some real good stuff here, Mrs. B."

"Me? Clay, it's truly amazing what life throws at you when you least expect it. We'll do all right by these kids, won't we?" Her eyes showed worry, her delicate brow wrinkled.

"You bet! They'll get taken care of, don't you worry."

Casually, as though Mrs. Bundle was the happy magnet, each child came into the room, like fireflies to the flame.

Jack entered first, holding Aineen in his arms, concern on his face. "Em, could I be getting you anythin', Mrs. B? Surely, now?

Are you getting tired? I'm ready to help you upstairs when you've had enough of this madness."

"No, Jack, dear, I'm fine. This has been such a *wonderful* surprise. I don't want it to end." She looked at him anxiously and motioned for him to bend down. He set Aineen down onto the rug and then leaned in, listening intently as Mrs. Bundle whispered, "How are *you* feeling? How do the blister scars look today? Is the balm working?"

He shrugged nonchalantly, "Aye, not to worry!" Although the concussion that Jack had sustained at the warehouse barn had been serious, it was the torturous cattle prod burns, in conjunction with the exposure to the frigid elements, that still required attention. Some of his injuries were third degree wounds and were taking some time to heal, leaving the remnants of scars in most places.

Doc Dot had applied a special aloe salve that she had concocted, and the cool ointment worked like a sorcerer's balm on the affected areas. Each wound seemed to be getting progressively better each day.

Mrs. Bundle was also concerned about the emotional scars left with Jack from such a trauma. After she had regained consciousness, she was distressed to learn Jack was in a hospital room in the next wing over, still in danger. His fingers and feet had been frostbitten and had required numerous warm baths until the white, waxy affected skin had turned bright red and then a healthy pink. After wrapping his feet and hands in sterile gauze, it had been necessary for him to remain immobile for a week while he recovered from the additional effects of hypothermia. All in all, he was a lucky fellow to be alive today and she hoped the memories of the cruelty he had endured would fade with time.

She stared with concern into those striking, clear blue eyes and he said, "Me? Ah, I'm right as rain, Mrs. B. There's nary anything to see now. Thank God, we're all as right as rain, aren't we now?" He bent down and planted a quick peck on the cheek, after which he blushed and gave her a lopsided smile, which was like heaven for Mrs. Bundle.

Aineen, her little legs wobbly as she took her new steps, cautiously held onto the door, then the coffee table. Like a bobbing, wobbly ocean buoy, she finally reached Mrs. Bundle and slurped a big wet kiss on her afghan-covered knees. She looked up expectantly for Mrs. Bundle's reaction. Curly chestnut wisps of hair shimmered and surrounded her luscious little face with an angelic halo, and Mrs. Bundle couldn't help but laugh.

"You are a pip, aren't you? You sweet girl!" The child gave her a gummy, wide smile.

"C'mere, you little pixie." Jack scooped up the child and hugged her to him. She wrestled her way back to the floor, giggling.

Erin and Angie entered laughing; Erin full of energy and effervescence as she looked up adoringly at Angie. She scampered to Mrs. Bundle and leaned on her good side, placing her arm lightly around Mrs. Bundle's shoulder.

"Angie's been teaching me how to play lacrosse, Mrs. B! See now, what she gave me for Christmas?"

She reached under the tree and held up a child-sized, molded-head lacrosse stick, bright yellow in color. Erin carefully balanced the accompanying white lacrosse ball in the pocket, cradling the stick back and forth. "See, I can do it, can't I, now?"

Jack jumped playfully in front of her, as though to try to steal the ball away from her. She flipped the ball with surprising agility toward Angie, who deftly caught it in one hand and then bounced it on the floor back to her. Erin scooped it up in the pocket of her stick and jumped up and down in excitement.

"We're quite a team, Erin!" Angie laughed.

"I'm going to be the best lacrosse player, just like Angie, the best in the world someday, sure and I am!" She smiled confidently at all the faces watching, taking in a quick breath, and asked, "Mrs. B, how's your shoulder? Would you be wanting another cup of tea? I can get it, you know. Aye, I helped Allie fill the teapot again, just now!"

So nice that the kids had bonded so well with everyone, Mrs. Bundle pondered happily, *and so funny the way everything has just fallen into place.*

Erin tossed her ball in the air, attempting to catch it with one hand like her mentor. Aineen tried to capture Erin's traveling ball, reaching back and forth as everyone followed the baby's antics. She weebled and wobbled in her haphazard fashion, wending her way back over toward Mrs. Bundle. Finally, she rested her head on Mrs. Bundle's lap and closed her eyes. Mrs. Bundle patted the curly head.

Suddenly, Aineen looked up coyly at Mrs. Bundle and, pointing her little stubby index finger at her, exclaimed very loudly and concisely, "Buh—Buh—Bee!"

"Holy Mother Mary! Did you hear that, now? Have y' ever seen the likes of it?" Jack crowed proudly, "She just said your name!"

There was a clamor as everyone was made aware of the baby's newest marvel.

As the rest straggled back into the parlor, everyone's noisy chatter filled the air. Will O'Malley's booming voice could be heard above the rest. When he reached Mrs. Bundle, he said, "Well now, I'll be getting along, Lettie. I'm headed up to Burlington for a few days of 'R 'n R'! Sorely needed after all this hubbub!"

Taking his outstretched hand, she said, "Give my love to Lizzie, would you? And, Will….I can't thank you enough…for everything."

"It's all right, Lettie. It's all turned out great for everyone," he grinned, looking around at the happy group.

As he left, snippets of conversations could be heard: farm talk, what someone's favorite present was, the secret ingredient for the chocolate chip cookies, and the best remedy for the latest flu—all were topics that filtered past Mrs. Bundle's ears as she sat and listened.

As if by design, the din suddenly receded and the room became silent. Mrs. Bundle took this opportunity to talk to the gathering. "I'd like to thank everyone for coming. And, a very special thank-you to you, Angie—and Allie, too, for planning this wonderful surprise—you both are the best! You have no idea how fantastical it is to be downstairs again! I think I've had enough of staring at those four walls of my bedroom!"

Everyone chuckled.

She went on, her eyes glistening. "I consider you all," she looked around the room expansively, "to be my extended family, and I want you to know," her voice broke slightly, "you all mean the world to me. Thank you again, everyone."

"We're just glad you're gettin' better!" Walter said.

"I plan on being fit as a fiddle here very shortly!"

He chided her mischievously, "Heck, there's a whole passel of crim'nals out there waitin' to be *lashshooed* by the best dang detector in...why, all of North Pillson Corners!"

Behind her sober countenance, Mrs. Bundle's eyes sparkled impishly, "Yes! Who *knows* where our next adventure will lead us?" She winked at Angie.

Walter's raised his furry eyebrows. "Hold up *jist* a dang minute. You ain't fixin' to get us into another hornet's nest anytime in the near by-and-by, are ya?"

"Well, Walter, I can't really say. Who knows what could happen next," she looked around the room, "here...in our little world?"

He paused, reluctantly shaking his head. "Hard tellin', not knowin'."

"Yuh-huh. Hard tellin', not knowin'." Mrs. Bundle returned dryly, tongue-in-cheek.

Angie squeaked, holding back a giggle, "Hard tellin'..."

Jack said matter-of-factly, "Aye, not knowin'."

Everyone broke up, especially Walter, who wiped his eyes, still chuckling, and said, "How 'bout that? *Hey*! Let's have a song, Jack!"

Carl picked up his guitar and began strumming the traditional

Christmas song's lively chords. As the music began, feet tapped in rhythm.

Jack and Erin both stood and began clapping; their voices filled the little farmhouse in Vermont with the melodious, Irish strains. The brother and sister's harmonies were exquisite, their voices true and wonderfully clear, and soon everyone joined in, clapping and singing along:

> *The holly green, the ivy green,*
> *The prettiest picture you've ever seen*
> *Is Christmas in Killarney,*
> *With all of the folks at home...*

Epilogue

IN A SEEMINGLY UNRELATED EVENT, a fascinating newspaper article in the London Times ran that same day. It referenced the quarter page obituary notice of real estate magnate Sidney Lambdin Johns Wesley, III, the misanthropic multimillionaire financier who had passed away five days earlier due to complications related to pneumonia and emphysema. A leader in London real estate development and banking for seven decades, Wesley left no survivors, bequeathing the entire volume of his estate, estimated to be in the range of £875 million, to the Museum of London, the largest city museum in the world. The Museum's Curator, Phillip Smythe-Whitton Graves, was quoted, saying, "Mr. Wesley was a fervent collector and generous benefactor whose extraordinary gifts supported the arts. At his request, the collections bestowed onto the museum will be exhibited at the Museum at Docklands opposite Canary Wharf, where he spent the last years of his life. His legacy will live on in the 'Sidney Lambdin Johns Wesley, III Exhibit and Collection'."

Of particular note was the donation of his extensive collection of 17th and 18th Century Celtic artifacts and antique jewelry, a collection of untold value; in particular, the works of the renowned Silversmith Joseph Johns, from whom the prominent reclusive entrepreneur claimed to be a direct descendant.

The End

Historical Notes

The Children of Lir legend is an integral part of the Celtic culture. One can easily find Children of Lir jewelry in Irish stores, or online.

The Travellers (aka Roma or Gypsies) are a distinct group of nomadic people that have been present throughout Europe for hundreds of years. According to the 1996 census, there were at least 24,000 Travellers still living in Ireland. Stereotyped often as criminals, the Travellers of Ireland are generally considered one of the most disadvantaged and discriminated against groups in that society, although, in the last two decades, less significantly so, according to human rights advocates. The Traveller way of life in Ireland is undergoing gradual changes as they are assimilated into the rest of Irish society. Their nomadic way of living is slowly declining as they move, with the government's help, into permanent housing. Despite this move into permanent housing, they still have managed to hang on to much of their culture, music, and traditions.

RECIPES
FROM THE FILES OF MRS. BUNDLE

MRS. BUNDLE'S SCONES
(afternoon tea with Angie and Mrs. Bundle)

1 cup unbleached white flour
1/2 cup whole wheat pastry flour
1/4 cup sucanant
1/4 tsp. salt
1 tbsp. non-aluminum baking powder
3 tbsp. soy margarine
½ cup soy milk

Optional ingredients:
1/3 cup dates, snipped into small pieces, or raisins, or chocolate bits, or blueberries*
1/3 cup walnut pieces
1/4 tsp. orange extract

Mix all dry ingredients thoroughly, (including dates, raisins and/or walnuts if so desired). Melt soy margarine and pour into dry mix along with the soymilk and orange extract. Mix with spoon until liquid is absorbed. *If adding chocolate bits or blueberries instead of dried fruit, add these now.

Using your hands, mix dough lightly until it is uniform. Pat into a round flattened wheel about 12" in diameter. Cut into 6 to 8 pie shapes, then place on an ungreased baking sheet with none of the scone edges touching.

Cook in a preheated 425° oven for about twelve minutes until scones are slightly browned at edges. Makes 6-8 scones.

Serve with lots of hot tea, honey, warm milk, and a variety of jams.

OLD-FASHIONED PARKER HOUSE DINNER ROLLS
(Thanksgiving)

This favorite yeast roll became famous during the late 19th century at the Parker House, a Boston hotel. It gets its special shape when an off-center crease is made in a round piece of dough before it is folded in half. The result after baking is a light, puffy bun.

2 cups soymilk, scalded lightly
3 tbsp. soymargarine
2 tbsp. sucanant
1 yeast cake
1 tsp. salt
4–5 cups flour

Mix soymargarine, sucanant, and salt in a bowl. Scald the milk, and let cool off until lukewarm. Add the yeast to the lukewarm soymilk by whisking in a little of the liquid at a time. Add yeast and milk mixture to soymargarine, sucanant and salt. . Add about 4 cups of flour. Whisk, then knead with a wooden spoon. Mixture should be doughy. Let rise, until double its original bulk (about 45 minutes). Knead by hand for about 3-5 minutes, adding flour to make it less sticky and easy to knead. Let rise until it doubles in size again. Roll out on floured board—use the remaining flour to flatten the dough to about 2". Cut with biscuit cutter or thin rim of a glass. Crease each roll with a knife, fold in half, and place them side-by-side in a greased baking pan so that they will keep their shape. Brush over with a little melted margarine. Cover and let rise again for about 20-25 minutes. Bake in hot oven (400-450°) for about 15 minutes.

(Author's note: Mrs. Bundle often substitutes the vegan ingredients of sucanant, soymargarine, and soymilk for sugar, butter, and milk, but all of these can be interchanged in the above recipes in equal quantities by her readers. Please note that Cracker, however, prefers his treats replete with eggs, dairy, seafood, and good ol' red meat.)

CRACKER'S
FAVORITE RECIPES AND TREATS

LIVER LOVER COOKIES

½ cup dry milk
½ cup wheat germ
1 tsp. honey

Preheat oven to 350°.

Combine dry milk and wheat germ. Pour honey on top.

Add a small jar of strained liver baby food or homemade blended liver and stir together just until everything is mixed well. By hand, form into small bite size balls, place on oiled cooked sheet and then flatten them with a fork. Bake 8-10 minutes.

These are soft and almost fudge-like. Cool and store in an airtight container in the fridge. They will keep for a few days, or freeze them and remove as needed. Loved by cats far and wide!

CRACKER'S FABULOUS COOKIES

1 12-oz can salmon with liquid
1 egg
1/2 cup flour
1/2 cup dry instant oatmeal

Combine the salmon and egg in blender. Mix for a few seconds, then add the oatmeal and blend well. Spray cooking spray on a 9"-by-13" inch pan and spread the mixture in the pan. Bake at 350°s for 30-35 minutes. Cool, then cut into cat bite-sized squares. Can easily store in freezer. Makes about 24 treats.

Note: Fine china optional

About the Author

ALLISON CESARIO PATON, author of the Mrs. Bundle Mystery Books, grew up in Vermont and has deep respect and love for Vermont, its rich history, and its people. She enjoys their unique views on life and the rest of the world.

Allison and her husband, John, a native Vermonter, divide their time between Scarborough, Maine and southern Vermont, where they thoroughly enjoyed the unique experience of rehabbing an 1830's brick cottage. They also love to ski, take long rides through back country roads, and try new wines.

Allison holds a Master's degree in Counseling and Education; she was a music educator in her first career, then moved into real estate sales in the 1980's, where she continues to work full-time while pursuing her passions of writing and the art of watercolor.

Her sojourn into the creative genre of mystery fiction began in early 2001 when she first created the "little world" of Mrs. Bundle and North Pillson Corners, a place that intertwines two families and their exploits and is rich with strong female protagonists, tradition, danger, local color, and intrigue.

Both the author and Mrs. Bundle agree on the old adage, "When someone shows you what they are, believe it."